HEARTS STILL BEATING

HEARTS STILL BEATING

BROOKE ARCHER

G. P. Putnam's Sons

G. P. Putnam's Sons
An imprint of Penguin Random House LLC, New York

First published in the United States of America by G. P. Putnam's Sons,
an imprint of Penguin Random House LLC, 2024

G. P. Putnam's Sons is a registered trademark of Penguin Random House LLC.
The Penguin colophon is a registered trademark of Penguin Books Limited.

Visit us online at PenguinRandomHouse.com.

Library of Congress Cataloging-in-Publication Data is available.

ISBN 9780593698327

1st Printing

Printed in the United States of America

LSCH

Design by Alex Campbell
Text set in Scala Pro

For the girls who've been told they're
too loud, too angry, too much.
You are exactly enough.

HEARTS
STILL
BEATING

PROLOGUE

MARA
THE DARK DAYS

I watch time unfold, and a whisper reminds me I used to concern myself with it, but the voice belongs to something too far out of reach to listen to. It belongs to someone who isn't here anymore, someone I will not find again.

A new voice, the girl with dark eyes and a wicked smile, is an echo, but her face is not. Her face, pressed next to another through a cloudy surface.

When I try to reach her, to rip her to pieces and erase the reminders she forces out of me, I smash into something. The faces don't disappear until the window—a word snatched from somewhere deep inside and lost as soon as it comes—is painted in a red so dark it looks black.

Her voice stays. The one I can't let go of. Her figure grows smaller, next to another familiar silhouette, until the second fades, and the girl does, too.

Then, the sound of metal breaking and the whine of a hinge. A familiar scent, lemon and salt and sweat, wafts through the house.

I am free. And so very hungry.

1

MARA

When the doctors ask what I remember, the answer they want to hear is "Nothing." If only that were true.

Dr. Benitez clears her throat, drawing my attention away from a poster of a lion with the word RESILIENCE typed beneath it. The doctor's hair is slicked back today, and she's wearing eyeshadow, an odd eggplant color pressed into her lids. I wonder if she has a big date tonight.

I'm not sure if people date anymore. Not that it matters, not to someone like me. My romantic prospects died when I did.

"How much do you remember of your time under the virus's influence, Mara?" She stands two feet from where I'm propped up on the rusting exam table, her brow creased in concern. I used to think her puckered expression meant something, but in my six months at the facility, I've come to understand Dr. Benitez defaults to anxiety the way I default to indifference.

We all had to find our own coping methods when the world ended. Some of us hardened. Some cracked. Some shattered.

I haven't figured out which applies to me yet. I didn't think I'd have to. I thought my time was up the moment the infected man closed his teeth around my wrist.

How much do you remember?

I shake my head. Speech was a mountain to climb in the beginning, the phrases and definitions unearthing themselves and clawing back to my tongue, so I slid into silence for my first month. It's become another default.

Dr. Benitez purses her lips, but she doesn't question me. I can't imagine I'm the first person between these walls to lie. Every single room in this building harbors monsters. Monsters with stories and secrets. Three hundred of us relearning humanity.

My heart beats on a semiregular basis and my lungs are teaching themselves to take in consistent breaths, but none of it matters.

A nasty scar traces down the doctor's neck from an old wound. The outline of a tranquilizer gun, tucked against her hip, is visible underneath her faded lab coat. I don't blame her for taking precautions. I don't trust myself, either, tossed back into this bright, loud, overwhelming world.

She jots something onto her cerulean plastic clipboard. "Dyebucetin varies in its effectiveness in the reparation of cells in the cerebral cortex. It'll take time."

Dr. Benitez isn't sure if the treatment will bring me back to life. For all the doctors know, the Altered might drop dead—really dead—one day, or grow third arms, or lose all our extremities. The last two are more my illogical fear than the doctors', but I used to think the living dead were illogical, and then I became one.

"And what about the nightmares?" she asks.

I grind my teeth. Admitting to the night terrors that have plagued me since I woke to my third life was an early day's mistake. Memories of the creature I was when the virus hijacked my body and the girl I was before.

What do I remember?

Jeans rolled up to asphalt-torn knees and four legs distorted by the pool water. The image pulses with the kick of her feet. She complains her eyes are muddy and boring, and if I were braver, I'd tell her how the sun pulls out flecks of gold and auburn in her irises; I'd tell her looking into them is like drowning. But I am not brave.

"Stopped," I lie. "Sweet dreams on this end."

"Please," the man says, and I know the word used to mean something, but I've long stopped caring. His garbled screams are a quiet hum behind his heartbeat and the blood pumping in his veins, warm and alive.

I take his skull between my hands, slamming down, down, down, until he stops screaming.

Dr. Benitez snorts a laugh, covering her mouth with a hand. With a shake of her head, she says, "I suppose it's a positive sign your sense of humor survived the virus."

The virus. It sounds so harmless when she says it. Like Letalis Tichnosis—the Tick—was the common cold and not an ancient disease trapped in a glacier, waiting for its chance to escape again. The virus didn't just gnaw on our brains; it chewed the world to shreds.

Instead of a response, I give her a tiny smile, because it's what she wants, and I almost mean it. She smiles back as if she's forgotten where she is, what I am. She does it often: treats me like I'm human.

I am anything but. I'm a patchwork quilt of lacerations and punctures and dry open wounds that have woken up and are protesting their existence as I shuffle back toward life.

Some time ago, I was shot straight through the shoulder, and blood oozes from the cut each time I raise my arm over my head. Three of the fingers on my left hand are gone, and until the doctors stitched it up, I'd worn the skin and muscle surrounding the bone like a gross-looking claw. To top it off, two large slashes make an X bisecting my nose. I am better off than most, and as pesky as the doctor's questions are, they are kinder than mine would be if the roles were reversed, so complaints are scarce.

"It was humor"—I pause to wrangle my occasionally rebellious tongue—"or my humanity."

It is a joke, a swing, and if it's a miss, all of our future sessions will be awkward. After another pause, Dr. Benitez smiles, rounding the desk and dropping into a peeling leather chair.

"Whatever the reason," she says, "those are the parts of you that you need to hold on to. The parts that are human." She falls silent, focusing on her clipboard long enough for my heart to thump out a soft beat.

"There's something else I wanted to discuss with you." There is no question mark, and so no obligation to answer. She sighs and continues, "I'm sure you've heard the rumors about the resettlement program."

She seems to realize I don't plan on saying anything. "It's true we intend to release some of you into the care of your guardians."

She's being cautious, circling a truth she isn't sure I'm aware of. I still say nothing, and though she takes the time to sigh dramatically once more, she doesn't press me.

"You're going home, Mara," she says. "That's what I'm telling you." She winces. "Not home, per se, but we have located some of your kin."

Home is not something that exists anymore. Not for me. The only blood I have left is my sister, if she's still alive. And if she is, she's the last person on this earth who'd want to see me.

"*Kin?*" I ask, and Dr. Benitez smiles, clearly proud to have coaxed the syllable off my lips, but it fades as fast as it came, and the following silence is strained.

"Your godparents. Unfortunately, your parents are—" I fix her with the coldest glare I can, and my monstrous state lends me the advantage, killing the rest of Dr. Benitez's sentence before it reaches air.

Dead. My parents are dead. And I killed them. But she doesn't know that.

"Your godparents are living a few hours south. In one of the coastal communities," she says.

Another *thump* ripples from my chest, a single beat of a bruised heart.

"Samantha and Isaac Blake."

"I know who they are." My words crackle like electricity. Dr. Benitez's brows arch to her hairline, and she drops her eyes to the paperwork on her desk, chipped-paint fingers ghosting across the inked letters.

"They'll be picking you up next Sunday. You'll be released into their custody."

I shake my head. "No." Anything but this, anyone but them. It can't be the Blakes. I'm not sure what I thought was waiting for me after all this, if I thought anything at all, but it didn't involve them.

I twist the fraying and stained woven-string bracelet on my wrist—all I have left from my first life, and from *her*. Aurora. Her name triggers a flurry of memories, bright and bursting with life, a happier time with a better me. *Me* before everything fell apart.

I put most of my energy into keeping her somewhere I can't see her, keeping her name locked deep in my gut, but it slips through and shrouds me in warmth. The name means remembering, which means *feeling*. It means wondering whether she survived and considering the possibility she didn't.

"I can't," I say.

Dr. Benitez purses her lips again. Always scribbling on her notepad, and always pursing her lips. "Mara, you have made immeasurable progress in the last six months. The team agrees you're ready for this."

I take a deep breath, lungs rattling as I finish exhaling. "And?"

"And what?"

"And if you're wrong?"

She says my name again, in the tone of hers I don't think is meant to be condescending but is—like I'm a toddler arguing the sky is yellow.

"We have complete faith in you," she says.

I don't have complete faith in me, but I don't have the patience to debate it, either, so I settle for the silence I know digs under her skin. It's much easier than asking questions.

She sits back in her chair, the old metal creaking. Her gaze darts to the desk and up.

"You're not the only one being resettled on the Island. Fifteen others will be joining you. Forty more are going to other settlements." She licks her lips. "You're not alone in this, Mara."

It's a nice thought, but still a lie. I nod, and she ends the session twenty minutes early, calling for one of the nameless soldiers to escort me back to the dormitory building. The old dorms resemble their former state in a way little else does. The rooms, which looked like prison cells long before we came, are bare and grimy and depressing, but they are dry and warm, too—both things I've recently come to care about again.

When I reach my dorm, my roommate, Vivian, has the windows up. She leans into the thick metal bars, a cigarette she bribed off a soldier tucked between her lips. From where I stand, she looks human. At my entrance, she turns, her reflexes a hair faster than they should be, and the resemblance disappears.

Her right ear was ripped clean off, leaving a dry mess of brown and red intermixed with tufts of dark hair. A bullet tore through one of her knees, shattering the bones and giving her an uneven gait. Her skin is as sunken and pale as mine.

She doesn't remember much, or she's pretending not to, and her body is far worse off than mine, but the fire in her eyes is the brightest I've seen in a long time. Since before everything fell apart. Most of the Altered still look empty, but Viv is wide awake.

Her bunk is stacked with a duffel bag.

"You, too?" I ask.

Viv pauses and straightens, blowing a strand of stringy hair out of her eyes. She stubs out the cigarette and flicks it past the bars. Her eyes are wild when they meet mine, like she's been staring at something for too long and forgot to blink.

I'm not sure if we need to blink. I still do.

Viv huffs. "Yeah."

"We have five days."

She snorts, rolls her eyes like I'm missing the punch line of the most obvious joke in the world, and reaches down to zip her duffel closed, joints clicking as she stuffs escaping fabric through the hole. "I'm getting the hell out of here. Tonight."

I frown.

Her heavy-lidded eyes close for a long moment. "I won't do it. Go from one prison to a slightly *bigger* prison."

"Viv," I say, "you're from Pacific Beach."

"You can't *honestly* tell me you want to go back to your family. Spend your days locked in the house playing solitaire. Stuck, forever. *Literally*."

"It won't be that bad." I don't believe it, but I don't know any other way this road can go. A happy ending left the cards a long time ago, and we're not flush with other options. "And it's better than a year ago."

Her eyes darken. "I'm not waiting to find out."

On her nightstand, a box with the label DYEBUCETIN sits unopened. I have only seen it through windows behind locked cabinet doors, but I don't get a chance to ask how she got it before she's rambling.

"We've been their lab rats for months. I'm not going to . . ." She shakes her head. "To go shack up with my cousins and play house."

"What choice do you have?"

"Any choice I want," she says, and the earnestness with which she speaks teeters too close to mania for my liking. "Second chance at life, right?"

"Wrong," I say. "You're not alive. Those meds"—I jab my stubbed pointer finger toward the box—"are keeping you from *killing* anyone with a heartbeat. Say you did make it out. Make it past the soldiers, past the electric fence, and into . . . whatever is left out there. What happens when you run out of the drugs?"

She says nothing.

"And even if you had enough for a thousand years, there's nowhere to go, Viv," I say.

Viv lifts her chin, using her height against me. I'm not short by any means, but Viv is nearly six feet tall and wields her four extra inches as a weapon. She steps toward me. It's as if she's trying to tell me something with her eyes, but I don't understand the language, so the meaning falls flat.

"Of course there is," she says. She sweeps a look around the room, her gaze stalling on the camera in the top right corner of the ceiling. We're near certain it doesn't have a microphone, but Viv lowers her voice when she continues. "There are others. Who can't go back to their families or won't. Who want to be free. They're leaving tonight. Heading to the mountains. There are thousands of cabins and campsites without a human for miles."

"That's not freedom," I say. "That's running."

A smile ghosts her cracked lips. "Is there a difference?"

Vivian has spoken little of her life before this, like most of the residents. We prefer to keep our skeletons in the closet, where they can't rise and rip our throats out. Her expression, and the twisted lilt of her tone, gives me the sense her skeletons would drown her before she got the chance to shake their hands.

I consider warning her she'll die out there, but unless she wanders into an angry human, she'll live until her body gives up.

It could be a year or a thousand. Maybe the meds are enough, or maybe they'll stop working in a week. Maybe if I had those answers, I'd make a different choice.

"How?" I ask the simplest question I have.

"The generator resets every night at midnight. Doors, lights, locks. For sixty seconds, this place is wide open."

"And the gate?"

"They shut it down to conserve generator power. It's soldiers, and

they can be avoided." Viv shifts her weight. "You could come, too."
She shrugs a shoulder, gives me a smile likely intended to be reassuring, but it makes me tense. The Tick slumbering in my head
knows danger when it sees it and senses something at the end of this
road I don't or can't. It urges me back, away, *anywhere* but down the
path Viv wants me to take.

"Be careful, okay?" I say, and I tell myself it isn't about her—about
Aurora—but I've always been as bad at telling myself lies as I am
good at seeing through others'.

Maybe it's not whatever is at the end of Viv's road. Maybe it's the
fact Aurora isn't on it.

For months, she has been the smoke billowing off a car crash up
the road, and the closer I get, the more I both dread and anticipate
what lies ahead. If I knew she was alive, if I knew anything, I could
look away.

But I don't. So I can't.

2

RORY

Standing at the bridge ledge feels a little bit like flying.

Not that it's really a bridge anymore. The bombs put most of the bright blue metal into the ocean and left a road ending abruptly three hundred feet in the air.

I ease up onto the dented hood of an old Toyota and stare out over the city. It, like the bridge, is not what it used to be.

Half the skyscrapers are mountains of ash and debris, burned or bombed or collapsed in the initial push to curb the spread of the Ticks downtown. San Diego was so loud before, constantly in motion and buzzing ahead at the speed of light, but it's a graveyard now.

I'm so busy staring at the charred wreckage of a dock on the mainland side of the bridge, I don't notice the footsteps crunching over the uncleared debris until they are ten feet away. At one point, it would have been a fatal mistake.

I slide off the car and pull my sword from its sheath, swinging for the Tick, my brain disregarding the fact the Island hasn't had an outbreak since before I arrived a year ago.

It's not a Tick. It's something worse. Carter Knight. The sole survivor of the Knight family, three years older than me and—

Three years older than me.

Carter ducks away from the blade. I lower the sword, resting it on my denim-covered thigh.

"You know you're not permitted to be up here," Carter says. Each time I speak to her, which is as little as physically possible, her voice is harder, her vocab more rigid, and her posture stiffer.

Carter and I have butted heads since we met. It was as if she took one look at me and decided I was a problem, and I made no efforts to convince her otherwise. The rest of the Knights were like family to me, but never Carter.

She's a soldier now, outfitted in aquaflage from the base's inventory, and while she plays the part well—inky hair pulled back into an immaculate sock bun, face expressionless, and tone authoritative—she will always be the teenager I watched projectile vomit wine coolers into the firepit in the backyard between our houses.

"You know you're not a *real* soldier, right?" I step back, leaning against the car door. The sun is pushing toward the horizon line, and the ocean breeze lifts the sticky hairs off the back of my neck.

Carter's nose wrinkles, and the familiarity of the expression makes my stomach wrench.

"It's for your own safety. And for the safety of—"

"The people and peace of the Island," I finish. "You and the rest of Mal's little clones should get that tattooed across your chests. Make it a bonding event. I heard some world-famous tattoo artist made it to Pacific Beach."

Carter's nostrils flare, and she folds her arms across her chest, showcasing an impressive belt stocked with various assorted hammers, pickaxes, ice picks, and a shiny revolver. The gun is for show, and probably doesn't have bullets. Gunshots draw Ticks faster than anything, and even on the Island, apocalyptic taboos aren't broken.

While Carter retorts with a comeback I don't have to hear to know is lousy, I consider how easy it would be to get into her quarters and pocket her collection after she falls asleep. She bunks with at least fifteen other girls, old soldiers and new volunteers, but I'm sneaky. It would be worth it to see the look on her face.

The old Rory would be ashamed of me. The thought makes me want to smile. I settle for rolling my eyes.

"This stuff isn't a joke, Au—" At my narrowed eyes, Carter clears her throat, reattempts. "*Rory.*"

"You didn't use to be this uptight," I say. "I mean, a little bit, but not this bad. What happened to you?"

Carter's eyes widen to the whites, and her lips pull back to bare her canines; it is remarkably difficult not to tell her how much she resembles her dead sister with the gnashing teeth.

"What happened? Oh, I don't know, the *apocalypse.*"

"Just because the world ends doesn't mean you automatically shove the largest stick you can find directly up your—"

"Rory, I swear to god—"

I tuck the sword back in its sheath, stretching out a foot to kick an old gas carton, poking the toe of my sneaker through a hole in its side. The plastic whines in protest, and an ache from the barely healed injury to my left leg forces me to stop. It's been a year since the Island's doctor, Fatimah, pried the fragments of bullet out of my thigh, but the one piece left behind still likes to remind me it's there. Or, really, it likes to remind me how close I came to dying.

"Like I said. Uptight," I say.

"Even if that were true, and it's *not*, I think I have reason to be."

"What reason?" I ask, feigning sincerity, sweeping a hand around at the wreckage of the city across the water and the frail house of cards we've built on the Island.

The blood drains out of Carter's face. Every part of her is rigid, and I can see the sentences forming and twisting around in her mouth like worms.

"What reason?" I repeat.

Carter may be the soldier here, but she made it to the Island months before I did. She knows as well as I do that, in any fight, she'll lose—again. Like she did in the Pit. Mal's gladiator-style fighting ring

13

was disbanded, but not before I was thrown in for breaking into the armory. It was a way to pay off crimes, but a way to earn prizes and show off, too; Carter was in with me for the latter.

She regains her composure, and her words are bitterly laced as she sneers, "You didn't hear."

Frustration pricks its sharp fingers into my sides, and I bite back the insult that flies to my tongue.

"Obviously not," I say. "Care to share with the class?"

Her lips pull into a thin line. She may be wearing new clothes, but I grew up with the girl beneath them, and I know what a terrified Carter Knight looks like. "The list of Ticks being resettled on the Island was released."

"How many?" Bile claws up the back of my throat, the real question I want to ask burning through my esophagus.

"Fifteen."

"Fifteen." I mirror her words so I don't say mine, though judging by the way Carter can't meet my eye, she has some clue as to what I really want to know.

She was there the last time I saw her. Carter brought me back to the house she trapped her undead sister in, and when she tried to kill her, I stopped her. She's never forgiven me for it. I haven't forgiven myself.

"Her name is on the list, Rory."

I flinch as if she's hit me.

Midnight-colored braids long enough to twirl around my finger five times, and a lopsided smile when I do. Grass tickles my thighs and calves, and at least six ant bites are cresting over my ankles, but I don't care. I don't care, I don't care, I don't care. She has her head on my stomach, and she's humming along with the pop song on the iPod blasting out beside us, and we are teetering on the edge of a cliff, and—

Her name is on the list.

"No, it's not," I say, blinking past the other memories.

Carter ignores my delusions. "They're coming home next week. Fifteen monsters, personally delivered."

"No, they're not," I press. "She's not."

Carter frowns. "Rory—"

"She's not—" I stop, take a breath. I am going to pass out, or throw up, or scream, or kill her, and none of those are good to do on a crumbling bridge. "She can't be. We saw her."

Silence hangs between us, squeezing, until Carter says, "You know what we saw. And you know what we should have done."

"Don't," I say.

"You're the reason she's still upright," Carter says. It's the cut I've been waiting for since she broke the news, but it still breaks skin. I didn't just stop Carter from killing her sister; I broke the lock on the door and released her, making the blood on her hands half my own. "You're the last person who should be surprised she's coming back."

"How long are you going to hold that over my head?"

"As long as it's still above the ground."

"Why here? Your parents—" I don't finish the sentence, but Carter flinches anyway. She knows what I'm going to say. She never told me exactly what happened to her parents, but they aren't here, which is answer enough. "Did they make you her guardian?"

"No," Carter says, and I swear she looks smug.

"Spit it out."

"She's being placed with your family. Your parents are her god-parents, and since she's not *technically* eighteen—"

"Not eighteen? She's dead."

"I'm the messenger," she snaps. "You think I'm happy about this? You think I want those things walking around here? If it was up to me, I'd throw them all in the Pit—"

"Mal signed off on this?" I ask before she says anything else and dredges up memories I work very hard to keep at bay.

One of Carter's brows twitches, and she shifts her weight between her feet, a hand coming to rest on the pickaxe tucked into her belt. The motion seems more comfort-based than intimidating.

"Mal didn't have a choice. The Island isn't his anymore," Carter says.

Colonel Mallory Gordon, one of the few of the original troops stationed at the base on the Island who managed to hold its perimeter, with an ego to match his vast accomplishments. Before the Island joined the Alliance, he had this island locked down tighter than the Pentagon. A pre-zombie Pentagon, at least.

"Becoming civilized again does typically mean ditching the dictator. The Alliance might frown on one."

When it started, the Alliance was an agreement between the heads of two communities: Oceanside and Solana Beach. They'd trade what they had, and in exchange, neither community would raid the other. Then Pacific Beach joined, and Point Loma, and it snowballed. Now the Alliance is the closest thing to a governing body we have in the region. It's the Alliance who coordinated this entire Tick resettlement program with the RPA. To stay in, every settlement had to agree.

Another twitch in Carter's jaw. Her buttons are so easy to press; for a moment, I forget why I avoid her so much. There are so few ways of blowing off steam these days, and here she is, prime for the pissing off.

Then she sighs in a way so much like her sister, and I remember. The girl I used to be starts banging her fists against my rib cage, screaming to be released, and if I remain here, staring at the wrong Knight daughter, everything in me will finally shatter.

"Just . . . get off the bridge, Rory," Carter says, seeming much older than her twenty years as she pinches the bridge of her nose and turns, heading back toward the old tollbooths.

As her silhouette grows smaller and smaller, the tidal wave I've been keeping at bay shoves through the floodgates and smashes into my chest.

Her name is on the list. The other Knight daughter, the girl I grew up alongside, the girl I have loved longer than I had the word for it. A monster, a creature, the very thing I've spent so long running from. It is everything I wanted drenched in rot like some sick, cosmic joke.

Hushed, snarky comments whispered in the back of classrooms. A smile no one else gets to see. My name turned into a poem on her lips.

Mara.

3

MARA

In another life, this reunion might still have taken place here, in the lobby of a college dorm.

However, in the other life, it would be my parents coming to pick me up. There wouldn't be four armed guards lining the walls. The girl sitting in the chair across from me certainly wouldn't have a stab wound in her forehead, and I wouldn't be drumming an uneven beat with finger stubs against stiff denim jeans.

"Miss Knight," barks Dr. Caldwell, buzzing herself through the front door, poking her head around the corner, and sweeping her pointed eyes around the room. She's not as sympathetic as her partner, Dr. Benitez, and perpetually upset about something, though I can't blame her for either. There isn't a person left untouched by the virus. We've all lost someone, or everyone.

The bags beneath Dr. Caldwell's eyes are especially deep today. They've been there, purple and persistent and growing, as long as I've been here, and some mornings, she looks as dead as I do. Acts it, too.

The last few days, though, she and the others have been especially rigid. Nineteen of their own medicated monsters vanished into the night, and those of us left behind won't say a word about where they went. But as uncomfortable as the interrogation was, it means Vivian and the others made it.

"Your guardians have arrived," she says, her tone reminiscent of a regal Victorian woman in a period piece, though she's from Idaho and not even forty.

I push off the cracking leather seat, ignoring the protest of the wound in my shoulder as the duffel strap grazes it, and don't meet the eyes of my fellow dischargees on my way to the door.

The sun swelters above us, summer setting up shop and turning its fury on those of us with sensitive eyes. I squint, stumbling after Dr. Caldwell through the path between two of the treatment buildings. All the windows are barred, the structures fortified, the roofs fitted with perches for snipers, but the buildings harbor traces of their old lives, as we do. Peeling and near-illegible stickers wrap around metal posts. Faded initials are carved into thin tree trunks. A molded poster urges attendance of an improv show this Friday at eight. Unfortunately, I think I've missed it by three years or so.

The only additions to the decor are the banners placed around the campus, frequent enough they are impossible to ignore. *Res PublicA* written in sharp edges, the *R*, *P*, and *A* always capitalized. It means "the commonwealth," the doctors remind us often, but it's a slogan and a name rolled into one. We call them the RPA.

The doctors aren't exactly forthcoming with information, but thin walls and heightened senses have made it clear the soldiers don't answer to them. Dr. Caldwell and Dr. Benitez and the others are soldiers in their own right, with RPA badges and lab coats instead of fatigues.

Vivian and I are pretty sure the soldiers are what's left of the National Guard and any military that didn't end up on a ship, but I doubt they'd tell me if I asked.

The path leads to a cracked, pothole-dominated parking lot packed with soldiers. The grounds are wrapped in fencing buzzing with enough electricity to flay the skin off someone's body.

Outside the gates, cars line up down the block, a thin trail of designated guardians coming to collect their medicated monsters. Officially diagnosed as Letalis Tichnosis survivors. The Altered.

If my heart still did what it was supposed to, it would be hammering. I miss that feeling sometimes, the nerves looping around my intestines and squeezing, the bile burning at the back of my tongue. I miss how my body reacted without a thought, only instinct. That, and my three fingers. I am already at a disadvantage, all creaky, stiff joints and tight muscles. Once upon a time, I was a musician, but now I couldn't form a chord if I wanted to.

Caldwell stops, and I catch myself before slamming into her back, forcing my attention to the lot.

On the far side of the lot, near one of the other buildings, a handful of soldiers stand with a stern-faced woman no older than her mid-thirties carrying an authority that makes her seem older. I've never seen her before. There are a dozen or so doctors here, and more soldiers, but I know I've never seen this woman.

The massive gate buzzes as it begins to open, but a loud whistle rings through the air.

With that single noise, the entire operation grinds to a halt. The gate slides back shut. Caldwell lifts an arm to keep me from moving forward. The soldiers around the lot stiffen, turn toward the gate.

Outside, two silhouettes are visible pushing out of the trees on either side of the road. I can make out the RPA fatigues on one of the Ticks, but the other is practically a skeleton, her skin so deteriorated it's peeling off her bones. Their attention is on the gate because it makes noise, but there are at least five cars with people in them close behind. They will notice them eventually.

This could go very, very badly.

Another whistle, this one sharper, from one of the snipers on the roof. I turn my head, craning to make out the soldier peering through his scope.

"Wait!" the unfamiliar woman yells. The sniper hesitates. The woman steps away from the soldiers, heading for the gate. No one moves, or speaks, or tries to stop her.

I may spend all my time inside the gates, but even I know the protocol. Subdue if possible, assassinate if not.

"Thalia!" an older soldier calls, but the woman, Thalia, ignores him. She pulls a thick baton from her belt, as well as a loop of thick rope.

"Open it back up!" she yells. The Ticks on the other side of the fence jerk at her voice, pushing toward the gate. One presses into it, seemingly unbothered by the electrical current it sends through his body, only stepping back when he realizes he won't get through.

No one moves.

Thalia stops at the tall gate. After a long minute, the gate buzzes and begins to slide back open. The Ticks rush for her.

An old anxiety, born in the ashes of this city, pricks at my insides. I don't know this woman, but that doesn't mean I want to watch her be eaten.

The gates begin to close again after the woman slips out, and when they clang shut behind her, she stops just outside them. She waits.

And so do we. No one makes a move to join her, to help her.

The soldier reaches her first. The newly turned are the most dangerous, the fastest. This one can't have been turned more than an hour or two ago.

But Thalia is unwavering, lifting her baton and letting the Tick approach her. His fingers grasp her collar, and she shoves at his chest, sending him back a step. He recovers quickly, snarling, lunging for her, and she jumps to the side, slipping behind the Tick. She swings the baton into the backs of his knees, buckling them, and when he tries to whirl on her, she swings the baton again, this time into the back of his head. It isn't a kill shot, but a stunner, one the Tick shakes off quickly. In the second between being hit and recovering, the woman unfurls her rope, throwing it around his neck, darting behind him, wrapping it around his torso and pinning his strong arms tight to his sides. With a light shove, he's on the ground. He writhes and snaps, but Thalia easily sidesteps his teeth.

The other Tick, slower, gets close enough to grab Thalia's attention, and she inspects her as she approaches. Then, in a blink, Thalia materializes a wicked-sharp knife from her belt, grabs the Tick by the collar of her shirt, and plunges the blade into one of her eyes.

She lets the body fall with a thud, returning to the soldier. She slips a hand around the ropes at his back, wrangling him onto his feet. Thalia couldn't be called gentle, but she's avoiding major injuries, too.

This isn't the first time a Tick has wandered too close. Through my room's window, I've seen a handful of them approach the fence, only to be wrangled with tranquilizers and cuffs. Some are taken inside. Some are killed, their bodies dragged away. The treatable, and the too far gone.

Thalia heads back for the gate, the Tick at her front, craning his head to snap uselessly at her. She doesn't need to ask for the gate to be opened again, and marches through.

Three soldiers from the lot break from their posts to meet her inside the gates as they creak shut again. One of them pulls out a catch pole, like those used by animal control in the old world, and loops it around their fallen comrade's neck.

The Tick is led away, and Thalia returns to her previous spot across the parking lot. She tucks the knife back into her belt, not even bothering to wipe the blood away.

And the operation carries on as if nothing has happened. The gate buzzes open, and the soldiers wave in the next vehicle. The one carrying Isaac and Sam, who didn't flee after what they just saw, though they had every reason to.

The car pulls up a few yards from the curb. The engine sputters to a stop, sending out a plume of smoke in dissent. Predatory instincts that don't belong to me flicker to life in the pit of my hollow belly, and I stomp them down, reminding myself *anxiety* and *danger* aren't synonymous.

For a moment, I don't recognize the two adults who climb out of the driver and passenger seats. My chipped memories of them are far brighter and shinier than the people coming to stand in front of the hood. Samantha and Isaac Blake, three years older than I remember them.

Samantha-call-me-Sam's silky black hair has faded, is streaked with gray and piled atop her head in a bun half the size it used to be. A black fabric eye patch covers one of her dark eyes, its straps stark against her washed-out hair. She is tall and gaunt, and the smile I once thought permanent is pulled into a thin line.

Isaac's once tight, bouncy curls have lost their volume, and his face is covered in scruff. He, too, is thinner than he was, and his dark skin is littered with tiny scars. The Isaac Blake I knew had a voice that carried down the block to draw us back into the warmth of our homes on summer days as the sun dipped beneath the trees. The type of person who had something to say about everything, but it was all nice, or true, so no one minded.

The Blakes may not be my blood, but they have been family for longer than I can remember. Sam's eye slides to me, her nostrils flaring and her pale lips parting. She touches Isaac's side, and he stiffens. Though her focus is trained on me, Isaac is looking between the soldiers and Dr. Caldwell, clearly unsure how to proceed.

"Mara." Dr. Caldwell clears her throat, and I resist the urge to look back at the dorm once more before stepping off the curb and slowly crossing the asphalt.

The soldiers lining the perimeter and perched on the rooftops with their tranquilizer guns have every scope trained on me. I don't have to turn to know it. I feel it, the hairs on my neck rising, the Tick twisting in warning. In moments like this, it is hardest to cling to being human.

If anyone here had a sense of humor, I'd remind them that, if I wanted to tear their throats out, I'd have done it by now. And I don't want to. Not really. All I want is to get the hell out of here. To get away from the guns before they decide to turn on us again.

I tell myself I don't want to know if she's okay. If she's alive. She has to be alive. If anyone survived this, it was—

"Isn't that right, Mara?" I don't realize Dr. Caldwell is speaking—has been for some time—until she's fixing me with that spiked scrutiny of hers, like she wants to pry me open and look inside.

I nod without a clue as to what I'm agreeing to, eyes trained on a spot of peeling white paint on the hood of the car. I'm looking anywhere but at the Blakes. And they're looking directly at me. The monster beneath my skin scratches to be released.

"As you were informed at the orientation sessions, your settlement's designated medical professional has been briefed on the circumstances. Fatimah will walk you through the important details. Any questions or concerns can be taken directly to her."

"Thank you," Isaac says, raspier than I remember. I still don't look at them, though it's more for their sake than because of my own nerves.

My eyes were a deep ivy once. The Tick ate that and left an unnerving gray. Coupled with the wounds that will never fully heal and the vaguely sickly pallor of my skin, I can't be a pretty sight.

"Mara," Isaac says. "Ready to head out?"

It has been so long since someone said my name like that, like it was a name and not a knife, like it belonged to a flower and not a weed, I lift my head without thought.

Isaac doesn't flinch. He might smile, but it's gone so fast I can't be sure.

I nod, looking to Sam, who still says nothing. Her lip quivers before she averts her gaze.

"Everyone will be excited to see you," Isaac says with a little too much enthusiasm to be believable.

Everyone. I stumble, trip, fall on the word. I want to ask about my sister, about the twins, about Aurora. Memories flash behind my eyelids, bathed in light. The debris in my chest thumps once. My heart still struggles to remember to beat, but it remembers her. Of course the busted thing remembers *her*.

It is evident Isaac has more to say, but the gun barrels are making us all tense. When Isaac takes my duffel and opens the back door for me, I climb in without hesitation, eager to be *anywhere* else.

After an agonizing two minutes pulling slowly toward the gate, and a ten-second period before it opens during which I'm convinced this was all a big trick and I'm about to be wrenched from the car and stuck back inside those antiseptic-laced halls, we make it onto the rubble-littered streets surrounding the facility.

The area isn't one I'm familiar with, but the decay is worse than I remember. The buildings and homes are more rotted, the roots and weeds more overgrown. It shouldn't be a shock to see how much things have changed, but it is. All my time as a Tick, stuck in place, and the world was moving on around me. Growing and falling apart at the same time.

Isaac is the picture of calm in the driver's seat, but I'm not so easily appeased. Being outside the gates, even in a car, has the Tick squirming around my skull. Being so exposed is dangerous, to a Tick and human alike. The last twenty minutes have been a stark reminder of that.

"Is it . . . safe out here?" I ask.

In the passenger seat, Sam jumps, as if she forgot I was here.

"Under the general definition, 'out here' "—Isaac lifts a hand from the wheel to make air quotes—"is never safe. But the major routes are clear. As long as we avoid the hotspots, we'll be fine."

"Hotspots?"

Isaac nods. "There's a pretty good radius around every settlement and RPA facility scrubbed for Ti—unmedicated Ticks. Go past it, or anywhere near a downtown, and you could walk right into a horde. But there are always the stragglers, like you saw."

It's like I'm a little kid, thrown into a strange world with new rules. I already feel out of touch, so I refrain from asking the dozen more questions battering around my skull.

"You won't need to worry once we're on the Island. The water keeps everything out," Isaac says, and I can tell he's trying to be reassuring. He's feigning normalcy as best he can, but we're so far from normal there's no chance he'll ever reach it.

"And everything in," Sam says, the first time she's spoken since they picked me up.

"Who was that woman?" I ask, images of the woman—Thalia—composed as she faced two Ticks, flickering behind my eyes.

"Thalia O'Neill," Isaac says. "I guess she makes house calls now."

Sam snorts a laugh, and for a minute, I can see a glimpse of the old Sam. Isaac is more or less as I remember, if not more muted, but Sam isn't someone I recognize. Quiet, sunken, with none of the fire she was known for.

I want to ask what happened, but I already know the answer. The thing in my head is the answer.

"She's Oceanside's head honcho," Isaac says. "She started the Alliance. She's the reason the Ticks are being resettled, too. Negotiated some deal for the medical supplies the RPA was hoarding."

This must be the Alliance the facility doctors talk about. Some agreement between the communities expanded to include Ticks when the RPA started treating us.

"From what I hear, she's on the intense side, but I suppose you can't blame her. Not with the weight of the Alliance sitting on her shoulders and the barrel of the RPA gun at her head," Isaac continues. "Besides. None of us survived through serenity."

The following silence hangs thick over the car. Isaac is waiting for me to ask more, or say something, from the way he keeps flicking looks at me in the rearview mirror. I can't figure out how to put everything I want to know into words. None of us have good stories to tell from our time apart.

"We lost Aria two years back," Isaac says suddenly, voicing the question burning the hottest on my tongue.

Stiffening, I find his eyes in the mirror, uncaring of the intensity of my expression or how unsettling it might be. All I can think about is little Aria, running barefoot around the front lawn with her sister, Raisa. They were adopted at a year old, and I have known them almost as long as they have been alive.

With big eyes, dark brows, glittering golden irises, cheekbones and an attitude belonging to someone thrice their age, copper skin always covered in dirt or sand or a combination of both, Aria and Raisa are the closest things I have to little sisters.

I want to ask *Who else?*, but emotions are still not fully acquainted with the virus living alongside them in my brain, and I don't trust them not to fumble on their way off my tongue.

And somehow, Isaac knows, glancing over his shoulder from the passenger seat.

He adds, "Raisa is ten now. And Aurora—" Another thump in my chest. Two in the span of an hour. Dr. Caldwell might actually smile if I told her. "—is still as feisty as ever."

Aurora is alive. Six billion people died, but Aurora didn't. I did, and she didn't. Maybe there is someone up there, looking after us. Or, at least, looking after her.

I clear my throat.

"My sister . . ."

Isaac's easy tone doesn't match his words when he says, "Carter is on the Island, too. You'll probably see her soon."

I may have a disease tucked into my brain, but I know a conversation ender when I hear it. Carter is alive. She may—probably does—hate me for what I did, but she's alive.

The awkward silence holds for a long minute before Isaac remembers the CD he found in the glove compartment, and then we're driving with Billy Joel accompanying us. The song is the first I learned to play on the old, scratched, and sticker-coated guitar I outgrew by thirteen. Isaac reaches out to take Sam's hand, their twined fingers resting on her thigh.

It isn't until we reach the bridge that it settles in.

I've blocked so much of it out. Especially that first month. The panic to contain the initial spread.

We think it's an earthquake at first. When the second bomb falls, Carter and I climb out onto the second-floor balcony, and we understand.

"They're blowing it up," Carter whispers, and slips her hands into mine. "All of it."

Downtown is on fire. Half the big blue bridge, too. A jet whizzes overhead, shaking the roof of the house we've been squatting in for the last two days. I've lost count of how many weeks we've spent trying to escape the city. Now all we're trying to do is make it back home. If there's a home left to return to.

"Get down!" Carter screams, as another jet darts overhead, so close my hair blows back and my lungs scream for air. She drags me down, both of us smacking the hard balcony as another bomb detonates. It is close enough the heat hits us like a tidal wave.

Four more explosions ricochet through the city before the silence falls again. When Carter and I climb back to our feet, we're dusted with ash like snow, and all we can see is fire.

No music or forced pleasant conversation can block out the reality of the last few years. The closer we draw to the water, the thicker the air in the car grows. And each time Isaac catches my eye in the mirror, he sucks in a tiny breath, like he's remembering all over again he has a monster in his back seat.

4

RORY

If Raisa notices me throwing up in the bathroom as she comes knocking on the door to let me know Sam and Isaac are back, nothing in her face gives her away. She was always the quieter one between her and her twin, but since we burned Aria, she hasn't said a word.

"Where's Noah?" I ask, exiting the bathroom, swallowing the nerves coiling like vipers in the back of my throat.

Raisa points in the direction of the living room, which is a few steps away. The Island is stocked with million-dollar mansions, but our house is small enough its surviving solar panels can power it. Before we fixed the place up, we were squashed in with five other families two blocks away, which killed the mansion vibe.

I can't complain, though. Our house, right along the water facing the cliffs, has a billion-dollar view and occasionally musters enough breeze to cool us down. Sam and Isaac made a point to pick a place apart from the residential streets a few blocks away where the rest of the Island lives. The house will always be missing a resident, but Aria never reached the Island, which makes it easier. Her ghost didn't follow us.

Others did, but after the end of the world, that's a given.

Silhouettes shift outside the front windows as I come into the living room. A beach house in every sense of the word, the walls are painted seafoam green, with still-life paintings of lighthouses and boat docks tacked to the walls. The furniture is ancient, muddy browns and oranges, with dirty throw pillows that survived the apocalypse for some godforsaken reason. We've tossed half the decorations and furniture, but unfortunately, the room had three times too much of everything to begin with.

Noah, five years old and all gangly limbs and long, black corkscrew curls, is perched on the couch, leafing through a magazine. His personal favorite is *Seventeen*, though we have to go through and rip out the more PG-13 pages before he gets to them.

His dark brown skin is flaked with sand, and he's managed to get it in his hair, too. He knows he shouldn't be down at the water on his own, but I'm the last person to scold him for breaking the rules.

"Come on, little monster," I say, earning the gap-toothed grin I knew it would. "You heard the elders. Upstairs, with Raisa."

"Raisa isn't upstairs," Noah says pointedly, his logic unflawed. He doesn't seem to notice my shaking hands, and I'm grateful. I cross the sage shag carpeting—the same color the wooden house is painted, and ugly as all hell.

"*Raisa* is waiting for you."

"But I want to meet her," he says, pouting.

I almost tell him, *Trust me, you don't*, but he has seen enough sadness and disappointment in his life, and I hate being the one to take the goofy smile off his face. We found him, three years old, parents dead or gone, in an old grocery store. He's adopted like the rest of us, without any of the paperwork.

"You will." His smile widens. *"Later."* It dims, by a fraction, but it's still there. "Now go. You don't want Raisa to be lonely up there, do you?"

I jerk a chin toward the doorway, where Raisa is waiting, hands on her hips, not needing to speak to pressure her brother into reluctantly joining her. They head for the stairs, Noah stomping up as he always does—he wasn't allowed to make noise for so long, now we're here, we let him hop about like a bull in a china shop. He's broken quite a few pieces of *actual* china that were likely precious treasures, but we're all so grateful to see him having some kind of childhood we let him.

Keys jingle outside the front door, and my sword is in my hand before the lock turns. Half instinct, but half justified.

The door opens slowly, Sam and Isaac stepping through first, finding me and my blade within an instant. Isaac looks disappointed, but a rare fire lights in Sam's eyes, and she hisses, "For the love of god, Rory, put the sword away—"

I barely hear her, not with a third figure entering the room.

I had enough days and nightmares to plan a method of attack or escape in any outcome, but now she's here, and I can't think. I can't breathe, can't move.

She steps into the door, sunlight illuminating pale, washed-out skin and blue veins resting beneath the surface. I knew she hadn't aged since being bitten after she turned seventeen, but it's still odd to see, like a living photograph.

Dying has accentuated her severe features, and I think now her jawline really could slice through paper. Her face is peppered with scars: the shape of a crude X across the bridge of her nose, a line through one side of her chin. The shadows beneath her eyes are purple, like a bruise halfway to healing. Which it will never do. Her once long, voluminous black hair has been chopped in a haphazard bob, and the jade eyes I dreamt circles around are a faded, pale gray.

I think I'm going to be sick again.

"Rory, put the blade away," Isaac says, his voice muffled by the ringing building in my ears.

Eighteen years of memories, eleven of them at her side, roll behind my eyes, and the stale cereal I choked down for breakfast threatens to resurface.

Mara.

Sam steps toward me, lunging toward my hand in a surprising show of authority, and I jerk it away, taking a step toward the door. A few more steps, a thrust, and it ends.

She broke the world. My grip on the sword tightens. *Do it.*

"Aurora."

Then my name falls off her lips, the name I don't let anyone call me because it belongs to her, and it is scratchy and raw but clear.

The sword falls back to my side like it heard a command in her syllables, and though it's still in a tight grip, Sam deflates, and Isaac scratches at the scruff lining his cheeks—his nervous tic. They know I'm no longer on the cliff's edge, but Mara has gone rigid.

This is not the girl I knew. Not the witty, loyal, inquisitive girl living in my memories, but a rotted, wretched creature with her face.

My heart threatens to crack my rib cage and spill out for everyone to see.

"No one cut your head off," I say. "Good for you."

Her nostrils flare—do zombies *need* to breathe?—and her hands curl into fists at her sides. She's missing three fingers.

"*Aurora Elizabeth Knight,*" Sam says, and the corner of Mara's mouth twitches up.

I want to stab something. Someone. *Her.* I don't understand how she can walk back in here, after what she's done and what she's become, like it's nothing.

"Everyone, *sit down.*" Isaac's voice isn't loud, but it's commanding. He looks tired, like he hasn't slept in days. I know the feeling.

Mara and I stare at each other, neither moving as Isaac cuts across the room to stand in front of the fireplace we neither need nor use. The *sit down* only applies to Mara and me, but we're stuck in place. Sam gets the door, turning all three locks, before retreating to a seat on the armchair, leaving the long couch for us. Like I'm sitting next to *her.*

"Sit down, Rory," Isaac says, and this time, it's more of a plea.

32

I set my jaw, dragging my feet across the living room.

Mara, still in front of the door, catches my gaze as I sink into the cushions. I narrow my eyes, lips curling back in a snarl more animal than human, like I'm the monster in the room.

"No one here is going to pretend things haven't changed since you last saw each other," Isaac says. I open my mouth to speak, but Isaac interrupts. "And yes, your oppositions to all of this have been noted, Rory." He looks to Mara. "I can't begin to imagine what you've been through in your time away—"

A snort busts out of me before I can stop it, but the irritated twist to Mara's lips almost makes it worth the exasperated sigh from Sam across the room. Not participating, but judging nonetheless. Isaac, ever the mediator, clears his throat.

"What I'm trying to say is no one expects this transition to be easy. But we're in this together, like we were before."

"Before Mara started chomping down on brains, you mean?" I hiss.

Isaac takes a long, deep breath.

"I'm fairly certain I wasn't picky with body parts," Mara says, voice low, not looking at me. It's the second time she's spoken, and it's like a cheese grater against my composure. I can barely see past the blood on my hands, and Mara is joking about her own, like they weren't really people. Maybe they aren't to her.

Sam's eyes are saucers, and I am swimming in anger, when Isaac does something none of us expect.

He laughs.

I make the mistake of looking at Mara, and the stitch between her brows and slight purse of her lips hauls me back in time to a fifteen-year-old with knobby knees and long braids and summers of sticky Popsicles and secrets we kept from ourselves and each other—

"Look, I know this isn't ideal," Isaac says. "We're all going to have to make some sacrifices. Rory, that means the—"

"If you say *the sword*, I will—"

"—sword. I'm not saying you have to get rid of it, but keep it in your room when you're home."

"Not a chance in hell." I consider pushing to my feet, but it isn't worth the show of weakness to Mara. "I am not sleeping in the same house as *her*"—a finger jabbed at Mara—"without something sharp next to my head." A tap on the sword I'm still gripping like a lifeline.

"Mara is sleeping in the basement." Isaac looks to her. "It's not as bad as it sounds. It's more spare bedroom than basement, but with a hefty lock on the steel door."

I set my jaw. A lock on a thick door. Because locks and doors were *so* helpful the first time around.

"I don't care," I say, standing and shoving the sword back into its sheath. "I'm keeping my sword. If you want it, you'll have to take it off me. Who's gonna do that?"

Isaac sighs.

"Rory—" he starts.

"No," I snap. "And when she tears out Raisa's or Noah's throat like Aria's, and I have to take care of it myself *again*, you'll be glad I have it."

Sam curls into herself, making a choked, painful sound. She shuts down like I've yanked her plug. Part of me knows I went too far, but I can't find any guilt.

Mara jerks. The twitch in her brow makes me think she's going to speak, but as quickly as it came, the emotion clears from her face.

I don't wait for the inevitable lecture or outraged responses as I storm toward the door and out into the cool evening night. But I don't make it out fast enough to miss Mara's flinch as I pass.

5

MARA

She would have killed me.

The thought cracks against my skull over and over. Aurora would have killed me.

If Isaac and Sam weren't there, she'd have killed me. Swung the blade and put me down the way she has clearly put down so many others.

And I would have deserved it. No one could say I don't. At the facility, one of the doctors' favorite mantras was we weren't responsible for what the Tick made us do, but it was clear they didn't believe it. There were moments I caught Dr. Benitez staring at me as if she regretted ever stepping foot in the building.

The Aurora of my memory wouldn't have touched a weapon if her life depended on it, but the girl who lifted the sword wielded it like a fifth limb. It wasn't my Aurora I found standing in the living room, but a strange facsimile. And one who hated me.

Isaac attempted pleasantries for a few minutes after Aurora left—how they fixed up the house themselves, and that eventually I'd be moved into the bedroom down the hall—but the bitter reunion seemed to have shattered whatever spell we'd found in the car. He went first; if he didn't go check on the kids, he said, they would come searching.

"They want to see you, but I think for tonight, it's best we play it safe. In case . . ." He hadn't finished, but he didn't need to.

In case Aurora came back, saw, and decided to finish the job she started.

And with Isaac gone, Sam was left to shift her weight and clear her throat until she finally retreated, too, with barely a glance my way. She hasn't looked at me for more than a few seconds since they picked me up, and I can't help but wonder if all she sees in my eyes is the monster who killed Aria.

As horrible as it is, I'm glad when she leaves, too. The look in her and Isaac's eyes is somehow worse than Aurora's white-hot rage. The curiosity combined with grief, the questions they want to ask about what I've done or what I remember are bulldozers on a door I keep locked.

Instead of going down to the basement, like it's clear I'm meant to, I head for the front door and slip out into the night. Neither Isaac nor Sam told me not to leave, though it was certainly an unspoken rule. Dr. Benitez warned us all reception from residents might be varied.

I was given my dose of Dyebucetin by the facility this morning and don't need to visit Fatimah, the Island's doctor, in the infirmary until tomorrow, but I feel trapped in the house. Meeting the woman who'll be giving me the drugs keeping me conscious is as good a distraction as any. It's far better than sitting and waiting for Aurora to return.

I pull out the folded map made by Isaac, scrawled in Sharpie on the back of the cover page of an old book. The page is faded and ripped at the edges, but the drawing is clear.

The Island is shaped like a mushroom, four miles all the way around. The beach on the left, and the bay and docks on the right. The wide half of the Island is marked as uninhabited—the old military base. There are a few buildings and streets marked with little stars: the residential streets and Main Street, the infirmary and the school. According to the crude map, the infirmary is inside the police station on Main, alongside the armory.

It's a quiet walk away from the Blakes'. Despite the residential streets two blocks away, the Blakes seem to be the only people living on the street along the ocean side.

We made it over to the Island a few times before, for beach days or trailing up and down the block to browse overly expensive boutiques and bike shops. When the street curves—the historic and now half-ash Hotel Del to the right—the idyllic town is a wasteland. I expected as much.

What I didn't expect were the hints of regrowth. Debris shoved off parts of the streets or piled in old storefronts. Obvious efforts at rebuilding some of the shops. Completely different than the mainland.

A pile of objects in a small park draws me to a stop. At first, I think it's more debris, but the pile is too organized. Like every item was placed with care. Everything from toys to backpacks to dusty, cracked photograph frames.

A shrine.

Some kind of pressure builds in my chest, enough to be noticeable, and fades away. I lift a hand to my heart like I can will it to beat.

I wonder if any of my parents' things are in this pile. Any of mine. I don't know if Carter left with anything but the clothes on her back when she fled.

Carter. Thinking about her makes the pressure return to my lungs.

It was different when I didn't know where she was, when she was too far for it to matter. After what I did, I can't imagine she wants anything to do with me, but I make myself a promise to find her tomorrow. My apologies might not be worth anything, but I still have to make them.

I don't see anyone for the next few blocks, even as I approach the old police station. With the infirmary and armory in the same building, and the school and the old theater where town hall meetings are held a block away, this is the new center of the Island, according to Isaac's map.

The front lights for the large, beige stucco building have probably been burned out for years, so I approach the station in the dark. Though I'm allowed to be here, it still feels odd to walk around without supervision. At the facility, we had to be accompanied at all times, but right now, not a soul knows where I am. It's a giddying thought after so long under people's eyes.

The big doors creak as I pull them open and slip into the building. The front hall is lit by a few hanging lanterns, casting menacing shadows over old photos of the Island posted on the walls. Smiling faces of long-dead residents watch me as I make my way toward an open door at the end of the hall with soft light spilling out.

As I draw closer, a tune carries out into the hall—someone is humming a song, and I can almost remember what it's called. I come to a stop outside the door, listening, but before I can identify it, the humming stops.

"Hello?" a voice calls. I chew on the inside of my cheek, about to turn around and abandon this little trek altogether when a woman steps into the doorway. She's on the shorter side, round and soft, with dark skin and hair down to her shoulders. She's wearing a pair of mismatched scrubs, blue on top and yellow on the bottom. Her eyes are kind when they meet mine.

This must be Fatimah, the Island's doctor. She is immediately not what I expected. Not hard-faced and stern like most of the RPA doctors, but like someone's mom.

"Oh, hello. You startled me." Her lips pull up. "I'm usually the only one here this late."

If I could blush, I think I would.

"I'm sorry. I was . . ." I clear my throat. "I wanted to meet you." Technically, I wanted to get the hell out of the Blakes' house, but this isn't a lie. "You're Fatimah, right?"

"I am." Fatimah steps forward, wrapping an arm around my shoulders as she guides me into the infirmary. "Come on in. Let me find your file." I'm so shocked at the voluntary touch I can do nothing but follow without thinking. She tosses a glance over her shoulder, into the hall, like she's searching for someone or something, before releasing me and pulling the infirmary door shut behind us.

"What's your name?" she asks, moving over to her desk. The room is small, with a dozen cots, and clearly used to be some kind of boardroom.

"Mara," I say.

"Mara Knight?"

I nod.

At her desk, Fatimah flips through a stack of papers before stopping on one, tapping it with a finger.

"Ah, you're staying with Isaac and Rory."

Isaac and Rory. Not Isaac and Sam. Not the Blakes. It raises the question that came to life when Sam and Isaac picked me up. The way Sam moves around like a ghost, the way she shrank into the living room as Aurora and Isaac argued.

The Sam I remember was confident and controlled. If Aurora or the twins got in trouble, it was Sam who leveled out punishments and lectures. Sam was the authority. I'm unsure what she is now.

I nod. I expect Fatimah to press and ask why I'm here now, but she doesn't. Instead, she pushes her papers aside and smiles at me.

"So, you'll need to stop by each morning for your dose. Once a week, you'll need a nutritional injection, as well, as your digestive system is still out of commission. I'm always here, but if for some reason I'm not, or you're unable to reach me—" She pauses, tossing a glance at the closed door like she's expecting someone to walk through it. Once she's satisfied no one is, she tugs open a desk drawer and pulls out a small plastic case. She unzips it to reveal six vials with bright purple liquid inside. Dyebucetin.

"There are six emergency doses in here. Don't lose it." She swallows. "But keep it between us, yes?"

I want to ask why, but one thing I've learned since waking up in the facility is that sometimes, if you pretend not to care, people volunteer the answers themselves.

Sure enough, after a few seconds of silence, Fatimah continues, "There have been a few town hall briefs by an RPA doctor for the Island's residents about your arrivals, but let's just say public opinion is still varied."

Translation: Some of the people here still want me dead, and eventually, they might try and do something about it.

"But they agreed to let us in?" I ask.

Her brows twitch.

"That's the thing about compromise. Everybody wins a little, but everybody loses a little, too."

The scales seem skewed to me, but I suppose I'm biased. No one is as familiar with my monstrosity as I am. And if I were still human, a resident on the Island, I don't know which side I'd come out on.

"I hate them," I say softly.

"Hmm?" Carter hums.

"I hate them," I say, louder. "The Ticks. Does that make me a horrible person?"

Carter looks up from her perch on the windowsill. She has a water-stained book, found in a gutted Target, spread open on her lap, but she's been staring at the same page for the last ten minutes. She sets the book aside, not bothering with a bookmark, and jerks her chin at the spot beside her.

I join her on the sill, drawing my knees to my chest.

"Hating the monsters who killed everyone we ever knew? No, it doesn't make you a horrible person. It makes you sane." She stretches out her foot to poke me in the sneaker, giving me a smile.

"But they weren't always monsters. They were people," I say.

Her smile flattens. "They're not now."

"But we don't know—"

"Mara . . ."

"We don't. What if they're still in there, trapped?"

Carter huffs a breath. "You're right. We don't know." She shrugs a shoulder. "But it's not like we can afford to find out."

"I don't understand," I say, not realizing I'm speaking aloud until Fatimah responds.

"Well, the RPA has medicine stocks beyond the Dyebucetin used to treat you. Things like antibiotics. The only way to get them is to allow the Altered to settle in the communities, clearing up space for more—"

"No," I say. "I mean . . . I don't get the whole thing. Why put so much energy into treating us? What happened to finding a cure?"

"They tried." Fatimah purses her lips. "How long after the Fall were you turned?"

"About a year," I say.

I remember the first news story about a random violent attack came in March of my freshman year. A massacre at a research station in Antarctica. By May, there were dozens of stories throughout Asia and Europe. The infection hit Los Angeles in June, and after, I stopped counting the days. Carter tried to keep track, and she thought we were somewhere in July of what should have been the summer before junior year when I was bitten.

Fatimah makes an approving hum.

"So you remember the beginning," she says. "The calls for epidemiologists and research scientists to report to the CDC."

The PSAs and emergency broadcasts ran all day, every day, until one day, they stopped altogether. I remember.

"But that was to find a vaccine."

"It was." Fatimah gives me a sad smile. "From my understanding, the scientists and researchers at what we now call RPA facilities exhausted every resource they had. Granted, they weren't near as expansive as they were before. Every possible combination of compounds was tested."

She doesn't go into how all these drugs were tested, but she doesn't

41

need to. Once or twice, before I turned, my family and I ran into Ticks with boils all over their skin, or worse, skin that seemed like it was melting right off. One's skin was an odd green color—after the green Tick's blood had splattered on Carter's face, she spent an hour spraying herself off with a broken fire hydrant and made jokes about radioactivity. Now, though, I don't know if it was a joke. Experimenting on Ticks is the only way to figure out how we, well, *tick*.

"It was an accident," I say, not a question.

Fatimah looks pleased I've come to the conclusion on my own, and says, "Yes."

"They weren't trying to treat us."

Something about it makes a phantom ache pulse inside me. I'd believed the treatment came out of a drive to save those of us infected with the virus—to bring us back. But it was never about saving us. It was about preventing *more* of us.

"No." Her smile falters. "They've yet to be successful in finding a vaccine, and it's unlikely they ever will be. But with the Dyebucetin, there's at least hope of a future. Perhaps not a future any of us imagined for ourselves, but a future still."

So, the other Altered and I are the consolation prize for the apocalypse.

Since Dr. Benitez told me I was being sent to the Island, I've wondered if it would be better to stay at the facility forever, where I can't hurt anyone ever again. Where I wouldn't have to face the people I've hurt and the things I've done. Maybe it would be better for everyone.

Instead, I'm here. Staring down the barrel of a future I don't think I deserve.

When I return to the house, I linger on the front porch, reveling in the quiet. I don't want to risk a run-in with Aurora.

The facility was never silent. Even in the middle of the night, the generators hummed or churned. Footsteps clicked down the hallways as the soldiers patrolled. Sometimes, screams and moans filtered through the vents from wings with new Ticks.

Minutes pass, and the wind carries the salty smell of the sea up the sand and across the street. The night air pricks with a chill that skitters over my skin; it's not cold, exactly, or uncomfortable. Simply there. An unnecessary instinct for warmth draws me to pull an old hoodie left on the chair over my head.

Before I turned and after the world ended, when my nights were spent huddled in abandoned apartments or decrepit stores with Carter and my parents, I ran myself ragged wondering about Aurora. Wondering if she made it out, if the rest of her family was okay, if she was thinking about me.

I don't know what I expected her to be when I learned she was alive, but it wasn't this.

Anger or frustration are what I should feel, but instead, I am sad. Sad this is what we are now. Because if anyone has changed, it's me. I'm the nightmare she has every reason to fear.

A thick, heavy ache sweeps through my chest. It's so sudden, so unfamiliar, so painful I think it's some side effect of the Dyebucetin, but then motion catches my eye—a blond girl approaching the house— and I realize it's Aurora.

She hurt before. Stubborn as ever, she still manages to hurt now.

6

RORY

The sun has dipped beneath the ocean by the time I trudge, panting and sweating, back through the sand and up to the house. The trek awakened, and pissed off, my left leg, still sore from the walk up the bridge today, but it was worth it.

Our home, with a zigzagged roof, chipped white fencing along the short grass yard, and old white metal railing up the handful of stairs to the porch, is straight out of the eighties. It is nothing like our old place. I love it for that.

I falter as I come up the drive. Noah and Raisa aren't allowed outside after dark, and Sam and Isaac are usually busy wrangling Noah into a bath by now, but the porch isn't empty.

A figure sits in one of two wooden chairs at the edge of the porch, looking out at the endless ocean across the street. Wearing one of Isaac's hoodies, her hair raked back like she's been carding her fingers through it—a human action, *too* human—is Mara.

I was hoping to avoid her. Ever since I found out the Altered were coming back, I've had a churning pit in my belly.

It's dangerous, and idiotic, but above all, it's unfair. The Ticks ended the world, ate it away like termites, and now all their slates have been wiped clean. They've been given a second chance at life, and the rest of us are stuck with this fragment of one.

Isaac likes to say the strongest of humanity survived, but I don't think it's true. I think the worst of us made it this far. And maybe we didn't start out that way, but years of stealing and killing and hurting have left us rotten. The Ticks, too, but now they get a free pass for it.

I wonder if Mara remembers anything from her time as a Tick, if it haunts her the way the last few years haunt me. Probably not. She probably sleeps easier than anyone.

Lucky her. I haven't gotten a full eight hours in years.

I stop at the top of the last stair, waiting for her to notice me. It takes me too long to realize she already has and is waiting for me to do something. Kill her, talk to her, leave her alone.

"You're going to get killed if you stay out here like a sitting duck," I say. I don't realize I've crossed the speckled-tile porch and pulled out the chair three feet from her until I'm lowering into it.

"By you?" she says eventually. I forgot what we were talking about, and it takes me a moment to recall my comeback.

"I'm thinking about it," I say.

Her mouth twists, but she doesn't take the bait. The old Mara would have. The old Mara wasn't this quiet, either. All she does is look out at the ocean with an odd, hollow look on her face.

"What?"

She shakes her head. "Nothing," she says, and shrugs. "You're not as different as I expected."

My heart skips a beat. Fucking traitor.

"Can't say the same for you, Joker," I say, gesturing to her face.

She makes a strangled noise I think might be a laugh.

"Really?"

"What?"

"Surely you can do better."

I scoff, folding my arms across my chest. "I think the resemblance is uncanny."

She inclines her head, fixes those disconcerting silver eyes on me, and deadpans, "See, I think Edward Scissorhands is more on the nose. Or Freddy Krueger."

"Well, I'm not going to sit here and be lectured on pop culture by a zombie."

Her fingers twitch where they rest on the table. Forcing my eyes onto the dark beach ahead of us, I press my lips together and pretend my stomach isn't twisted into knots.

"What happened to your parents, Mara?" I say, poking at her facade, trying to punch through it.

She freezes in my peripheral vision. Her voice is clipped as she says, ignoring my question, "Your parents told me Carter is on the Island."

"I heard a rumor. About how they died." It is a low blow, an unspoken post-apocalyptic taboo, but anger is rising in me like a tidal wave, threatening to bust past the seawall and drown us both.

It's her turn to avoid my gaze. A muscle ticks in her jaw.

"Please just tell me if she's okay, Aurora," she says. The name vacuums the air from my lungs, and I'm grateful she's not looking at me. I can't look at her anymore.

I don't like the way she says it. Like it's a joke, or a weapon, or a metaphor I can't understand. The small ache that has sat like a stone in my gut for three years grows and shifts into my lungs. I swallow dryly.

"She's fine," I say. "And don't call me that."

"Your name?" Her silver gaze slides to mine. "And define *fine*."

"*Fine* as in she's as arrogant as ever, and no, she doesn't want to see you." I sit back in the chair, feigning calm. "As for the other thing, nobody calls me that." I clear my throat. "It's Rory."

She studies me.

"*Just* . . . don't call me that." I'm not sure why I say it—her silence is suffocating, and I think she's doing it on purpose. "And if you're going to be here, there are going to be rules."

Mara's odd, hoarse laugh sounds again.

"You're not part of this family. You're not welcome here. I don't give a shit what Isaac says. If I'm not around, you stay away from Raisa and Noah, or I *will* kill you. Do you understand me? I'll kill you, and I won't lose any sleep over it."

Again, she is quiet. Staring at me, inquisitive as ever, and god, I want to stab her, if only to make her stop looking at me like this.

"See, *Rory*," she says, and I hate the way it sounds, too, "I think we both know that's not true."

I push to my feet. I tower when I face her, though she's unbothered. My attempts to intimidate a monster are unsuccessful, but it doesn't stop me from trying.

"You are not my Mara," I say.

"No," she says. "I'm not." She pauses. "You called them Sam and Isaac. Not *Mom and Dad*. Why?"

She wasn't this confrontational before—she circled conflict until it, or I, dragged her inside. I'm so surprised by the question, I don't think before answering.

"Because my parents are dead," I say, "and so is Aurora." As I turn to leave, a faded woven bracelet wrapped around Mara's wrist catches my attention, and I stall, heart thudding like a kick drum.

I knotted it around her wrist the day before everything ended. She asked why I made it, but she really meant to ask why I made it for *her*, and I couldn't find the words. Instead of trying, I bent toward her, and I kissed her.

My anger deflates, and I'm not Rory anymore, but Aurora, and I am fifteen, and Mara's eyes are green.

Before I do anything stupid, like cry, I head for the door.

She broke the world. I can't forget it.

7

MARA

I've never had a room to myself like this. In our old house, Carter's and my Jack-and-Jill-style rooms shared a bathroom, and her music always filtered in through the closed door, or the television my parents were watching in the front room carried down the short hall.

The basement is quiet. Not like outside, where the wind and lapping waves swirl through the air. Without any background noise, it's hard not to think about all the people who aren't above me. My parents. Carter. I wonder what my parents would think of the Island. Of me. I wonder what it was like for Carter, all alone. I wonder how she ended up on the Island.

Squeaky wooden steps lead down to the tiled floor of the basement, and an old and broken washer-and-dryer set faces the staircase. Tubs marked with their contents—supplies, medical, clothing, blankets, and so on—line the walls, and a myriad of candles with flickering flames take up every flat surface.

In the far corner, a futon is pressed against the wall, a stack of folded blankets and a pillow perched atop it. To its side, a chipped wooden dresser and a lamp without a bulb.

At the top of the stairs, the locks click into place. One, two, three trapping me until morning. Ignoring the flash of panic at the temporary incarceration, I shift my good fingers through as many basic chords as I can remember on my other arm. C, D, Em, E, and on and on until the Tick settles in my thoughts.

I wander over to the long rectangular window above the futon. Thick curtains cover it, and I draw back the fabric. Flimsy boards are held in place by rusting nails, and without thinking, I use one of my good fingers to test the boards. The wood comes away, splintering in my hands, wood dust billowing up and into my eyes. I blink it away and peer through the window into the dark, still night.

Not completely still. A flash of white to the left draws my gaze, and a beat later, Aurora crosses the grass, hair pulled up. She's shed her jacket for a tank top, and pale scars down her arms shine in the moonlight. One of her hands brushes over the hilt of her sword, like she's reassuring herself it's there. According to Sam and Isaac, the Island's curfew falls at sunset. I'm not surprised Aurora is breaking it, but I am curious as to why. Curious, and restless.

The rest of the boards come off easily. It's stupid, I remind myself with each passing minute, but I don't stop. The logic dies when my feet touch the grass and set after Aurora.

Aurora walks down the grassy median of the main avenue slowly, a slight limp to her gait. Her pace is calm, like she's taking a midnight stroll. With each step, the hilt of the sword she treats like a fifth limb brandishes itself, and I remember where we are, who she is.

You are not my Mara, she said, but she is not my Aurora, either. She's Rory. My Aurora always had a lopsided grin and a joke to crack. When she spoke, she didn't care if anyone agreed with what she had to say. That first moment we met eyes in the living room, and again on the deck of the house, I could see her. It's in her little motions: a trace of the girl under the patchwork armor.

Seeing her for the first time in three years, neither of us who we thought we'd be, felt a little bit like dying all over again. Like seeing someone I grew up with change so much hammered in my own differences.

I slow my pace, tucking into the shadows behind her, hidden by awning skeletons and darkness as we push through the remnants of the town. Cars stripped of parts and tires and siphoned to their last drops are scattered about the street. When I inhale, the wind smells of salt and ash.

By the time Rory reaches the block-sized park halfway down the main street, her limp is more pronounced. I can hear her huff and puff, and her shoulders rise and fall with the effort. Her skin glistens with a sheen of sweat despite the cool night.

The park is mostly grass, save for a now-crumbling metal jungle gym, bricked bathrooms that have definitely seen better days, and a white-flecked gazebo in the center.

Rory moves to join the group of people lingering at the base of the gazebo steps, their attention focused on the uniformed man at the top. I slink between trees and don't inch closer than I need to. The Tick turned my senses up on high, and what should be unintelligible noise is clear conversation. The discussion—more accurately, heated debate—has at least twenty heads, ashen and edged faces contorted with rage or fear or both. They range from middle-aged to older teens like us.

"—have children here! And the RPA expects us to welcome these monsters into our community?"

"The *RPA* won't even come out of their barricaded headquarters because they're afraid! They don't speak for us. 'Every man for himself' doesn't extend to *Ticks*."

"Would you be calling them that if it were your son coming home, Ollie? Or your husband?"

"And how will you justify it when your son tears his sister's throat out over the dinner table?"

Back and forth the arguments go, emotions rising and cresting. The air is thick with tension, even back here in my subtle hiding spot behind a tree.

I keep waiting for Rory to pop in, to agree with the majority who believe the Altered are uncontrollable, bloodthirsty monsters who deserve no more than a bullet to the brain, but she remains silent and motionless at the back of the pack.

I shouldn't be surprised she's here, among people who would gladly take my head off without question. I shouldn't care. I shouldn't need to dig my remaining fingers into the bark until a single tiny spark of pain flickers in one fingertip, and I draw them all back.

Rory has made it clear she wants nothing to do with me, and it's hard to be angry at her for it. But try as I might, I haven't figured out how to do the same. She's grown up, and I am a buzzing preteen drunk in her presence. Nothing between us is the same—we are not the same—but the infuriating, ill-timed feeling is.

The man beneath the gazebo awning wears a navy-blue camouflage uniform, and even if he weren't standing on an elevated surface, his presence is dominating enough to make me believe he's the leader of this little gathering. Whatever it is. Black hair is cropped close to his skull, and his face is clean shaven. His dark eyes are narrowed, like they got stuck. The same way his lips seem to have been stuck in a judgmental scowl.

Two stern-faced women flank him, standing on the top steps, like secret service officers. One is middle-aged, the other younger, closer to Carter's age.

"I understand your concerns," the man says. His voice is gravel against cement. "And I share them. These . . . *creatures* are not welcome here. Not in a community they destroyed without remorse, without thought, and without punishment."

His words are true, but they still sting. And I do feel remorse. So much I think I'll drown in it.

I don't know any of their names, but I remember all of their faces. An old woman and her granddaughter with the same wide blue eyes. A man wearing glasses with no lenses. A girl with green hair and enough metal in her face to set off a metal detector. More, too, and I slaughtered each one. I tore out throats with my blunt teeth. My hands punched through rib cages and ripped out intestines.

There is no sugarcoating any of it.

"And the *Alliance*"—the word is thrown out like a curse—"will not prevent us from maintaining the safety and security of those who *haven't* killed with their bare hands!"

His energy is infecting the crowd, and the small group is buzzing with anticipation. The Tick squirms and writhes in my skull, every nerve ending alight and aware, preparing for a perceived threat.

It's harder to talk the voice down when the people across the grass are chatting about how badly they want me dead. Truly dead.

"We are one of the last pockets of civilization in this state"—I'm pretty sure this is an exaggeration, as at least ten major settlements are scattered across Southern California alone—"and we will not fall under the rules given by those who survived the Fall by hiding in a bunker."

He's a captivating public speaker. More dangerously, he believes what he's saying.

"Fifteen of these creatures have been dropped in our laps," he says. Dropped. Even I, with my limited knowledge, know the resettlement was part of a trade earning each community badly needed pharmaceuticals from the RPA. But these people don't seem to know, or don't seem to care. "It is up to us to keep them monitored and controlled. Their names will be distributed, and shifts will be assigned for watches until this *mess* can be cleaned up—"

Vivian was right. I've jumped from one prison to another bigger one. I'm beginning to wonder if she was right about running, too—if it isn't too late to do it myself.

I shift closer to hear over the rising voices, and a small twig crunches under my sneaker. I freeze, dropping to my knees and ducking behind the tree.

A handful of the voices falter, the leader's stopping with it. Silence settles quickly over the group. In the span of three seconds, I've pictured a dozen ways these people can punish me for the sin of still being alive.

"The hell was that?" a deep voice asks.

I don't wait to hear more, slipping through the darkness back to the street. I run until I reach the beach, and I make it to the Blakes' block without interruption. I almost miss the voice calling out behind me.

Almost.

The tone is familiar, more tempered, a bit deeper. If I hadn't grown up hearing it across the dinner table, I wouldn't distinguish it in its differences.

"I said *stop*," Carter repeats.

Whatever is left of my mangled stomach is in my throat, clawing its way up my tongue. I slow, turn, and find a nail gun pointed straight at my face, held by a version of my sister I barely recognize.

She's going to shoot me. With a nail. It's so ridiculous, so impossible, I have to stifle a laugh.

My movements, however small, wind Carter tighter, and she pushes the sharp tip of the nail closer.

A plea curdles on my tongue, and I swallow it with the realization that the Carter I knew is also long gone, further away than I am. I can't find a trace of my sister in her steel-green eyes. Her hair, bouncing and shining in all my memories, is pulled and slicked back into a bun, and she's wearing those blue camouflage pants she used to make fun of the sailors in town for.

The Carter I remember was bright and loud and opinionated. Her filter was abysmal, and her curses came too quickly. She couldn't show up on time if you threatened her. She was fierce, and she was loyal, and she was my sister. And I was hers.

"Do you think this is really the end? Like . . . The End, capital letters,"

I whisper. Carter and I are squished into a sleeping bag in the corner of a stripped loft. Across the small room, our parents sleep fitfully, weapons lined on either side of them like railings.

Carter is silent for a moment, and I wonder if she's fallen asleep when she asks, "Have you ever heard of the green flash?"

I'm not sure where she's going with this, but I know I'm supposed to follow the trail.

"I think so."

"Mom told me about it, this one time we were at the beach. She said if you looked out at the ocean when the sun was setting, right when the sun disappeared under the water, a green flash would appear. And I stared at the ocean so hard I thought my eyes would pop out, but I didn't see it. Every time I went to the beach, I looked for it, and every time, I didn't see it."

"I know," I say. "You won't let us leave until it's good and dark."

Carter smiles. She doesn't do it much anymore, and I realize I don't, either.

"That last time," Carter says, and her smile fades, "I remember asking myself, 'How long are you gonna stare at the frigging ocean, looking for nothing?' And when I was about to call it quits on the whole green flash bullshit . . ." She lets out a breath. "I saw it. I saw it." The sleeping bag crinkles as she shifts closer, twining her fingers through mine and squeezing. "I don't know if this is really the end of it all. The grand finale for humankind. But I want to believe it's not. I'm going to believe it's not." She squeezes my hand again. "Maybe if we believe long enough, we'll get our own green flash."

"If you so much as breathe, you're getting an eight-inch stud to the brain." Even her voice is different, slick like rain on asphalt and sharp against my faltering defenses.

"Carter," I say.

A shudder ripples through her, and for a second, I swear she's going to do it and this fever dream will end. I can't decide whether

I want it to. In all my daydreams about leaving the facility, I never landed here, with them. With Carter and Rory and all these ghosts.

"Quiet." Her hand wavers. She might kill me by accident. "You don't get to call me that."

"Carter—" Her grip on the nail gun tightens, and I clamp my mouth shut, try again. "I know. I shouldn't be out here. I'm going back to the Blakes' right now—"

"I don't think you are," she says, taking a step forward as I take one back.

I'm not sure if I want to laugh or cry. I killed my family, and what's left of it is going to kill me. Once again, I'm suppressing a wildly inappropriate smile.

It's always been a bad habit of mine. Discomfort or awkwardness or tension draws laughter out of me in the worst of moments. And this is definitely the worst moment.

"Please don't do this," I say. "You don't have to do this." I stumble back, but my unrecognizable sister matches my stride. I smack into the skeleton of an SUV, the rims rattling as I collide with them. The cool plastic of the nail gun digs into my forehead. I will myself to sink into the debris.

Carter's eyes, green like mine used to be, are wide, the pupils blown, and her strong jaw is clenched tight. Her aim is steady.

She wants to kill me. And part of me is relieved. After all this, it ends where it begins, with my blood. Literally and figuratively. I killed our parents. I left my sister alone in a burning world. The girl I love thinks I'm a monster, and she isn't the only one who believes so. I can't blame her, or Carter, or any of the people who want me dead.

No one can say I didn't deserve this. If the situations were reversed, I might take the shot. I remember what it was to hate the Ticks before, and I know what it is to hate them now.

"Oh, Jesus Christ." This voice, too, is familiar.

Rory comes to a halt half a foot from where Carter has me trapped against the vehicle. I risk a glance in her direction. Her dark brows are drawn together, plump pink lips pursed, but I can't read any intent in her eyes.

"Go home, Rory. This isn't your business," Carter spits through clenched teeth. Her glare stays focused on me.

"It will be when whoever's on patrol finds a body in the street outside my house," Rory says.

My heart gives a solitary thump against my ribs.

Carter inclines her head. "I'll burn it."

"And when they notice the fire?"

Carter drops the nail gun so quickly I flinch. She shifts partially, keeping half her attention on me as she addresses Rory. Neither of us is short, but Rory, as tall as Viv, towers over her.

"What the hell are you defending this thing for?" Carter snaps. "It doesn't matter what she looks like. She's not—"

"*I'm not.* I'm trying to avoid the awkward conversations you're going to drag me into after you kill your sister."

"She is not my—"

"Shut up for five seconds!" And to my surprise, Carter does. Rory rakes a hand through her blond hair, now loose and hanging like tangled strands of white silk, the breeze lifting it off her bare shoulders. "I'm not defending her. I'm also not arguing with you. I'm telling you. Let her go." With a blink, she transforms, solidifies into cement. This quiet, calm wrath is not directed at me, and I resist the urge to shrink against it.

"Go home, Carter," Rory says, and it is not a proposition, but an order.

Carter relents, tucks the gun back into place on her belt. She throws a single murderous glance my way before huffing and trudging down the street.

Rory doesn't look at me, and I think she's going to leave, depart into the darkness. At least she doesn't seem intent on killing me herself right now.

"That thing in your brain didn't eat your common sense, did it?" she asks suddenly. I stiffen, lips parting, though no words fall out. "Curfew isn't a suggestion."

I cock a brow, gesture between us.

"Curfew isn't for humans. And *I* am not a"—she waves a hand dismissively—"whatever you are." She releases a deep breath. Presses her lips together. "Half this island wants you dead. And next time they get you, I won't stop them."

"Why did you this time?" I ask, not because I think she'll tell me, but because I'm trying to make sense of the words. Trying to make sense of what she did. Why she would do it.

"I didn't do it for you," she sneers. I knew snark was coming, but I'm still wounded by it. Even if it's a little too venomous to be true. "Because, unfortunately, as much as I'd love to let the next trigger-happy survivor with a weapon who crosses your path end both of our suffering . . ." She pauses. Like she's not sure if she wants to continue. "My family needs this. After everything they've lost, they need you."

But do you? I want to ask. *Did you need me before?*

"So maybe try not to get yourself murdered," she says. "I've lit enough funeral pyres."

She turns, heads in the direction of the house. Her departure is a clear end to the conversation, but I have too many questions, and I get the feeling Sam and Isaac don't have the answers.

I push after her, not daring to touch her, and slow at her side. "Who was that back there?"

Her brow twitches; there is a thin line through it, a pink scar stretching half a centimeter up.

"That would be a pissed-off Carter Knight. Surely you remember your own sister."

The honesty is something I remember—the cruelty is new. But I have my own talents, and I still know the girl walking beside me. Not all of her, not anymore, but enough to throw my own spear.

It takes thirty seconds and precisely half a block of silence for Rory to speak again, answering my initial question.

"Colonel Mallory Gordon," she says. The tone drips with false sincerity. "He was on the Island when the outbreak hit. There were fifteen thousand people here, you know. I may not trust him, but I'll give him credit for this." She gestures around us. "He and a dozen people cleared this entire island. Only he, Fatimah, and a few others are left from day one, but since then, most everyone's treated him like a god."

We're a few feet from the porch, and I'm reluctant to reach it. The porch signals the end of the conversation, and I am not likely to get another one soon.

"He's in charge?" I ask. "What about Thalia?"

Rory's nose scrunches—an old habit. "Thalia O'Neill?" She shakes her head. "She started the Alliance, and I guess if anyone's technically its leader, it'd be her, but everyone in the Alliance has their own . . . system. The RPA is entirely their own thing, and no one knows much about how they work or who's in charge, but Pacific Beach and Solana elected mayors. Point Loma has a council, I think. Mal just never gave up his reins."

His radiating anger from the gazebo flashes behind my eyes. His twisting of the truth.

"He doesn't want the Altered here," I say, and it isn't phrased as a question, but it is one.

She nods.

"He won't outright admit it, but he wants to lock this place down again, like it was before the Alliance. No mainland influence. And he's got everyone here wrapped around his finger."

"But not you?" I ask. Her disdain for the man is clear, but she still snuck out to listen to him speak.

"No," she says, glowering at me—we've returned to full hatred. "I don't need Mal to convince me not to trust you."

"Is a straight answer impossible for you?"

"A straight *anything* is impossible for me—"

I scoff. I'm grateful I can't blush.

"I like to keep an eye on things," she says. Her shoulders are tense.

We've reached the Blakes' porch, coming to a stop before the first step. Above us, the moon is half-full and surrounded by endless black. The dark and moonlight make the green home a pale gray.

Rory turns to face me. "It isn't just monsters who end the world. It's men. Men like Mal. And next time, I'm going to be ready."

"You're so sure there's going to be a next time?"

"What's the alternative?" she asks. "A happily ever after?"

I'd like to contradict her, to elongate this small moment of normalcy, but she's right. I'm fairly sure our happy endings died with most of the population. And those of us left don't deserve them, anyway.

8

MARA

When I push through the infirmary door, a college-aged Altered boy is sitting behind Fatimah's desk, leaning back with his sneakers up on the corner of the wood.

I stop, letting the door swing shut behind me, and frown at him.

He looks up at my entrance, hands stilling over the papers he's riffling through in his lap. Files, like the one Fatimah read my name out of last night.

He can't be older than twenty, with tight, dark curls spilling over his forehead. A scar on one side of his mouth gives him a tiny permanent smirk.

"Mornin'," the boy says, like we're old friends. The other Altered and I have been here for a day, but he lounges with the familiarity of a local.

"What are you doing in here?" I ask. I'm being rude, but I can't find it in me to care.

"Same thing you are." The boy leans farther back in the chair, so far I swear he's going to topple over. "Waiting for Fatimah to get back."

At my deepening frown, the boy continues, "She said something about jerky, and she seemed pretty excited about it. I don't know." He shrugs. "She should be back soon."

I say nothing. The boy removes his feet from the desk and sits forward, inspecting me.

"I remember you from the facility," he says. "Didn't realize you were from the Island." He gets out of the chair and comes around to lean into the front of the desk, folding his arms over his chest. "I'm Emir."

"Mara," I say. "And I'm not. From here, I mean." I step farther into the room and drop onto the edge of the nearest cot. "I'm staying with the Blakes. My godparents. My family is from North Park."

Emir nods.

"My parents were out on some whale-watching tour when it all went down. Them and a dozen other old farts hung out on the water for like a week and then came to the Island." He scoffs. "I was a mile out of downtown when the infection hit the city." He gestures to himself. He's covered in gashes and lacerations like I am, the worst of it a mangled area of skin covering half his right arm. "Clearly didn't work out for me."

"Short end of the stick, huh?" I ask.

Emir laughs, and a smile tugs on my lips.

Down the hall, the door whines open and shut, followed by the chatter of two voices. A few seconds later, the infirmary door opens, and Fatimah walks in carrying a black tote bag filled with dried jerky. At her side is an Altered girl around thirteen years old with sheet-white hair. She has a tote bag with jerky, too.

"Emir. I see you've made yourself at home," Fatimah says with a smile. "Mara. Good morning. I see I have another early bird."

"They always get the worm," Emir says.

"That doesn't make sense," the girl says. "I mean, who cares when the bird gets there? It's not like worms are some endangered species."

"That's actually a pretty good point, Dolly," Emir says.

Fatimah claps her hands once. "Alright, alright. Come on, time for your doses." She takes the tote from the girl, Dolly, and sets both on top of her desk and heads to the other side of the infirmary, past the cots, to a door. A supply closet behind it is piled with boxes.

Fatimah lifts the flap on the closest box and removes three syringes

61

filled with bright purple liquid. She makes her way back to her desk and sets two of the needles down.

"I hate this part," Dolly moans.

"Just get it over with," Emir says, and his voice is gentle.

Dolly grits her teeth and crosses to Fatimah.

"Where do you want it?" Fatimah asks.

"Nowhere," Dolly says. She sighs. "Neck is fine."

Fatimah gives Dolly's shoulder a squeeze before brushing the hairs to one side.

Dolly's fingers curl so tightly around the nearest edge of the desk the whole thing shakes.

Fatimah plunges the needle into Dolly's neck. Dolly flinches, eyes clamped shut, but she relaxes when Fatimah removes the syringe. Her shoulders slump.

Fatimah deposits the needle in a tiny trash bin with a lid near the desk. Biohazard containers are a luxury lost to the apocalypse.

"You're good to go," Fatimah says. Dolly opens her eyes and shudders.

"Emir, you're up."

"I know, I know," Emir says, waving a hand as he rounds the desk, taking Dolly's place as she retreats to sink onto a cot across from me. Emir kneels slightly so Fatimah can reach his neck, craning his head toward her. He stiffens but doesn't flinch when she injects him.

Then it's my turn. I hold myself still as Fatimah plunges the needle in, familiar with the routine, even comforted by it. A little pressure, a pinch, and the certainty of another day as myself.

Fatimah tosses the third syringe into the bin.

"You're all set," she says.

Dolly gives a disgruntled hum, and the sound reminds me so much of myself at that age I think it would hurt if it could. "Until tomorrow," she says, and stands, marching out the door without another word.

At her exit, Emir says, "Well, I guess we're going." He gives Fatimah a smile. "Thanks. See you in the morning."

"See you in the morning," Fatimah says.

Emir heads for the door, and I follow his and Dolly's lead.

"I'll see you tomorrow," I say.

"See you tomorrow, Mara," Fatimah says. Before I've turned all the way, she's uncapping a pen—probably recording our doses.

Outside the station, Emir is still heading down the steps, Dolly a few yards ahead of him on the sidewalk. He looks back as I push through the doors and slows down in a silent invitation to join.

I jog to join him, falling into step at his side.

My gaze strays to Dolly, walking ahead like she's making a point not to stand with us.

As if reading my thoughts, Emir says, "Her dad works with chickens or something during the day, so she's hanging out with me and my parents until he gets home."

"I don't need a babysitter!" Dolly calls. I shouldn't be surprised she's listening. The Tick gave us heightened senses, cranked everything up a few notches.

"Take it up with the wardens!" Emir yells back. Dolly lifts a hand, one finger raised.

Emir tosses me a grin. "Personally, if I was the Tick, I'd steer clear of hormonal thirteen-year-olds. Give the Tick a run for its money."

I snort a laugh despite myself, and it pleases Emir. I can't remember the last time I laughed. The noise feels odd coming out.

"Pissed-off teenager versus monster? I'd pay to see that fight," Emir says.

Emir doesn't seem to mind my quiet, either. He fills the silence so I don't have to.

"Who are you putting money on, though?" I ask.

"Oh, Dolly, for sure," he says.

Dolly glances over her shoulder, one side of her mouth lifting in a smile.

"Damn right," she calls.

"Do you kiss your mother with that mouth, Dolly?"

Dolly laughs and slows down a bit, letting us catch up to her.

As we walk through the old town, it feels like I'm a kid again, walking with Rory and our neighborhood friends down to the grocery store to rack up snacks and caffeine, giggling as we go.

In another life, I might still do those things. Dolly certainly would. Emir, maybe, would walk down this block holding someone's hand.

But in this life, it is us, three monsters walking down Main Street.

9

RORY

I come down the hall the next morning to find Mara perched on the arm of the couch, her sleeve hiked up to her shoulder. She leans to the side, and black strands of hair, shining in the morning sun, hang long enough to graze the moss-colored fabric she's sitting on.

She gets her treatment every morning from Fatimah in the infirmary, but for some reason, Isaac stands at her side, a capped syringe in one hand, the other steady around Mara's bicep. Sam hovers behind them, watching intently, gnawing on her thumbnail the way she does when she's nervous.

"You shouldn't have to, but in case Fatimah can't give it to me. It doesn't really matter where you inject it," says Mara. "Just don't hit an artery with the needle."

"Or what, you'll die?" I ask. Sam stiffens, and Isaac lets out a deep sigh. Mara tenses, shifts forward, looks me up and down in a way that makes something inside me boil.

"And good morning to you, kiddo," Isaac says. Sam catches his eye, a silent exchange passing between them. After so many years together, they have their own secret language. Once upon a time, I knew someone that well.

Just as I note how quiet it is, Noah barrels through the doorway from the kitchen, screaming like a banshee. Raisa is hot on his heels, a smile on her lips as she chases after him. He launches across the living room and onto the couch across from Mara, and Raisa climbs up next to him, catching him and tickling him into submission.

Once he's been properly subdued, Raisa sits up, blowing strands of hair out of her face. Her cheeks are flushed a deep red, and she—Noah, too, his eyes and smile wide—is happier than I've seen her in a while.

Good things don't happen much around here. And for some reason, to everyone else in this house, Mara's arrival is a good thing. It's nauseating. I don't understand how I'm the only one who can see we've let Death in the door.

"Does it hurt?" Noah asks, staring at the needle Isaac tucks back into its case. Pulled by an invisible tether, I join Raisa and Noah on the couch, dropping down between them. Noah tucks himself into my side, getting comfortable. I catch Sam's eyes and roll my own.

Then Mara talks, and reality slams back into focus.

"No," she says. "It's a little pinch."

I slip a protective arm around him. Raisa, sensing my tension, shifts closer to me. She gives me a tiny, supportive smile.

Noah pouts, a little disappointed, but quickly, he smiles again. "Your eyes are pretty." He leans forward, giving Raisa an inquisitive look. "Do you think they're pretty, Raisa?"

Raisa hesitates, flicks a glance at Mara—I wonder how much Raisa remembers of her; she was seven last she saw her—and nods.

"Raisa thinks so, too," Noah says, satisfied. I might find it adorable if I weren't scolding myself for leaving the sword on my nightstand. The endless no-weapons-in-the-house argument has found a single compromise: no blades before breakfast.

Mara smiles at him, as lopsided as ever. Something deep in my chest wrenches, and I stamp it back down.

"Rory," Sam says. She and Isaac have come around to settle on the couches and chairs, like this is some normal family morning. Like there isn't a monster on the settee. "Eliza mentioned last night she'd be dropping the jerky off later this morning. You're not still going to the Bay, are you?"

"Course I am. The trade was set up weeks ago," I say. "If you paid a little more attention around here, you might know that."

Sam barely hides a flinch. I almost feel bad for the jab. Almost. But the mom I knew died the day Aria did, and while she might make brief appearances, she's Sam now. She dropped the mantle and left me to pick it up. Her attempts to take it back when it pleases her are more nuisance than anything.

"It's a risk—" Sam begins.

"You don't think I can handle myself?"

"Of course I think you can handle yourself. But it's still dangerous. We have enough going on without another trip to the mainland."

"We need these meds. And if I don't show up, the Bay doesn't get the jerky. We might not get any more trades. If I leave now, I can make it before sunset. In the morning, I hit the road, and I'm back by nightfall. Easy done."

"It is never 'easy done,'" Sam says. I tense, and Noah slips his hand into mine. Raisa, too, has silently taken my side. Only the latter understands what we're truly talking about. We've done our best to drown out Noah's mainland memories with Island ones.

I straighten, lean forward. "This isn't some jaunt to the mainland. Mal ordered me to go." I have my own questions about why Mal would send me when he has a dozen soldiers to choose from. "Maybe if someone stood up to him once in a while, I wouldn't have to listen, but that's not how things work here, is it?"

Her composure cracks briefly, and guilt flares in my gut, hot and sharp. But I need out of this house, off this island, away from Mara and the tension slowly coiling around us all like a python squeezing its prey.

"You're taking a walkie," Sam says.

"Sure," I say. "Seeing how this island gets absolutely zero reception, that'll go *swimmingly*."

Sam opens her mouth to argue, probably, but Isaac touches her arms and draws her gaze.

"She has a point," he says.

"Isaac—"

"We know these people," he says. "This isn't Oceanside or Pacific Beach we're sending her off to. We spent a week in the Bay. As far as we know, it's safe."

"Yeah, and *as far as we know* is what I don't like," Sam says. Looks at me. I look away.

"She's going to be fine." Isaac gives me an encouraging smile.

"Isaac's right. I'm going to be fine," I say, forcing some of the hardness out of my tone. I look between Sam and Isaac. "I always am."

Sam frowns. "It rained hard all last night. The roads could be—"

Isaac's watch, which has been around longer than Noah, screeches its alarm, making us all jump. Sam lets her sentence die in the air.

"Time for school, rascals," Isaac says to Raisa and Noah.

Sam sighs, drawing a hand down her face. She pushes to her feet, Isaac beside her, and fixes me with a take-no-shit stare I haven't seen in ages. Something about Mara's arrival has woken her up.

It makes me hate Mara more. I tried for months to drag Sam out of the dark hole she fell into, but one day with Mara and she's remembered she used to be a parent.

Sam crosses the living room to wrap me in a quick hug. I stand stiffly with my arms at my sides. She squeezes tightly once before releasing me. Isaac pulls me into his arms next, dropping a kiss to the crown of my head.

"Be safe," he hums as he lets me go. I give him a mock salute, and he rolls his eyes with a smile, pulling Sam and the kids toward the door.

We don't do drawn-out, dramatic goodbyes anymore. I guess we all said so many to people we never saw again that doing it still feels like a self-fulfilling prophecy. Like maybe if we don't say anything at all, the universe won't realize we have something to lose.

❂

With Isaac and Sam helping out at one of the residents' community gardens and the kids at school—it's a dozen kids of different ages and two graduate students in the old gym, but it's something—it's only Mara and me at the house. It's never felt so small. As if the walls have gotten thinner and her footsteps and quiet breaths follow me everywhere.

Eventually, I give up trying to escape her and settle in the living room waiting for Eliza Heath and her jerky. Most of the houses have some form of garden in the yard, but the larger mansions, occupied by multiple families, use their large yards as makeshift farms. The Heaths and Zavalas raise pigs. The Cantus, the McAllisters, and the Wangs have a dozen cows. The Walshes, a few dozen chickens.

Mara sits perched on the far side of the room, thumbing through a magazine at least five years old and missing half its pages. Suddenly, she stiffens like a rod, her head snapping toward the door.

"Someone is coming," she says.

"It's Eliza," I say.

"No," Mara says, standing. "I can hear boots. They're too heavy. It's a man."

"Since when do you have superhuman hearing?" I ask.

Mara shoots me a patronizing look. "It's not superhuman. It's just better than your—" She freezes, and a half second later, there is a single commanding knock on the front door.

I jerk to my feet and instinctually reach for my sheath. Empty. I curse inwardly and take careful steps to the door.

One lock. Two, three, and the door swings open.

Mallory Gordon stands on the other side, a large wagon piled high with packaged jerky behind him.

He's sent me on a trade one other time, after Carter and I returned from the supply sweep on the mainland. It was a thinly veiled punishment that didn't land. Most residents want nothing to do with the mainland, but it was a badly needed escape, and not one Mal gave me again.

Mal wouldn't admit it, but I know Carter told him I stopped her from shooting Mara. God knows what he'd have done if he learned I let her out.

"What the hell are you doing here?" I ask.

Mal scowls. In the early light, his hair is exceptionally greasy, like he dumped olive oil onto his scalp.

"A shame you were never taught manners," he says. "My girls never spoke disrespectfully to authority."

"Lot of good it did them in the end," I say.

Mal stiffens, and a vein pulses in his forehead. It's massive, and I think if he doesn't get control of himself, he'll break a blood vessel.

It takes everything in me not to keep poking this particular bear. Instead, I ask, "Where is Eliza?"

"I wanted to handle this personally," he says. He flicks a glance over my shoulder, toward Mara, and I step into his way without thinking. "Check in with all of you. See how the transition is going." He cocks a brow.

"Yeah, well, my parents aren't here, and I'm not really in the mood for small talk. Leave the jerky on the porch." I go to shut the door, but Mal throws out a hand, stopping it halfway. He nudges it back open, taking a half step inside, a grin on his lips.

"Let's not be hasty, Rory." He looks at Mara again. She still hasn't moved, as if someone nailed her to the floor.

Mal pushes his way past me and approaches Mara in the living room. I'm too shocked to do anything but let him.

Mara doesn't blink as Mal slinks up to her like a predator approaching prey, though I'm not sure if it's because she's dead or brave. But when she doesn't cower beneath him, he straightens, his chest broadening and nostrils flaring.

The living room has turned into a powder keg, and either one of them is likely to set it off.

We spent a few months on the Island before the Alliance became official, but those months were enough to see what kind of world Mal had created. A hybrid of the mainland, still fueled by intimidation and fear and survival but without the Ticks. A place he owned. He walked around this place like he moved the sea and bombed the bridge himself to protect the people who lived here.

And most of them looked at him like he had. Still do.

"Don't do this," I say, though I learned a long time ago begging gets you nowhere. When it comes down to it, and my weapons are gone and I'm all alone, standing at the edge of an empty swimming pool stained in blood, I'm no better than the many people I've heard beg for their lives since this started.

It always seemed stupid to me to plead with a Tick as it attacked. Mindless creatures can't be reasoned with. I'm not standing in front of a Tick now, but finally, I understand.

"You did this to yourself," Mal says. I've been trying to find some semblance of humanity in those dark, empty eyes of his since the day I woke in the infirmary to him standing over my cot. I still haven't found anything.

Did this to myself. I took back weapons stolen from my family when we got here. Surely it isn't worth dying for.

Mal nods to the soldiers at my back. The thundering roar of the crowd screams louder, like they're hungrier for my blood than any Tick.

Before running becomes an option, hands close around my arms, hauling me forward.

"So. This is the infamous Mara Knight," he says. He does a slow circle around Mara, who turns her head to watch him. "Your sister has told me all about you."

One of Mara's fingers twitches, but otherwise, she acts like she doesn't hear him.

"Tell us what you want and get on with it," I say.

Mal stops. Faces me. That same disgusting grin is still on his face, and I want to smack it off him more than I want anything. More than I want a milkshake and French fries and a hot shower.

"You're bringing the Tick"—he nods at Mara—"with you to the mainland."

"I don't need backup," I snap. "I can handle myself."

"Oh, I am aware of your capabilities, Rory," Mal says. "After all, you've been running your very own little black market for well over a year now."

Heat rushes up my cheeks, and whatever retort I might have had dies on my tongue.

"You thought I didn't know?" Mal asks. His lip curls. "I know everything that happens on this island."

Supply runs led by Mal or Carter go out in search of big things like gas and construction supplies, or to make larger trades with other Alliance members. But the runs have become less frequent as the mainland is picked over. Anything accessible has been cleaned out by now. It's just trades, which occur every other month, sometimes more.

Mal has all the boat keys—except one spare, the one I have and thought he didn't know about—so while it isn't exactly forbidden to leave, it isn't an option, either. But I make monthly trips for smaller things, from toys and books to tampons, which are like gold in this world. The notebook hidden under my mattress has a long list of requested items and names beside them.

At first, it was a way to escape the suffocation of the Island and my family. Out in the mainland, things are simpler. It is kill or be killed.

And the other reason, the one I won't even admit to my family, is sometimes, when I'm out there, I see my sister. Aria never made it to the Island, and we barely talk about her. But out there, I can see her in the toy stores she loved and the peeling billboards she always laughed at.

Going out there won't bring her back, but at least I can feel her. Like the moment I step foot on the mainland, her ghost sidles up beside me.

I can't go back and save her, but I can bring back toys she loved for the kids who are still alive, for her siblings—for Noah, who she never met. I can bring back books for the school, or ridiculously expensive makeup, or the lemon shampoo Raisa and I like. Once, I found a bulk-sized roll of wrapping paper. It still gets passed around for birthdays when we remember them.

"Mara can't come," I say. "She has to get her Dyebucetin from Fatimah in the morning. If she went feral on the Bay, I bet we'd be out of the Alliance in hours."

Mal's lip curls.

"The Bay has Ticks. She can get her drugs from them. Less of a strain on our resources anyway."

I snort, folding my arms over my chest. If any of our resources are scarce, it's not Dyebucetin. A shipment of boxes taller than me and as wide was brought over to the Island a week before the Altered. Another is due in a few months. If we had that much of anything else, we wouldn't need the Alliance or the Altered.

"Part of this program is reintegration," Mal continues. "So the Tick goes with you. Just in case." I doubt the words would sound so condescending coming from someone else.

"I still don't get why you're sending me in the first place." There are probably a dozen names ahead of mine on a list of Mal's first choices.

"You're well equipped for the journey," Mal says, and his tone drips of condescension; it's an odd contrast to the veiled compliment. "And my soldiers are busy enough as it is."

He must be really worried about the Altered if he isn't willing to let one or two of his people leave for a day. But he doesn't care what happens to me, nor does he need me. Punishment and convenience all rolled into one. Making Mara come with me is an added bonus. Punishment on top of punishment.

The underlying threat isn't lost on me.

I see you. I control you. You are mine.

And in all the ways that matter, he does, and I am. Because if I had said no to this trip, it wouldn't have mattered—the choice to go is an illusion. I have to do what Mal tells me, like the rest of us, and he wants to make sure I know it. Maybe he wants to make sure Mara knows, too.

"You'll be back by sunset tomorrow, or you'll never step foot off this island again. Understood?" he asks.

Everything in me wants to scream, or smack him, but Mal still owns this island, and the people on it, Alliance or no Alliance. And my family isn't the hardened group of survivors we once were. All this time playing house, I'm not sure we could stand up to Mal if it came down to it.

"Understood," I bite out.

Mal makes a *humph* sound. He digs a hand into his pocket and pulls out a key on a keychain with a neon foam float for the boat; I don't mention the stolen spare. He tosses the key my way. Then he leaves, not bothering to haul the wagon in as he slams the door behind him and stomps away.

It isn't until Mara says in a low voice, "He's gone," I start to breathe again, and I'm so rattled by the whole thing I don't realize she's moved until she's standing beside me.

With a shiver, I jerk away from her.

"He can't do this," I snap. "I'm not doing this. I'm not some baby-sitter."

"Tell that to him," Mara says.

"This isn't a joke," I say, whirling on her.

"Actually, I think it is," Mara says. "And it's on you."

All I can do is stare at her, mouth open and gaping, until my legs remember they're connected to my body, and I trudge out of the room.

It's a ten-minute walk to the docks, during all of which Mara trails behind me. A smart move on her part.

A while back, before we came, Mal and his clones went around collecting leftovers from the base's armory and the police station. We're down to about twenty guns now, apart from all those hidden. After my stunt in the Pit, Isaac was given his pistol back. He lets me take it because I'm a better shot. All those years of weaving bracelets for a local boutique until my eyes went blurry gave me a steady hand.

There's no reason to keep the pistol out of my bag. It's too noisy to use on the mainland, for emergencies only. But holding it keeps Mara five paces back and out of my periphery, where my mind blurs the line between now and then—the old Mara and the new.

We've gotten lucky, those of us who managed to get to the Island and peninsula communities, where the borders are easily maintained. Oceanside, Pacific Beach, and Solana have none of the natural barriers we do and still know a life of watching their backs. I can't forget to watch mine. I sure as hell don't trust Mara to do it.

When we reach the docks, she draws closer, whipping her head around and scanning the rusted boats tethered to the docks. She sucks in a breath.

"Not quite the yacht club you remember?" I ask. There used to be hundreds of boats here, all fancy and dripping with wealth.

There are fifteen now. And they are not yachts. Fishing boats, deck boats and bowriders, a catamaran, even a houseboat. A sad collection, but it gets us where we need to go.

Mara says nothing. She has never been loud, but if you paid attention, she had something to say. But I am too far to hear, and the way her mouth stays firmly shut is so different—too different.

With a huff, I push forward, following the cracked cement path down to the wooden docks. The slats creak beneath my weight. Mara follows, closer than I'd like, though the dock isn't wide enough for me to complain.

Maybe if I push her into the water, I can make it to the boat before she catches up. I meet her eyes, and I swear it's like she knows what I'm thinking. A tiny crease forms between her brows, and she purses her lips, her gray eyes boring into mine.

I clear my throat and turn back to the deck boat at the end of the dock. She isn't anything special, twenty feet and more rust than white paint after all this time. But she gets me off the Island, making her perfect.

"Get in," I say, stopping in front of the slip and waving at the boat. Mara considers me a moment, probably wondering if I'm going to untie the line and send her drifting away without the key. I'd love to, but I love this boat more. It's the new-world equivalent of getting a car. And I so rarely get to drive it.

"I know what you're thinking, and no, I'm not going to do it." I slide off my pack, grabbing the ledge to steady myself as I toss the bag and the pistol onto the driver's seat. "Although, if you don't get in the boat, I might."

Mara grumbles something I don't catch and climbs into the boat with an ease I'm jealous of. Despite dying, or almost dying, or whatever, she seems to be in the best shape of her life. Good for her.

I bend over, not attempting to kneel, and untie the line, tossing it over and clambering over the side. Even using my right leg, it is awkward, and I slam hard into the hollow floorboards, which sends a sharp pang up my left leg.

Mara, to her credit—or awareness of all the knives I packed—doesn't comment. Instead, she settles into the leather passenger seat. They were white, but now are grayish brown. The thing runs, and it's fast.

As soon as we reach the small dock on the other side, I dig out the key for the ugly red Sedona, instructing Mara to fill the tank with the cartons we keep stashed in the sand and beneath the brush. The car is as shitty as the boat, but it runs, too.

The engine rumbles and grumbles in protest, but it quickly realizes I've fed it and sputters to life. In the passenger seat, Mara is frozen. She breathes, blinks, but the rest of her is like a photograph.

When I was younger and couldn't fall asleep, I'd imagine Mara and myself driving, the ocean on one side, wind blowing in our hair. In my fantasies, I was always brave enough to reach out and take her hand, and she always squeezed my fingers when I did. But that dream is as dead as everything else.

I must be staring, because her head snaps my way, a question in the twist of her mouth. Ignoring her, I switch gears and ease my foot off the brake, pulling through the gravel and onto the road.

10

MARA

Sam wasn't making light of last night's storm. As soon as we make it onto the main road, the asphalt turns slick with mud. An already tedious journey is doubled as Rory cautiously maneuvers past fallen trees and around shifted debris, picking our way north.

She doesn't speak, but her grip on the steering wheel is viselike, and her jaw is clenched so tight I worry she'll crack a tooth.

When we reach the exit to take us around downtown, it's clogged with debris and cars that shifted in the storm. The other road is less packed but cuts straight through the downtown. And it isn't an option.

When everything fell apart, the military piled onto ships and set off into the ocean, leaving the national guard to contain the infection. They threw up barricades and rickety fences around the big cities and population hubs. Evacuation centers were set up in stadiums and universities and hospitals in the beginning, too. My family and I spent a few months on the move in our failed attempt to escape the city and eventual retreat home, but after we found two alleged safe zones burned to ash, we avoided them like we avoided Ticks.

Then the military came back, not on ships, but in fast, whizzing planes outfitted with explosives. I found out later, from Dr. Benitez, every large city was bombed in one day. I was still alive when it happened. The rotted scent of bodies and ash hung over the ground for weeks. We wore scarves over our faces and rubbed petroleum jelly beneath our noses.

But bad memories aren't the only things lurking downtown. A hundred thousand people were downtown when the bombs dropped, and no one knows exactly how many Ticks are still in the heart of the city.

Rory pulls the car to a stop in the center of the road, a few yards from the row of cars that shifted into the exit during the storm.

"What are you doing?" I ask.

She ignores me, turning off the engine.

"Rory. Don't get out of the car," I say.

"We have to move it." She stares at the abandoned vehicles, rusted and grimy after so many years exposed to the elements. "We need enough space to squeeze through."

The hairs spike on the back of my neck. I can feel the Ticks around us, hidden behind corners and in shadows. We're too close to downtown, too tucked up into neighborhoods of sardine-packed houses, all of which are liable to have something lurking inside.

"That's a bad idea," I say. "The storm will have the Ticks wide awake." It feels weird to say the word, though it didn't used to be. I spat the label with as much venom as Rory does. "There has to be another way around."

"What, do you have a private jet you haven't mentioned? Or a tank?"

"It's not a joke."

"This isn't my first time out here," Rory snaps. "We won't make it to the Bay before nightfall if we have to go farther east. And we're not turning around."

Anger is a cool, slick vine crawling up my skin. I have not shuffled my way back to her after all these years to watch a Tick catch her by surprise and tear her apart because she refused to change paths.

"You've always been stubborn, but I didn't realize you were stupid," I say.

"Don't remember asking for your opinion," Rory says.

"I'm not letting you wander out there to ring the dinner bell!"

"That's not your choice to make. And if you try and stop me, I'll—"

"Kill me?" I don't know where this calm confidence comes from, and it surprises Rory, too, judging by the flare of her nostrils. "Do it, then."

She jolts back and stares at me like she's actually considering it. She keeps staring.

"But you won't, will you? Because you can't," I say.

When she looks at me, she still sees someone else. It's her she won't kill. The ghost in my skin.

Rory's nostrils flare, but she doesn't take the bait. She grumbles beneath her breath as she pops open the door and cautiously slips out onto the pavement. She tugs open the back door and riffles through the floor, returning to the open front door with a metal baseball bat studded with nails in her hand. Her eyes, still wild and angry, find mine.

"Are you coming or not?" she asks. She's playing cocky, but her voice is low, and her words are stilted.

"I'm coming." I open my door with a quiet snick and ease out onto the concrete, turning my ear to the crumbling debris on our right. It's the biggest blind spot—a pileup of at least ten cars blocking the view of the collapsed median and hundreds of businesses and homes behind it.

I meet Rory at the front of the van.

"What do you expect me to do when you go and get yourself killed?"

"I don't know." Rory shrugs and swings the bat up to rest on her shoulder. She doesn't meet my eyes as she says, "I guess you'll know what it feels like then."

A lump pushes up and down my throat, like my body remembers hurt but can't quite replicate it.

Rory sets forward before I can respond, though I doubt I would have.

I hadn't thought about the people I loved finding out what I became. Carter watched it happen, slammed the door and locked me inside, but Rory may have spent months more wondering if I was still alive. She had to be told I wasn't. I wonder if she cried, or screamed, or tried to deny it. If I found out she was gone, I think I'd have hit the ground and never figured out how to stand up again.

Rory's shoe scuffs the asphalt, and the soft noise snaps me back to reality. In an hour, the sunlight will be gone.

I jog to join her, and she jumps when I fall in step beside her. A lifetime ago, I'd have chided her for making noise. I don't dare do it now.

There are dozens of cars scattered up the road, zigzagging across the highway exit. A handful are tipped over or busted up from accidents, the rest abandoned as their owners fled the hordes exiting downtown.

Rory pauses a yard from the blockage and turns her ear toward it. She goes still, impressively so, and moves forward again. Her motions exude confidence, but there is a hesitation to her she didn't have on the Island.

This is the Rory of the mainland. The hunter.

I don't know what that makes me.

"Are your Tick senses tingling or anything?" Rory asks, looking over her shoulder.

I frown. "It's not, like, an exact science. I can feel them out there, but I don't know how close."

"Some help you are," Rory says. She jerks a chin toward the car farther to the right, its bumper kissing the tall cement median. "Alright, let's make this quick."

"As opposed to?"

"Stop talking."

We approach the car slower than I'd like, but I'm not going to criticize Rory with the bat in her hand.

I step up to the mangled bumper. Rory sets her bat on the road and joins me, eyeing it warily.

"It's one car. Surely the great Rory Blake has seen worse."

She gives me a bemused smile. "On three."

I nod.

"One, two, three," Rory says. On the last count, we both plant our hands on the trunk and shove. A piece of bumper hanging off the back screeches against the asphalt, and the sound blasts through the silent night. I jump back as Rory does and meet her wide-eyed gaze.

"Again," she says, her voice edged with fear.

I joked about ringing the dinner bell, but we have. I can hear them already, the closest a block away—Ticks, following the sound of life.

Rory inhales, looks at me, and nods. I dig my toes into the asphalt and shove, ignoring the sliced metal threatening to rip open my skin.

The car moves, but not fast enough. Ten seconds earns us a foot, and we have at least ten more to go before we have space to squeeze through.

Rory breathes heavily and sweat shines on her upper lip. To her credit, she doesn't complain or acknowledge the exertion.

I give her five seconds, and say, "Again."

Over the course of a minute, we gain a few feet of open asphalt, but a piece of the car's front molding catches on a divot in the road. Rory has deserted all efforts at staying quiet; she grunts and pants as we shove against the car.

Across the road, a piece of rock hits the ground with a loud crash. Rory eases some of her weight off the car, but I push us a few inches farther.

"We've got company," she hisses, pushing off the car and picking up her bat. I pull my aching fingers off the bumper and straighten, but I sense the Tick before I see it. Like a feather across the back of my neck. I hear its footsteps, too, shuffling across the gravel.

His skin is as gray as the cloudy sky above us, and his hair hangs in oily clumps half covering his face. After years exposed to the elements, he could be thirty years old or seventy.

Not every Tick responds to the Dyebucetin. The more recently turned, or less deteriorated, the more likely it is to work. This man must have been infected early on, and is too far gone for a facility, if we could get him to one.

The wind shifts. The man jolts like he's been electrocuted, freezes, and jerks toward us—toward Rory. He lets out a hollow moan. The thing in my head writhes like a beached fish.

It brings other things, too: flashes of my family and me hunkered behind barricaded doors, of nights falling asleep to those moans beyond walls we hoped would hold. Of those very moans coming from my lips.

"The car, Mara," Rory says over her shoulder, voice clipped.

Another silhouette pushes through the crumbling median. I can hear more behind it. Others, farther away but coming closer.

Rory hasn't noticed it yet, but I have to trust she will. If she can trust me to move this car, I can trust her to stay alive long enough for me to do it.

The moan rises to a half roar, and the footsteps scuffing across the ground are no more than fifteen feet away. Just before I throw my weight against the car, I hear the squelch of Rory's bat smashing into a Tick's head.

The car whines and shrieks against the asphalt, and I think I may be yelling, too. My bones threaten to shatter and leave me limp against the metal, but the snippets of noise I catch from where I last clocked Rory keep me pushing.

Finally, the space between cars opens, and I give the car one final shove. The sensation rolling through my limbs is like the ghost of exhaustion—I am heavy and warm.

Something metal smacks the ground and rolls, clattering as it goes.

The warmth turns to ice.

"Mara!" Rory's voice is shrill. It plucks the weight out of my tired limbs, and I bolt around the car to find Rory surrounded by bodies. Three are on the ground, heads bludgeoned, but another four have Rory circled. She spins, thrusting a knife at each one when they lunge for her. Half her hair has come out of her ponytail, like it was yanked. Her eyes are wild, and her movements are jerky. Her bat is outside the circle.

Three more Ticks amble toward us.

"I could use a hand here!" Staring death in the face, literally, and still giving me hell.

I wrench the closest Tick off her, sending the woman careening into the nearest car, and intercept the next a breath before his nails slice into Rory's arm. I wrestle him back, arms looped around his waist.

"Start the car!" The Tick claws at my arms, but it doesn't try to bite me. It wants to get away from me.

A wave of newfound strength pushes through me, and I slam an elbow up and back into the Tick's face. Its rotted nasal passages crunch and shatter, and a bone must puncture brain, because the Tick drops.

Rory's bat arcs through the air and smashes into the third Tick, but two more replace it.

"Go!"

"Shut up!" Rory yells.

She swings again. The nail lodges into a skull, but when Rory tries to pull it back, it refuses to give. She curses, sending a panicked look over her shoulder in the direction of the next closest Tick.

She's going to get herself killed. And for what?

I kick the Tick square in the chest. The impact sends it back, freeing the bat, and the momentum makes Rory stumble a step. The Tick's thick, dark blood splatters across my face. The liquid is warm but wrong, all wrong. Rotten and decayed.

Rory's grip slides all the way up on the handle, and she cries out, dropping the bat with a clang. She's sliced open her hand. Red pools over her palm before she presses it against her pant leg.

"Mara," she says, like she can sense the shift rolling through me like a cold front.

I can't look away from her bloody hand, her fingers, the veins in her arms and the freckled skin. It would be so, so easy to tear through—

I force myself back a step, shaking my head as hard as I can.

"Start the car," I say, half Mara and half Tick. "Now."

Rory stills, and for a moment, all my brain sees is the rabbit realizing it's been caught. Then she moves, jogging for the van. It takes everything in me not to chase after her, and not for reasons I want to admit.

The engine rumbles to life behind me.

"Let's go!" Rory yells, drawing the Ticks toward her. The three remaining set their sights on her. The rest of the bodies litter the ground.

Blocking the gap.

"Just go!"

"What?" I can make out half her face through the dusty windshield. Her features are contorted—confusion and rage and panic.

"Go, Rory."

She holds my gaze for one more second. The car jumps as she shifts gears.

I run for the gap, shoving a Tick aside so hard it cracks its own head open on the street. The bodies littering the ground are heavy and limp, but I haven't come this far to let my broken body give up now.

More moans rumble behind me. One of the Ticks heads for Rory, but two have gotten distracted by me. They may not want to eat me, but they seem to have realized I'm keeping them from their meal and want me out of the way.

Tires peel off the asphalt, and the van tips onto two wheels as Rory cranks the wheel. Instead of heading for the gap, she veers the car straight toward me and the Ticks.

I jump back right as she slams the car into the Ticks, sending them flying across the road. They don't move again once they land.

The passenger door flies open. In the driver's seat, Rory grips the wheel like she's trying to strangle it.

"Are you waiting for an invitation?" she exclaims. "Get in the damn car."

Swallowing a wildly inappropriate smile, I climb into the car and pull the door shut. Rory slams on the gas the second it closes, and the car lurches forward. The mirror on one car scrapes against the side of our van, but we squeeze through with little space to spare.

"You didn't leave me," I say.

Rory's jaw clicks. "You saved me. Figured I should return the favor," she says.

I almost ask her why, but her fingers tap erratically against the wheel, and she drives a little too fast. We still aren't in the clear.

She didn't leave me. She could have driven away, gone on to the Bay and then back to the Island and told some story, but instead, she came back for me.

The thread between us is still rotted, but maybe it hasn't snapped yet.

11

RORY

The rest of our drive is uneventful, but the adrenaline hangs over my shoulders like a second skin, only peeling away when we take the exit leading to the animal park in Mission Bay. Signs of life creep up in minutes.

Rows of cars and chipped concrete roadblocks ride along the land's edge of the only road to the park, narrowing the closer the van crawls to the park's entrance. The long, dry ravine on the left is deeper, too—dug out.

A year and a half ago, as my family tried to reach the Island, a horde of Ticks from the north forced us to hole up at the Bay for over a week. Four days hunkered down in a storm shelter as the horde tore through the city and half the Bay's walls. Another six days trying to help repair the perimeter.

Even back then, as a year-old community of fifteen hundred—at least before the horde—the Bay was impressive. The ocean spoils us on the Island. This peninsula may be on the water, like all the coastal communities, but it's close enough to the nightmare of downtown that peaceful sleep is hard to find.

When we reach the parking lot, littered with more roadblocks and cars and a lot of old bloodstains, I pull the car into a spot halfway to the gates. My leg is already protesting after the road stunt.

Mara finally speaks: "Are we here for the dolphin show?"

I turn off the engine and jam the keys into my pocket, refusing her the satisfaction of acknowledging the horrible joke.

"The park was empty when the first group moved in." I pop open the door and cock a brow at her. "Well, not totally empty. But they cleared it out pretty fast." I jab a finger toward a massive ring of singed parking lot, like someone held the world's biggest bonfire.

Mara clenches her teeth but doesn't take the bait and climbs out of the car. With a sharp exhale, I slide out onto the asphalt and slam the door harder than necessary. Mara is already at the back of the car, unloading the wagon and piling massive packs of jerky into it. Her motions are rigid and mechanical.

"What's your problem?"

She straightens too fast, and the severity of her expression makes me want—need—to look away. I don't give her that satisfaction, either.

"Nothing," she says, which even I can tell is a lie. "I'm fine."

I scramble for some comeback, but the words fizzle out on my tongue. Before I find anything, Mara is slamming the back door shut and lifting the wagon handle. She heads across the lot, and I set after her, a sick feeling in my stomach. I risk a glance behind us. Menacing dark clouds are much closer than they were a few minutes ago.

The blue gates at the park's entrance are double the size they used to be. Only one turnstile remains, at the break in the wall, but it sits behind a sliding gate. At least three crossbow arrows peek over the top of the wall. There are more bloodstains the closer we get, too.

A low whistle echoes beyond the wall.

Mara slows and falls behind me. Like a traitor, one of the knots in my belly untwists. It should be the opposite. I should encourage the archer to finish the job.

"I shouldn't be here," Mara says in a low voice, making the hairs on the back of my neck rise. I shake off a shudder and brush my fingers over the hilt of my sword.

I agree with her but still say, "It's one night. And we have meat.

The great unifier." A silhouette shifts beyond the gate. The knot returns. "Just . . . put up your hood."

"My hood? Really?"

"And be quiet."

Mara huffs but flips her hood anyway. I figure it buys us about twenty seconds.

"That's far enough," a deep voice booms from beyond the gate. A man steps up to the metal slats, his red curls catching the light of a flickering bulb. I let out a sigh of relief.

"Benjamin."

A smile spreads across the guard's freckled face.

"Is that Rory Blake?" His eyes dart to the wagon Mara pulls. "And is that what I think it is?"

"Pure, one hundred percent pork," I say.

Ben moans. It's an off-putting noise from a twenty-something the size of a linebacker.

Meat on the mainland is a delicacy. Any clump of humans draws Ticks, but animals are another story. The Ticks come like flies to honey. And there are still enough Ticks wandering around that a farm puts up a bull's-eye. Animals may not turn, but I've never seen a Tick refuse a living meal.

The appeal overshadows Mara's presence for a few seconds, but not as long as I predicted. Benjamin stills.

"Who's your friend?" he asks.

She's not my friend. "New to the Island. Mal made me bring her along."

He's hesitant, and I don't blame him. I probably wouldn't let us through the gate, either. Everything about Mara screams *run*.

"You. Take your hood down," Ben says.

I risk a glance over my shoulder. Mara lifts her head to meet my eyes. At my nod, she straightens and removes her hood. Her silver eyes practically shine.

I wait for an explosion, but it never comes.

I've brought a monster to their door, and I'm asking them to let it inside, but instead of lunging for a weapon like I expected, Ben stiffens for a moment and nods curtly.

"She's—" I start, with absolutely no clue where I'm headed.

"Save it," Ben says. "I don't want to know." He jerks a chin toward the park, gaze darting over my shoulder, not at Mara, but at the vast parking lot behind us, and the approaching storm clouds. "Get in."

Definitely not what I expected. Mara keeps trying to catch my eye, but I avoid her as we both stumble past the bright yellow line on the concrete and up to the turnstiles.

I turn instantly, waiting for Ben to reach for a weapon with Mara's back turned, but he doesn't. He's more amused by my jumpiness than anything, smirking and folding his arms.

"You're just . . . letting her in?" I ask.

Ben tilts his head with a frown. His eyes widen slightly, and he glances at Mara, then back at me. He doesn't look at her like he wants to blow her head off. He doesn't try to cuff her, which would be my first move.

He simply says, "Been a long time since you were here, Blake," and punches a button inside the gate. A loud buzz screams through an old speaker, and the slats groan as they roll up and click into place.

He gestures us forward, and a second set of gates rolls down behind us, triggered by another patrolman. Again, I can do nothing but follow him wordlessly into the park and wonder what the hell I'm walking into.

12

RORY

The week my family and I spent trapped in this park was the third time I'd been here. The first, Aria and Raisa had turned five and were obsessed with anything living under the water. The second, on a field trip when Mara and I were thirteen. The moment our teacher broke out the worksheet packets, Mara and I snuck away. We rode the roller coaster until she announced she was going to throw up. After we got off, she planted herself on a bench with her head between her knees, and I sat beside her, staring at a huge map on the wall of all the evacuation routes and emergency plans. That map—the storm shelters my brain held on to—saved all of our lives two years later.

Despite the wildly overgrown weeds and the obvious bloodstains, the bones of the park still poke out as Ben leads Mara and me down the chipped concrete path. Bleached posters advertise shows, and pale blue paint and signs lead to enclosures for animals who died years ago. Clearly, we've missed peak season.

Ben directs us toward the old café and under an overhang with a sign spray-painted to read MESS HALL.

Every step we take makes the ground beneath my feet more unsteady. This isn't the ramshackle group of survivors my family and I left over a year ago.

I risk a glance at Mara, but apart from the clenched jaw she's had since she walked in our door a few days ago, she doesn't seem shaken.

"Where are you taking us? I ask.

Ben shrugs, and says, "To see Daphne."

Daphne. I have a dozen more questions, but they all fall away as we reach the mess hall door. Ben pulls it open, and the chattering of voices and the soft music from a speaker spills out into the cold night. He gestures for us to go in.

Thunder booms in the dark sky, rumbling the ground, making me flinch. I count the seconds between the thunder and a bright flash of lightning, trying and failing to remember the rule about seconds and distance.

"You're going back to the wall?" I ask, eyeing the sky.

"The ferals don't care about a little thunder, Blake. Neither can we," he says. "We're waiting on a transport crew anyway. They were supposed to be back an hour ago, but with last night's storm . . ."

"A roadblock nearly took us out on our way," I say. "I hope they get back soon."

"So do I," Ben says. He clears his throat, clearly trying to hide the concern on his face, and lets the door fall into my hand. I take it, and Mara and I watch him walk away. Once he's gone, I meet her eyes and cock a brow.

"After you," I say.

She exhales through her nose. It almost seems like she wants to say something but decides against it. I consider pushing her on it, but the noise from inside the building has me walking a razor blade's edge. It takes everything I have not to pull out my sword as we head in.

Neither of us makes it more than a few feet inside before we stop.

Even the mess hall is different. For one, it isn't damp and dark, serving as a sad infirmary like it used to. Now it looks like a cafeteria again, with mismatched tables and chairs, armchairs, even a few couches. Crudely barred floor-to-ceiling windows stretch up to the high, dark vaulted roof, and a dozen strings of fairy lights hang across the beams. Soft-white bulbs, bright pastels, a string of plastic stars, and another line of glowing plastic cacti.

There are at least three hundred people inside. Sitting in chairs or on the tables or perched on the stall countertops. Talking and eating and smiling. A handful of kids weave around tables and screech with laughter.

A deep, heavy ache presses on my lungs.

The only place on the Island that ever attracted this many people at once was the Pit.

"Look," Mara says. She's staring at a tall slab of stone on one side of the door. The words *In Memoriam* are scrawled in huge letters across the top, and the stone beneath it is covered in photographs, notes, scraps of receipts or pages from yearbooks, slivers of clothing.

It's been a long time since I've seen a shrine like this. They used to be everywhere, but I guess we all ran out of people to hang pictures of. The shrine on the Island is just objects, but no faces.

Tears prick at the backs of my eyes, and I blink them away.

Mara turns, her brow furrowing as she takes a few steps to the side.

Another stone on the other side of the door is covered like the first, but this wall isn't honoring the dead. It's full of Polaroids of people smiling, their arms around each other. I need a single glance around the room to realize the photos are of the survivors. At the top, it reads *Dum spiro spero.*

"While I breathe, I hope," Mara says, gesturing to the words. Her mom was a Latin teacher a lifetime ago. I didn't realize Mara knew any.

I try to form a response, but the words, and the photographs, awaken all the ghosts living under my skin. I'm scared if I open my mouth, they'll come spilling out.

Fortunately, the rest of the room notices us before I have to say anything. All at once, the chatter trickles out like a spigot.

Mara stiffens.

My hand flies to the hilt of my sword.

Every eye is on us when we turn around.

No, not on us. On Mara. But like at the gate, the reaction is the opposite of what I expect. There aren't exactly looks of love, but no one goes for a weapon or seems like they're imagining what Mara's head might look like separated from her body.

Instead, they seem curious.

I scan for someone familiar, but being around so many people makes focusing on anything impossible. I have to wrangle back the instinct to turn and run the hell out of here, medicine be damned.

"Rory?"

Relief pushes warmth through my stiff, icy limbs, and I let out a sharp breath as a friendly face rises from a massive beanbag a few yards to our right.

Daphne Turner. She retired exactly a month before the end of the world, which is a pretty shitty retirement, if you ask me. But after forty years as a nurse, and raising four daughters, it's no surprise she was picked to lead the Bay after the horde took out its previous iteration.

"Rory Blake," she says, crossing the shiny stone floor to wrap me in a hug. "I thought you were dead." She pulls back to look at me, flicking a stray hair off my forehead. Her own hair, piled in a bun on her head, is more gray than black now, and she has more wrinkles, but the fierceness in her eyes is the same as it was over a year ago. Her smile is just as kind, if not a little sadder. It quickly turns to a frown. "We heard the distress call a few days after you left. I sent a group out as soon as I could, but we were still mending our own perimeter and dealing with stragglers from the horde—"

"It's okay," I say, surprising myself by taking her hands in mine and squeezing.

She presses her lips together and shakes her head. "By the time my people got to the beach, it was empty. All they found was blood in the sand and tracks to the water. We had no idea whether—"

"I survived," I say, heat flushing my cheeks. "We made it to the Island. Isaac, Sam, Raisa, and Noah are there now." I'd promised to come back and visit, before I got shot and thrown into the Pit. Before we found out the Ticks were coming back.

"Well, I'm incredibly happy to see you," she says, and I can tell she means it. "Joyful reunions are much too infrequent these days."

I swallow the urge to look at Mara as the three of us settle in chairs around a rickety card table. "It's good to see you, too." I clear my throat and gesture to the wagon sitting at Mara's side. "And I brought gifts."

Daphne laughs, and though her eyes widen a bit as she takes Mara in, she doesn't falter as much as I expect. Not that Daphne was ever on the anti-Tick train. According to her, no one was beyond saving, not even the Ticks. Killing them instead of trying to help them may have been necessary for survival, but she didn't like doing it.

"Oh, lovely. I must say, ladies, as much as I appreciate a good to-mato, I've been dreaming about this jerky." She smiles at Mara. "I'm Daphne. Daphne Turner. It's good to meet you." She leans over and holds out a hand.

Mara stares at it for a moment before she takes it, and shakes it once before quickly dropping it.

"Mara Knight," she says. She pauses. "You, too."

Daphne's gaze slides between the two of us. A knowing smile plays on her lips. "*Mara*. What a beautiful name."

My cheeks burn.

On one of the nights we spent trapped in the park's storm shelters as the horde tore through the Bay, Daphne asked me why my family was so intent on making it farther south. For my parents, the Island was the chance to find the lives they lost. Mara's parents were best friends with mine, had been since college. But by the time we got there, only Carter was left. For me, though, it was always about Mara.

And because it was dark and cold and I was afraid, I told Daphne about the dream I had at least once a week, about finding the girl I left behind alive and well. A stupid dream, and I knew it.

"What's her name?" Daphne asks. Her voice is hoarse, and it'll be gone soon if she doesn't stop talking, but I'm not going to be the one to tell her to.

"Doesn't matter," I say. "She's probably dead."

"Or she's not."

"Or she is."

It's too dark in the shelter to see Daphne's face, but the silence is telling enough. I huff a breath and whisper, "Mara."

"Mara," Daphne says. "What a beautiful name."

Mara looks between us. Her expression is too smug for my liking. She opens her mouth to speak, and I quickly interrupt.

"Since when did everyone here board the peace train?" I ask.

Daphne's gaze fogs over, and I know she's thinking of that awful week. Of squeezing like sardines into storm shelters and passing around stale chips and waiting to die. For the first two days, the chatter of people praying to every conceivable god was endless and infuriating. Then it stopped, and I kind of missed it. I haven't heard a prayer of any kind, from anyone, since.

"Yes, well, after the horde, we all looked around and realized we were—and do pardon my language, ladies—screwed beyond belief. We lost four hundred people in three days." Daphne rubs at her chest, face going slack. My stomach lurches as she speaks; it had been chaos the night the horde hit. Not everyone made it to safety, and not all of the shelters held. "Our gardens were gone. Inventory was next to nothing. Even our main generator was trampled."

We're lucky, far enough south bad weather is more nuisance than danger, but each year, the winter gets a little colder. Not deadly, but painful.

"You joined the Alliance," Mara says.

"We did," she says. "Not at first, of course, but I convinced the people here to listen to the woman from Oceanside. We'd only heard her last name, you know. O'Neill."

"Thalia O'Neill," I say. I straighten. "Wait—Thalia? Wasn't she one of your—"

"My eldest daughter." Daphne smiles. "It seems she took on my maiden name when she entered the politics game. She says it sounded more official than *Thalia Turner*."

"The politics game? Is that what we're calling it now?" I ask, lips turning up.

Daphne laughs, and says, "Well, the surprise reunion turned out to be quite convincing." Her expression softens. "I think it gave the community more hope than any promise of supplies ever could. By the time Thalia got around to making her pitch, the majority jumped on board, and the rest had no leg to stand on, so they stayed quiet."

Her expression stays neutral throughout the conversation, but she's looked at the door four times in the last minute alone. I recall Ben's comment about the transport crew. I almost ask but don't want to deal with the explanations to Mara.

"Your guard Ben mentioned you were expecting people from some kind of supply run?" Mara asks.

Once again, Mara takes the words from my mouth, but I'm more surprised she's talking at all. She's been tight-lipped since she got to the Island, but for some reason, being here is opening her up.

"One of our transport crews," Daphne corrects, and I understand what Mara is doing.

"Transport?" Mara's brow furrows slightly. "What are they transporting?"

Daphne stills, and the tops of her cheeks go pink. She leans her elbows into the table.

"Do you know how the RPA facilities get their patients?" she asks. "The ferals don't exactly line up at the doors for their shots."

"Roundups," Mara says as she figures it out. "RPA soldiers are still clearing neighborhoods."

"Not enough soldiers anymore, hon. The RPA sent them to the facilities," Daphne says, but she doesn't sound condescending, just sad. "*We're* clearing them now. Delivery of an intact Tick to a facility for treatment earns a reward. Medicine, gas, or anything extra they're willing to give. And if you know where to go and you bring them enough bodies, you can negotiate additional trades for things we don't get in the bigger swaps."

Mara's hand curls in and out of a fist at her side, where Daphne can't see.

"Oh," Mara says.

I struggle to find a way to change the subject, but before I can, Mara snaps her head toward the door. I frown, following her gaze, but the rest of the cafeteria is undisturbed, chatting and laughing away.

"What are you—" I start.

The glass doors swing open, and at least two dozen people spill inside. They're all in dire need of a shower, and their clothes could use a scrubbing, too.

Daphne jumps to her feet, faster than I expect from a woman nearing seventy. Her face lights up. She glances between me and Mara, torn.

"If you girls will excuse me—" Daphne says.

"Go," I say, waving her off, and she gives me a grateful smile before rushing for the door.

"Oh my god," Mara says softly after Daphne leaves. I frown, squinting at the survivors pushing inside. People throughout the room have risen from their seats and make for the front of the cafeteria, calling out their loved ones' names, catching them in tight hugs.

I follow Mara's gaze to a man around Isaac's age who tugs off a beanie and rakes a hand through his dark hair, scanning the crowd for someone. A girl no older than seven halfway across the cafeteria yells, "Daddy!" as she runs and leaps into his arms. The man wraps his arms around her and twirls her, gripping her tightly.

A warm, fuzzy feeling blooms in my chest, but it turns cold.

The man isn't a man. The dirt on his skin momentarily distracted me from how pale he is, and the extra layers of clothes hide his injuries, but when I really look, it becomes clear. The man is Altered, like Mara.

They're Altered. Of the thirty or so people who walked into the building, ninety percent of them are dead.

From far away, though, it looks like a bunch of people reuniting with their family and friends. And it's a much happier reunion than I'm used to seeing. No apparent injuries. No extra backpack from a body who didn't make it home.

"What the hell?" I muse aloud, jumping when Mara actually responds to me.

"Genius," she says, though her expression makes me think she didn't mean to speak, either.

"What?"

"The Ticks," she says. "The Altered, I mean. I think they're doing the roundups."

I shake my head, widening my eyes, not following.

Mara clears her throat, and is sheepish as she says, "Who better to round up ferals than the one thing they don't want to eat?"

"Wait, they don't want to eat you?" I ask, and realize it's the first time I've considered the Altered and the Ticks to be different creatures.

"No. I mean, I haven't tested the theory myself, but the doctors at the facility said we're . . . *unappetizing*." Mara frowns. "They don't want anything to do with us."

"What, so you're, like, tainted meat?"

"That's disgusting." Mara scrunches her nose and groans softly. "But I guess."

"So you're not really a Tick, then," I say. "And you're not human."

She pauses. Her gaze lingers on the people hugging at the doors. "I guess not," she says.

I could so easily take that and run with it, but I, too, can't take my eyes off the people at the front of the building.

Hugging. Talking. Laughing and smiling. Even with the storm they outran and whatever horrors they must have seen outside the park.

It feels like stepping back in time, to a world not revolving around loss. It's a world I barely remember, and one I never expected to see again.

I thought we had it better on the Island. Safe and isolated and protected from a backslide into the Dark Days. But looking around, I don't think the Island is safe at all. It's stagnant. And stagnancy is as dangerous as the backslide, if not more.

13

RORY

Daphne leads us to the animal hospital, which she tells us she's converted into a makeshift clinic—or it will be a clinic, eventually, if they play their cards right. It looks more like a real doctor's office than I've seen in years. Daphne says half the rooms are full of medical equipment she and some others are coaxing back to life, but the other rooms are for storage or for the occasional guest.

"Tourism's back in swing, yeah?" I ask, which earns a smile out of Daphne. Mara, of course, doesn't react.

Daphne lets Mara into a storage closet to change before leading me into another room.

"You and Mara can stay in here tonight," Daphne says.

The examination-turned-guest-room is cleared of all furniture besides the metal cabinets tacked to the walls. They've all been emptied, the shattered glass cleared away. All that remains in the room is a small folding table and a large, lumpy mattress piled with blankets and two pillows. Someone nailed up a dark blanket to cover the window facing the hallway.

One bed. Not only am I supposed to spend the night in here with Mara, Daphne thinks we're going to curl up next to each other like we're at sleepaway camp.

I slam to a halt a few feet into the room, looking between Daphne and the bed.

Daphne frowns. "Is something wrong?"

I open my mouth and clamp it back shut.

"All the doors lock from the inside," Daphne says, "if it makes you feel safer, but we haven't been breached in months. You're safe in here."

"No, it's not—" I stop, the words getting stuck behind my teeth.

Daphne's frown deepens, confusion pulling at her brows, and then understanding dawns in her eyes, and the frown takes on a disappointed twist.

Hot shame surges in my blood, and I'm angry at myself for it, and at Daphne for looking at me like that. Like I'm in the wrong for not wanting to bunk with a monster.

I want to push further, ask for another room, but Daphne and her kind eyes and disappointed frown make me swallow the rest of my protests.

One night. I can survive one night.

Mara wanders into the room, and I instantly regret my decision, but Daphne is already stepping back into the doorway.

"I'm down the hall, three doors down. If you need anything, holler." Daphne smiles softly. It reminds me of slumber parties as a kid and makes my stomach roll. "Good night, girls."

"Good night," Mara says.

I don't say anything.

Daphne lingers a beat longer, then pulls the door shut behind her, leaving Mara and me alone.

The tense silence balloons and threatens to crush me in seconds. I clear my throat and kick off my boots, risking a glance Mara's way.

She's wearing a pair of gray sweats and a green sweatshirt that reminds me of her old eyes. The clothes dwarf her, and she looks younger, the way she would have if this was one of our many past sleepovers.

Where I sit, perched on the mattress edge, arms slung around one drawn knee, it occurs to me I'm incredibly vulnerable from this angle—if she wanted to kill me, she could, and I couldn't stop her.

"What are you waiting for? I don't bite," I say. "Unlike some of us."

She drags her tongue across her lips, pulling them into her teeth. Without replying, she comes to the other side of the mattress, drops down, kicks off her sneakers, and slips her legs beneath the quilts spread out over the bed.

I ease down onto my back slowly. I woke up aching this morning, and spending the day on my feet hasn't helped. The ache has morphed into a hot, sharp pain radiating down my left leg. I'd chop off my finger for an aspirin.

Mara shifts down beside me, letting out a soft breath as she relaxes, the raggedy mattress giving slightly under our combined weight. We're both flat, hands at our sides, staring at the dusty ceiling, and it feels so much like before, I have to blink back tears.

There are no more than five inches between our hands. Back then, I spent every sleepover exactly like this, willing myself to reach out and take her fingers in mine.

"Why are these meds so important to you?" Mara asks. The question sounds rhetorical, like she doesn't expect me to reply.

"They're not just important to me," I say. "They're not for me at all. They're for the Island. The infirmary—"

"It's more than that," she says. "It's like you're trying to . . . prove something. Or make up for something."

I am, but I don't have to admit it to her. I don't have to admit I'm trying to replenish a medicine supply that was used to save my life, leaving a gaping deficit behind. Fatimah still hasn't restocked her infirmary. A vicious strep infection ran through the Island a few months back, and two people died because the antibiotics were gone.

But tomorrow, with the medicine from the Bay, the infirmary will be a little fuller. The next person who needs help might get it.

"You still haven't asked how my family got to the Island," I say. I don't expect her to reply, but she does, breaking my rhythm.

"You wouldn't tell me if I did," she says, which is true.

"You were nosier before, you know."

"Still am. Just better at it." I think she might be smiling, the way the words curl and tilt on their way off her lips, but I can't bring myself to look.

"Does that mean you don't want to know?"

"Of course I want to know." She brings her hands to settle on her stomach. "But I figured, if I want real answers, I should ask Noah. He'll give it to me straight."

I laugh, surprising us both. I'm not sure why I decide to tell her the truth, but in this small, dark room, it suddenly feels ridiculous not to.

"We never made it past Oceanside. Got stuck for a month and spent six more making our way back south. We heard Carter's name tossed around with the Island's when we were in the Pacific Beach settlement and figured, if she was alive, maybe your parents and—" I pause. Roll my shoulders. "The cities were still so congested it wasn't like we could drive. We had to walk. Got news of the horde, ended up here until it passed. Noah was still a baby, basically, and Isaac had him in this souped-up BabyBjörn thing, and—" I stop again, memories poking through the fray. "Aria was already . . . already gone. We made it all the way past downtown, almost to the water, when they were on us."

"Ticks."

I have used the word on her and in my daily life for so long it is second nature, but it sounds plastic off her lips. My tongue tastes like ash.

"No," I say. "People."

She doesn't speak again, forcing me forward.

"We don't know whether they thought we were Ticks or not." A grimace pulls on my lips. "Probably not. They nearly killed Sam, nicked her right across her neck, and one of them got me in the back of the leg with a shotgun. I was pretty out of it, don't remember how they got us away. I remember a beach, and Isaac sending out an SOS on his walkie to every goddamn station he could. There aren't any boats on the mainland side, not working ones."

I sneak a glance at Mara to see if she's still listening, though I know she is.

"Next thing I know, I'm on a boat, and this old lady is yapping about how she's barely stitched up cuts, how is she supposed to pull birdshot out of somebody's—" I stop, pulling in a breath. "It was touch-and-go for a while. Or so they tell me. I only woke up once before they had me stitched up and pumped with their inventory of narcotics."

"Once?" Mara asks. I was hoping she didn't catch that. Stupid of me.

"When they took the first piece out." Fire, carving me open and shredding my insides. The sharp, intense pressure in my leg, the tip of the flaming knife. "It wasn't Fatimah's fault. She's not a surgeon. And I'm not a great patient."

Isaac left midway through. It hurt as much as the flame, the way he turned, hands over his ears as he pushed through the doors.

"Fatimah thinks I should be dead." It comes out more sarcastic than I intend. "I thought I was for a while."

"You always were stubborn," Mara says.

"Stubborn." I scoff.

"Too stubborn to die."

"Pretty sure *you've* got that market cornered, Mara," I say, and I realize it's the first time I've called her by her name. I've missed the way it rolls off my tongue. But I'd rather get shot again than admit it.

14

MARA

My hand is warm—there are calloused fingers resting on top of mine. The pressure is gentle, soft, different from anything I've felt in so long my nerves don't quite know what to do with it, how to process it. Tenderness has become a foreign language to my skin.

Rory slumbers beside me. She's curled up, facing me, one of her hands on mine. Her stern face is slack in sleep, pink lips parted, dark lashes brushing freckled cheeks, a tiny spot of drool on the ratty pillow beneath her head.

My heart gives two distinctive thumps, both harder than they're supposed to be, like it's new to the job.

Red for love, pink for attachment, blue for loyalty. The lover's trio, Aurora calls it, which I'm fairly sure she read on the internet somewhere, but the where doesn't matter. What matters is she's given the tricolored bracelet to me. Red, pink, and blue.

I ask a stupid question, and she looks at me for so long I stop expecting an answer. And technically, she doesn't answer. She doesn't say anything at all. She leans forward and kisses me.

A third beat of my fractured heart.

I untangle my fingers from hers and sit up, sliding off the bed. My knees dig into the hard floor as I roll over and push to my feet. I consider going to find Daphne, who must administer the Dyebucetin to the Altered here, but the idea of Rory waking up to me gone bothers me, though I don't think it should.

Rory stirs at the movement but doesn't wake as I inch across the room and unzip my pack, tugging out the small, tough case Fatimah made me promise to keep on me at all times.

Inside the case, six vials of Dyebucetin are held carefully in place. I free one of the syringes, straightening and stepping back, leaning into the plastic-coated countertop.

The realization I've never done this to myself before gives me pause. I had to practice self-injection with a needle a few times before I left the facility, but I've never actually given myself a dose. Asking Rory is out of the question. I'm not naive enough to believe last night's honesty was anything more than a way to fill the time.

For a moment, I wonder what it would be like to walk through the doors, past the park's gates, and never look back. The Island wouldn't miss me. Rory wouldn't.

The vials clink as I shift my fingers. Wondering means nothing without enough of the drugs to back it up and keep me conscious. I don't know if there's anywhere to go.

A tiny part of me thinks I could stay here, with Daphne. I could make a place for myself, maybe do some good. But hiding from my ghosts is no better than running from them. The place isn't the problem. It's me. What I am. What I've done.

The long, thin syringe cap pops off, and I toss it aside, ignoring the stone pushing up my throat and the little raw voice in the center of my skull saying *screw it.*

"What the hell are you doing?" Rory's voice is loud, making my fingers tighten around the handle of the syringe. I turn, brows knitted, and she's pulling herself to her feet, unbalanced and favoring her left leg. Her eyes are on the needle and the part of my sleeve I have shoved up.

Dropping my chin, I loosen my grip on the syringe and bring it to my arm. I expect my hands to shake, but they are rigid in their quest.

Rory is across the room in half a blink, faster than she should be, and snatches the needle out of my hand.

"I don't—" I protest.

"Shut up and hold still." Her eyes dart up to my face, briefly, and I keep my head forward. One of her hands settles beneath my elbow, holding it steady. Calloused as they were when I woke up holding them, but with a rougher grip. Not hurtful, but tight, her thumb digging into the crook of my wrist.

Her hair is mussed from sleep, platinum waves double their normal size, and there are bags beneath her eyes. She was always beautiful, but she's grown into it, into herself, into something more otherworldly than me. Scarred and bruised and bent and still devastatingly beautiful.

Thump goes my heart, and then something else—

I lunge back, ripping my arm free, choking back the urge to—

To *something*. I don't know what this feeling is, this twisting, yanking, gnashing thing unfolding in my gut. Not hunger, but related to it. A gag travels up my throat, and a hand flies to my mouth.

Rory doesn't go for her sword. She must realize I don't mean to kill her but to get away from her. I can't read anything else on her face, can't think past the warmth in the pit of my stomach.

"If you're going to go feral on me, at least wait until I've had breakfast," she says.

"Sorry." I clear my throat and immediately regret it, the sound reminiscent of chalk screeching across a splintered board. "Sorry." Stepping back toward her, I lift my arm as an olive branch. Rory looks at it, and up at me, before letting out a sigh that could mean a million things and taking my arm.

My eyes fall shut as she plunges the needle into my arm, but the rush of heat as the drugs race through my veins is nothing compared to the fire everywhere her fingers are.

I don't thank her when she's finished, don't know what to say, where to go from here, but Rory makes the move for me, zipping the vial container shut.

"We should get going. It rained again last night. We don't need a repeat of yesterday." Rory clears her throat. "Daphne loaded the meds into the wagon last night."

I nod. We pack up in silence, and it is heavier than normal.

15

RORY

Sunset comes and goes as we dock the boat on the Island side and load the boxed medicine into a wobbly wagon. Our drive back is uneventful but slow to avoid slipping on the muddy roads. Isaac is going to kill me or, at the very least, lecture the hell out of me.

Mara takes the wagon handle without a word or a glance. Our walk from the docks and up past the Del toward the infirmary is quiet, borderline peaceful. It's unsettling. The mainland is stuck to me like pollen and will be for days. Especially after yesterday's incident.

It's been months since I've seen so many Ticks at once. In some ways, it felt like the first time.

The headlights of hundreds of cars light up the interstate like a football field. Smoke billows from the pileup a dozen cars up where the vehicles on the other side of the median crashed through it.

Metal screeches ahead, and our sedan jostles as the rear of the truck in front of us slams into our bumper.

"Get out of the car!" Dad yells, throwing open the driver's-side door. I've only heard him yell a few times in my life, and it lights a fire under my feet. "Everybody, out!"

I brace my shoulders on the backs of my parents' seats and reach to undo Raisa's seatbelt. She frees Aria while I kick open the dented back door.

Hot air blasts me in the face, and I can't hear my parents over the screeching tires and loud voices and—

"What the hell is that?" an unknown voice calls.

The moans pierce through my skin, right down to my bones. Every inch of me stills.

Then the screaming starts.

I grab my sisters' hands, one on each side, and drag them close.

"Don't let go," I say.

And we run.

Mara's abrupt stop hauls me back to reality. The wagon handle clatters to the ground, and Mara's head snaps forward.

"What?" I ask.

She is frozen for a long second before she says quietly, "Something's wrong."

I frown, swallowing the itchy sensation creeping up my throat. "Tonight is town hall. Everyone is in the theater. You probably hear—"

"No." She gives a curt shake of her head. "No." She meets my eyes, and I can't quite identify her expression, but it makes my blood run cold.

She stills again, head cocked as she listens, then runs without another word, bolting down Main Street.

"Where the hell are you—" I start, but she's gone. We're still a good five blocks from the school, and seven from the theater and police station. Too far for me to hear anything, but not for Mara.

And whatever she hears is enough to scare her.

"Damn it," I curse, pulling the wagon out of the way and beside a decayed bench. I take off after Mara at an awkward jog.

I'm panting after one block and limping after two. I can't see Mara anymore. I don't know if she stopped at the school, or continued on to the theater—

A high-pitched scream from the school, a block away now, makes the decision for me.

In an instant, I've fallen back in time and am standing in a dim alleyway, watching my sister die.

It happens too fast to stop it. Sam and I are up front, Isaac at our back, Raisa and Aria sandwiched between us.

Maybe Isaac is going too slow, or we're going too fast. Maybe it's chance. But when the arm snakes out from the alley as we pass it, wrenching Aria into the shadows, none of us can stop it.

Raisa screams as Aria is ripped away from her, and then Aria is screaming, too, but it's a different scream, one that plucks the air from my lungs.

Sam lunges, and Isaac raises his mallet. My sword is halfway out of its sheath. But we aren't fast enough.

The Tick ducks his chin, sinks his teeth into Aria's neck, and rips out her throat.

Noah. Raisa. Images of them, lifeless and bloody like Aria, in my head are so overwhelming my knees threaten to buckle.

I can't lose them. I won't.

Ignoring the protest in my leg, I sprint to the school, sword unsheathed and in my hand.

I can hear the screams before I have the door open.

The school isn't technically a school at all; it's an old gym cleared of all its workout equipment except a few pull-up bars and gymnastic rings. Despite its origins, every time I've been inside, it's looked a little more like a real classroom. The cement floor is sporadically covered in mismatched rugs: woven bamboo, pastel Berber, yellow-and-gold Persian, even a bleached roads-and-cities map likely taken from the elementary school on the mainland. There are tables and chairs and an old chalkboard.

It doesn't look like a classroom now. Inside, the room has been torn apart, the furniture is upended, and blood splatters the walls and chalkboard. At least two bodies lie scattered around. Noah and Raisa are nowhere to be seen. Neither is Mara.

Three Ticks chase a dozen kids around the room, though there should be at least twenty children, even with the ones on the ground. Pretty much everyone attends town halls, and during the meetings, the Island's kids hang out in the school with their two teachers. Technically, they're graduate students, one of which was studying education, but they're all we have.

Make that *had*. The teachers, a man and a woman, both with mauled chests and necks—they must have been bitten less than an hour ago and just turned—sprint after the panicked children. The third Tick is a young girl I've never seen before. The unfamiliarity raises alarms, but the thought files itself away before I can get stuck on it.

I refuse to let myself look at the fallen kids' faces and focus instead on the closest Tick.

The male Tick, a few feet away, catches a young girl, Violet, by the wrist, but before I can move toward them, there is a flash of movement, and a figure tears the Tick off Violet, sending them in opposite directions.

Mara. A surprising rush of relief pulses through me.

She grabs the Tick as it tries to run for Violet again and kicks him hard into the brick wall. He rears back up, but I intercept him as he bolts for Violet, swinging the sword into his neck. The Tick screeches, recoiling toward me, and I throw the sword up again, plunging the blade into its skull.

Every part of me wants to drop everything and find my siblings, but there are a dozen kids in this building. The longer the Ticks are up and walking, the more likely this island is a hotspot by morning.

"Mara," I yell, "get the rest of the kids out!"

It goes against my instincts, but the logical part of me born on the mainland recognizes I can't do this alone. And I've seen Mara fight. I may not like it, but I can trust her to get them out safely.

She doesn't say anything to acknowledge my words, but when she moves, it's to pull a little boy named Javier, no older than six, from where he's curled up beneath a table and push him for the door. Mara grabs Violet next, practically carrying her to the doorway.

I head for the third Tick, the little girl I don't recognize. She's in the far corner, where two of the wooden tables have been upended and shoved together like the front of a ship. She struggles against the tall, flat slab, too short to see over the top.

I slink up behind her, grab her by the collar of her filthy, holey nightgown, and spin her around. Half her face is ripped away, giving one side of her mouth a permanent menacing smile. As she pushes toward me, I lift my sword, driving it through her right eye. I rip the sword out, and she falls to the ground, black blood seeping onto the patterned blue-and-green rug beneath her.

Through the crack between the tables, a pair of dark eyes latches onto mine, and a fraction of my fear falls away.

Raisa. Noah squeezed behind her. I shift to get a better look and see at least seven kids, including my siblings, crouched behind the tables. Raisa and a boy around her age kneel near the front, the younger kids pressed into the wall behind them.

Pride swells in my chest.

"Is anyone hurt?" I ask. Ten separate headshakes, though it's clear some of them are injured. Their *no*s do not mean they're alright; it means they haven't been bitten.

I hesitate long enough to find Mara, shepherding the last of the other kids—three young girls—through the door, using her body as a shield. The last Tick, the female teacher, slams into Mara, and the pair go stumbling to the side. The Tick tries to scramble away from Mara, toward the open door and the kids waiting outside. All I can do is hope the town hall meeting is ending and they've heard the chaos or one of the kids has the thought to go for help. With an animalistic yell, Mara kicks the door shut and grabs the Tick by the arm, wrenching so hard the bone snapping echoes throughout the large room. She throws her arms around the Tick's waist and holds her thrashing form in place.

"Rory!" she calls—she seemed in her own world, but she yells in my direction, like she knows where I am without having to look.

I lunge, have to avoid tripping over a small body I don't let myself look at, and jam my sword up through the Tick's chin, into her brain. She goes limp, and Mara lets her smack the floor with a thud.

It doesn't occur to me until I shove the bloody sword back into its sheath that this Tick—the woman she was an hour or two ago—might have been savable. The Dyebucetin Mara is injected with each morning might have been able to prevent this end if I'd had time to think about it. If I'd subdued instead of slaughtered.

And there's the biggest part, the thing we still haven't gotten past. The reason Mara and I killed the Ticks on the mainland, and the reason I killed these. Because there wasn't time. There wasn't the luxury of consideration.

Put it away. The old mantra comes rushing back, and I shove my train of thought off its track. I can't let myself think about all this.

With the Tick down, Mara goes to work dragging apart the table barricade. She pushes the tables open, revealing the children hiding behind them, Raisa at the head.

Only Raisa and Noah move once they see Mara. Noah barrels into her, throwing his arms around her waist and hugging her fiercely. She stiffens, meeting my eyes for a brief moment before hugging Noah back, her expression softening.

"You're alright," she murmurs into his curls. "You're safe."

Raisa picks her way out of the debris to me, and though the fear still has her pupils blown and her limbs are a little shaky, she looks determined. She takes my hand, squeezes once, and gives me what I think is a reassuring smile.

"Get your brother and the kids out of here," I say. "Find Isaac." I look to Noah, who has extricated himself from Mara and makes his way over to me. "Tell the others what happened and get help. Okay?"

Noah nods, and I can tell he's grateful for a task—he keeps glancing at the bodies on the floor and averting his gaze.

Raisa takes his hand, guiding him toward the other children still hiding behind the tables. Like a small mayor, she claps her hands and gathers the other kids, leading them toward the door and out into the night. I have to force myself not to trail after them, reminding myself the Ticks are down and aren't getting back up.

When I break myself out of the thoughts, Mara is already across the room, dragging the male Tick by the shoulders, pulling him toward the door, where she deposits him. I join her at the female Tick on the other side of the room. She catches my eye, gives me a thin-lipped smile, and takes one arm as I take the other. We haul the body over to the first, near the door—though the chances of infection are slim to none with a dead Tick, the bodies will be burned.

Neither of us speaks as we move the children's bodies. We're gentler, transporting them with care, lowering them softly onto the ground on the other side of the floor.

Alice. Paulo. Neither of them older than ten years old. Practically babies still. I have to blink through the tears blurring my vision.

"Do you think . . ." I start.

Mara freezes. She won't meet my eyes as she says, "They're too far gone. It wouldn't work."

I'd hoped maybe we'd find them put together enough they could be taken to a facility, but both have their throats torn out, their chests ripped open. I'm far from squeamish these days, but looking at them makes my belly flip.

Not everyone responds to the Dyebucetin. The better condition the body is in, the better the chances of response to the treatment.

"They're going to turn soon," she says.

"I know."

"I can do—" Mara starts, reaching for my sword, but I step back.

"No," I say. "I'll handle it."

"You don't have to," she says, and I hate how she says it, like I'm a baby cow struggling to find its legs.

I ignore her and pull out the diving knife I keep tucked into my boot.

"I said I'll handle it."

And I do.

Neither of us speaks again until we're standing over the third Tick—the young girl. She's more deteriorated than I thought. Her skin is gray, not like Mara's gray tinge, but gray like dark, forbidding clouds. One side of her body is burned. The skin around her wrists and ankles is worn raw, like she's been in cuffs. Her neck is covered in tiny little holes. Needle marks, like the ones on Mara.

"She's not from the facility," Mara says.

Her words awaken the pit in my stomach, one that spilled open when I first saw the girl.

"That's not possible," I say, aware it's false even as I do.

"She's not," Mara says. "I'm telling you, I've never seen her before."

"Well, she's not from the Island."

"Then where did she come from?"

I shake my head.

"She looks like she was turned years ago," Mara says. "I don't understand. How is . . ."

"I don't know," I say. "I don't know."

Mal's words from the day before ring in my head. *You'll be back before sunset tomorrow, or you'll never step foot off this island again.*

His insistence that Mara come with me—that I make this trade at all. That we be back before sunset, when the rest of the Island's residents are in the soundproofed theater and the children are a block away, mostly unprotected.

The justice system may be in pieces, but the concept of an alibi still exists, and neither I nor the Altered have one.

Bile burns the back of my throat.

Shouts from outside the building, down the block, draw both our attention. Mara's face is stricken as she stares at the cracked door across the room.

"You need to get out of here," I say suddenly, my stomach wrenching. I point to the girl at our feet. "And you need to take her with you."

"What?" Mara asks, with the audacity to act horrified.

"This wasn't an accident," I say.

She pauses. "You think Mal did this," she says.

"I don't know," I say. "Yes. Maybe. I mean, who else has motive?"

Mara frowns, but before she can protest, I continue, "She's leverage. So take her to the house next to ours. I've gone in a dozen times, and it's empty. Put her in the basement, get back into the house as fast as you can, and stay there."

Mara opens her mouth. Closes it. She licks her lips and says, "You can't be serious."

"I shouldn't have to tell you what this looks like," I say. "An attack, a few days after the Altered get here."

"But it wasn't us." She looks down at the girl. "It was her."

"We don't know where she came from," I say. "We don't know how she turned, or when, or who she is. But when the rest of the Island gets here, all they're going to see is you and five bodies."

Mara's nostrils flare. She stares down at the girl for a long second, so long I don't know if she heard me. And then she stiffens, and says, "Okay. Fine. I'm going." Her brow furrows. "Noah and Raisa—"

"I'll find them, if Isaac and Sam haven't already."

She shifts her weight.

"Go, Mara."

She hesitates another moment. Chews on the inside of her cheek. Finally, she kneels, picks up the girl, and runs, letting the door slam shut behind her.

Then it's me and the dead, waiting for the Island to find us.

●

Locating Isaac and Sam in the aftermath of the attack is near impossible. It's more chaotic out in the street outside the school than it was inside. All panicked voices and parents rushing about to locate their

118

kids and the crackling of flames as someone starts a fire for the bodies.

Isaac, Sam, Raisa, and Noah are at the far edge of the throng. I pull Noah and Raisa into fierce hugs and don't protest when Sam pulls me into her arms. To my relief, Isaac sends her and the kids back to the house, and as soon as they're out of sight, I turn to Isaac, telling him to find Fatimah and meet me at the neighboring house. He doesn't question it, nor does he need specifics, trusting I'll give him the answers later. A rush of affection pushes through me as he walks away from me, but part of me recognizes it shouldn't be like this. I shouldn't be doling out commands, and he shouldn't be taking them. We should be arguing over whatever teenage girls bicker with their dads about. I wouldn't know. I never got the chance to find out.

Being a carefree teen was never in the cards for me. I vaulted from kid to adult, and now that I'm on the other side, all I can see is the life I missed out on.

⬤

The house next to ours, on the corner of the block, is empty, like the rest of the street. Island occupants get to choose where they live, under the condition they fix it up themselves. Some families cohabitate a few blocks down, where the big yards are used for raising livestock, but for the most part, people live on the residential streets a few blocks away. My family and a few others live elsewhere, but no one is far from the main street. Despite the Island's size, most of it is uninhabited.

The cream-colored house is three times the size of ours, and its front is made entirely of long-broken windows. As I walk up the driveway, an uneasy feeling skitters over my skin, and I stop, whipping around. The street is empty and dark, but I can't shake the sensation of eyes on me.

I shrug off the paranoia and make for the front door.

It's cracked open, and I head into the dark entryway. Like whoever owned our house, this place's original occupant was stuck forty years in the past, evident in the decor and the god-awful patterned shag rug leading through the foyer.

The basement door is open, too, and I ease down the stairs to a moonlit room. Isaac, Sam, and I have taken all the usable linens and clothes, but the basement is still packed with sports equipment.

In the center of the room, a small corpse is laid on the floor.

The girl from the school. The one who killed four people tonight. And I haven't the slightest idea where she came from.

I put the blade through her skull myself, but I still expect her to open her eyes and lunge. My fingers curl around the hilt of my sword like a child with a blanket.

Within a few minutes, noise above signals someone's entrance into the house. Isaac. Footsteps creak, and a tentative "Rory?" echoes down the stairs.

"Down here," I call.

Isaac descends the stairs slowly, Fatimah at his back, both slightly confused and weary as all hell.

"Rory?" Isaac asks. "What are we—" He stops at the base of the stairs, gaze landing on the figure at my feet.

Fatimah, joining him on the basement floor, inhales sharply.

"Rory, please tell me what the hell you're doing with a dead body," Isaac says.

"I'm not loving the judgment in your tone," I say. At his displeased expression, I continue, nudging the girl lightly with my shoe. "She started the attack at the school. I've never seen her before, and it seems like she turned a long, long time ago, but—"

"Juliette," Fatimah says suddenly.

Isaac and I look at her.

Fatimah clears her throat, looking between us, then back at the girl.

"Her name is Juliette," Fatimah says. "Juliette Gordon."

I exhale sharply.

"This is Mal's youngest daughter."

Horror makes my gut churn and lurch. "How?"

"I thought his family died during the Fall," Isaac says, and I'm grateful he can form coherent sentences, because all I can do is stare at the Tick's face. I can see Mal in the sharp line of her jaw, in her thick, dark hair.

"His wife died on day one. But not his daughters." Fatimah moves to sit on one of the stairs, elbows on her knees. "It couldn't have been more than a month after the infection hit. Right before the cities were bombed. We thought everything was contained, but . . ." She swallows visibly. "By the time it was over, a dozen more were dead. Juliette and Rose included. I saw him bring Rose to the pyre, and I never asked, but I always assumed . . ."

She doesn't have to finish her sentence.

She always assumed there wasn't enough left of Juliette to be burned.

"He kept her confined," Isaac says, kneeling before the body like a detective from those old shows. He reaches out to turn one of her wrists, his fingers fluttering over the bruised, gray skin. "These look like cuff marks."

"He's kept a Tick locked up on the Island for three years," I say. The fury living beneath my throat flares upward, and I don't realize I'm curling my hands into fists until my nails dig into my palms.

All his talk about the Altered bringing danger onto the Island, and he's had a ticking time bomb tucked away all this time.

"Look at these," Isaac says. He points to the girl's neck.

Fatimah curses beneath her breath.

"I swore there were doses missing from the shipment," she says, standing and coming to kneel beside Isaac. She keeps a wider berth and doesn't touch the body. "He's been giving her Dyebucetin."

Isaac stands, and Fatimah rises, too, the pair of them frowning.

"He's been trying to treat her himself," Isaac says.

"Yeah, key word there is *try*," I say. "Why the hell wouldn't he send her to a facility?" Though I can tell from looking at her she was too far gone a long time ago. The Tick who infected her all those years ago took more than a few chunks out of her.

But he could have tried. He should have. He should have done anything but keep her locked up, blocks away from sleeping families.

"I didn't know Mal before the Fall," Fatimah says. "But the man I met the first day, the one who saved me from a Tick, is not the man who burned his daughter's body. Whatever happened to his girls, it broke him."

"We have to tell someone," I say. "We have to tell *everyone*. Mal's been keeping a Tick here all this time—"

"No," Isaac and Fatimah say at once.

"No?"

"No," Isaac says. "If we run out there and start hurling accusations at Mal, we'll be shut down faster than we can speak. He'll call us liars, and the Island will believe him."

"We're not lying!"

"Isaac is right," Fatimah says. "No one out there will be receptive to an accusation toward Mal, certainly not tonight. Grief negates logic. You know that." She takes a breath. "Plus, we have no way to prove this is Mal's daughter. Could be somebody you brought back with you from the mainland to set loose."

"You can identify her. You're the proof."

"I'm not exactly a creditable source at the moment," Fatimah says. "Mal has me aligned with the Altered, which means my word is as good as dirt."

"There were kids there," I say. "They saw Juliette, too."

"Children's testimonies were unreliable pre-apocalypse," Isaac says. "And a child against Mal? There's no question."

"So we sit here and do nothing?" I snap.

"We aren't doing nothing," Isaac says. "We can't make a rash decision here. There are lives at stake."

"I'll try and get a message out to Daphne. She can contact Thalia for Alliance help," Fatimah says. "But for now, the best thing to do is lie low and keep our mouths shut, unless Mal decides to shut them for us."

"Mal won't get away with this," Isaac says, and I can't decide if he's trying to reassure me or himself. "But we're going to be smart."

Fatimah licks her lips, looking between Isaac and me. "Keep an eye on Mara. Mal will be looking for someone to blame for all this, and Mara was there during the attack. She's the easiest target. I'll be around in the morning to administer her Dyebucetin. It's best she stays inside."

Anxiety loops tight around my throat, and I dig my nails into my palms, letting the sting ground me to the present.

"Be safe," Isaac says.

"You do the same." Fatimah gives him a thin smile and squeezes me on the shoulder once before she heads for the stairs.

I exhale and cross the basement to a pile of plastic tarps, dragging one off the top and spreading it over the body.

"Let's keep this between us for now," Isaac says. "No use causing unnecessary panic until we have a plan."

Essentially, don't tell Sam yet. It's not really a lie, nor is it the first time we've kept something from her. When we were running low on food, when I got a nasty cut on my arm that almost became a problem, when Isaac's tooth bugged him so much he finally asked me to take a pair of pliers and yank it out. The realities we swallowed so Sam and my siblings didn't have to.

"I hate it," I say.

"I know," Isaac says. "I do, too."

It goes against the instincts the last few years drilled into my bones—when there's danger, run the hell away. And if you can't run, fight. Do something, or you're dead.

But Isaac and Fatimah have made up their minds, and I see the logic in it. I hate it, but I see it.

So when Isaac heads up the basement stairs, I force myself to follow him, shutting the door and closing the body in the dark.

16

RORY

Juliette's body is gone.

When I went next door the morning after the attack, the only trace left in the basement was the tarp I'd pulled over her. Neither Isaac nor Fatimah has a clue what happened to it, but both their expressions were grave when I told them.

Which means someone else knows and our evidence is gone. All we have now to prove Mal's daughter was behind the attack is my, Mara's, and Fatimah's word. None of which carry any weight.

I want to scour the Island for the body or trail Mal and see if he took it, but Isaac orders me to stand back and give Fatimah time to reach help on the radio. Apparently, I'm an instigator, and Isaac places me under unofficial house arrest alongside Mara.

On the third day of mind-numbing nothing, I am perched on the couch, pretending there is no glass between me and the broad ocean beyond the street. Mara is down the hall in the guest bedroom.

The house is uncharacteristically empty, with Isaac and Sam taking the kids to the park for the afternoon. With a bloodstained schoolhouse and dead teachers, school has been shut down, and Noah was practically bouncing off the walls.

One of the Altered was killed last night. He made the mistake of walking outside his house, and this morning, his skull was cracked open on the asphalt. A warning, or retaliation for the outbreak, and one I can't figure out how to tell Mara.

I've avoided her all day in the hopes of not having to.

It's like the first day she was here, the sticky feeling in my limbs urging me to run until I couldn't anymore. I'd hoped she'd be the first to break, but instead, I'm the one who takes advantage of the quiet and slips out the front door.

The flimsy line of no patrols is still holding outside the house, and with no neighbors—a choice I already approved of and now appreciate—the street is soundless as I cross it.

Walking down the sand is a pain, and I curse the town this island used to be for not installing walkways through the sand all down the beach. It's nearly half a mile to the water in some places and near inaccessible to anyone, save for a single rubber mat stretching halfway down the sand a mile down the beach.

I took it for granted before. The freedom to move without thought. I don't anymore.

Huffing and puffing down the sand takes a good ten minutes, exhaustion added by the constant looking over my shoulder to ensure I'm not being followed, but the journey is worth it. It's always worth it.

The ocean stretches for miles in each direction, endless straight ahead. Lacy white waves break against the shore, water bursting ten feet tall. Seaweed swaths the beach, drifting in the surf, and the wet sand glitters in the sunlight.

I scan the waterline, blood running cold at the silhouette ten yards down the beach. My hand stalls on my sword as recognition dawns. Mara. She must have snuck out before I did.

She's shed her sneakers and one of the big billowing tees she's always wearing, standing barefoot in the surf in yoga pants and a tank with her head tipped back.

A deep, dark hole is set into one shoulder blade, the edges blurred with purples and blues and reds, the wound as dried as the one on her face. There is barely an inch of skin unmarred by an old scar or a new wound or a scratch or a bruise.

Strands of hair, different lengths, lift and sway in the breeze. Half of her face is visible from here, and her eyes are closed, her lips parted slightly.

Something in my chest gives a great tug.

"Are you actively trying to get yourself killed?" I call.

If she's surprised, she doesn't show it, and turns to face me casually. She holds my eyes as she steps back to her sneakers and the balled-up shirt in the sand, tugging it over her head, hiding the patchwork quilt of her skin.

"Is this your way of telling me to go home?" Mara asks.

When I say nothing, she turns to face the water again. I move to stand beside her. We're close enough our arms could touch if they weren't both crossed against our chests.

"For the record," I say when the quiet becomes unbearable, "you probably *are* going to get killed if you stay out here too long."

She says nothing.

"Unless that's what you want," I continue.

Again, with the *nothing*.

"Fine. Whatever." I ease down onto the sand, legs spread out in front of me, and dig my fingers into the damp sand at my sides. After a beat, Mara sits beside me.

She lapses into her characteristic refusal to speak, but two can play her game, and I have the time to sit here, with no risk in doing it. Mara has to go home sometime.

I've dug two significant holes in the sand with my heels by the time she talks.

"I'm sorry," she says. "About Aria. I should have said it before."

The name presses deep into the hollows of my chest. The sound of her laughter, drowned by the scream she let loose as the Tick tore into her neck.

"Go, Aurora. Now." Mom crouches over Aria's limp form, a protective-ness to her stance setting off alarm bells in my head. We can't have more than a few minutes until she . . .

Dad and Raisa are upstairs, where I am supposed to be, but Mom is here, and Aria is here, and she is . . .

"No," I say. Mom stiffens, snaps upward, fixes me with a stare I've never seen before. It trails up and down me like a sharp nail. In one of her hands, a blade trembles so hard I think she's going to cut herself.

"Get out," she snarls. "Get out!" If she keeps yelling, she'll draw un-wanted attention. But I'm not brave enough to scold her, and she wouldn't listen anyway. Not when she's swallowing sorrow with every breath.

So I don't scold her, and I don't leave—part of me is beginning to know my mom as more than a mother and recognizes the cry for help. Kneel-ing at her side, keeping my eyes off Aria—no, not Aria anymore, but the body—I pull the knife from her hands.

She releases it with a sob that hits me like an icy wind. She reaches to take back the knife, but I don't give her a chance.

I bite down on my tongue until I taste metallic, bitter blood, and sink the blade into Aria's skull. When I drop the knife to the ground, it is not my mom who picks it up, but Sam. And it isn't Aurora who stands, but Rory.

"What are you sorry for?" I say, shaking off the memory. Grief rises and crashes against me like a wave, then retreats with the tide. "You didn't bite her."

Mara flinches. Shakes her head. "I'm sorry she's gone."

"So am I," I say. Mara looks away, closing up like a zipped fleece. I bite my tongue and clench my fists in the sand. If anything has stayed the same between us, it is this, the endless jamming of my own foot in my mouth.

Mara is quiet for a long time before she speaks again. "There isn't a place for me here," she says.

"You sound like Mal."

"I'm serious." She draws her knees up, slings her arms around her legs. "I don't think I can stay here. Not much longer."

"You're not leaving."

Mara doesn't say anything. Typical.

"You're not leaving," I repeat. "I'm not letting you."

"It's not up to you. You're not all-powerful, Rory, no matter what you think. And, sooner or later, this is going to come down on my head, and it'll come down on yours, too, if I don't go. It'll come down on Sam's and Isaac's. Raisa's and Noah's. I am not worth it."

"I'm serious," I say. "You're not leaving the Island."

Mara lifts her chin. "You don't get to do that," she says, jaw set. "You don't get to ask me to stay when you've been pushing me to go since the second I got here. If you hate me so much, Rory, why the fuck won't you let me *leave*?"

The cap on the anger with Mara's name on it rattles, pops off, and everything I've swallowed to survive comes rushing to the surface. I can barely speak through the tightness in my throat.

"Because you *left me*," I say, with all the poise of a dribbling, whining child. "You left me, and you didn't say anything. And then you died, and now—" My mouth, saving me some inevitable embarrassment, stitches itself shut. I pull in a shaking breath, holding back the memories threatening to crack me in two. "I kissed you, and you . . . stared at me like I had three heads, and then you left."

"I left?" Mara explodes a second after I do, her voice rising to meet mine. "Me? If you think that's what happened, Rory, then you're forgetting some pretty crucial facts. If anyone left, it wasn't me. It was you."

"The hell are you talking about?"

Her gray eyes are wide, pupils blown, anger making them look black. "The next morning. I woke up to my parents arguing in the kitchen, to Carter crying in the front room. By the time I found out you were gone, your car was halfway down the street. We never saw you again."

I tear my gaze away and force my eyes shut, memories poking through my carefully constructed walls like bloody fingers.

"The world was ending. My grandma called us from Los Angeles, told us it was bad, and before I knew it, Isaac was stuffing all of us in the van. They didn't exactly give me a choice. I didn't *leave*." Mara scoffs, and I clear my throat, try again.

"We didn't make it," I say. "LA fell first, you know. The farther north we got, the worse it got. We had to ditch the car, and all of our stuff, right there on the interstate." A bitter laugh slips past my lips. "It wouldn't have mattered. The phone lines went down the same night."

"I know," Mara says, and an image of a young, living Mara dialing my number until she lost service altogether flickers behind my eyes. I force them shut, blinking hard enough to scatter the picture, and open my eyes again.

"I was going to come back," I say. "No matter what, I was going to come back to you. Even after what happened."

"By *what happened*, you mean you kissing me and Carter running out five seconds later dragging me to dinner?"

"Five seconds? More like five minutes!"

"What, we have one awkward moment and you hate me?"

I called her the coward before, but looking at her is the scariest thing I've ever done.

"Of course not!" I rake a hand through my hair, fingers catching in knots. With a groan of frustration, I wrench my hand away. "I hate you because I loved you for *ten years*, and you died, and you never said goodbye. You never said anything."

"You can't blame me for—" She stops. Pins me with her metal gaze.

The words I've admitted aloud for the first time hit us both seconds after they hit the air, and we both hang still in their wake. *I loved you.* I have felt and known them longer than I can remember, but letting them be heard is a different kind of acknowledgment.

My gaze slides to the water, the waves breaking against the sand and being pulled back into the depths. I can feel Mara's eyes on me, grating against my skin, digging through bone to reach my thoughts.

I open my mouth to speak, but fingers brush my jaw, and I turn my head. Silver holds me in its grasp, the irises of my memory seeming to flash in place of the new ones. In place of the new Mara.

Then it is her again, all pale skin and slashed face and haunting eyes. I am a statue as she shifts closer, close enough her warm breath tickles my nose, and I can't find the strength to pull air into my lungs.

Her fingers, soft and gentle, settle against the line of my jaw. I am so sure she's going to kiss me my chin lifts on instinct, eyes fluttering. It doesn't come. I open my eyes to gray, to Mara.

Her lips purse. "I should have kissed you back."

My heart stutters and skips.

Before I can say anything, Mara is on her feet, looking down at me, lines of sunlight streaming around her. I think she's going to say more, explain, but she shakes her head and walks away.

17

MARA

There is an Aria-shaped hole in the Blake home. Her echo is everywhere: in the instinctual glances Raisa makes to the side before remembering her twin is no longer there; in the anecdotes tossed out across the chipped table at dinner, which I don't eat but attend for social and civilized purposes; in the stack of three worn books sitting untouched atop a similarly untouched piano in the living room corner, a series I remember Aria talking about for months.

It is still a happy house, impressively so considering the circumstances. A CD player has a constant tune filtering through the halls, often eighties music by Sam and Isaac's decree. Tonight, Rory put up a fight and has a Taylor Swift album pumping from the kitchen, where she's on dish duty. It reminds me of being fifteen and learning to play her favorite songs on my guitar.

I've avoided the kitchen so she doesn't see the smile the small act has left on my face. The Rory I knew, still unapologetically herself in every way.

She hasn't spoken to me since the confession on the beach—another reason to avoid her. Though she's already doing a fine job of ignoring me all on her own. And I can't find it in me to blame her. *I loved you.* Not *I love you*, but *I used to love you.* I thought it'd be a relief to know that, at some point, she felt the same as I did, but it was more like a punch to the chest. As if I needed any more proof things are different now.

Sam and Isaac are out in the backyard, stringing up clothes to dry on the lines, their chatter and laughter drifting through the open door at the back of the kitchen. In a surprising show of trust, Rory didn't blow a gasket when she passed through the room a few minutes ago and saw me sitting opposite Raisa and Noah on the couch, a book spread open on their laps.

The first notes of the next song on the album ring from the kitchen, and I don't realize I'm moving until I am standing in front of the piano. A second later, I am sitting at the bench. The old me could never resist an open instrument.

I lift the fallboard and brush my fingers across the keys. It takes a moment for muscle memory I thought I'd forgotten to kick in, and the melody joins the crackling music flooding down the hall.

The overcompensating fingers on my left hand skip over the keys, and I yank my hand back, as if the ivory will shock me. From the kitchen, the song continues on like I never joined in at all.

I let out a huff of frustration and drop my hands to the wooden bench.

Two sets of footsteps approach my back. Noah on the left and Raisa on the right. A soft poke hits the back of my left arm, and I turn to find Noah wearing a shy smile.

"Do you need help?" he asks.

The *no* forms behind my teeth, but Noah's expression is so earnest and Raisa's gaze darts up to me and down to the keys so eagerly I can't get the word out.

I had barely begun teaching Aria and Raisa to play before the Fall. We made it to the basics, and I remember Aria's giddy smile when she figured out which keys were which and the determined purse to Raisa's lips as she played "Twinkle, Twinkle, Little Star."

"Yes," I say. I wiggle the remaining fingers on my left hand. "Want to be my left?"

A smile lights up Noah's face, and he nods. Raisa moves to stand beside him on my left.

"Okay, Noah, you're going to play this key"—a G note rings through the room—"like this." I gesture to the music coming down the hall. "Do you hear it?"

Noah nods, closing his eyes. A beat later, his eyes snap open, and he tentatively tests the keys. It takes a few notes for him to find the rhythm, but once he does, he grabs on tight.

"You're a natural," I tell him, and he pulls his hand back with a wide grin.

He nudges his sister. "Okay, Raisa's turn."

Raisa rolls her eyes but looks at me expectantly.

I sneak a glance toward the kitchen doorway and beyond, where Rory is. I simultaneously hope she can and can't hear us.

Clearing my throat, I say to Raisa, "It's the same idea for you, but it's"—I demonstrate an A and a B flat in quick succession—"like this. Does that make sense?"

Raisa tests out the keys but latches onto the beat as quickly as her younger brother.

"Exactly," I say, giving her a smile. "Now, Noah, you play, and then Raisa, and then go again. Okay?"

Raisa nods.

Noah takes a deep breath, biting down on his lip in concentration, and the expression is all Sam. I have to stifle a smile.

He plays his note, and Raisa follows, and after a few beats, I let my right hand fall to the keys.

The CD player sings the last notes of the song from the kitchen, but Raisa, Noah, and I keep going. Rory can surely hear us now.

The beginning of the next song doesn't come, though my somewhat-decayed brain knows it wasn't the final track.

I can't bring myself to stop. Even with one hand on the piano and the offbeat tune we're playing, the music puts me in a trance.

Piano. The word flits around my skull, unimportant and ignored as I chase the man around the large black object taking up half the room. Still, some part of me recognizes the object, remembers it makes noise.

Not as much noise as the man makes when I catch him, slamming him into the piano. His screams join the screeching notes as he grapples for a hold on the keys, filling the room with sound. I catch him by the ankles, dragging him back, and the last notes of the chaotic song die with him.

Two or so blocks away, too far for the Blakes to hear but too close for my comfort, muffled yells rise. I jerk my hand back and jump off the bench.

My abrupt abandonment of the piano triggers some alarm in the kids. Noah stops, stiffening, and Raisa finds my eyes, her round nose scrunched in concern.

The loud voices outside must get close enough for them to hear, because Raisa pushes to her feet, worrying the end of one of her braids between her fingers. She gestures for Noah, who frowns but steps away from the piano bench to join her.

"What is it?" he asks, looking between me and Raisa. Neither of us has an answer. Even if we did, more shouts, inching closer by the breath, steal our opportunity.

Raisa rushes around the couch to press her face against the glass, hands cupping her eyes as if it will enhance her vision. The innocence of the gesture stirs venom in my gut, burning through ruined intestines.

"Mara," Noah says softly, slipping his hand into mine. The pit deepens, churns. "What's goin' on?"

Feigning the calm I wished to have seen from my parents in the Dark Days, I turn to face him, squeezing his little hand and kneeling to put myself at his level. I brush a finger down his chin, pulling on a smile.

"Don't you worry 'bout a thing, chicken wing." A small, quick giggle bubbles out of him, and the sick feeling in me cools. "Whatever it is, us big people can handle it."

His concern slides back to the forefront. "It's not . . ." He flicks a glance at Raisa, at me, at the window, as if the word he's chewing on is dangerous. "*Ticks?* Again?"

There is far too much fear in one syllable for a five-year-old boy, a boy who should know school buses and recess and whiteboards, not death and loss and decay.

Three days ago, he watched two of his friends die. His teachers. He shouldn't have to see any more.

It gives me pause, sending an old, fleeting sensation dancing through my veins. After so long in place, something shifts, like the surge of fire when the Dye lights up my brain like a firework. Only there are no drugs. There is just me.

For a second, only a second, I can taste the *life* this entire island is clutching—the thing I have been reaching for without knowing. And then it slips away.

"No," I say. "The Ticks are gone. At least from here."

"But you're not gone."

Raisa hums a disapproving note and comes to join her brother, who tosses her an apologetic smile.

"Raisa doesn't think you're a Tick anymore, but Rory does." He lifts his big brown eyes to mine, long dark lashes touching his thick brows. "What do *you* think?"

What do you think?

I haven't been asked to think. I've done a good job of avoiding it, for sanity's sake. What *do* I think?

"I—"

"Raisa, Noah, downstairs, right now." Rory storms through the doorway. She has what looks like a military-grade crossbow in her hands.

I expect some argument, but the crossbow and Rory's sharp tone have transformed every person in the room. Raisa and Noah are tiny soldiers, linking hands and running for the hall to the basement door. Before they disappear, I glimpse a small, long blade tucked into a sheath at Raisa's side.

Isaac and Sam burst through the back door, pausing on their way through the kitchen long enough for Sam to pull a small pistol from the cabinet beneath the sink. She passes it to Isaac before giving him a curt nod and departing in the direction of the basement door.

"Isaac," Rory says.

"Meet me outside," Isaac says, not seeming to notice me as he heads for the front door and out.

With the others gone, Rory's wrath finds a new target.

"Away from the window." Rory crosses the room to take my arm and pull me to the side, pushing me into the corner against the front door with her free hand. Her grip on the crossbow is white-knuckled, her breaths coming in fast puffs. "I am getting *really* sick of you trying to get yourself killed."

"It's them, isn't it? Mal and . . ." The name sticks to my dry tongue. "Carter. And the others."

"It's sure as shit not Christmas carolers," she says.

"*Rory.*"

She has her teeth clenched so tight it's a miracle she hasn't chipped a tooth. Stepping back, she stares through the window, tensing until every inch of her is hardened steel.

"Go downstairs with Sam and Raisa and Noah. Isaac and I will handle this." She reaches for the door handle, and I shove myself between her and the door, swatting her arm aside.

"Not a chance." Her eyes go wide, confusion quickly replaced by fury. She opens her mouth to speak, likely to tell me to screw off, but I don't give her the chance. "They're here for me. Not you. Not the others."

"If you go out there, they'll kill you."

"I'm hard to kill, remember?"

"Damn it, Mara! This isn't a game! One of you is *nothing* against a mob of them."

I don't point out that if anyone here has perfected killing, it's me. There is so much blood on my hands I couldn't begin to keep track.

"I can take a hit. I don't need you and Isaac fighting my battles—"

"The little girl from the school is Mal's daughter."

My train of thought careens off its track. "What?"

"She was Mal's daughter. He's kept her locked up for years. She must have escaped," Rory says, the exasperation in her tone culling all of my retorts. "But her body disappeared, so now we can't prove Mal is responsible. He's blaming this all on the Altered. Dolly Winsleigh's arm was ripped off." She takes a heaving breath. "You and I both know it will never heal. And they shot her father in the leg for trying to stop them." Her composure falters for a half second. An image of Dolly, crying with no tears, cradling her own arm, flashes in my head. "They don't care who gets hurt on their way to the target, and in this case, *you* are the target."

"But if Mal is the reason those kids died, we could tell everyone—"

"Oh, yeah, because they'll believe you."

"Then you tell them. Or Isaac."

"I don't know if you've noticed, but we aren't exactly on Mal's good side. If I go out there accusing him of keeping his infected daughter locked up for years and letting her escape and kill a bunch of kids, it's going to land me in a cell at the station."

"We have to try," I say.

If it could, steam would be pumping out of her ears. Every inch of exposed freckled skin is flushed.

"*No.* I said no. Just . . . stay inside, will you?" she says, and does what she does best: walk away and take the last word with her. This time, she walks out the front door and into the waiting throng of an angry mob.

Rory and Isaac will not take fire directed at me. I'm the one who deserves to burn for it. Not them. Never them.

If the Tick has made me anything, it is impulsive, and I am momentarily grateful. Without it, I'd never make it past the threshold. Unhesitating, I open the door and plunge into the cool night air to find a standoff settling into place on the street.

At the top of the driveway, side by side, weapons raised, stand Rory and Isaac.

Scattered down the drive, spilling into the lawn and onto the street, are at least thirty faces. They wield clubs, bats, bows, and other customized weapons which could easily obliterate me. Varying ages, some outfitted in ill-fitting uniforms and some in casual wear, identical in their unwavering anger.

And as much as I want to hate them for what they're doing, part of me understands it. I have lost everything to make it here, but so have they. Everyone on this island lost everything and everyone, and no one is equipped for it. For a lot of people, it's too much to bear. It's easier to tack the blame onto something they can see and cut down than to accept the world as it is now.

There are a few torches in the mix—a little excessive, in my opinion. I force the inappropriately timed smile off my face, cursing the Tick for not eating that embarrassing habit.

Standing directly opposite Rory and Isaac are the leaders of this little group, and the only ones with guns: Mal and Carter. The two women from the first night stand at their backs but wield clubs.

Carter. My sister is a shell of the girl who coached me in crushes and let me sleep in her room when I had nightmares. Gone, further away than I am.

My exit from the house has ramped up the friction in the air a thousandfold, and every weapon rises.

I raise my shoulders, stare straight ahead, and let myself be the monster they believe I am, placing myself between the mob and the closest thing I will ever find to family again.

Mal's scowl is twisted so deep I wonder if it hurts. A hulking beast of a man, he could probably snap my neck if he got his hands around me long enough. He could definitely snap a human's.

There is a current running beneath his anger, a desperation and grief he is trying to pass as something else. His movements are too jerky, his voice too sharp and loud when he speaks.

"And there she is! The undead star of the show." Mal pauses, ensuring he's keeping his people invested. His next words address the man at my back. "Was that so hard, Isaac?"

"I won't play your game, Gordon. Leave my property, and leave it now."

"Give me the Tick, and I'm gone." He holds up his hands in a false surrender.

Isaac flicks the safety off on the pistol, and the click echoes through the night. The kind, calm man from inside the house—the mediator—is long gone.

"Not happening."

"She will pay for what she's done," Mal says.

"Bullshit," Rory calls.

"Have you ever heard of the 'make my day' law, Mallory?" Isaac asks. "I'd recommend getting off my lawn before you get a one-on-one lesson."

"I see arrogance is a family trait," Mal sneers. "Don't play high and mighty, Blake. Your stories from the mainland are infamous."

"Survival and mob rule aren't the same thing."

"Big words, but they don't mean a damn," Mal says. A smile flashes over Carter's lips at his side. She hasn't just sipped the Kool-Aid. She's drunk on it. "Words didn't save us before, and they won't save us now."

"It doesn't have to be this way," Isaac says. "Just walk away, Mal."

"Not going to happen," Mal says, and a shiver runs down my spine. A man capable of manipulating the masses is a scary thing. A man capable of manipulating himself alongside them is more frightening. More dangerous.

I can't see her, but I sense Rory's movements behind me—hear the soft shuffle of her steps as she moves closer to Isaac, feel the brush of air and smell the scent of lemon. The desire to reach for her, protect her from anything that would dare look her way, is almost impossible not to act on. It is not just me who wants her safe, but the monster in my head. Maybe the monster the infection in my head has turned me into.

My senses spark with stimuli, a predator's observations in preparation of an attack. That numbness I'd started to forget flows through me, softens the edges of my thoughts, chips at them until fragments remain.

Rory and Isaac take a step closer to me, and I can smell the fear in their blood, in the sweat collecting on their skin. Thirty-four heartbeats skittering around the street, a symphony in my head. Rory's behind me, as fast as a hummingbird's.

"What happens when the Alliance finds out? You'll condemn this whole island."

"I'll tell them the truth," Mal says. "That the Ticks attacked our people and we dealt with it."

"There's no proof the attack at the school was started by an Altered. In fact, I have it on good authority—"

"Enough," Mal snarls. I see his desperation for what it is: not fear of the Altered, but fear of being found out.

The attack at the school, the kids who died, it was Mal's fault. He kept his daughter locked up. And he knows it.

"You know, I think I'm done with this conversation." Rory steps forward, pauses at my side, and raises the crossbow. She doesn't look at me, but her elbow grazes my shoulder on its way up in a move I can't decide is intentional or not. "It's late, and I've had a long day." A humorless, somehow menacing laugh fills the air. "Actually, I've had a long three years. So I'm going to ask you to leave, politely, and if you don't, someone is going to get an arrow to the leg." She inclines her head. "Isaac?"

Something infinitesimal shifts between them. Whatever control Isaac has slides to Rory, and they are not father and daughter, but two soldiers on a battlefield.

I am not the only one who notices. Mal's gaze darts between them once, twice.

"Seems reasonable to me," Isaac says. He and Rory sound identical in their stony tone.

"Alrighty, then," Rory says. "You heard him, clones."

Ten or so of Mal's soldiers shift as if to leave but halt when Mal remains steady. He looks at my sister, leans over to speak softly to her. When she meets my eyes, it's to aim a pistol at my head.

"Rory," Isaac says. It makes the dozens of people in the driveway nock arrows in their bows and lift their blades.

Rory moves faster, pulling the crossbow's trigger. It's aimed low, the arrow plunging into Carter's knee. Carter screams, slamming into the asphalt, and around her, chaos erupts.

She shot her. She actually shot her. I can't decide if she did it for me or not, nor can I decide whether or not I feel bad for my sister. I think I should.

"Nobody move!" Mal barks.

Carter's wound is not deadly, but it serves its purpose. No one moves past the invisible line in the concrete, not even Mal. He stares at Rory, and she stares at him. Only half her face is visible from this angle, but it is bright and flushed and unafraid.

"Next one is to the skull," Rory says.

The pressure builds, presses on my scarred lungs, pushes until I'm sure they're going to burst and the sun will rise to a driveway bathed in blood. But after one of the longest minutes of my life, accentuated by the soft, painful hisses coming from Carter, Mal lowers his weapon.

"Stand down," Mal says, raising a hand. "Tonight is not the night."

"I think you're forgetting something," Isaac says.

"Don't think I am," Mal says.

Rory raises the crossbow.

"Try again," Isaac says.

A muscle twitches in Mal's jaw. "Anyone found on the Blake property will be placed in a cell indefinitely." I don't have to know the Colonel to miss the lie, and Isaac and Rory don't seem assuaged, either.

"Keep your dog leashed, Isaac," Mal barks, jerking a chin at Rory, who spits an extremely creative expletive at him. "Or she'll be put down."

"Lay a hand on her, and I'll use your carotid as a ponytail holder," I say. Rory doesn't hide her smile.

"I would expect nothing less from a Tick," Mal says, and though looking at him is like being shoved under a microscope and inspected, I don't break. He is the one to turn first, whistling at a handful of soldiers, who rush to my sister's side, carefully pulling her into their arms. I'm unsurprised but a little sad to realize I feel no sympathy for her.

"Move out," Mal says, and turns on his heel, stomping down the drive. The group disperses into the night after him with little dallying, though their jabs and insults echo down the street until they fade into the darkness. Only when they're gone do I turn to face Isaac. Rory shifts away from me.

Isaac clears his throat, and like she's been given permission, Rory lets out a sigh, and says, "We're fucked."

Isaac frowns. "Nothing's going to happen to you," he says to me. "You're safe here. We protect our own."

"You shouldn't," I say. A stone is lodged in my throat, making speech difficult. "I'm not worth it."

Isaac's brow furrows. "That's not for you to decide, kiddo." He turns and heads back up the drive, toward the door.

When he is out of earshot, Rory says, "That 'no one on the Blake property' crap won't last beyond dawn, but it gives us some breathing room." As if this somehow covers it, she turns back toward the porch.

"Rory."

She ignores me.

Anger skitters across my skin, and I say, "*Aurora.*"

She halts. Turns to face me. Closes the gap between us.

"Don't call me that," she says, suddenly an entity I've only seen traces of or heard from behind. This burns hotter than I can bear.

"Isaac won't admit it, but you know it's true. Mal is going to get to me, and he'll hurt all of you to do it. *I am not worth it.*" I am frantic, images of the Blake family spread open, bone and muscle scattered around the street, of their blood on my hands and in my mouth. Half memory, half nightmare.

"Don't flatter yourself, Knight." Rory sweeps a look around the street, and when she continues up the porch to the house, I follow her—this is an argument we can have inside. It stalls until we've closed the door behind us and Rory faces me.

"Standing up to Mal isn't about saving you. Because, let's be honest, is that even possible?" It's harsh but valid. "It's about setting an example. This island is one step away from crumbling into chaos. If everyone lets Mal's soldiers walk into our homes and walk out with our people, then this place is lost. We didn't have a choice. We didn't do it for you."

I don't have any proof it's a lie. I just know it is. Know it like I know the color of her eyes.

"How many times do you think you'll have to tell yourself that before you believe it?" I ask.

"Probably as many times as you tell yourself you're not still a monster."

I've wondered for days why Rory is so angry with me, but I realize I am mad at her, too. Mad, period. Mad at her for waiting so long to kiss me and at myself for not doing it first and at the Tick who bit me for taking my future and at the world for breaking apart. I'm so mad I think it'll burn me, maybe this whole island, down to ash.

Someone clears their throat in the doorway. I'm unsure how long Isaac has been standing there, but I also don't know how long we've been standing *here*, bickering like the children we didn't have enough time to be.

Rory swallows and strides across the room, headed down the hall, without a word to Isaac. When her door slams shut behind her, he gives me a sympathetic smile.

"Noah fell asleep on your cot. You'll have to sleep downstairs for the time being, for your protection, but I'll carry Noah up before you head down. He kicks like a mule in his sleep," he says with a tiny, sad smile. His tone is soothing, making me think of my own father, of his soft voice singing me to sleep when I was small. Of scarlet blood and the metal of canines scraping against his jugular—

"Don't chase the rabbit," Isaac says. I snap myself back to the present, meeting his eyes, and his smile is kind, a little sad. "You follow it too far, you get stuck in the past. Never come back."

"Would it be such a bad thing?" I ask without meaning to.

A dull, hollow glaze passes through his eyes. "The world hasn't completely ended yet, Mara," he says. "It might not completely end at all. Don't you want to see what it could be? What the new world could look like?"

"What if I don't deserve to see it?"

He frowns and looks much older than his forty years as he speaks. "You're not the only one who became a monster to survive. But you *are* the only one of us who had some kind of a reason."

"It's not an *excuse*. I still kil—" I choke on the end of the sentence. Isaac sighs deeply, his brows knitted and his eyes thoughtful.

"I don't know if anyone has taken the time to tell you this, Mara, at least anyone who truly meant it, but *it was not your fault.*"

I have heard the words before, but they've never been genuine. The person who said them has never believed them. Until now.

My eyes burn, trying to shed tears and failing, and air catches in my ruined chest. A sob, maybe one that has been lodged in my esophagus for so long I forgot it was there.

As I crumple, Isaac steps forward, pulls me into his arms, holds me the way my dad held me, like I am a child, like I am someone safe enough to touch and care for, and though my body can't figure out how to cry, it dry sobs until it loses the ability to do that. For a little while, I am not a monster, not a drugged beast. I am Mara.

●

With the kids being put to bed by Sam, Isaac takes up post in the living room, settling on the couch near the window with a book.

Watching for Mal and his soldiers.

We broke skin and shed blood. Carter's blood. They will retaliate, and they will do it soon. Rory thinks we have until dawn. Isaac is a bit more optimistic.

Personally, I am tired. When I first woke in the facility, I was as sleepless as a vampire. Still, sleeplessness didn't last long. With every passing week, I spend more and more hours unconscious. Never dreams. Memories. Rust-soaked and raw. I told Dr. Benitez the night terrors stopped, but really, they've gotten worse.

When I am able to escape to the basement, having gathered my measly belongings from the guest room I lasted a few nights in, it is as I left it. The blankets on the futon are rumpled from Noah's nap, and the sight makes me smile.

Kicking off my sneakers, I exchange my clothes for a pair of shorts and a big tee, grateful my hair doesn't grow anymore. It used to be exhausting, wrangling it. Carter took a pair of scissors to it a few weeks before I turned. It hasn't changed since.

I fall back onto the futon, socked feet planted on the cement floor. Cracks trace vines through the ceiling above me, as thin as hairs, fading into the spackled corners.

Footsteps creak above my head, and I wait for the clicking of the locks into place. Instead of locks, the door whines open, and someone comes down the stairs. An uneven gait, every other step noisier.

When I push up, I know it is Rory standing at the bottom of the staircase, but my heart still does its traitorous thump when it sees her—it doesn't seem to care how much disdain her eyes shine with when they trail over me.

She's in pajamas, a pair of pants with yellow ducklings and a faded tee with SAN DIEGO written across the chest. Her socks are fuzzy and purple. She has a pillow beneath one arm and a blanket balled up beneath the other.

"Duck pants? Really?" I say.

"I'll still kill you," she says. As if to prove her point, she lifts her shirt, pulls a diving knife from her waistband, and comes to toss it onto the bed beside me. She throws the pillow and blanket down, too.

The unspoken request—not really a request, nor is anything where Rory is concerned—is at odds with the show of force. It's hard to be intimidating as you get ready to climb into bed with someone.

Which is what's happening here. For some reason. I am not opposed, but I *am* confused. I may be hallucinating.

"What are you doing here?"

She sighs. "I may not be all on board with this whole 'protect Mara even if it gets us all killed' thing, but that doesn't mean I'm going to let someone walk in here and . . ." She gestures to my head. "You know." She draws a finger across her throat and pokes out her tongue.

My laugh surprises us both.

"Besides, Sam's not thrilled I shot your sister, and I'm not in the mood for a lecture. Isaac's talking her down."

"Isaac listens to you," I say. "Why?"

Rory doesn't say anything for a long time.

"Things were different out there," she says eventually. "Sam's the one who got us back from LA alive, which was a miracle, because it was like nothing I—" Rory stops. Turns her head away. "But after Aria . . . she shut down. And I stepped up, I guess. Isaac already had his hands full. We found Noah a few months after Aria died, and he was so little, and Sam was barely holding it together, and at some point, Sam stopped calling the shots, and I started." She pauses. "My parents like to forget who we were out there. Me shooting Carter through the kneecap makes that kind of hard."

"To be fair, Carter had it coming," I say.

"She's still your sister, you know."

"Fairly sure she doesn't see it that way."

"Do you?" Rory shuffles to the bed, sits down at least two feet away from me. She leans back onto her elbows, and instead of answering her, I'm thinking about how the futon is smaller than the blow-up mattress, especially tucked into the wall the way it is.

Rory reaches out to tap my shoulder expectantly, and I remember she's waiting for a reply. It takes a long time to find it.

I shrug. "That girl out there, that's not my sister. Maybe she's in there somewhere, but it's not her."

"So, you're saying you're *not* pissed I shot her?"

"Would you really care if I was?"

"No." She scoffs. Flashes me a grin as if we're in on some joke. It feels like being small again. Like standing on the edge of a cliff, the two of us, and trying to be brave enough to jump.

Rory eases down onto her back, and after a moment, I lie beside her. The candles spread around the room cast the space in shadow and flickering yellow light.

"What was it like?" she asks eventually, voice low. I don't pretend not to understand what she's talking about.

"Like watching through someone else's eyes," I say. "The scariest movie you've ever seen, but you're the villain, and you can't close your eyes or take your hand off the knife."

"You remember?"

"I remember."

"How much?"

"Everything."

I simmer in the aftermath of the admission, sure I'm going to die in it, when Rory says, "That sounds like hell."

Rotted butterflies flit about in my chest, battering against my rib cage. A strangled laugh slips past my lips.

"Hell could take a few notes from the Tick," I say.

Rory doesn't say anything, and I can tell she wants to ask another question. I wait for her to let it out.

"Carter never actually said what happened to your parents. Just that they're gone," she says. Not a question. An opening for me to fill in the blanks.

I can't. I can't turn the reality into words.

"What happened to your mom and dad, Mara?"

"What happened to everyone."

"You know what I mean."

I push to a seated position, meeting her eyes over my shoulder. "And I think you know what I mean, too."

Her thick brows knit as she puzzles it together. I expect horror when she does. And there is horror. Blinding and sharp, flashing across her features and filling me with lead. And then there is more, so much more I can't pick it apart or identify it. All I know is it is not the unwavering loathing of the first day. It is something different altogether.

"It was you," she says.

I rip my gaze away. Draw my legs up onto the bed, sitting cross-legged, eyes straight forward.

In my peripheral vision, Rory sits up. One of her hands seeks out her knife, fingers tracing over it.

She doesn't poke me for the story, and for that reason, I tell it to her. I've never said it out loud before.

"Carter and I were out scavenging. We were stuck by that point, the bomb fallout on one side and the hordes on the other. Had no choice but to go farther and farther into the dead zones to find food and water. We found some convenience store, thought it was empty, and when we finally figured out it wasn't, there were twenty Ticks in there. It was a bloodbath. And by the time I realized the blood on my arm was mine"—my hand drifts over the fabric covering the oldest wound I have, a half-moon of teeth set into my wrist—"it was too late. We were so damn busy trying to get away that we missed it. *I* missed it. And I . . ." I trail off and don't pick the path back up.

Rory doesn't say anything. Doesn't say anything as we curl up on opposite sides of the futon, facing away from each other. Doesn't say anything before she drifts off, her hand gripping the blade beneath her pillow.

But she stays.

18

RORY

While it's hard to blame Mara for doing the very thing I've been doing the last few nights—sneaking out of the house, in my case, to perch on the rocks across the street and watch the black waves hit the beach—it's not hard to be mad at her in general, so I manage.

Half the reason I've been camping out on the futon downstairs the past two nights is to stop Mara from doing something stupid or selfless. And of course, I sleep through half of her escape. When she slips out the window, her sneakers smack the pane, startling me awake, my fingers closing around my blade.

Blinking the daze out of my eyes and cursing myself for falling asleep, I stumble out of bed. I left the door unlocked when I came down, and I wonder why Mara didn't use the stairs. The creaking floors remind me.

I inch through the house, cursing the Ticks for taking yet another thing from me: teenage rebellion. I could have been a master at sneaking out with proper training. Still, I've managed to make do with what I have. And silence still is necessary on the mainland. Even after the bullet, I can move soundlessly if need be. Slowly, but soundlessly.

I use the beach to slink around the soldiers Mal has stationed at the end of the block. A figure blurs in the darkness ahead of me: Mara. She's taken the same path of evasion I have.

It makes keeping track of her easy, and I need it easy with the combination of the thick sand and a full day's worth of being on my feet that I haven't properly slept off. The dull ache in my leg grows heavier with each step.

Mara walks all the way down toward the Del, taking the cracked sidewalk path and hugging it up the street, slipping in and out of the darkness. Tracking her is difficult, and my speed is lagging, but I have eyes on her when she slips into the alleyway of one of the residential streets.

A few of Mal's soldiers are positioned outside one of the houses along the street, their chatter echoing before I dart into the alley after Mara.

The alleys aren't lit by torch, but by moonlight, which works in my favor as I press myself into the fences and tiptoe after Mara. She stops halfway down the alley, behind a house with candlelight flickering beyond curtain-covered windows. It takes a moment to place the home.

The Joshi family and their adult son, an Altered man of twenty named Emir.

Mara's silhouette shifts, her hand rising to her lips. She lets out a low, hollow whistle that makes my stomach turn. It hangs in the air like fog and fades into nothing, and the night carries on around it.

Before I can approach and confront her, a door whines open at the back of the house, and a second silhouette joins the darkness. The father is too short and stocky, the mother too tall and thin. It has to be Emir, standing across from Mara in the black alley, exchanging words too soft for me to hear.

I'm already too close, though, and any closer would slap a neon sign right over my head.

At some points, their soft chatter rises enough for me to catch snippets—*mountains* and *die here* and *Vivian*.

They speak softly for at least ten minutes, and Emir turns and ducks back inside, the door whining shut behind him. Before Mara can turn around, I rake in a deep breath, will my body to obey, and take off in an awkward jog down the alley toward the beach.

My leg is screaming within breaths, but I keep up for the four blocks it takes to reach the sidewalk along the beach, ducking behind the rocks and allowing myself ten seconds to huff and puff.

The moment Mara reaches the sand again, covered from the street by the rocky path lining the sidewalk all the way down the beach, I tackle her. I'll regret it in the morning.

She's strong enough to hold her ground, but I surprise her and manage to take her down into the sand before she reacts. With a growl and a burst of inhuman speed, she writhes underneath me, jostling my grip. She hooks her leg around my right side and yanks, rolling me beneath her in a fluid movement. My hands fly up to shove her off, but she catches my wrists in a vise grip, slamming them into the sand. She's straddling me, knees against my ribs, hips holding me in place.

I fight for a long ten seconds as she watches, a predator inspecting prey, not loosening her hold by an inch. With a frustrated sigh, I relax into the sand, her grip on my wrists pressing me deeper into the dunes.

With a lopsided smile, she leans down, warm breath on my chin, and murmurs, "That wasn't very smart."

For pride's sake, I struggle against her for a moment before giving in again. Her smile widens. It's so smug, so pleased, I want to scream.

"Done?"

My head falls back against the sand. Mara relaxes, settling gently on my ribs, the pressure making traitorous moths flutter around my belly.

Mara releases my wrists and waits, like she expects me to try something else. With a blink, she rolls off me, righting herself in the sand and drawing her knees up. The abrupt absence makes my heart skip a beat.

"What the hell are you doing out here, Mara? Did you somehow miss the 'everyone wants to kill you' memo?"

She snorts softly. Turns her attention to the water, far across the sand. "Everyone has wanted to kill me for a while now. You get used to it." At her side, her thumb twitches.

"Still avoiding the subject."

She shrugs. "I had a question."

"Jesus Christ, this is like pulling teeth."

"Maybe you should stop, then."

"Yeah, I think I'm good," I say. "What was the question?"

She gives me a long, withering look and brushes the stray hairs from her eyes, shrugging and leaning farther back in the sand, propped on her hands. I have to shift sideways to see her.

"I asked him if he knew where my old roommate, Vivian, was," she says. I think that's all she's going to say, and I'm three seconds from throttling her when she goes on, "If he knew where she went. If he was going after her."

There are multiple flags, but of course, I choose the least important one.

"Vivian? Why?"

Mara's brow twitches, and she says, "She took off with a few others a couple of days before I was released. I guess she figured whatever was out there had to be better than what was waiting at home. Or what was *left* at home."

"You didn't go with her?"

"No."

"Why not?"

She frowns. "I don't know anymore."

"And does he know where they went? Emir?"

Her features go slack for a half second before she admits, "Anza-Borrego. There are dozens of abandoned cabins and campsites out there." She pauses again. "He almost left before but wanted to see his parents one last time. And with what happened to Dolly . . . Tomorrow, as soon as the sun sets, he's leaving."

"Stealing a boat?" I accuse.

She squints. "*No.* His parents have a two-person kayak or something. It doesn't matter. All that matters is getting to shore."

Two-person. And there it is, the thing I have wanted since the moment I found out she was coming back—for her to leave and go far enough that I can forget and burn the rest of *before* away.

If anyone left, it was you. And who's leaving now? I push up onto my feet, rage spilling over and lighting me up.

"Got it. Great plan, Mara. What could *possibly* go wrong?"

"He doesn't need a great plan; it just has to be possible. And it—" I turn and walk away before she can finish, and her half-finished sentence hangs in the air. "What are you— Wait, where are you going?"

An ear-splitting ringing builds in my ears, like the battering of the waves against the sand fifty feet away.

"Rory, would you stop for a second?"

The sand makes the storming away less impactful than I'd like, but any step is one more away from her. After all we've done, after the standoffs, after I shot her sister, after all of it, she's going to leave. She's going to leave me—

"Aurora."

I stop as she catches up, lunging in front of me. Her nostrils are flared, and her eyes are wide and shining gray in the moonlight, and she shifts her weight back and forth as if to block me from moving.

I shouldn't care that she's going, should be escorting her to the boats myself, but I do. I do, I always fucking do, and it always ends here, a million miles between us even if we're an inch apart.

"Stop saying my name like that," I say, raising my hands to push her aside, but she catches my wrists, holds me in place.

"Like what?" she asks, brows arched.

"Like it means something." I yank my hands back.

Mara stills, shoulders slumping. She opens her mouth, but nothing comes out. A pause. "Can you listen, for a second? Please?"

I fold my arms across my chest and divert my gaze—I should have let her get caught out here and solved all my problems in one fell swoop.

"Look at me," she says, and I do. Her commanding tone softens. "I'm not leaving. Emir is. I tried to convince him to go to the Bay and see if Daphne would let him stay, but he's set on finding Viv and the others." She cards a hand through her hair and her sleeve falls, moonlight catching on the jagged circle that has to be the bite that made her. It is like she is: half healed, dried out. "I could never actually go. There's no Dye out there. Not enough, at least." She shrugs.

"You could go to the Bay, though. Daphne wouldn't turn you away."

"I could," Mara says.

I gnaw at the worn skin of my lips, unable to hold her eyes and unable to stop finding them.

"But you're not going."

She hesitates. "No," she says.

I don't believe her, and I don't think she believes herself, either.

Neither of us knows what side she's on.

19

MARA

Noah and Raisa have shaken off the attack at the school like it was nothing. There was a memorial, which I wasn't allowed to attend, and though both Noah and Raisa came back puffy faced, they've gone on like nothing happened. I envy them their ability to carry on. Kids are like that: elastic, maybe stronger than the rest of us.

These are the children of the new world. I thought that was a disadvantage, but it might be the opposite. No one is better equipped for our new reality than the ones who don't remember anything different.

"And you got lost?" Noah asks, perched on the arm of the couch like a cat, listening intently as Rory and I tell stories. Raisa pulled out an old photograph she managed to hold on to—the Blakes and the Knights on a family vacation once upon a time.

"I didn't get lost," Rory emphasizes. Her hair, usually pulled into a bun or ponytail or tucked back in braids, falls loose around her shoulders, platinum waves dancing as she gesticulates. "*Someone* had to pee halfway through a hike, and I went with them so they didn't, like, walk off a cliff or something."

"A cliff? In Colorado?" I ask. The glare she throws is more teasing than threatening, and I think she might be suppressing a smile.

"Or walk into a mountain lion. Or something else that wants to eat you. You should have thanked me."

"Was she scared, Mara?" Noah asks, big brown eyes inquisitive. I've learned stories are the entertainment Noah has been raised on—tales from a dead world. Places that have been bombed or burned and people that he will never have a chance to meet.

Raisa nudges Noah and makes an exaggerated sad face, using her fists to represent tears. Noah giggles, and Rory's protests surface.

"I did not cry—"

"You did," I say. I smile at Noah. "We saw a snake. Rory doesn't like snakes."

"Does anyone like snakes?" Rory asks.

"I like snakes," Noah says.

"You've never *seen* a snake," Rory says, waving a hand dismissively. "And I screamed, I didn't cry."

I can still hear her complaining as we picked through the forestry, Rory taking the lead. After two hours of wandering, we found our way back to camp, exhausted and dirty and furious.

Something I never told Rory: we weren't lost. Camping in Colorado was a tradition, and long before the Blake family started joining, my family took the trip once a year. I knew that section of woods as well as my backyard.

We'd spent days in an RV to reach the campsite, and with both sets of parents, our siblings, and three dogs, I couldn't find a split second alone with her. So I wandered off, and I took Rory with me, and I wasted two hours taking wrong turns and trying to convince myself to speak the words that had recently exploded into existence.

I almost confessed I was in love with Rory on that hike. Almost. And four months later, Rory kissed me, and one day after that, the world ended.

And now I am three years too late.

"Did you survive?" Noah asks, such a little kid it makes my hollow chest ache. The Ticks—we—have taken so much, but we haven't taken it all. There are still kids asking silly questions.

"Nope," Rory says, reaching out to tug Noah onto her lap. He's all elbows, a hair too tall to sit comfortably, but he is writhing anyway, laughing as Rory tickles his sides. "I've been a ghost this whole time."

"Ghosts aren't real," Noah says. "Raisa said."

Raisa gives him a patronizing look as if to say, *Like hell I did.*

"Raisa said that because she accidentally saw *Paranormal Activity* and had to sleep in Ari's bed for a month. She doesn't believe in ghosts because she doesn't want to."

Across the couch, Raisa lifts a hand, holding up a finger she should not know how to use. Fortunately, Noah is too busy wrangling himself away from Rory's hands to notice.

"Put that down before I chop it off," Rory says pointedly, to which Raisa lifts the finger higher for a breath and lets it fall with a smug smile. Her thick brows rise as if she's challenging her sister.

"I think ghosts are real," Noah says, extricating himself from Rory's lap and falling into the cushions beside Raisa. His gaze flicks to mine, childlike innocence in his features. "Zombies are real."

"They're not technically zombies," Rory says. Raisa draws a finger across her throat and shakes her head as if to second Rory. "Zombies are dead. Ticks aren't."

"What are they?" Noah looks to me, the professional on the subject. His undivided focus, followed by Raisa's and Rory's, makes me squirm, and the ruins of my gut give a single twist.

"Almost dead," I say, and it tastes like blood. Seemingly reminded of itself by the conversation, the wound at my shoulder has begun oozing, dark blood staining the corner of my tee. My awareness of it brings it to the attention of everyone.

"Does it hurt?" Noah asks. Rory shoots him a glare, but I think she wanted to ask, too. Has wanted to ask for a while.

"No," I say, shaking my head. I can feel the wound, like a displaced pressure, but it isn't a painful sensation. It's more of a reminder of who—what—I am.

Noah's curious eyes linger on the maroon stain, and I avoid Rory's gaze as I tug the shirt over my head, leaving me in a gray tank. Without the fabric to cover it, all of my scars and slashes reach the air.

The deepest, a bullet hole through my right shoulder blade, has left two identical marks in the skin: entry and exit. The hole, half the size of a quarter, is dry and cracked around the edges, but movement brings blood to the surface. Black and red, unnatural as I am.

"Woah." Noah climbs off the couch and comes to stand in front of where I'm curled on the armchair, leaning close to get a good look at the wound. I expect disgust, but there is only awe. "It's so cool."

"Noah," Rory chides.

"It *is*," he says.

Even Raisa is drawn across the room, though she stands farther back than Noah.

"We have Band-Aids," Noah says. "If you want one."

Rory barks a laugh. Noah smiles, unaware what the punchline is but wanting to be included anyway.

"I think I'm alright, but thank you," I say.

Noah nods, content, and climbs up onto the armchair next to me. It is a small chair, leaving a few inches between us. His lack of fear is heartwarming. I don't trust me, but this little boy, one who has known little else but loss, does. He doesn't see me as a monster, but as Mara.

Risking a glance at Rory, I find her gaze fixed on the bullet hole, a line between her brows. Phantom nerves skitter up my spine, so gentle I barely register them.

I pull my tee back over my head. Red creeps over Rory's cheeks as she straightens, shifts back.

The stomping of footsteps—two pairs, Sam and Isaac, returning from one of the gardens they help tend during the day—prevent any further interrogation, and I'm grateful. As nice as it is to talk and be talked to, doing so in front of Rory feels like cracking my chest open and letting her dig inside. I can see her cataloging everything I say and do. Filing it away to use against me when she realizes I am more trouble than I'm worth.

Isaac marches through the front door, Sam slipping in behind him, their faces ashen and movements jerky, like something is running behind them. It sucks the sun out of the room. Noah goes rigid, reaching for Raisa's hand in my periphery. On the end of the couch, Rory pulls her sword and pushes unsteadily to her feet.

"Raisa, take your brother upstairs, please," Isaac says. His tone is clipped, his shoulders stiff as he slams all three locks on the door closed. I've never seen him like this, dripping in false bravado.

Raisa nods, leading a concerned Noah out of the room. No one moves until their path up the stairs echoes down the hall.

Sam lets out a harsh exhale, falling onto the couch and dropping her face into her hands. Her shoulders are curled forward, chest caving in, like she wants to fold in on herself until nothing remains.

"What's going on?" Rory asks.

Sam merely shakes her head.

Isaac answers. "Mal's lost it. He's collecting the Altered and sticking them in the Pit cages. After what happened at the school, he has all the ammo he needs to take action."

"There has to be a way to prove that the Altered weren't behind the attack," Sam says.

"Oh, sure, let's check the security tapes," Rory says.

Isaac purses his lips. He and Rory exchange a look I can't decipher. To Sam, he says, "Mal's daughter was behind the attack at the school."

"What?" Sam whispers, her eyes widening and glazing over.

Rory ignores her, and asks Isaac, "What about the Altered's families? They can't be standing by as Mal drags their people out of their houses."

Isaac licks his lips. "Dolly Winsleigh's father is in a cell at the station. The Joshis, too, since they tried to help Emir off the Island."

"He can't keep every relative of an Altered locked up forever," Rory says.

Dolly. Emir. All the other Altered. We may not have created the ghosts on this island, but we have made enough. And we're the perfect scapegoats because we're here to blame. Trapped with water on all sides.

The puzzle pieces slide into place, and the floor splits open beneath my feet.

"He doesn't need to," I say.

"Someone want to clue me in?" Rory asks, and her voice is shrill.

Sam's lips part, but she doesn't say anything. Her mouth gapes like a fish, opening and closing as she tries and fails to speak. Isaac, too, says nothing.

"He's going to kill us. All of us. And when we're dead, it won't matter what anyone thinks," Mara says.

"He can't do that. *He can't do that*," Rory says. She's back on her feet, head snapping between Sam and Isaac. She is waiting for them to contradict me. "He can't do that."

It's a plea more than anything—her desire for someone to say *You're right, of course he can't do that.*

Isaac looks all the weary warrior he is in the stories I've heard of the mainland, and Rory's features slacken to mirror them as the seconds drag by and no one speaks the obvious truth.

Mal can do what he wants. And he'll do what he needs to do to gain back the power that the Altered's arrival took from him. Covering his own tracks is an added bonus.

"How long do we have?" Rory says eventually, all traces of emotion sapped from her form. It's scary how easily she slips back into that persona. As if she's been waiting for the other shoe to drop, as if part of her wants it. The soldier who doesn't know what to do without a war to fight.

"Not long," Isaac says. "I'd give it an hour, maybe more."

"Then what the hell are we doing? We have to get Mara out of here. Or hide her. *Something.*"

Her sudden defense—more pivotal than the other night on the driveway, than the encounter with Carter in those first days—has us all stunned. She is taking my side without being forced to do it, and as thoughtful as it is, her panic is clouding the instincts I know she has.

"Rory . . ." Isaac starts. Sam reaches out a hand for her, but Rory wrenches back, eyes on me. The desperation that flashes before she throws her walls back up makes me want to gag.

Something passes between Isaac and Sam, an understanding. It reminds me of my parents, of nights on the couch watching old sitcoms and listening to eighties music as we cleaned.

It reminds me of the fountain of red that arced from my father's throat as I tore it out. Of my mother, falling to the ground. Of Carter, slamming every door and locking me inside.

A dark figure shifts into my vision, dragging me out of the bloodshed. Rory has moved to lean against the arm of my chair, another surprising show of commitment.

In a low voice, Sam says, "The crawlspace."

"Crawlspace?" Rory asks.

"Under the basement. It's small," Sam says, not meeting anyone's eyes for longer than a second.

Rory huffs. "That'll work." She taps my arm, and I have no choice but to let her lead me out of the living room. Sam trails after us, and we are all silent as we follow Rory. She's moving slower than usual— either her leg is bothering her or she is dreading the next few hours as much as I am.

Sam moves to kneel in front of the patterned rug, peeling it back to reveal a hatch. A wooden door, set into the concrete floor, no bigger than two square feet. She tugs it open to expose a pitch-black space beneath the house. I don't want to think about how many spiders and rats have made a home down there in the last three years.

"Jesus Christ," Rory says. I meet her eyes, and she looks as nauseated as I should be.

Sam grimaces. "In you go."

Rolling my shoulders, I drop to sit on the edge, sliding slowly into the darkness. My sneakers hit ground, and when I stand, my shoulders and head are still in the basement.

"As soon as they're gone, we'll get you out," Rory says.

I nod, taking a breath and bending my knees, lowering into the dim space. The crawlspace is roughly three feet high, stretching into blackness, at least ten feet long. I pull myself into the corner, lying on my back, the rough concrete digging into my spine and shoulder blades. The bullet wound twinges with something reminiscent of pain.

"Rory, can you close this up?" Sam asks.

Rory nods, not looking at her mother, and it seems like Sam wants to say something else, but instead, she heads for the stairs with a tense expression. With her gone, Rory kneels in front of me, her hair falling down in waves.

"It isn't too late to let me make a run for it," I say. "The Bay isn't that far." Rory gives me a stern look.

"You'd never make it off the Island alone," she says. Her lips pull thin, brows knitting together in concentration. "They won't find you, Mara."

I can see the lie in her face, but it's still nice to hear, nice that she goes through the effort of telling it. It makes me remember before, every false promise or assurance she made over the years to comfort me. A smile creeps over my lips without my realizing, and surprise makes Rory's lips part before they curve up.

"Now, be quiet," she says, standing with a small groan—she doesn't hide it from me—and grabbing the edge of the hatch door. It falls shut with a *click*, leaving the scent of lemon shampoo and sea salt behind.

And as the dark settles over me, Rory's face flickering behind my lids, I remember something.

Lemons and salt. I smelled it when I heard the locks break at the house, all that time ago. It had been familiar, but I didn't have the words to explain why. Didn't have the connection to memory to figure out where I knew it from.

I think I've known, deep down, it was her. I knew *someone* let me out, because I remember a locked door, and then breaking metal. Maybe I was hiding it from myself.

Rory was at the house after Carter locked me away. And she wasn't just there. She opened the door and let me out.

20

RORY

We hear them coming up the street five minutes after I've pulled the rug over the crawlspace hatch. It's nearly a repeat of the other night, but now it's me with my sword and Isaac with the spiked bat I'm glad I brought from the mainland. A parent and the eldest child of the Blake family, wreathed in death. What a family photo that would be.

Mal's posse is small, and missing Carter. I've been kept in the house as much as Mara, but Isaac let it slip that Mara's sister has been cooped up in Fatimah's infirmary since the "incident."

Twelve soldiers behind him. I recognize each one—twelve faces supposedly committed to protecting the Island. Protecting me.

Their weapons outnumber us four to one, but we won't give up easy.

"Don't make this a problem. Bring the Tick out, and we'll take it off your hands," Mal says, palms stretched up as if in surrender. The weapons behind him indicate anything but. He wants war, and he knows how to stoke its fire.

"She's not here," Isaac snaps.

A smile ghosts Mal's lips, and he gives a casual shrug, snapping a finger.

"We gave 'em a chance, didn't we?" he calls. "Can't say we didn't."

"Can't say, boss," someone coos. My stomach churns.

"I said Mara isn't here," Isaac calls, authority booming. He doesn't raise his voice often, but when he does, people listen. "She fled with the Joshi boy the other night. Took a kayak and paddled across the bay."

Mal narrows his eyes. He has always looked carved from stone to me, like the statues in old museums, a towering boulder of a man. I've never been convinced a bullet to the heart could take him down. He might even survive a shot to the head through pure will.

"You think I'm going to believe that heaping crock of shit?" he asks, and his laughter has my skin crawling. It takes considerable effort not to shudder at the sound. "The Tick left alone. Or *tried* to leave."

"My children are in this house, Mal," Isaac says.

"Children were brutally murdered by the Alliance's little monsters a few nights ago. That thing will pay for what it did." Mal's eyes find mine, and I know he's talking about how we killed Juliette. How *I* killed her. He jerks his chin at us. "Restrain them."

Bodies leap into motion, splitting into groups to apprehend us. Three of Mal's people take Isaac. He's tall, strong despite a wiry frame, and more ruthless than they are prepared for, and while he gets at least two broken noses in, he ends up cuffed.

A middle-aged woman named Tara, a girl my age named Lily, and another whose name I never bothered learning rush me. Mal's favorites. All silent and fast and underestimated as women, they are the most dangerous of his collection.

None deadlier than Carter, though.

I lift my sword, but Lily is swift and disarms me with ease, the blade clattering to the concrete three feet away. Her onyx eyes spark with bloodlust as she swipes out with her weapon of choice: a diving knife, serrated and sharpened constantly by the stone slab she keeps in her pocket. The blade slices through the fabric of my shirt, ripping into the tender skin of my belly, fire flaring through my gut. It is not deep enough to do much damage but ruins any semblance of balance I was clinging to.

Staggering back a step, I regain my footing, thrusting an arm up to block the bronze fist Tara is swinging at my face, but get caught at the base of my spine by a metal bat: the third in their trio, coming in for the metaphorical kill.

The impact ripples through my left leg, awakening the angry wound left by the bullet, and my knees slam hard into the concrete.

"This is *madness*," Isaac says. He's on his knees, and I am quickly deposited beside him. Lily doesn't bother helping me, and I am still riding the waves of pain from the bat, leaving me to curl like a helpless child on the driveway. "Mara is a seventeen-year-old girl."

"She is far more than that," Mal snaps, spit flying. "She is a monster. And she will be dealt with as such."

With a shuddering sigh, I shove up into a seated position, swallowing vomit. "She's not here. She told us she was leaving with Emir. How would we know if she didn't? You stupid, brainless sack of—" The insult is knocked out of my mouth by Lily's fist, and I choke on the words, falling into Isaac. A sob builds up in my chest, but there is no room for weakness here. I tighten my gut and push up onto my knees, pausing to spit a mouthful of blood onto the drive. Stars dance in the corner of my vision, but I blink past them, clenching my teeth to steady my head.

"Don't do this, Mal!" Isaac yells. Mal holds up a hand, halting the barrage of soldiers—excluding Lily and two men, who stand behind us—from their approach to the door.

"Where are Raisa and Noah?" he asks.

"Master bedroom closet," Isaac growls. "If you touch a hair on their heads, I promise I won't stop until—"

"Save it. I'm not interested in anyone whose heart is still beating." Mal whistles. "You heard him. You touch a kid and there's a knife with your name on it. Understood?"

"Understood" echoes through the soldiers, and I hope they follow Mal's order. Unfortunately, I'm not all that great at hope.

While Mal and his soldiers tear through the house, Sam crouches in the corner, trembling, and Isaac and I are unceremoniously dropped onto the couch. My leg pulses with a dull throb each time my heart beats, and each breath grates the sticky fabric of my tee over my slashed stomach. Isaac is allowed a single call up the stairs to warn Raisa and Noah not to make any sudden moves.

I've never felt so useless. The metal cuffs pinch the tender skin around my wrists. Sweat trickles down my brow despite the cool breeze coming in through the open front door. How courteous; they didn't knock it off its hinges upon entry.

The clones don't leave a single stone unturned, like they'll find Mara beneath a mismatched throw cushion or behind a book. Destruction is the real goal, and they're managing it flawlessly.

Each item that hits the floor chips away at my composure. Sentimentality is something I left behind—I thought I left it behind—but when one of the women knocks the stack of Aria's books off the piano, I have to blink back tears.

Put it away. Put it somewhere it can't hurt you. They don't deserve to see you break. A motto I haven't had to pull out much in the last year, but a comfortable, worn coat to shrug into.

Mara, hidden and curled beneath the house, comes uninvited into my head, her gray eyes laced with barely suppressed fear—

Put it away.

I catch Sam's eye. "You can't let this happen." To my utter relief, my voice comes out low and even.

Sam lets out a hard sigh, closes her eyes. When she opens them, they are blazing. "What the hell do you expect me to do, Rory?"

What if they find her?

"I haven't asked you for anything," I say. "All this time, since the

169

day Aria died, I haven't asked for anything." Tears well in my eyes, but they're angry tears. "You shut down on us, and I was the one who went out and risked my ass. I killed Ticks while you hid." I close my eyes. "I killed Aria because you couldn't. I kept all of us alive. I kept *you* alive when it should have been the other way around." Sam flinches, and Isaac says my name in a tight whisper, but I ignore it. "So, please, for once, *do* something. Stop this."

Sam's mouth opens and closes, and tears spill down her own cheeks, but I can't find a shred of guilt for the words.

"Rory—" Sam starts.

"Don't," I snap.

"Rory, please."

"You're a coward, Samantha," I say, and she jerks back.

It's not the time for crap apologies, and I don't want one anyway. I want a time machine.

As the rest of the soldiers comb the house, Lily and her counterparts remain in the living room with their guns trained on us. The first leans into the armchair across the coffee table, the second against the piano near the door, and the third paces like he's hopped up on caffeine. It doesn't seem possible that a few nights ago, Mara was at that piano with Raisa and Noah, stumbling through the notes.

"Clear!" a voice calls from upstairs, footsteps thundering down the hall and back down the stairs. The back hall is declared empty, and the kitchen, and the back room. The hammering of my heart has reached deafening levels when the men return from the basement and announce, "She's not down there."

Sam exhales softly, but neither Isaac nor I react to the news.

One by one, all twelve uniforms file back into the living room, each new body and attached weapon making me jumpier. Mal stalks back in, and I am so wired I flinch.

"If you've got that Tick stashed somewhere, watch yourself," Mal says. "Fatimah won't be giving out any more injections."

Fatimah. The Dyebucetin. My stomach sinks.

He has put Mara's and every Altered's life—the remnants of their humanity—on a deadline. And when time runs out, I will lose Mara all over again, and this time, there will be no way to bring her back.

●

Mal releases us from our cuffs once the soldiers leave, though a few linger, posting up on the driveway—three threatening silhouettes through the window. Our weapons, he says, have been confiscated. The pistol, my sword, and anything bigger than a pocketknife. All gone.

Stolen. The things we have to protect ourselves. It is a new taboo, one the three remaining guards were visibly uneasy with as they added our weaponry to their collection.

"Consider yourselves under official house arrest," Mal says. "Step foot outside and I'm not responsible for what my guys decide to do."

"Like you haven't given them the order to kill on sight," I say.

His lips curl, dead eyes wreathing me in cold. To Sam and Isaac, he says, "Keep a leash on that one. She might be the death of you." And before I can hit him with one of my admittedly impressive insults, he stomps out the door and slams it behind him, shaking the very foundation.

No one moves. I am lost, drowning in deep and unknown waters.

There are five doses tucked at the bottom of Mara's pack downstairs. That is five days until—

Put it away.

"Rory," Isaac says, too calm, always too calm—matches to my kindling. "I'm going to check on the kids. Round up any spare weapons we have hidden, will you?"

"No." As I rise to my feet, the throb in my back increases to an unavoidable presence. Sweat makes my clothes stick to my skin and stray hairs cling to my neck. The sob that has been building in my chest is seconds from breaking loose.

"Excuse me?" Sam asks. Like they've told me to do the dishes and I refused. Like the sky isn't splitting open above us all over again.

"No." Nausea pools in my gut, and I suppress a gag as I take a step on my left leg, almost sinking to the carpet. "I'm taking a shower. The dog is off duty."

"Rory, you know that's not—" Isaac says.

"Deal with it yourself," I say, limping from the room and down the dark hall.

"Five minutes!" Isaac calls. "No hot water!"

A scream punches at my teeth. *I know.* I know the rules. I wish like hell I could forget them, but I can't.

I can't forget anything.

21

MARA

The face behind the hatch when it whines open is not Rory or Isaac, but Sam. She steps back, giving me room to climb out, and she doesn't hold out a hand, but she doesn't flee the scene, either. Sam has made a point to exit any room we are left alone in. But instead of heading for the stairs, she lingers, shifting her weight. She's clearly waiting for me to say something. I don't.

"We told Mal you left," she says eventually. "But I can't tell whether or not he bought it. You'll have to stay hidden, at least in the house, for the time being."

"Okay," I say, and I have more questions about the noises I heard above me before the hatch opened and about what comes next, but they're not for Sam. I doubt she has the answers. And honestly, as uncomfortable as I make her, the feeling is mutual. I prefer the hatred of Mal and Carter. Talking to Sam is like staring at my own grief personified. She wears everything she's lost like a bloody, tattered coat.

And part of me resents her for the way she looks at me. Resents every set of eyes that narrow when they land on me.

I didn't ask for this. I didn't ask to die, nor did I ask to come back. But I'm here, for better or worse.

"My parents never blamed you for leaving that day," I say, not meaning to.

Sam stiffens.

"We used to play this game to pass the time. 'Where are the Blakes now?' Carter said you all were surfing in Australia. I figured sightseeing in Europe. My mom and dad were set on Barcelona." I shrug. "It got a little extravagant, but I think it made us feel better to pretend you made it somewhere all this didn't matter."

Contact with other continents dropped off before it did with Canada and South America, but no country was untouched. It's likely nothing is left. But maybe there is a pocket of Earth somewhere where a Tick is still a bug.

"I always wanted to see London," Sam says.

"I wanted to see all the states," I say.

Sam almost smiles. Almost.

Another tense silence falls. In another world, Sam might reassure me that my childhood wish is a possibility, but in this one, we both know we'll never make it.

22

MARA

I have accumulated more in two weeks on the Island than I did in six months at the facility. Once upon a time, I had gadgets strapped to my hips and in bags, had a wardrobe full of things that belonged to me and me alone, had shelves full of knickknacks and books. When you own that many things, you forget you have any of them. Until they're gone.

Everything I own can fit easily into a backpack, but it feels like a heap. Four oversized long-sleeved tees, two pairs of jeans, two pairs of yoga pants, and the sneakers on my feet. Two books Noah gave me, the first Percy Jackson and *Goodnight Moon*—because "someone should always tell you goodnight." A diving knife gifted to me by Sam, one I don't need but didn't have the heart to say no to.

I fold and tuck it all carefully into the bag, zipping it up and setting it on the futon. A water-stained notebook and pen sit on one of the closed tubs, and I've picked it up three times now without writing anything.

The Dyebucetin tethering me to this semblance of life is gone. When I dug the small pack of emergency vials from the bottom of my bag, I found them shattered. My fingers are stained purple with my last chance.

Upstairs, the floors creak as someone steps on them, and I go still, waiting for the sound to fade as they head down the hall. Instead, the door opens and closes, Rory's uneven gait following as she descends. Slower than usual, with suppressed grunts I can still hear.

She clocks the backpack before I can toss the blanket over it. Her hair is damp from a shower—thanks to a well servicing the four houses on the block and mechanics that are lost on me—and she's outfitted in a tank top and shorts, showcasing long toned legs. The left is slightly weaker than the right but strong, like the rest of her.

I keep my focus on her face, a choice I regret instantly. Her eyes are blazing, the anger from last night times a thousand. I can imagine how it looks: like I lied to her face, like I'm ditching her. And I did, technically. I am.

"You don't have to do this," she says, but the words come out soft instead of sharp.

"I have to go," I say. "You know that."

She shakes her head, cheeks flushing. "You still have five doses. That's five days to find more."

It takes everything in me not to say, *There are no more doses*, but the truth will make her fight me harder. And she is already battling like her life is on the line.

"Or it's five days to find a way off the Island and get to the Bay. If I can get to Daphne, she can call Thalia for help. Or tell someone what Mal is doing and stop all this." My hands find my hips, shoulders tall, but Rory still has four inches on me—something I resent now more than ever.

Something like horror flashes in her eyes.

"You won't make it," she says, and I know she wants to say something else; maybe she wants to ask me to stay, or maybe I'm already delusional.

"I won't make it here," I say.

Rory waves a hand dismissively, crosses the room to lean into the stack of boxes. I'd ask if she wants to sit, but if she did, she would have already. "We'll find more Dyebucetin. There are a dozen boxes in the infirmary. What are the chances Mal got rid of it all already?"

It's admirable, the attempt to lie, but I spent a decade memorizing Aurora Blake. A couple years with a disease gnawing on my brain didn't erase *that*.

"He's probably tossed it all into the ocean."

"Fatimah gave the other Altered emergency doses like yours, right? Ones Mal doesn't know about?"

The gears are turning in her head, sending her in a dangerous direction.

"Yes, but—"

"So we'll check their houses. Find their doses. Buy you some more time."

"No. I won't take their Dye."

"It's not like they're using it."

"I said no."

She lifts her chin. "It's better than you going feral—"

"No. No, Rory. We're not taking something meant for someone else." I take a deep breath. "I've ended enough lives. I won't end any more."

"Five doses is nothing if something goes wrong. If the car finally dies, or you take a wrong turn—"

"I'll make it."

Rory lets out an exasperated breath.

"Why do you care so much all of a sudden?" I ask.

"Not everything is about you. There are other Altered on the Island. And we both know what happens when they turn back. Do you trust a few flimsy cages?" she says.

I shake my head. "They'll be dead before they get a chance to turn. And if I don't leave, I will be, too."

"We won't let anything happen." Her teeth are clenched, and her neck is corded. Does she believe the line she's spitting?

"You can't protect me, Rory," I say. "And we both know you don't want to. The only way to stop this is to get to someone who can help. If I stay, this entire island is damned."

"I can't let you walk away."

"It's not forever. I might be able to come back if Daphne calls for help—"

"No."

"Why not?"

"You know why."

"No. I *don't* know why." I cross the room in a blink, half a foot from her, somehow towering. "You spend ninety-five percent of your time acting like you hate me. The rest of the time you're that same fifteen-year-old who was too scared to kiss me. Which is it?" I'm not near as accusatory as I wish, but it is effective. Finally, I've done it, pushed too far and too hard, and I'm glad. Her anger means mine can surface, can find a target.

"I do hate you! You never say what you're thinking, and it's like you're constantly gathering information like some kind of weird *super-agent*, and you sit here staring at me like it's your sole purpose in life to remind me of all the horrible things I lost."

The six inches between us have been halved, and her hot, furious breaths puff against my chin. Her mouth is so close to mine; it would be so easy to—

Easy to get myself stabbed. *Stop thinking about her mouth.*

"You don't hate me, Rory. You told me as much on the beach." I shake my head. "You don't hate me . . . You just wish you did."

"You don't know what you're talking about," she says, and for once, I can't tell whether she's lying.

"I still have to go," I say.

Rory's shoulders sink. She doesn't contradict me. She huffs, then refocuses. "You can't leave without more Dye. Even with five days. The van is out of gas, so you'll have to walk, and it's too risky. And chances are Mal hasn't gotten rid of all the boxes yet." This, frenzied and shifting like a wild animal, isn't what I expected, and I think I prefer her angry with me. She is so close I can see myself reflected in her irises. Neither of us is recognizable anymore. "And you can't—" The sentence hangs off parted lips. Slender and calloused fingers—more beautiful than they should or have any right to be, like the rest of her—lift to my face, pointer tracing down the bridge of my nose so slowly my heart thumps twice.

"*Can't?*" I breathe, willing myself back to silence.

Her umber eyes slide shut. She opens them, hand falling away, and says, "I won't lose you again." She is swaying, and I'm reminded of her slow shuffle across the room. A bad day made worse by Mal and his clones.

I take her arms gently, shocked she lets me, and guide her to the bed. She flashes me a look, lips forming the beginning of an opposition, but before she can release it, I say, "Sit down or be sat."

Not quite what I was going for, but Rory moves anyway. She drops onto the edge of the futon, nose wrinkling as her mouth twitches into a grin. "Be sat? That's the best you can do?"

"It's been a long day," I say. I lower down beside her and tap her arm, a silent request. She scratches at her cheek, lips pursing—her eyes widen as she realizes what I want, but she gives a curt nod.

I gently coax up the fabric of her tank to reveal a swollen, angry patch of skin on her back. The contusion is the colors of the sky before the sun sets, bubblegum pinks and baby blues and deep maroons.

Unthinking, I ghost my fingers over the lifetime printed into her skin, not realizing she's staring at me until she sucks in a breath and my head snaps up. Her pupils are blown so wide her already dark eyes shine obsidian—the whites are bloodshot, glistening with unshed tears. Fear, pain, doubt, and all the other dark and scary things she keeps tucked away.

The Tick jerks awake in my head, a wave of fury and hunger rolling through the debris of my system.

"*I'll kill him,*" I hiss, pushing to my feet, going nowhere but desperate to move—if I don't, I think I might do something stupid, something absurd—

Fingers close around my wrist.

Tear him apart, an urge that isn't mine hums in my throat.

"Sit down," she says, and with two words, the authority is hers. She drops my hand and I lower down, curling the fingers on my right hand into a fist. The left, with its missing three, doesn't cooperate with the request given to the right and rests on my thigh, plucking invisible guitar strings.

"As much as I'd like to rip Mal apart"—a glance my way—"or let you do it yourself, right now we have bigger problems."

When my mouth stays closed, she presses forward. "Before you step foot on that beach, we have to get the weapons from the armory, the keys to one of the boats, and since you'll be in the damn building, it's probably worth looking for some of the medicine that keeps you from turning into a vicious creature. You know. *If* you feel like it. And you won't make it off this island without my help."

I ignore her pointed jab. I can still feel it lurking in the corners of my mind, the virus struggling to shove past the barriers to my sanity. "You lost the keys?"

"They took the keys, thank you very much." Her lips twist down.

"Isaac said they took the weapons. You're barely on your feet. How on earth do you expect to pull this off?"

"I'm fine," she says pointedly. A wicked grin pulls on her lips—conspiratorial—and once again, we're on the same side. "And they didn't take *all* the weapons."

I squint. "So, what, I'm your hired muscle?"

"You think you're getting paid?"

"You're serious about this."

"Damn straight."

"I thought *straight* wasn't possible for you," I say. Her grin shifts.

I might even call it goofy. Something deep in my belly shakes off dust and flushes with warmth for a second, long enough to notice it.

"Fuck off," she says.

"Why are you doing this?" I ask.

Rory closes her eyes for a long time. When she opens them, she says, "When I figure that out, I'll let you know."

●

Rory takes an hour-long nap on the futon, looking more peaceful than I've seen her in a long, long time, and when she flinches as I shake her awake, it ripples through me. She doesn't speak as she climbs the stairs, doesn't say anything until she comes back down half an hour later changed into tight ivy cargo pants and a black tee, her blond hair plaited down her back. For the first time since I came back, I can't see a weapon of any kind on her. Though I wouldn't doubt she has one hidden somewhere.

Sam and Isaac accompany her, grave looks on their faces. They have been filled in on the suicide mission we plan to undertake, and while I consider assuring them this stupidity was solely Rory's idea, it feels like a betrayal to open my mouth. Like before, like it's still the two of us against the world.

"Raisa and Noah?" Rory asks her parents with barely disguised hope. Sam averts her eyes. Isaac touches Rory's arm, his shoulders drooping.

"You know we can't risk it. Kids are kids. Secrets are dangerous in their hands."

"Raisa hasn't said a word in over a year," Rory emphasizes.

"No," Isaac says, expression pained. "But she is safer in the dark."

"I have to say goodbye," Rory says, and her voice is hard. "Aria didn't get a chance, and because she didn't, Raisa never said another word."

"You know it's more complicated than that, love," Isaac says, and pulls a stiff Rory into his arms. She is a statue for a long moment before sinking into him, unmoving, fingers curled in his hoodie. "And you know your sister knows you love her. If something happens"—he pulls away, hands moving up to her shoulders—"and that is an *if*, I promise I will tell her, and Noah, that we didn't let you say anything. And that you love them."

Rory hesitates, clearly thinking about fighting it, but she steps back and turns to Sam. Mother and daughter stare at each other until Sam reaches out, tugging Rory against her. Rory is a little too stiff, but Sam hugs her anyway.

Isaac and Sam join me atop the rug hiding the crawlspace, and for a moment, I wonder if it might not be better to stuff me back down there and lock it up tight. If it would be more mercy than a blade.

When Isaac's hand brushes my shoulder, my instinct to snap is near overwhelming. I am usually asleep by now, or trying to be, and the leftover Dye is leaking out of me.

No, the crawlspace wouldn't work. I'd find a way out. The Tick, once it regains full control, and I will rip this house and every living thing inside it apart—it will let the blood of the only family I have left linger like flecks of meat caught in my teeth.

My parents weren't close to their relatives. A Christmas here and there, the occasional reunion we couldn't get out of, but for the most part, our family encompassed the two homes on a small plot in the middle of bustling San Diego. Riviera Drive. I can barely picture the houses now, ours facing front, the Blakes' facing the alley, the large, grassy shared area between the back porches always humming with children.

Isaac comes to squeeze my shoulder. "Your parents would be proud of you, you know," he says, ruffling my hair in the way he might Noah or Raisa.

The bitter laugh that comes out is unintended and strained. "For becoming a monster?"

It isn't funny, but I catch glimpses of Rory hiding a smirk behind her hand.

"You're not a monster. You're Mara Knight," Isaac says.

Is there a difference anymore?

"And if you've survived this far, you will survive what comes next," Isaac says.

"Thank you," I say in a hollow voice. "For letting me stay, for trying to keep me safe." My eyes burn, a dry heat, as if stretching out in search of tears to cry and finding nothing.

"You're family," Isaac says in a fierce tone. His eyes find mine and hold them, the expression so intense I want to look away. "Listen to me. At the end of the day, when push comes to shove, *you* get to decide what you are. No one else."

"Positive thinking won't stop 'em from putting a blade between her eyes," Rory says. I might not have before, but I agree with her now.

"Pot calling the kettle black, Miss Positivity," Isaac says. Rory grins and waves a hand in dismissal. "Besides. A blade between the eyes just hits bone."

"You're lecturing me on fighting form now?" Rory asks.

He laughs.

"You'll be home before you know it," Isaac says. "The Alliance will step in. Mal won't get away with this. When this ends, things will go back to normal."

When this ends. I could tell them the truth, that nothing ever ends. That it shifts, twists, morphs into something we might not recognize, but it doesn't end. *We* never end. I am walking proof of that.

I don't—instead, for a moment, I let myself exist in a world where coming home isn't an impossibility and there is something for me to come back to.

23

MARA

"If you think there's a chance in hell you and I are riding tandem like we're taking a jaunt through Disneyland . . ." Rory huffs, glaring at the tandem bike I dragged from behind a dumpster. We've made it to the old bike shop a few blocks from the Blakes' house, and Rory's limp is more pronounced, her breathing heavier than normal. Her strength and capabilities aren't in question, but she's already been through enough tonight, and I'm not naive enough to believe we've hit the last of our roadblocks. A walk all that way will sap whatever Mal didn't already take.

She says the police station halfway down the main street serves as the new unofficial heart of the town. The home base for Mal's soldiers, the meeting rooms the council uses, the armory, and the infirmary. All conveniently under one roof.

The tandem bike, possibly baby blue once but rusted beyond visibility, is wobbly, and its wheels are in desperate need of air, but the thing doesn't fall apart the moment I touch it, which puts it miles ahead of any other transport left in the open.

"You," I say, whirling to face her, letting the bike tip into the dumpster, "can hardly walk." The next words are cruel, but I know what pushes Rory onward. "Unless you want to do the honors and slit my throat yourself, you'll get on the bike so we can make it to the station before this entire island wakes up and comes after us."

Rory gapes at me, her eyes narrowed. After a beat, she inquires, "Would that even work?"

"What?"

She drags a finger across her jugular. "You know. Slitting your throat. The parasite is in the brain, yeah?"

"Really? That's what you want to talk about?"

"I don't want to ride a bike with you if that's—"

"Please, Rory, just get on the bike."

She turns her nose up. A mischievous glimmer shines in her eyes, and I realize she's screwing with me. It's been so long I forgot what that looked like.

"You're an asshole, you know," I say, and reach for the bike, steadying it.

Rory grins. "I know," she says.

I swing a leg over the front seat and stretch up on my toes to keep the bike in place. With a grumble and a curse just loud enough for me to hear, Rory painstakingly eases herself up. The bike jostles, and one of her hands closes around my shoulder rather than the bike handle. One finger digs into the bullet hole, and the feeling is like a metal rod jammed into my skin, but if I hit the ground, Rory does.

I flick a look over my shoulder, and a pink-cheeked Rory wrenches her hand away. Her hands find iron vises around the bars.

If I didn't know her, I'd think she was angry. When it comes to Rory, most things look like anger. They take the same form, but if you poke, if you look long enough, you can tell the difference.

"I won't let you fall, Rory," I say. It's so sincere I want to jam it back in my mouth and sew my lips shut. For every bullet she fires, I toss back a flower.

Rather than tell me off, she takes a breath, nods, and says, "I know you won't."

The confession hangs between us like sheets fluttering on a line.

I push off the ground, feet finding the pedals, the bike tipping as I adjust to my and Rory's weight on it. Her sharp inhale is the last protest she makes before we are coursing through the silent, black night.

●

The station feels different, though it's been no more than a few days since I was here. For the first time, I notice three tattered flags flapping in the wind: country, state, city.

"God bless America, yeah?" Rory murmurs.

Both patrollers, drooping in lawn chairs on the grassy median down the center of the street, are busier with the flask they're passing between them than keeping watch. We go unnoticed as we pull the bike around the back of the block and tuck it into the alley. A few yards in, fencing encases a small parking lot filled with three civilian cars, one police SUV, and an old Harley-Davidson.

The back door had a scanner to enter the building before, but the pad has been smashed to pieces. Without a word, Rory squats awkwardly with her left leg straight to the side—a half lunge, not comfortable. She digs a small black pouch from her pocket: a lockpick set.

I'm grateful the dark hides my smile. This Rory, the one I've spent weeks thinking is the remains of the girl I lost, looks more comfortable in her skin than I've ever seen her. I wonder what the old Mara would say if she saw this Rory. I wonder what the old *Rory* would say if she saw herself.

The lock clicks, and Rory stands, murmuring, "Idiots," and tucking the pouch away. Her eyes dart to mine, and she nods once before she tugs the door open and plunges into the dark.

24

RORY

The first lie I told on the Island was within these walls.

In the bullpen-turned-infirmary, sweating bullets through stained cotton sheets on a rickety cot, I awoke from one of many fits of slumber to a roaring pain pulsing through my left leg. Sam, gauze still covering one eye, grasped my hands in hers. Her cheeks were splotchy and red, and behind her, Isaac dozed sitting up in a chair, head tipped back against the wall.

"What happened?" I asked, slogging through blood-soaked memories.

"What do you remember?" Her eyes were hopeful in a way I didn't fully understand, like we were actors in a play with lines to speak—lines I knew without realizing.

"Nothing," I said. *"Nothing."*

I remembered everything. I remembered the fraying straps made from dead men's belts digging into my wrists and ankles as Fatimah strapped me face-first to an old cot, the burning that turned me to ash from the inside out, the mangled screams I spat until someone shoved a rubber spatula between my teeth as Fatimah dug the bullet fragments from my leg.

"Where is everyone?" Mara whispers, though the dimly lit halls make it sound louder. Electricity is a luxury, and using it at night is for emergencies. The candle business has been booming.

Still, it's quieter than I think it should be. I've avoided this place since my stay, but Mal practically lives here. He sleeps in the unofficial "barracks" up the block, on the first floor of a small apartment complex, but the apartment spends most of its time unoccupied.

Fatimah, too, is usually here, tucked over some patient in the infirmary or dozing on a cot.

Every footstep feels thunderous down the linoleum hall and past the dark waiting area. Mara is the self-proclaimed muscle of the mission and has been here enough to navigate, but she follows closely behind me.

"I don't know," I say softly, pausing before the first hallway opening on the right. "It shouldn't be this empty."

"Bad sign?"

"Probably not a good one," I say. "I don't want to stay long enough to find out."

Mara hums affirmatively. "Lead the way."

The armory down the hall, its original weapons gone and replaced by whatever the survivors scrounged up, has a handful of guns. Even fewer blades. I've been in the room once, when Sam and I came to try and get our weapons back—they'd been confiscated when we first arrived—but I remember it more stocked. Not full, because nothing here is ever full of anything, but certainly not as scant as this.

It isn't the emptiness that keeps my attention, though. It's the rectangular box taking up half the bottom shelf, some kind of homemade technology the size of a big speaker. Four large, mismatched antennas stick out from the top. It reminds me of a radio, with dials, but not one I've ever seen before. I don't know what it is, but it makes the knot in my stomach wrench tight.

"Rory?" Mara asks.

I've been staring at the odd box for at least ten seconds. My attempt to shake off the sick feeling is unsuccessful, but I don't have time to get lost in my train of disastrous thoughts and career off the track.

"I'm guessing you don't want one?" I ask, crossing to the shelves and scanning the dozen or so leftover firearms. Relief sings in my blood at the sight of the pistol on a shelf near the floor. Before I can crouch down to grab it, Mara ducks and snags it.

I whirl, prepared to lay into her. "What the *hell* do you think you're—"

The gun sits in one outstretched palm, and my sword is gripped in the other. My cheeks burn. I take them, averting my gaze, huffing a "thank you," and tucking the sword back into its holder. I keep the pistol in my hand.

With a tiny smirk, Mara says, "Boat keys?"

Directly next door, in a thin rectangular room, is what used to be a records room and now serves as storage. All the file folders have been removed, the files probably burned, and the room furnished with bookshelves holding cardboard boxes full of random things.

A box of keys is tucked near the door, and while Mara watches the hall, I sift through the pile of boat, car, motorcycle, even golf cart keys, tugging out the familiar neon green key float. I jam it into the pocket on the side of my right thigh and pull the zipper, securing it inside.

"One step closer to the hard part," I say, turning to face Mara, my voice drawing her through the doorway. She frowns, tucking a strand of inky hair behind her ear only for it to fall again, swaying past her chin.

"What aren't you telling me?" she asks.

I shrug a shoulder dismissively and say, "There's someone in the infirmary."

Her eyes narrow, and I have to suppress a shiver. In the shadow and moonlight, she looks monstrous. There is something painful about looking at her, like staring directly into the sun. Ever the angsty preteen, I remarked in many failed diary attempts that Mara Knight was so beautiful it hurt.

"Who, Rory?" she presses.

"Carter," I say, wishing the truth wasn't up the hall and through the doors.

Mara's eyes bulge, and she jerks her head around, scanning the hall before marching forward, the momentum making me stumble back, farther into the room.

"What on god's green Earth is my sister doing here?"

"She's been held up in a cot since—"

"Since you shot her."

"Which you said you were cool about," I snap. "And she's probably fast asleep." Her lips form the beginning of a protest. "*And* I didn't tell you because I knew you'd freak out, and if we're lucky, Carter will never know we were here."

"When have we ever been lucky?" Mara asks.

My stomach wrenches. "It doesn't matter whether she's there or not. We need to get into that storage room, and the only way is through the infirmary."

"Where my sister, who you shot in the knee, and who definitely wants us both dead, is lying, probably plotting her revenge, as we speak?"

I snort. "And they call me the drama queen."

"This isn't a joke—"

"I know that." The intensity of the response renders her silent, her mouth pulling into a thin line. "I know what happens if you turn back, Mara. Maybe better than you do."

Her expression is venomous for a beat before it softens, like she's flipped a switch, and she lets out a breath.

"What happens if she's not asleep?"

"Why do you think I got the gun and sword first?"

"You're not planning on murdering my sister."

"I'm not *not* planning on it."

The judgment and protest I'm prepared for don't come. Instead, a wicked, lopsided smile plays on Mara's lips.

A small rack of keys directly beside the door, made from crudely hammered nails, sports the keychains allowing entrance to any and all still usable buildings on the Island. As expected, the nail with a scrap of duct tape reading STATION, as in where we are, is empty. Mal keeps the spare set of keys on him at all times.

Other fobs dangle from their nails: base gate entrance, the old and wholly unstocked grocery store we use for large storage, a big boutique converted to a thrift shop, on and on. One other peg is missing a key. It is labeled simply as THE PIT.

My stomach bottoms out, panic racing down my spine and scattering into my veins.

I've stopped, a hand hanging limp in the air, and Mara's voice shocks me so badly I nearly slice her remaining fingers off. I am no longer in the dim records room, but gathered around the deck of a drained pool.

"On your feet," Carter hisses. Moans from the other side of the pool nearly drown out her voice.

I spit a glob of blood onto the tile, shoving up onto my hands and knees. My left pant leg is sticky and damp. Fatimah restitched it last week, after Carter's and my trip to the mainland, and I can already hear her lecture. Like the fire racing up my thigh isn't punishment enough. That, or the whole "being tossed into a pit of the dead" thing.

I jerk my head up, and instead of Carter's outstretched hand like I expect, I find the heavy end of a sledgehammer leveled at my throat.

There could be a million reasons the key to the Pit is gone. They could be securing the structure. They could be sweeping for anything usable they left when they shut it down eight months ago.

"*Rory*," Mara says again. I seek out her cloudy gaze, grounding myself in the color. Gray, not green. I am still here.

"What is it?" she asks.

The words wouldn't come together in a legible sentence if I wanted them to, and I don't.

Mara has only survived a year in this new world. She doesn't know what all of us did to survive, whether it was on this island or not—me, Sam, and Isaac included. We killed and stole, and we let others die so we wouldn't.

To her, the Island must seem like a monstrous place, but it's the best we've found, and we've made a home here. I'm not sure I know how to let that go. My parents surely don't.

"Nothing," I say. "Nothing."

●

The door to the infirmary is cracked, yellow candlelight casting shadows along the hall outside. They dance as silhouettes in the corners of my vision—a building of ghosts in a town of spirits.

Fatimah's characteristic humming is absent, home for the night already. She sat with me for a week straight after the surgery, but Carter's wound had to have been sewn up two days ago, and she's likely toward the end of her forced bed rest. With Carter having what I imagine is a shattered kneecap and no reason to expect us, we have the advantage if there is one to be had. But a tired, injured Carter is still dangerous. And with the pulsing in my leg and the headache slowly easing over my skull, we are evenly matched. Or we would be if I weren't carting a zombie along behind me.

Altered person. Tick. Whatever you want to call her. Whatever I think of her, her strength and ability aren't in question. If Carter makes a move, Mara can stop her.

But I've had that shot lined up before: staring at the person you love through a lens. It both is and isn't as simple as pulling the trigger. I never pulled it.

Slipping through the crack in the door, Mara at my back, we enter the infirmary without a sound. Atop each bedside cupboard sits a thick, misshapen candle.

Twelve dark green cots line the dingy walls, but only one holds a body. Carter Knight, sleeping with her hands folded over her belly like some goddamn mummy, a thick and sharp knife resting on the blue plastic cupboard beside her.

Mara's fingers graze my elbow. Her dark brows are arched in question. With a single nod from me, she slinks into the room, all predator as she advances on the cot. She leans over, stares at her sister's face, and takes a deep breath like she's listening or smelling or doing something inhuman that should scare me but instead fascinates me.

A lion looks different when it isn't hunting you. Sleek and stealthy, every move instinctual. Bewitching and beautiful. When she straightens and finds my eyes, she is Mara Knight again—whoever that is now. She gives a curt nod; Carter is sleeping.

I am not as silent as she is, and she's way too smug as I cross the floor. My boots squeak twice before I reach the office door, and I'm three ideas deep into ways to *quietly* smack the grin off her lips. The door opens with a whine that makes me freeze, head whipping around to Mara, who inspects her sister intensely. Her shoulders dip as she exhales, and she meets my eyes, one side of her mouth twitching up.

I step inside the small office, scanning the shelves for the Dyebucetin. The infirmary isn't as well stocked as a real one would have been, and most of the time, it is in dire need of supplies, but right now, after Mara's and my trip, the shelves are comfortably full. Syringes, dressings, swabs, ointments and pill bottles, boxes of packaged pills and vials.

On the lowest shelf at the back of the room are six large boxes with tape stretching across them that reads DYEBUCETIN.

If there is someone up above that sky of wheeling stars, they get thanks for this. Relief pushes a sigh out of me, and I ignore the ache as I bend down and heft up one of the boxes. I set the gun atop the closed box. Awkward, but not too heavy to carry. It's certainly enough to get Mara to the Bay.

"Aurora." *Speak of the devil*. Her voice is hushed but louder than it should be.

Content with the pickings, I move for the door—and stop.

Mara is silence in a pair of sneakers, and if she needed my attention, she'd have joined me in the closet. The irony of that thought isn't lost on me, but those three syllables run through my head.

Aurora. Not Rory. A name she uses with purpose: to piss me off, to get or hold my attention. To warn me.

Just as I go to set the box down, a voice arcs across the room. "Don't do something stupid, Rory."

Carter. Great lookout, Mara.

Heaving a breath, I swallow a wave of nausea and step out of the room at a snail's pace. Mara stands in the middle of the aisle with her hands raised. Carter is at her side, a knife tucked against her younger sister's throat. Both pairs of fierce eyes are locked on me.

She's barely on her feet and favoring her leg. Sweat forms a thin sheen across her skin—she's wearing a tee and shorts, her skin peppered with scars like mine. Like Mara's.

My gaze falls to the gun resting on top of the box in my hands.

Carter shakes her head. "Tip it onto the ground. Now."

Tensing, I look between her and Mara, who gives me the tiniest of nods like she's saying, *It's okay, it's okay.* It isn't, but it will be a lot *less* okay if Carter shoves the knife into her skull. I rifle through all the possible moves to make, rounding back to *you're screwed* in three fast seconds.

The gun clatters to the floor at my feet. I make to set the box down on the cot to my left, but Carter snaps, "Don't."

With a sigh, I straighten, fix her with a patronizing smile. "Come on, Carter. We're all friends here. Family, if we want to get specific," I say, sarcasm looping through my vowels and consonants.

"Kick the gun away. Then set the box down slowly."

"And if I don't?"

Mara's nostrils flare. Carter jams the tip of the knife up against Mara's throat, hard enough to break skin.

"This isn't a game, Rory," Carter says. "I know Mal stopped by the house earlier. Came for"—her gaze darts over to Mara, then back to me—"her."

"What's Mal's plan for when this gets out? When the Alliance cuts you all off? When the RPA finds out you're killing their test subjects?"

"As far as the Alliance and the RPA are concerned, they'll learn that the remainder of the *Altered*"—the word is a weapon off Carter's lips—"fled the Island. Or something like that. Doesn't really matter what happens to them, does it?"

Mara's eyes flutter shut for a long moment.

"It's not like you've ever cared," Carter continues. "How many do you think you've killed since it all started? A hundred? A thousand?"

Nausea creeps through my insides, and I recall the feeling I had the night of the outbreak, when I swore I was being watched outside the house with Juliette's body in the basement. It's the same way I feel now, with Carter's eyes on me.

"It was you, wasn't it?" I say suddenly. "You followed me from the school. Why?"

"Mal had me tail you," she says. "And it's a good thing I did."

"You took Juliette from the basement. Mal's daughter—"

"That wasn't his daughter," Carter says, and I can't tell who she's trying to convince.

She has no idea what she's done. What she's doing. She's so under Mal's spell, so certain he's the road to safety, it's given her tunnel vision. And it's going to get all of us killed.

"You don't want to do this, Carter," I say.

"Don't I?" she asks. Her eyes are frenzied, hungry. "Don't tell me you haven't thought about it. Dropping her in the Pit, where she belongs. Finishing what we started that day on the mainland."

She has to stop talking. Stop planting questions like poisonous seeds in Mara's head that I will have to answer.

Mara's eyes, gray like ash, are empty and ravenous through grimy windows.

"We have to end it," Carter huffs, tears streaming down her dirty cheeks.

"End what?" I ask the question like it will change the answer.

She doesn't say anything. Instead, she lifts a trembling gun and aims it at the window, where Mara has broken her own skin trying to claw through to us. Bile burns up my throat, and I heave into the grass, the world spinning around me.

"No," I say, stumbling forward, reaching for the gun in Carter's hands. There is nothing but a monster on the other side of that glass, but I can't let her pull the trigger. I can't.

We hit the torn-up dirt in a tangle of limbs, and my barely healed leg screams in protest, but I don't stop until I've wrangled the revolver out of Carter's hands. I clamber back to my feet a half second before her. She tries to go for the gun, and I stumble back a step.

There are a few yards between me and the house and the thing inside it wearing Mara's skin.

Carter jerks sideways, headed for the front door, though she has to know there's no way into the house that doesn't draw the attention of every dead thing in this neighborhood. She'll be dead before she gets her revenge.

I raise the gun and aim it at her forehead.

Stop, stop, *stop*—

"Say her name, Carter." Speaking makes it impossible to think, and I ease into my false bravado, though it hasn't been all that successful lately. "Not *Tick*. Not Altered. Say her *name*."

Mara's head tilts up with the pressure of the blade against it, but she isn't looking at Carter. She's looking at me.

"Put down the box. Pull any of your usual crap and this goes into her brain," Carter commands.

The instinctual *You won't* rises, but I force it back down my throat. She will. She tried once.

"Do what she says, Rory." Mara's smoky voice keeps me in the present.

Holding Carter's eyes, I give the gun a swift push, sending it skidding to a stop a few feet from the door.

"Box," Carter says. I sneer, falling back into the role of snarky teenager long enough to crinkle my nose and shake my head. The slow dropping of the box to the cot beside me is a comedy routine lost on the Knight sisters. If they have anything in common, it is the disdain flickering over their features.

"Hands up. And I swear to god if you reach for that sword—"

"Trust issues, much?" I lift my hands slowly.

"Can we skip the peacock dances?" Mara interjects. A single syllable wavers.

"*Quiet,*" Carter says. Mara ignores her, and it pulls a smile onto my lips. As Carter turns her focus back to me, I squash the grin and plant a hand on my hip.

"How do you see this ending?" I gesture around the empty room. "No one is coming. Not until morning if the Pit"—I pointedly avoid Mara's eyes, and they singe a hole in my cheek—"is really opening back up. Too much to do."

"You," Carter says, "are going to lie facedown on the floor with your hands behind your back while I secure the Tick—"

"Do you remember Camp Bumblebee?" Mara asks. Its randomness makes Carter and me freeze, giving Mara equally perplexed looks. "We played that game. Cat, Cat, Dog." Her stare is layered, an unspoken plea lying beneath.

"I would say the virus ate away your common sense, but you never really had any," Carter snarls. "One more word and it's lights out."

Mara acts like Carter hasn't spoken, attention fixed on me.

"It's Duck, Duck, Goose," Mara whispers, lips brushing my ear, making my stomach tumble. "Why not call it that?"

We're sitting cross-legged on the grass in a circle, a dozen other eleven-year-olds chattering around us. The counselor, an energetic seventeen-year-old girl named Jimena with big, round glasses, stands in the center.

I flash her a brace-toothed smile. "Everyone wants to be original."

Mara shrugs. "It all means the same thing."

And I understand.

Carter's head whips between us, her black brows knitting together as she struggles to decipher our silent conversation.

"*Cat!*" Mara says, and the unspoken *duck* is stitched to its syllables. I drop flat, knees slamming hard into the linoleum, diving to the right and onto my back on my good side. The gun is still yards away, but the distance doesn't stop me scrambling for it, searing pain and all.

Above me, Mara swipes a hand up, knocking the blade from her sister's hand and sending it sprawling. Carter reacts instantly, twisting and throwing a punch with the other hand. Mara catches her fist, squeezing tightly, and while pain puts wrinkles on Carter's face, she doesn't relent, doesn't slow down.

Another blade appears from beneath Carter's waistband, metal flashing in the candlelight, aimed at Mara's neck. Mara rears her head back and steps forward, using the momentum to send Carter tumbling back into the cupboard between two cots.

Mara is pulling her punches. She could have made at least three fatal blows by this point, but Carter is still standing. I have no clue how she's still up fighting; blood seeps through the bandage around her knee, and she sways on her feet.

My focus lands on Carter's gun, eight feet from me and a few more from her, as she lunges for it. I scrabble across the floor, fingers grazing the barrel as Carter pulls it from the ground.

Dread ices down my spine, and I clamber back, trying to clock Carter and Mara, and keep from ramming into a metal cot at the same time.

Carter raises her gun and points it at my temple. Her finger twitches over the trigger, and—

Pale, slender fingers close around Carter's arm, one hand on her wrist, one around her bicep. With a terrifying ease, Mara holds Carter's arm in place as she drives her knee up and through her elbow, snapping the bone in two with a sickening crunch. Pearl shines through scarlet, the bone protruding from Carter's flesh, and she drops like a sack of potatoes. Her scream pierces through the walls holding my memories at bay, and red-soaked flashbacks of the bullet lodged in my leg threaten to punch through and drag me back.

For a horrifying moment, Mara stares at her sister writhing on the floor and at the blood dripping from the gore of her arm. Only half her face is visible, but I can see enough.

A science teacher once showed our class a documentary about sharks. Their eyesight is so horrible they mistake humans for seals. They attack before realizing they chose the wrong meal. One wrong move and I am bloody chum in the water. Who knows if she'll be able to tell the difference between me and the seal.

"Mara," I say, approaching her the way I would a wild dog.

Her eyes snap to mine, wide and unfocused. She blinks, heaves a breath, and when she looks to Carter again, she is simply Mara.

On the ground, Carter cradles her bloody arm, her face flushed red. She seethes, a strip of saliva flicking off her teeth.

"Kill me," Carter says. "Finish it. End the Knight line."

Mara shakes her head. "If Mom and Dad could see you—"

"You don't get to talk about them," Carter spits. "Not after what you did. Their blood is on *your* hands."

Mara flinches, tears her focus away from Carter with visible effort. "We need to go, Rory."

Those five words send a writhing Carter scrambling across the floor after the gun. Mara leaps after her, and I don't wait for another cue to exit.

I lunge for the box, fingers closing around the cardboard as a gunshot echoes through the room. The bullet slams into the box, and the sound is like a car crash as the vials explode, a dozen tiny pieces of glass slicing open my fingers. I can't tell if the stinging is from the cuts or whatever was in the vials, and I don't want to know. The box tumbles out of my hands and onto the floor.

The office. There are more boxes in the office, five of them packed with Dyebucetin, and if I can reach them—

"Leave it, Rory!" Mara yells, scrabbling to knock the gun from her sister's hand, but Carter is prepared now, and her rage seems to have numbed her injuries.

"We need it!"

"It isn't worth *dying* for!" She slams her body into Carter, using her weight to send the two of them tumbling back and into the cot. Her fist makes contact with Carter's nose once, but the gun is still clasped in her hand, and it's rising.

Mara doesn't see it. She's as furious as Carter now, and as she rears back for another hit—a fatal one—I lunge. Mara gives up easily and goes limp the moment my fingers wrap around her wrist.

The meds are screaming behind me, reminding me what happens if Mara's drugs run out.

Another shot blasts through the doorway as we race through. By some miracle, we make it to the front door, shoving out and into the cold night. Before she can suggest the bike, I wrench us in the opposite direction, toward the heart of the main street.

We are out of the alley when Carter's call for help pierces the sky.

We keep running.

25

RORY

I lead Mara to the school. It's the last place anyone will look for us. Apart from removing the bodies, I'd wager it's been untouched since the attack.

A spare key sits under a rock near the door, as I knew it would, and as we close the door behind us, the first shouts echo down the streets. The manhunt is in full swing.

The large room is mostly dark, but the furniture is as it was a few days ago. I fumble across the room to the open office door, flicking the light switch on instinct. I'm surprised for a beat when light floods the small, windowless room and spills out into the gym.

The studio, now school, has solar panels and is one of few on the Island with electricity. And with no windows in the building, we can afford at least this luxury.

"We're staying here?" Mara asks. I don't have to turn to know she's frowning. But as little as I want to spend the night here, pretending not to see the places blood has seeped into the cement floor, it's better than a night in a cell. Or a cage, in Mara's case.

I nod. "For tonight. Don't get too comfortable."

"Imagine that." She slips past me into the office, shrugging the pack off her back and setting it on the desk. Sea-worn, beige planks, and the only furniture in the room. The office is unused, serving as more of a time-out or quiet zone—the first in the silent but rebellious Raisa's case, and the second in Noah's.

Mara's navy-blue sleeves stretch up to her palms, fingers curled against the fabric as she reaches up to brush the black hairs from her eyes. "Is it safe?"

The instinct to lie is immediate, but I've never been all that good at lying to her.

"The locks on the doors of any place people use are updated. More locks, and sturdier ones. So, if they don't come knocking down the door, we'll probably make it to morning."

"That's reassuring," she says.

I shrug. "You always were a pessimist."

One dark brow cocks. "Says the most pessimistic person I've ever met."

"The world ended when we were fifteen. How many people have you really met?"

"I'm technically still older than you," she says. "By eight months."

"Technically, you're dead."

One side of her mouth twitches up, and my stomach twists.

I almost smile back, but the hollow look in her eye as she stared at Carter sticks like tar behind my eyelids.

"I'm going to go track down some of those nap mats. It's no mattress, but it's better than the stone floor," I say, turning from the office before I fall directly off the cliff that is Mara Knight.

Stacked in the far corner of the small building are blue-and-red fabric-covered foam mats. They were shifted in the attack but are shockingly clean. I pile four beneath my arm, shuffling to a wooden table near the office door that's still standing and setting them atop it.

In the office, there is nothing to do but talk to Mara, and talking to her will make it harder to let her climb off the boat on the mainland and walk away from me.

Avoiding her is justifiable for the first five minutes, as I slam the locks shut on the door and double-check the ones on the tall roll-up door, inoperable, but an added sixty seconds of bullshitting on my part. I shove the thickest metal chair in the room up and under the handle of the door, adding a fourth layer of difficulty. With this, the locks on the office door, and a chair against that, too, I might sleep.

With no more methods of evasion and a growing throb in my leg, I ease up onto the table, the soles of my boots grazing the rug beneath it.

As if sensing my moment of weakness, Mara steps into the doorway of the office, tipping her hip into the frame. Her stare lacks warmth, and she folds her arms over her chest. One set of fingers shifts in odd shapes against her bicep, and it takes me a moment to realize and remember the way she was surrounded by music. If she wasn't playing it, it sputtered out of a phone speaker.

"Tell me about the Pit," she says, scattering my thoughts.

My heart leaps into my throat. "The tar pits? You're the one who visited La Brea, not me—"

"You know what I'm talking about."

When I don't respond, simply gaping at her, she says, "There was a key missing from the rack in the station. Then Carter mentioned it, and it was like someone punched you in the stomach. So." She gestures a hand, waiting for me to speak. "Don't be shy."

"I promise you don't want to know."

"Tell me, or I'll stop asking nicely," she says.

"You don't scare me."

"Yes," Mara says, "I do."

I heave a breath, swallowing the bile burning the back of my throat.

"Mal started the Pit way before Carter came to the Island. A stress reliever," I say. "By the time I got here, it was more than that. It was like some sick, twisted version of wrestling. And the prize was food, ammo, meds, supplies, you name it."

"Fighting pits," Mara says flatly. I nod, avert my gaze.

"At first, they threw a Tick and a volunteer or two in. Then Mal realized he could use the Pit as punishment. Anyone who breaks his rules goes in, and if they survive, they win their freedom. If they don't—"

"They die." I catch her gaze, the regret instantaneous. That vulturous look has settled in her eyes, and staring too long feels like being picked apart.

"Mal kept our pistol. Only he and a few others get guns, safety reasons or whatever, which I thought was crap—"

"Obviously."

"—so I broke into the armory and took it back."

"Weren't you shot?" Mara asks.

My mouth turns up in a crooked half smile, half grimace. "It had been a few months. Besides, I'm resilient."

"Don't know if that's what I'd call it."

"Good thing you're not telling the story," I say, and she rolls her eyes but keeps her mouth shut. "Mal caught me, told me I could fight off the charge in the Pit. I told him he could shove it where the sun doesn't shine, but I guess Carter spoke for me." I shake my head. "Should have known I was screwed right there. It was the two of us, volunteer and prisoner, on two Ticks. Really, Carter and two Ticks on me."

The one part of that night I allow myself to remember: the look on Carter's face when she knew I had her beat. I was thrown into the Pit so they could prove I wasn't a threat. The limping girl with an attitude. The one who took down both Ticks.

"So it didn't go well for Carter, I'm guessing?" Mara asks.

"No," I say. "I did get the gun back, though."

Mara leans farther into the doorframe. "Before, you said opening it *back* up."

"The Alliance made him shut it down when we joined. Mal's been angling to get it back up and running ever since."

"And that's why Carter hates you? Because you beat her in some medieval gladiator competition?"

A bitter laugh bursts from my lips. "Carter's never been my biggest fan, but that certainly doesn't help."

She purses her lips, eyes glazing over. I am desperate to both stop talking to her and carry it forward forever. She's a Venus flytrap, coaxing me in to snap shut over my head.

Mara's brows draw together, every ounce of her penetrating gaze locked intently on mine. A shiver tries to roll through me, but I threaten it within an inch of its life and remain steady.

"A few months after I got here, before that night at the Pit, before they figured out how to make you guys stop eating us"—she averts her eyes, and my stomach flutters—"Mal let me go on a supply run. This was before the trades were as commonplace. It was too risky to go in big groups, so we split into pairs. You can guess who volunteered to be my partner. Anyway, we ended up in North Park, looking for something that hadn't been picked clean."

Mara's jaw goes slack.

"I didn't recognize my own damn house. I didn't realize where we were until we were walking through the yard." My limbs urge me to bolt, to get as far from the past as I can make it, but there is nowhere to run. "Carter told me she'd been trying to come back and—" Mara's nostrils flare, and I swallow. "Come back to end it. I didn't know you were still . . ."

The memory of that night shines in brilliant, sharp colors, every edge barbed and forever slicing against my interior. A tear snakes down my cheek, and I swipe it away angrily.

"She wanted someone there when she did it. Wanted to put half of that—that weight on me. I mean, it wasn't you, that was obvious. You practically ripped your hand off trying to claw through the glass to get to us," I say. Mara's features contort, her chin dropping, two-fingered hand rising. Now, and maybe forever, bound in gauze. My breath hitches. "Guns are pretty much off-limits on the mainland, but

Carter pulled out this pistol, and it was like I—" All of my thoughts are a tangled web of mangled words that get lodged in my throat on their way up.

Mara used to be able to untangle them. It was as easy as breathing. I miss that as much as I miss her, and she's standing right in front of me.

"Why didn't you tell me?" she asks.

"Everything you've done, all the blood on your hands, it's because of me. You were in hell, dead or killing yourself, and I couldn't end it. I couldn't let Carter end it, and I'm sorry." Anger surges through me, but it isn't at her. Or it is, but not only at her. I am angry at me, too, for panicking and carving the path that led us here.

Mara is quiet for a long moment before she says, "All the things I did—that's not your fault, Rory."

"It is," I say. "It is, because I didn't just stop Carter from shooting you. After she left, I broke the lock off the door. I let you out."

Her face shows no surprise.

"You knew," I say.

"My hands weren't exactly clean when you opened that door," she says.

I clench my teeth.

"For what it's worth, I'm glad you didn't kill me," Mara adds.

I scoff.

"I'm serious." She licks her lips—they are less chapped than they were, might be soft. "But it does explain the Carter thing."

I curse the warmth that blooms in my chest. I nod and drop my eyes.

Mara's footsteps patter as she comes to climb up onto the table beside me. She eases back, farther from me—something I am grateful for and resentful of—and draws her legs beneath her, sitting cross-legged.

"That's the real reason, then," she says. "The real reason you can't look me in the eye anymore." As her head turns my way, I drop my gaze to my lap.

I lift my chin. The startling gray of her eyes holds me hostage.

"I look at you," I say, "and I see the end of the world. And I don't know how to make that go away."

Mara rips her gaze away from me, letting out a long, low sigh. I don't know what she's thinking, if she's thinking anything at all.

"Sometimes I wonder what things might be like if you guys hadn't left," she says, staring blankly at the wall opposite her.

"But we did."

"But you did," she says, and doesn't say anything else.

She is not the Mara of my memories, but I am not the Aurora she knew, either. We are what rose from the ashes of a burning world—we are what is left, for better or for worse.

26

RORY

"Do you have any sixes?" Mara asks, batting her dark lashes innocently.

"Fuck you."

"Is that a request?"

Heat rushes up my neck, and I strangle it back down. With a grumble and a quick flash of my middle finger, I wrench all three sixes from my hand and flick them toward Mara. Her grin is lopsided, and she lets out a laugh like a villain in an old cartoon, piling the numbers into her deck and pulling three pairs out, placing them before her.

Three cards in her hands. Twelve in mine.

We slept a little bit but have twenty-four hours to kill before we can contemplate leaving. Mal knows we took the boat keys. The waterline will be crawling with his guys today.

"Any queens?"

Mara waggles her brows. "Go fish."

We dragged the nap mats to the corner of the office, and I'm propped against it, Mara sitting with her long legs stretched in front of her. Every so often, she lets her ankle tip to the side, tapping my right knee with her sneaker.

"Got any fours?"

I drop my eyes to the cards in my hand. One nine, two fours.

"You're cheating."

She snorts. "Nope. I do know your tells, though."

"It's Go Fish," I say. "Not poker."

She shrugs and says, "Go Fish was our poker." Her eyes lift to mine, one side of her mouth quirking up. "You do this weird thing where you blink the number of the card you picked up. I've never seen anything like it."

"I do *not*—"

"Oh, you absolutely do. You never realized you were doing it, either." She waves her deck. "How else do you think I beat you all those years?"

"I thought you were cheating," I say pointedly. "Still do."

"No, you just have a really, really weird habit."

I don't dignify her with a response, turning my attention back to my cards, holding out the fours. She doesn't take them, and I find her eyes.

"What?"

She shakes her head. "This is usually the part where you threaten to kill me."

I frown and say, "Did you want me to?"

"Think I'm good," she says, and takes my cards, cool fingers brushing mine—lingering, for a moment. Her gaze darts to the sheathed sword sitting a few inches from me. "Why the sword?"

I'm surprised she hasn't asked until now. It's not exactly the most normal weapon these days. Most people have anything from axes to knives to their own inventions.

Not many people carry around an antique sword.

I reach out to run my fingers along the tough leather.

"It saved my life," I say. "Saved Raisa's and Aria's, too."

The cases are locked. All of them. A dozen glass boxes, bronze and stone and wood weaponry sitting inside, and I can't reach a single thing. So much for antique weaponry to keep us all alive if our guns couldn't. This museum is going to become a tomb.

Two pairs of eyes stare out at me from under the cabinet. Aria and Raisa, their limbs trembling. Raisa's gaze darts past me, toward the door.

"Don't move," I whisper.

Aria looks at her sister. Like she can't agree until Raisa does.

"But what if he—" Raisa begins, her voice barely audible.

"He won't get me," I say, and I don't believe it, but I need them to. I need them to believe so that they'll run, and so that they'll live. "Don't move." I straighten as slow and silent as I can, clocking the silhouette pressed against the door. Just that, my tiny motion, makes the man—not a man anymore, a Tick—freeze. His head snaps my way.

Doors slam down the hall, followed by the unmistakable crack of a weapon against a skull, but the Tick doesn't take his beady gaze off me. His eyes have already turned that unnerving silver that cuts straight through my muscles, all the way down to the bone.

There is a flash of movement as the Tick lunges, and a shrill shriek sounds from under the cabinet.

Fear unfurls in my chest and threatens to swallow me whole, and I think, This is it. This is the end.

Then Aria screams again, and the Tick stills. Turns. And redirects for the cases my sisters are hiding beneath.

Whatever fear I might have felt burns away as adrenaline rushes into its place. My body isn't entirely mine when I bring my elbow down into a glass case, slicing open my skin and sending glass shards scattered across the ground. I watch myself lift a hundred-or-more-year-old sword out of the case. Watch myself grab the Tick by the collar of his shirt. Watch myself swing the blade into his neck again and again until he falls and doesn't get back up.

"Since when are you the sentimental type?" Mara asks, tearing me out of the memory.

"I thought it was kind of ridiculous to carry around, but Aria asked me to—to hold on to it for her. Until she was big enough to use it." Needles prick at the backs of my eyes, and I blink them back, clearing my throat and looking anywhere but at her. "But it turns out it's a damn good sword."

I can feel her eyes on me, but she doesn't press any harder. Instead, she asks, "Got any nines?"

She beats me in two more moves, to no one's surprise, and we pile the cards back into one deck. I take it into my lap and shuffle it rhythmically. I used to do it everywhere, to the point where Sam and Isaac refused to let me leave the house with a deck. That was when the bracelets started, something to fill my fidgeting fingers with.

It is something to look at other than her, but the muscle memory is so ingrained I don't need visuals.

Eventually, after an agonizing three minutes, she speaks. And I immediately wish she hadn't.

"Why didn't you tell me sooner?" she asks, lifting the wrist with the bracelet, and I can't pretend not to know what she means.

"It took ten years to convince myself to—" I lose the words, stop, try again. I don't meet her eyes as I speak. "You know, you ruined my life the day you moved into the house behind me. I was this angry, lonely kid, and you blew into my world and made me forget what being lonely felt like."

A stone lodges itself in my throat, and I struggle to breathe around it. "I tried for years not to feel it. I tried so hard not to love you, Mara. I really did." I shrug, let out a wavering breath. "I knew you were too good for me, that I was already lucky enough to know you, to be close to you, but I—I felt like I was going to explode, and then there you were, sitting in our backyard like you were . . . I don't know, *waiting for me*, and all of a sudden, I didn't care if it ruined everything. I sat down next to you, and I gave you that bracelet, and I kissed you. You know the rest."

I risk a glance in her direction, but she's not looking at me—she's staring at the blue mat she's sitting on, picking at a stray thread between her fingers.

"You can't tell me you didn't know," I say.

Her eyes snap to mine.

"I didn't," she says. She shakes her head.

My heart is a thunderous roar, and if it doesn't quit, it'll draw Mal straight to us.

"I wanted you, too. For longer than I knew. So long I—" She pauses, and I can see the gears turning in her head, pulling more confessions forth.

I have been waiting for this for over a decade, and now that it's here, all I want is for it to stop. For her to stop. Stop making me remember the way it felt to love Mara Knight.

"It's not like it matters," I say before she can push the knife deeper into my chest. I pretend the words don't taste like poison. "Those girls don't exist anymore."

"You don't really think that," she says. A breath passes. "Do you?"

"Yeah, I do. That Mara and that Rory died a long time ago. If you can't see that, you're delusional."

"You're wrong. Maybe part of them did die that day, with everything else, but not all of us."

"You don't really think that," I imitate.

"I have to," she says. "What the hell is the point if I don't?"

I don't have an answer for her. And I don't have the courage to consider that she might be right.

Mara was always the brave one. Maybe she still is.

27

MARA

The woman does not scream. They usually scream. Their moans and cries batter against my ears, the sound so full of life I can do nothing but lunge, tear through their skin—silence the noise before it shreds me to ribbon.

But she is still, quiet beneath me, wide eyes locked on mine as her blood turns the asphalt a deep, dark red. She dies that way, her eyes haunting, unseeing but open as I rip into her.

The woman doesn't scream as she dies, but the little girl, running out from a hiding place, does. She screams and never stops.

"Wake up, Mara." The voice, the one that always drags me out of that cool, comfortable darkness, stretches down a hand and yanks my consciousness forward.

"It's a dream, Mara. *Wake up.*"

Mara. The word should mean something, I think. It should connect to another tangle of fragmented sounds. It is nothing, I am nothing, it is all—

That sound. Breath and heartbeat and movement. So loud, always so loud. Life, brimming and bubbling over the edge of a glass—

A palm cracks across my cheek, and my eyes fly open, rage settling into my fisted hands.

The bright fluorescents hum above my head, and I blink past the dizziness the stimuli brings. The girl, whose name I can't remember, sits awkwardly at my side.

I find her gaze again, struggling to understand why she bothered waking me. An image of my fingers peeling back the skin of her gut comes unbidden, and I strangle it down.

Almost two days since my last dose. The Tick skitters and dances over my skin. Her closeness keeps the wheels turning, keeps the monster beneath the surface.

You can make it all go away, the Tick urges. *You can make her go away.*

The girl's hand grazes my arm, a gentle touch, and I lurch back, scramble across the linoleum until I slam into the beige wall. The space between us is stretched to three feet, as far as I can make it without breaking the door down.

"Mara." The girl draws my focus back, a noisy bundle of life blinking in my face, begging to be silenced.

What is her name?

"It was a dream. You're okay." Her hand rises again as if she means to reach and brush against me again. Hunger snaps its jaws and writhes behind my teeth.

"Don't touch me," I gasp. Her hand freezes. Her brows knit. I expect her to ignore me, to keep coming forward, but instead, she sits back. Settles on the mat. Draws her knees up, loops her arms around them. And waits.

We stay like that, tense and still, her gaze boring into me—it pokes into something I don't have words for. Remembrance pricks at me until finally, eventually, three syllables slip out from the shadow they're hiding behind.

Aurora.

I don't dare move, holding back the parasite fighting to retake center stage.

Mine. You are mine. You will always be mine.

The urge to smack my palms against my skull until the Tick comes crawling out is near overwhelming. If only it were that simple. If only the solution were that easy to grasp.

Mine. Mine, you are mine, you are—

Get out of my head. I scream it through my thoughts, letting anger sizzle them to ash, letting the Tick sweep them up and go staggering back to its hiding place. When my mind is my own again, I meet Rory's eyes. She squirms and shifts for a moment, and I don't realize she's building to a question until her lips part.

"Was it a nightmare?" she asks. Gestures at nothing. "Or . . ."

"The other one."

Her brows lift, eyes widen briefly, and she nods as she says, "Memories. Way fuckin' worse than anything our brains could cook up."

A smile tries to tug on my lips, but it loses steam before it's successful. The little girl, whose name I will never know, screams in the back of my head, a violent song on repeat.

It was easier then. Easier to be numb and quiet and gray. To follow a path taken by a million Ticks around me and let thought and feeling rot behind me.

"Do you . . ." Rory clears her throat. "I don't know, do you wanna talk about it?"

"Do you want to hear about it?"

She shrugs again. "Can't be anything worse than I've seen." She stops. Frowns. "Or I guess it can, actually."

"Being a monster doesn't make for good dream fodder."

"I didn't realize you *could* dream. Did you sleep when you were . . ." Her nose crinkles. "You know."

Her curiosity feels out of place. Maybe it's the night, or the fact that we're both tired, or maybe she's been saving these sentiments. Waiting until she knew I wouldn't murder her before answering her questions.

The jury is still out on that, but I can't bring myself to tell her, not yet. What can Rory do about the Dyebucetin? Why should she do anything? I am the monster under the bed. Not the stuffed animal you hug to fall asleep.

"Ticks don't sleep, but when I woke up in the facility"—a stitch forms between Rory's brows at my words, but I force them out—"I was pretty much up all the time, at first. For a long time, I didn't realize I could sleep. I don't get all that tired, but sometimes—sometimes it's nice to get out of your head for a while. To not have to think."

A shadow passes over Rory's face, her dark eyes a deep well of loss as she nods and tears her gaze from mine.

"I know the feeling," Rory says.

"It's mostly nightmares these days, though," I say.

"The apocalypse will do that," she says, and though it's clear she tries to form the words neutrally, they drip with resentment—not at me, but at all of it. Everything we've lost and might have found.

"Can I ask you a question?" Something about the lateness or the small, isolated feeling of the office makes me braver.

"Shoot."

I press my lips together for a long moment. I haven't asked for specifics about what happened to Aria, but the pieces have put themselves together since I arrived. Aria was bitten, and because Sam couldn't keep her from coming back as a Tick, Rory had to do it.

"You made sure Aria didn't turn," I say slowly, aware I'm veering near the edge of a cliff. "But when Carter brought you to the house, you had a chance to kill me, and you didn't."

She ended Aria's life, but she didn't end mine, and for the life—or technically, unlife—of me, I can't figure out why.

"That's not a question," Rory says, a muscle twitching in her jaw.

"You did it for Aria. But not for me. Why?"

Rory recoils like I've slapped her. A fire lights in her eyes, and I expect her to chew me out, but instead, she says, "I couldn't do it *because* of Aria." The anger slips out of her. "Not again."

Rory takes a shaking breath. "Aria was—she was so torn up. Dyebucetin didn't exist, but even if she had lasted that long, it wouldn't have worked. She would have been like Juliette." She clenches her fists. "But my family was in that building, and Sam had this look in her eyes, and I knew that she couldn't do it. Aria was going to wake up, and Sam wasn't going to be able to stop it." She speaks through gritted teeth. "So I did."

I think she's done talking, but she continues, "Sam never looked at me the same way, and every night before I closed my eyes, I'd wonder if I made the right call." She blinks rapidly, and I realize she's holding back tears. "And then Carter brought me to your house, and you were standing in that window, and it was like I was back with Aria, and I just . . ." Tears spill down her cheeks, and she swats them away like she's mad they exist.

"I don't want to be this way," she says. "So angry I could burn the fucking world down. But anger is safer than anything else. I think if I did let myself feel it, all that grief and sadness, I'd never stop. I wouldn't survive all this." Rory clears her throat, swiping beneath her eyes again. She stretches her left leg straight, and a wince flutters over her face. "The drugs, resettlement, the Alliance, all of it, it's a . . . a Band-Aid on a bullet hole, and eventually, we'll hemorrhage."

"I don't believe that," I say.

She shakes her head. "That's why I hate you," she says, but there's no venom in it.

Opposition rears its head, and I want to refute her, but the words turn to dust on my dry tongue. Taking a breath, I shift back to my mat, easing down onto my side. Fortunately, Rory takes it as the unspoken end of the conversation and slowly rises, flipping off the light. Her boots scuff the floor as she steps back slowly, lowering onto the mat.

The space between us has never felt so vast.

28

MARA

I have no clue what time it is when I wake up again. Darkness has its arms wrapped protectively around us; no windows in the building, Rory said.

The front of my body is scalding, like I'm hugging a space heater. Hair, not my own, tickles my nose where my chin is tucked against someone's shoulder.

Rory.

Curled up, her back flush against my front, holding my hand hostage to her chest. Her figure moves slowly with the rhythmic rise and fall of her breath. The instant stuttering thumps of my heart send a rush of dizziness through me, and I clamp my eyes shut.

Mine, the Tick murmurs. *You are mine.*

How simple it would be. Lift my chin, brush the hair from her neck, and crack her skull wide open. The hollow hunger tugs on my insides.

Fingers thread tentatively through mine, dragging the parasite into a cage and slamming the door shut behind it. *Mara. You are Mara.*

My thumb traces a hesitant circle over her skin.

She doesn't pull away. Be it the dark, or the circumstances, or Rory's lack of full consciousness, she doesn't pull away.

The foam mats beneath us give as she turns in to me. The dark is unyielding, and I only know she's still here from the hot puffs of breath on my chin.

Her fingers fumble over my cheeks and ghost over the X slashed through my face—they pause on my lips, and I lose my breath. My heart beats once, twice.

There is no longer a world where someone touches me this way. My skin is so accustomed to pain it has forgotten about all the rest, and every brush of Rory's fingertips wakes something up.

When her hands dip to my collarbones, fingers curling around the collar of my tee, the hunger that yawns open inside me is different, painted in deep reds and oranges.

My lips find her cheek, grazing it and moving up to her brows. Each touch is a chance for her to shove me aside, to scream or stab me—to remind me that I don't deserve this or her—but nothing comes. Down to her cheek, across the line of her jaw. I linger at the hollow of her neck, and a shiver runs through her, the fabric of my shirt straining as she twists it in her grasp.

She tugs me up, nose bumping mine, but she pauses. I don't know who moves first. I blink, and we're kissing.

If that peck at fifteen was a spark, this is a wildfire. The first kiss we might have found years ago if we'd gotten the chance. If we had the time. If we were braver.

She kisses me slowly, like this moment will unfold ahead of us endlessly. And I want it to, so badly. I want to pluck this second and tuck it somewhere safe, and stay there forever.

Rory's hands slide up my shoulders, slipping around my neck, her fingers curling into the hairs at the nape of my neck and drawing me closer. The thrum of her heart against my chest is rapid, and she melts into me, tongue flicking against my teeth.

"I thought you hated me," I murmur, ever the idiot, making her mouth stall on mine.

"I do," she says, and traces a finger down my collarbone, releasing a groan from the back of my throat that horrifies me and greatly pleases her. "And I don't."

Mal and Carter and all the rest might be right about me. Rory herself. I might still be a monster. But right now I want to pretend I'm not. I want to kiss a girl until I'm just a girl, too.

I realize it's been too long since I took a breath when Rory pulls back and takes a shaky one of her own.

I inhale, but the smell shifts. Not the lemon of her shampoo. Not sweat.

Smoke.

I scramble back, and in any other circumstances, the soft, disappointed noise Rory makes would turn my limbs to jelly, but each breath out of her orbit clues me in to all the signs I've missed.

The sound, low crackling—too low for Rory to notice. The heat that doesn't fit with the cool morning breeze that should seep like ice through the walls. And that scent, acrid and stinging against my nostrils.

Rory has caught on, shuffling and stumbling as she struggles to find the light switch. Harsh artificial lights pierce my sensitive corneas, and I squint.

Even with my eyes closed to slits, I can see the tendrils of smoke slipping like fingers beneath the closed office door.

Rory's gaze latches onto mine, and it feels impossible that, seconds ago, she was pressed against my chest. Panic tenses her slender muscles as she wrenches on the chair she's propped beneath the door handle, and I blink the daze away, lunging to help her.

Our combined effort sends the chair crashing into the wall, two of the legs cracking and flying to the floor.

Rory reaches for the doorknob, crying out and yanking her hand back. Her breath comes in fast pants, and the smoke has painted red rings around her eyes.

"*Mara*," she says.

Nodding, I grasp the knob in my good hand, ignoring the sizzling that screams through my palm. By the time the knob turns, the pain has sparked in my skull, forcing black spots into my vision.

I throw the door open to a room on fire.

Heat smacks me in the face, sending me stumbling back and into Rory. Her fingers close around my shoulders, and I dip as she digs into the wound, another fire igniting under my skin.

The Tick slams to the forefront of my head, turning me to Rory in a blink, and she tugs her hands away, staring past me with wide eyes. Her attention is so fixated on the billowing flames outside the room she doesn't see the monster bubbling to life beside her.

Two days since my last dose, and the pieces of my sanity are quickly chipping and crumbling away. The corners of my head are pleasantly fuzzy, that familiar numbness threatening to unleash and wrap itself around me once more. Rory's fear, raw and real and raging, tethers me to my false humanity, and the ghost of her mouth on mine shoves the ravenous hunger back.

"Don't look out there," I command, surprised when she listens, gaze flicking to mine. "Look at me. Just me."

"We're trapped. The door. There's no way through—" Her eyes drift, and I take her face in my hands, not half as gentle as I was mere minutes ago. It is not just Mara running the show, but the monster, too, both battling for the reins of the carriage.

"We have to run. When I move, you move. Understand?" I ask.

She doesn't, her eyes glassy, fixed on the flames beyond my head. The unshakeable Rory Blake, drowning in a sea of fire.

"*Move*," I say, and take her arm.

"Mara—" Whatever she was going to say dies as I step forward, plunging into the blaze.

The fifty feet to the doorway could be fifty miles with the flames licking up the walls and consuming the rugs. Above our heads, a small hatch spits morning sunlight into the room. Directly below it, the heart of the blaze, are three plastic gas cans.

"*Bastards.*" Rory brings a hand to her mouth, hacking into her elbow, and sways on her feet. Before she can tip all the way over, I slip an arm around her waist and drag her onward.

Ten steps take a full minute; so much of the floor up in flames and so much of Rory's weight dipping into me that each inch is arduous. I haven't risked a breath since we crossed the office doorway, afraid to burn through the remainders of my lungs.

Rory's breathing grows labored as the air switches itself out for smoke. I can barely see through the smog and roaring flame—now stretching all the way up to the exposed-pipe ceiling, crawling over our heads.

An instinctual inhale lights my chest in pain, and I stagger to the side, Rory weaving with me as a cough rolls through my lungs. Her fingers scrabble for purchase on the fabric of my clothing, and I straighten, pull her closer to me, force us forward.

The roof gives a thunderous creak, and a pipe crashes to the floor in front of us, spitting flames into my face and arms as I crane to shield Rory. I don't bother stamping the flames away, dragging her and myself around and forward. Forward is the only way, the one thing I can think about. Absently, I note Rory's hands smacking at my singed sleeve and swiping embers away.

The tables have all melted or collapsed, and the chair propped against the door has melted into the handle and the wood.

Easing away from Rory, I grapple with the chair as she struggles with the steaming locks. By the time she manages to flip all three of them up with minor damage to her hands, my palm is bright red, and the chair has barely budged.

Rory pulls back, her pink fingers curling in and out of fists as she shakes off the heat. Her breath is scratchy, loud, heavier by the second.

A wave of coughs rack Rory's chest, and she drops to her knees before I can catch her. I hoist her back up, and her dark eyes find mine, orange and yellow flames reflected in the blown black pupils.

"Mara," she wheezes. "I can't breathe." The words are half sob, half plea and rip all of me into tiny, little pieces.

The Tick lights me up with buzzing adrenaline, but *my* hands are looped through the ropes. My feet are still my own.

Rory is dying. Eyes fluttering, shoulders drooping. *Rory is dying.*

The realization turns my vision to a blinding white, and the burn of the chair is a faint sensation.

The ears and top rails of the chair splinter beneath my hands, and the rest of the pieces fall away. I don't bother trying the melted mess of a doorknob, taking a deep breath of flame and stepping back before throwing my good shoulder into the wood with every ounce of force I can muster.

Hinges whine and snap as the door gives and turns to long, sharp shreds. I tumble through it and onto the concrete. Cool, fresh air lifts the scorching heat from my skin, and I gasp it into my ruined lungs, pushing up in the wreckage of the door.

A rasping cough echoes behind me.

Panic leaps into my throat, and I stagger up, losing my footing over the wood chunks but not faltering. Smoke pulses from the doorway like the mouth of a sleeping dragon.

I don't hesitate, plunging back into the darkness, falling at Rory's side, hoisting her half-conscious form into my arms. Though her eyes don't open, her grip on me is tight.

My mistake is breathing. So focused on hefting her out the door, I suck in gulp after gulp of stinging air and am swimming in darkness as we step back into the sunlight. I fall to my knees, letting Rory down beside me. Her blurry figure squirms, strains, straightens until all I can see are her legs.

Get up. *Get up.* The thoughts get stuck on their way to my limbs, leaving me limp on the concrete.

"Out come the roaches!" a gruff voice calls, followed by hoots and cheers. At least five people, maybe more. My thoughts have turned sluggish, sloshing like muddy water. The sounds are muffled. Whoever drew us out didn't want to risk being caught in the blaze, it would seem. They're far away.

A hand closes around my bicep, roughly dragging me up and onto my feet. Rory, the terror gone from her eyes, replaced with fierce determination. Limping, coated in ash, but still wielding her sword like a fifth limb.

"Move," she says, like I did, and now it is my turn to listen.

The second we step forward, a shot splits the air around us. Rory lets out a huff of pain, then stumbles. A spot of red blooms through the dark denim covering her thigh. It's a graze, but enough to make her falter.

Footsteps thunder on the asphalt, echoing around the side of the building one door down.

Mal and his soldiers coming to collect their prize.

"Come on," I urge, slipping an arm around her shoulders, carrying most of her weight. We make it three steps before she's begging to stop.

"Rory, we have to—"

"I can't," she snaps, shoving me away. Her head whips in the direction of the uniforms, a block away from us now. When she looks at me again and opens her mouth to speak, her tone is pleading. "I can't."

"We have to move. We're not dying here—" I move to pull her back into my grasp, to pick her up and march her out of here if I have to, but the cold, empty glaze in her eyes traps me in place.

"You go," she says. "Now."

Horror unfolds in my gut, and its acid eats through my intestines. Her instructions don't make sense, can't make sense.

She lurches forward, swaying but steady handed, biting hard on her lower lip, shaking her head.

An image flickers behind my eyes: the sword in her hand, wrenched from her grip, and her skin peeled back—

A frustrated scream slips through her gritted teeth, and she pulls me back, dragging us around the building and into the alley. Even that show of force dies out with the shake of her step and the slow loosening of her grip as pain takes precedence over anything else.

"Mara, you have to go." Desperation bleeds into her words, and every half second, she glances back, waiting for the soldiers who will be upon us in seconds. "Take the boat keys, find Daphne—"

"I said *no*."

Rage paints her red, and she shoves at my shoulders, but I hold my ground. She pushes, pushes twice more until she can't push again. And she shifts tactics again. She unsheathes her sword and presses the tip between my eyes.

"Go, Mara!" she yells—pinpointing our exact location to the soldiers. "Go!"

"Do it," I say, a hand flying up to hold the sword in place. I acknowledge but don't feel the blade slice through my palm. Rory's breath hitches. "If someone's going to, it should be you. It has to be you."

She tries to pull the blade back and stops at the trickle of dark blood that gathers around it. Her nostrils flare, and her eyes shine with moisture—from the smoke, from the fire.

"I can't," she says, frustrated.

"And I can't leave you," I say, gentler. I release the sword, and her hand falls to her side.

A sad smile pulls on my lips.

Oh, Rory. Don't you get it now? There is nowhere to run. The past will always catch you.

Her face falls, and her response is stolen as the soldiers spring forth like ants from every direction.

The animal slumbering in my skin snaps awake as they descend, no longer names and faces but enemies, creatures trying to pull me from the girl at my side.

Back in the facilities, the RPA soldiers had a special sedative reserved for the ones who snapped. It was a more frequent occurrence in the beginning, but it's hard to forget the feral screams and the empty eyes that punched at something newly quiet in my head.

"Keep your hands off her," I snap, pulling a wobbling Rory into my side as Mal and the soldiers approach us. "Touch her and I swear to god I'll rip your eyeballs out of your head and make you watch as I stuff them down your throat."

Rory coughs, fingers gripping the back of my shirt. Her knees finally give out, and I drop, arms hooked beneath her armpits, pulling her up before she slams into the ground.

"You can't do this," Rory says. "When people find out what you've done, they'll retaliate."

"What happens next isn't really your concern now, is it?" Mal asks, stepping toward us. He breaches three feet, and I lunge as a woman with a tranquilizer gun pulls the trigger. The dart lodges in my arm with a tiny prick and sends cement through my veins.

I briefly register the smack of my knees on the concrete, the weight of Rory's hands gripping my shoulders as she falls next to me. The world blurs like I'm underwater in the deep end of a pool, watching the swimmers wade and kick past.

"If you hurt her, I promise you I will hunt you down—" Rory starts.

A slap reverberates through the air, followed by the sharp intake of Rory's breath and her angry, trembling form against me.

"Cuff them both. Ankles and wrists," Mal says. A pause. "Hit Blake with one of those tranq darts, too."

Rory inhales, building what will inevitably be an elaborate and impressive insult, but before it reaches air, a whiz buzzes past my ear. She sinks into me.

"Get them into the truck," Mal calls.

The drugs aren't strong enough to put us under, but will slow us down for a few minutes, like our limbs are encased in Jell-O. Even swaying, I hold Rory's eyes and grab on to the fear, the underlying ferocity and fortitude, in her expression until we're hauled to our feet and I can no longer look at her.

29

RORY

To keep from screaming expletives until I'm blue in the face as four soldiers load me and Mara into the bed of an old Chevy truck, I make a mental list of the best ways to kill Mal Gordon. The bastard stole my weapons, along with zip-tying us and tossing us into the truck like dead pigs. I've decided his precious pistol is the most fitting method of revenge. Nothing tastes worse than a stolen bullet.

He climbs into the cabin with Lily, the others staying behind to ensure that the fire won't spread. If it does, we don't have the water to put it out. It could take out the entire block. And they lit it up anyway. Wasted a couple gallons of precious gas to do it, too.

I'm oddly flattered.

"What on *earth* are you smiling for?" Mara grumbles, leaning against the corner of the truck bed, legs bent awkwardly. She's always pale, but I'm noticing now how pale. The shadows under her eyes have doubled in size, and her cheeks are more sunken, like whatever life was seeping back into her skin hit reverse.

"I'm not," I say. She exhales sharply through her nose, gaze darting to the back window of the truck. The engine rumbles to life, and she tenses, as if the noise hurts her ears.

Mal pulls the truck through the alley, turning onto D Avenue—the one street cleared of debris all the way from First to Tenth, and the only one fully drivable.

The Pit rests to the side of the high school, five or so blocks away from the burning school, but Mal takes his time. We aren't going more than five miles an hour; we're being shown off like a parade float, though the streets are empty.

"Smoke," Mara says out of nowhere.

"Yeah. I know. I'm still coughing it out," I say.

"No." Mara shakes her head, and I follow her gaze up.

There is smoke, a lot of it, pumping into the sky, but it's not coming from the gym we left. Even if the whole block caught, it wouldn't create a fire that put off smoke like that without gallons of accelerant poured on top of it.

"The docks," I say, bile clawing its way up my tongue.

"What? Why—" Mara stops, inhaling sharply. "The boats."

"The boats," I say. I have to resist the urge to retch. "They're burning the boats."

Mara shakes her head. She doesn't have to ask what this means— we're being cut off. She tips her head back against the glass windows, her eyes falling shut.

Her lack of a reaction hammers in the reality. It doesn't matter what happens next to two girls who are about to die.

Dread curdles deep in my stomach, keeping me focused on Mal's head through the back window. I imagine I could punch through the glass, stretch an arm through and yank him back. Slip an arm around his throat and squeeze until he stilled.

Mara could probably do it. A few days ago, certainly. Now something is different, something she refuses to acknowledge or talk about. She can't hide the tremors, or the snappiness, or that blank glint in her eyes for a moment after she meets mine.

"What's going on with you?" I ask. "And don't tell me you're fine—"

"I'm fine," she interjects, and a shudder rolls through her.

"—because you're not." I narrow my eyes. "What is it? Side effects? General being-dead stuff?"

"Not funny."

"I'm not joking," I snap. "Something is wrong with you."

"Rory." I meet her eyes and regret it; they are drenched in despair. "Please don't. Just don't."

"Whatever it is, you're doing a shit job of hiding it, for the record," I say. "And if I notice, they're going to notice. They'll think you're weak. And weak doesn't survive the Pit."

"Rory—"

"I'm done playing this game. If you don't—"

"The drugs," she spits. "I ran out."

The words are nonsense, ill-fitting puzzle pieces I can't jam into place.

I ran out.

My heartbeat rises to a deafening level, and I can see all the signs I tossed aside or outright missed. The shaking. The look in her eyes. The way she threw herself across the room when I woke her last night.

We're not running low on time. We don't have any left.

"How long ago?" I ask, breathless.

"Two days," she says.

I don't get the chance to lay into her the way I want. The moment I open my mouth, Mal slams the truck into park outside the old high school. For months and months, I have avoided this place like it harbored ghosts, and just like that, I'm back in cuffs.

The Pit.

We are hauled up the concrete sidewalk, the deserted football field to our right, and through rusted metal doors to the entrances to the locker rooms. Two guards are assigned to each of us, gripping us tightly now that the sedatives have worn off—Mara makes a show out of dragging her feet and going limp, being as difficult to maneuver as possible. I take the other extreme on the scale, thrashing and kicking and cursing like a wild animal.

It doesn't get us anywhere, but that's not why we're doing it. There's victory in fighting at all.

The men's locker room has been cleared of its benches, and the shower curtains have been torn away. Shattered mirrors rest above cracked sinks, and the showers probably have bacteria that could kill me faster than a Tick ever could. I don't want to know what the stains on the faded tile floor are.

My stomach churns as I rake in a sour, rancid breath, and if I had free hands, I'd clap them over my face.

The ruined state of the room isn't what catches my attention. It's the cages. A dozen of them, crudely made and pressed together in the center of the room, each large enough to fit a lion and sturdy enough to hold it. The metal bars are twice as thick as my fingers, and wide enough for a fist to fit through.

Six are occupied. Emir, the boy from the other night, leans heavily against the side of one, half-conscious and twitching every few seconds. Another holds a young girl with one arm. Four pairs of gray eyes stare out from the others.

"Emir," Mara says. *"Dolly—"*

One of the men holding Mara shoves her forward.

There is one more locker room down this hall. Are the rest of the Altered there or already dead?

"Watching you squirm is so satisfying," Mal says, poking me in the back with the barrel of his pistol.

Mara jerks against the men holding her and growls.

"Get them locked up." He holsters his gun. "Quick. They're feisty."

"I'm going to rip your fingers off one by one—" Mara's threats are silenced with an elbow to the face, and she stumbles to the side, into me. As she straightens, she catches my gaze for the briefest of seconds; she is unfocused, glassy-eyed.

Out of time.

Mal pops open the door on the first cage, and the soldiers shove Mara inside. She catches herself on her knees before her face smashes into the metal.

"In," Lily says, and delivers a swift kick to her lower back. Mara tumbles in, drawing her legs back as the door slams shut. Lily locks a heavy padlock and stands, giving me a wicked smile. "Next up."

I am placed in a cage between Mara and a grumbling, shaking Tick—a middle-aged woman who presses her face so hard against the bars her skin is rubbing raw.

I can't stand in the cage and have no choice but to press as far into Mara's as I can, my legs stretched out diagonally in front of me— barely long enough for my left leg not to screech in protest.

"Raise your hands to the bars," Lily commands, lifting a knife from her belt and crossing to Mara's cage. Mara fixes the woman with a murderous glare but does as told. Only when the zip ties fall to her feet does she sit, falling against the corner opposite me, sneakers tipped against the bars near my hip. The toe of one rubber shoe brushes my thigh through the bar.

Lily takes my ties next, and though Mara is the literal monster between the two of us, she is more cautious in removing mine.

"Lily, you and Tara take post outside the door. The rest of you, with me." Mal snaps his fingers and heads for the door, all but Tara trailing behind him.

"Last night on Earth," Tara croons, too-big mouth contorted in what might be a smile. "Any plans?"

"Using your guts as a jump rope," I say, and Mara snorts like she's drunk.

Rage flashes in Tara's eyes. For a second, I'm sure she's going to kill us both, but she turns, stomps to the door, lets it slam shut behind her.

The whine and *crack* of the door stirs Emir and the teen girl. Emir's eyes flash briefly with remorse at the sight of us, but there is nothing behind the expressions of the girl, Dolly, or the Altered in the other cages but hunger.

This is what two days without Dyebucetin has made them.

This is what *Mara* will be. And from the looks of her, shaking like a leaf in the cage beside mine, it will be sooner rather than later.

30

RORY

"For the love of god," Mara grumbles for the fifth time, "make it stop."

I sit back, fingers falling from the loose nail in the corner of the cage I've been trying in vain to pry free for half an hour, and huff, blowing hair from my eyes and dropping my chin.

"You've been at this for ages. Face it. That nail isn't coming out."

The knot that has been growing inside me pulses. A stinging sensation registers in my fingers, and I realize the pads are bleeding. With a sigh, I settle back into the bars, wiping my prickling fingers on my pants. Maybe tetanus will kill me before the Pit does.

"So that's it?" I ask. "You're giving up?"

"I am not giving up." Her intensity makes the others shift in their cages. They've stopped actively trying to squeeze through the bars to reach me, but if the metal weren't between us, I'd certainly be dead. Mara makes a point not to look at Emir or the young girl, Dolly. "It feels like my brain is trying to punch through my skull, and I'm trying very hard not to imagine cracking your head open on the tile and taking a bite. So I'm sorry if I'm not leading the escape effort, but I don't have anything left to give."

"You could have been across the water by now. Instead, you're here, and now we're both going to die."

"I was half-dead from the fire," she says, leaning forward, glaring at me. "The one that I dragged you out of. You're welcome."

"You saved me once. You've nearly gotten me killed like five times."

"You and I both know I could save you fifty times over and you'd still be angry at me."

"None of this would have happened if—" I huff. "God, sometimes I wish you'd just—"

"Just what?"

"Stayed dead."

There is no sugarcoating the cruelty, and I don't try. The storm I've been holding at bay since the day Carter told me Mara was coming back is splintering the already-rickety foundation of my composure. I am angry and afraid and sad and sick and a million other things all at once. Mara isn't the only ticking time bomb.

"I miss it, you know," I say. "Being out on the mainland. I actually miss the Dark Days sometimes." A bitter laugh slips out of me, and as it does, tears start to trickle down my cheeks. I ignore them. "And I know how that sounds, but I do. Like, when you're living for the next hour, you stop thinking about who you're going to be when it's over. It doesn't matter. All that matters is surviving the day. And that was easier. But now . . ."

"Now it's like looking in a mirror and not recognizing the person staring back," Mara says. Her shoulders sink, and she dips back against the bars, hunched.

"But it's not a mirror. It's you," I say, honesty spilling out of me. "I look at you, and all I can see is everything I'm not."

"That's not my fault," she says.

"I know," I say, deflating. "I know it's not."

She opens her mouth to speak, then stops, expelling a pained hiss, squeezing her eyes shut, and leaning back. "God, get out of my head." The sentence isn't directed at me, and whatever anger or sadness I have left follows Mara's out the door, leaving a concern that I wish I could scrape away.

"Mara—"

"I'm fine," she says, pushing into the far side of her crate. I couldn't reach her if I wanted.

The frustration comes rushing back in a way only Mara can trigger, but before I get the chance to respond, seven pairs of eyes snap in the direction of the door. A noise I can't hear.

My pulse has enough time to spike as the door opens across the dank room, hinges whining. Lily's, Tara's, and Tara's boyfriend's pounding footsteps have woken the half-conscious Ticks around me and have them banging at the bars. The woman in the crate on my left is clawing at the six inches between her fingers and my boot like I'm the quarter she dropped between washing machines.

"Time for the show?" I ask.

The soldiers ignore me. Tara's boyfriend, whose name I never bothered to learn, pulls a set of metal cuffs from his pocket and tosses them to Lily. Tara raises the tranquilizer gun.

My theatrics falter, and I shift toward Mara instinctively.

"What are you doing?" Mara asks before I can.

Lily inserts a small silver key into the padlock of my cage—no key ring, so probably one key for all the kennels. The scrape of the bars as she pulls the door open wrings me so tight I barely keep from springing out of the crate and shaking my aching limbs free. I'm not in a hurry to be cuffed, and I would be stabbed or taken out with another tranquilizer before I could straighten, so I settle for slowly climbing out.

As my eyes reach Lily's shoulders, she whips me around, yanks my arms behind my back, and cinches the cuffs painfully around my wrists. An involuntary yelp slips past my lips, and heat snakes up my neck.

Mara's cage rattles as she smashes her fists against its bars, spitting curses.

Weak doesn't survive the Pit.

"What is this?" I ask. Lily ignores me, grasping my cuffed hands and yanking me forward. I stumble, pain sparking in my leg, and catch my footing. She has to hold me up, and for once, I don't bother trying to steady myself. Let her drag me.

"Where are you taking her?" Mara says, holding the bars in a vise grip. "What are you doing?" She is as frantic as I am, shaking her cage, her gaze darting around and around—but always returning to me. And I keep holding on when it lands, a warmth and courage swelling each time the gray settles on me.

I'm as eager for that feeling to die as I am for the soldiers themselves to die, but I'm helpless against either.

"Mal wants a word with you," Tara says in her velvety voice, holding one of my arms.

"If you hurt her—" Mara says.

"Quiet, Tick, or I'll cut out your tongue." Tara flips a combat knife deftly between her fingers.

Two can play at this game, even in cuffs.

Don't think.

I dig in my heels, slow us until Tara catches up, and lunge, catching her earlobe between my teeth.

Don't think. Don't think—

I bite down, hard, and jerk my head back. Her lobe comes clean off, hot blood splattering my face, and I spit the glob of skin and blood onto the floor. Lily wrenches me back, slams me against the wall—I must look mad, laughing through a scarlet grin as Tara screeches, a hand coming up to her ear like she's going to find it whole again.

"Get her the hell out of here," Lily barks. "Tara, get to Fatimah's. Let her sew up what's left of that ear."

Tara, pushing to her feet, starts in on me instead, but her boyfriend stops her. He has at least a hundred pounds on her and pulls her away like it's nothing at all.

"I promise you, Rory Blake, next time I see you—" Tara says.

"Looking forward to it," I interrupt. The man has her through the door before she can respond; her infuriated shriek makes the whole thing worth it.

That, and the look on Mara's face. It's a brief glance, and I'm being dragged away by Lily, but I see it—pride.

31

MARA

"Emir," I say. Emir, in his cage, is wholly uninterested in me now that Rory isn't at my side. He isn't Emir right now. He's the Tick.

Dolly, too. She curls against the side of her cage and shivers every few seconds. The bright, fierce girl I met has been stashed away by the Tick.

Despair rolls around on my dry tongue, making a long-gone gag reflex pulse like a phantom pain. If I want to keep Rory alive, I'll have to kill them. All of them.

"Emir," I say, louder.

Footsteps down the hall stop my pointless endeavor. The door swings open, and I go rigid, preparing for the inevitable enemy to walk in. It is an enemy, but it is my sister, too.

Carter. Leaning heavily on a crutch, one arm tightly wrapped in gauze and tucked to her side in a sling. Her face is dotted with bruises, but her emerald eyes are fierce and flaming.

The click of the door sliding into place sparks adrenaline up and down my spine. I'm a caged animal with a poacher stalking my enclosure.

Carter doesn't speak as she slowly crosses the room, pulling a plastic folding chair from its spot in the corner. It whines as it trails across the floor, rousing the Ticks around me, but they could be flies for all Carter cares. She props the chair up three feet from my cage, lowers into it, sets the crutch on the floor at her feet. For a long, long time, she doesn't say anything or look at me.

The Tick and I are on mutual footing about the anxiety swirling through my veins—human nerves and predatory awareness all scrambled together. I gnaw on the insides of my mouth until I taste bitter blood.

"Are you here to kill me?" I ask.

She lets out a mirthless laugh.

"Still don't have the guts?"

She scoffs and leans back, the veins in her neck straining, her gaze skating over me and away. "I didn't come here to argue."

"What did you come for, then?"

"I wanted to look you in the eyes. One last time. I wanted to hear you say it."

"Say . . ."

"Say it's your fault."

"What?"

"You know what." Spit flies from her mouth and lands inches from my cage.

"Fine. That's what you want?" I throw my hands up. "I killed our parents. I got bitten, and I was too late, and I killed them. I did it. I wish I hadn't, and I wish I could change it, but I can't. And I'm sorry. And there's nothing I can ever say to make anyone understand how much I—"

A voice batters against my skull, but it isn't the Tick's—it's Rory's. *Weak doesn't survive the Pit.*

Weak won't survive my sister, or whoever she's become.

"It isn't about me, though. You're not angry that I died, Carter."

"No?" she seethes.

I shake my head. "You're angry you couldn't stop it and angry about everything that came after," I say. This hardened, carved thing in front of me wants my head on a pike, but beneath it all, she's the

Carter who let me crawl into her bed when I had nightmares, the one who belted off-key lyrics in her beat-up car, the one who assured me it was okay to like boys and girls, who punched the boy down the street that said otherwise.

"You blame me because it's easier than facing what you couldn't do," I say.

I have to call her name three times before she sighs, turns her gaze to me, really looks at me for the first time in years. She flinches as if she'd forgotten what I look like. I forget sometimes, too.

"I didn't know I'd been bitten. Whatever you think of me now, you know the Mara that went on that run with you that night. You know I'd *never* have stepped foot in that house if I knew."

"How could you not know?" she asks. Her jaw ticks, and I wonder absently whether she still wears her night guard; she used to grind her teeth to dust. "The living dead bite you on the goddamn arm, and you miss it?"

We won't miss when we go for your throat, the Tick croons.

Quiet.

"You were there," I say, leaning forward, legs tucked under me. "We were swarmed. Barely made it out of that place running, dodging hordes on the way back. I . . . I missed it. That's the truth. It's horrible, but that's what it is. I tried to get out in time, but we had everything boarded up, and I—"

"I know what happened," Carter says.

"And I know that you came back," I say. "Rory told me."

Her lip curls. "Of course she did."

"Look at me, Carter." I have no expectations and am shocked when she listens. If she's right and this is the last chance I have to talk to her, the old Mara has things she never got to say. "I forgive you."

She recoils like I've reached across the room to slap her, shaking her head. The chair whines as it shifts back, scraping the floor, but Carter doesn't stand and storm out the way I expect.

"What the hell would you have to forgive me for?"

"I'm still alive—"

"You're not alive—"

I toss her a sinister stare and am both disgusted and thrilled when she stops. "I'm still alive, and you blame yourself for not killing me when you had the chance, but you were a kid, too, Carter-pillar." An ancient nickname, dredged from the weathered ruins of childhood memories, but it strikes her where I want it to. I watch her defenses shudder down momentarily, and she is the girl I remember—the sister I loved so much.

Just as fast, she stiffens and clears her throat, once again the blank-slate soldier she's beaten herself into. Not my Carter.

"We stopped being kids the day everything fell apart," she says, and pushes to her feet.

"Wait—"

"We're done, Mara." My name is a throbbing, thorny thing in her mouth, but at least she's using it.

"What are they doing to Rory?" I ask. Carter pauses, and I risk another question. "Are they hurting her?"

Her brow furrows, then releases. "She'll be fine. Mal has questions. Sam disappeared two days ago, right after you two. He wants to see what she knows."

The Island isn't big enough to disappear on—I've been here long enough to know that. Which means she's not on the Island.

She left. Sam abandoned her family.

"You seriously care what happens to her?" Carter asks, staring at me.

I frown, nod. It feels like a test, and I doubt there's a right answer.

A grimace strains her face for a heartbeat—one of my own, so longer than a normal one, I think. She shakes her head, limps to the door. With a hand on the knob, she looks over her shoulder.

"Goodbye, Mara," she says. My broken eyes prick but fail to draw tears. The finality of it is a battering ram to my rib cage.

"Mal burned the boats," I say, and to my surprise, she listens.

She arches a brow. "Is there a question in there somewhere?"

"You know this is wrong," I say. "Mal was behind the attack at the school, and you know it. You can do something. Stop him."

Carter looks at me for a long moment. Eventually, she shakes her head and slips through the door, leaving me truly alone with the Tick. I am too tired to fight against it any longer.

32

RORY

I'm slammed into a folding chair in front of a table in a small room. A caged light bulb flickers above my head—the high school's generator must have enough juice to turn the lights on periodically. Convenient; it powers the bright, heavy lights on the pool deck.

Lily leaves once my cuffs have been secured to the leg of the heavy table, and I've counted to fifty at least four times when the door opens again. In march Mal, Lily, and Tara's boyfriend. Like a scene out of an old crime show.

"How's Tara doing?" I ask, faking calm like it will somehow make me feel it.

Mal waves me off like a gnat, boots squeaking as he comes around the table and leans into the metal tabletop. His hulking chest is a foot from my face. Perfect place to plunge a blade, if I had one.

"No earrings for her birthday, I'm guessing?" I ask the boyfriend. He lunges half a step before he is intercepted by Lily, who effortlessly pushes him through the door.

"If you know what's good for you," she hisses at him, "you'll stay out here."

Satisfaction momentarily warms my frigid and aching joints as the door swings shut in his face, but a hand catches my chin, thick fingers wrenching my head to the side. Mal's eyes are black and poisonous.

"That mouth of yours . . ." He makes a *tsk* sound. "Going to get you in trouble."

"Careful," I say, and I know my teeth are stained with blood when I flash them. "Get too close and you might lose something."

The glint of gratification in his eyes kills my bravado. I have no way to protect myself and no time to prepare before his fist slams into my chest, scattering my thoughts like a bag of marbles.

"Like I said." He flexes his fingers. I hope they sting—actually, I hope someone rips them off one by one and forces them down his throat.

I take a shuddering breath. "What do you want?" *Keep your big mouth shut,* I remind myself, but I'm having trouble remembering why poking the bear is such a bad thing.

Lily comes to stand across the room, leaning against the wall beyond the table—a better vantage point for what is quickly becoming an interrogation.

"Tell me." Mal sits back, towering over me. "Where has your mother run off to?"

The words make a sentence, but it isn't one I understand. I look to Lily and back to Mal as if I'll find the explanation in one of their faces, but they are slabs of metal.

If they won't reveal anything, I won't, either. Even if I know nothing. Even if hearing Mal's words cracks open something inside me.

Sam's gone.

I cock my head, frowning. "Sam's gone?"

Lily huffs a laugh. She steps to the table, leans into it. Her disdain for me is as palpable as Mal's and Tara's, and while I understand theirs, I'm not sure what I did to earn hers. To be fair, though, I've earned the reputation of always aiming for maximum annoyance.

"Disappeared the same night you did," Mal says with a sniff. His scowl makes him uglier than usual. Or maybe his personality does that for him. "Quite a coincidence."

Disappeared. Wheels are turning and blowing smoke in my head, but it is easy to keep it confined. I was good at that before all this.

Your mother, he said, not *mother and father,* no mention of Raisa and Noah. Which means they are likely still at home, if not under lock and key.

Sam is gone. I thought I'd run out of anger fighting with Mara, but it floods back into my veins, and I am furious at my mom for leaving when I need her most. For not being here to make me brave, whether or not I really feel it.

She abandoned us. After two years of trailing behind us like our own pet ghost, she's finally decided to cut and run. Bile burns the back of my throat.

Sam is gone, running for the hills. Tears burn my eyes, and I stamp them back, refusing to let any of these people see me cry. Refusing to cry for Sam, period.

A finger snaps in my face, making me jump. Mal's pointed glare pulls me back to the present—as horrifying as my train of thought.

"The same night you and your little monster left," he presses. "See how this is all coming up with an arrow pointed at your head?"

"I have no idea what you're talking about," I say, and it's the truth, but it doesn't matter.

"Don't lie to me."

"I don't know where she went. I didn't know she was gone." I almost refrain from cracking open the wasp's nest. "And even if I did, I'd die before I told you—"

Another punch rams into me, and this one pulls stars into my vision. Something in my chest gives a nauseating *crack*, and I gasp, leaning forward, heaving for breath.

"Tell me where she is," Mal says, grabbing my hair with his fist and jerking my head back up.

The lacerating pressure on my lungs slices through whatever strength I have left. A broken rib, maybe two. A death sentence in the Pit, where I already have my leg weighing me down.

"I d-don't—" I suck in air like it's—well, *air*. "I don't know."

And it's true. I don't have the slightest idea where Sam would go. What hole she'd slink into to hide.

"Three people don't flee into the night, on the same night, for no reason. And they don't all make that decision on their own," he says.

I risk a glance at Lily, not that there's any help to be found from the stone-faced girl three feet away.

"Make this easy for yourself, Blake," Mal spits. "Tell me where Samantha is and you won't step foot in that Pit. You'll be released into Isaac's custody, and once Samantha is located, you and your family will be allowed to leave the Island and resettle."

"And Mara?"

"The Tick isn't part of this."

A laugh bubbles out of my ruined chest. "That's your deal? Really? And how exactly will we leave the Island, *Mallory*? You burned all the boats." More pieces slip into place as I talk, like all the hits have knocked the truths I've ignored for far too long into the light. "You cut us off. That thing in the station. It's a frequency jammer, isn't it? That's why our walkies never work on the mainland."

He bristles. Imagining him with steam pulsing out of his ears makes me want to smile.

"You are no better than I am. *You are nothing*, Aurora Blake." He leans closer. "And I did not burn *all* of the boats."

I throw up every wall I have in defense of the cruelty, but it slips past, shreds pieces of me, because he's right. He's right, and I hate him for it, and I hate me for it more.

His loathsome eyes pin me in place, and in his irises, I see myself reflected back. I see him, too. The second spans an eternity, a heartbeat pulled by a thread, and I remember every piece of information about Mallory Gordon I've tucked away.

"It was me, you know," I say. "At the school, I was the one who killed her. Juliette. I killed your daughter, and I didn't blink." A grin, merciless and bloody, pulls on my lips. "Do you think there was anything left of her in there? Think she felt it when the blade pierced her brain?"

The first hit has me choking on my tongue, and with the next, I am too dazed and blinded by pain to feel shame for the cry that slips out of me. He lands two more punches—one more to the chest that almost rips me from consciousness, and one to the jaw, splitting my lip open—before Lily tears him off me.

"I need help here, now!"

"It's your fault," I scream, not caring how hysterical I look; I want everyone on the block to hear. "You're the reason those kids are dead. You kept a Tick—"

Mal's fingers close around my throat, cutting off my words. The reluctant watchman finally makes it in, pulling Mal and his iron grip away from me. I collapse, gasping for breath, my hands tugging uselessly against their binds.

Mal thrashes in the soldier's grip, rage centered on me; my mad grin doesn't help the situation.

The soldier wrangles Mal into the hallway, but when he's gone, the racing of my heart doesn't stop, and the pit in my belly doesn't fade.

Watching Mal snap should be like opening birthday presents. Not like looking into a mirror.

●

The pain in my throat and chest and the collective surrender of my leg force Lily and the soldier to half carry me back to the cages. The relief those horrendous dog cages bring might shame me another time, but one of them holds Mara.

Lily shoves me through the cage door, igniting the stabbing in my ribs, and I can't hold back a cry.

Neither Lily nor Mara seems to notice. The first is too busy unlocking my cuffs, slamming the door, and securing the lock. The latter is slumped against the corner of the crate, head drooping into her shoulder. A shudder rolls through her, and the fluorescent light casts a sickly sheen over her skin.

Lily lingers again as Mal's other soldier leaves. She dips a hand into one of her pockets. Her lips pull into a thin line as she holds out a fist. I cock a brow, going for arrogant rather than confused.

"Take it."

With a frown, I lift a hand, and Lily drops three small pills into it. Tiny and red, like ladybugs with no spots.

"Tell anyone I gave you this, I'll kill you," she says. Her cheeks flush. She doesn't voice the unspoken: that soon, I really will be dead.

With a sigh, Lily is gone, too, and I'm too shocked and dizzy with pain to thank her before she goes. I don't bother considering what she's given me, tossing the pills into my mouth and swallowing them dry. Pain meds if I'm lucky. Poison if I'm not. Though poison might be better than the Pit.

Two empty stares track my slow movements as I try to get comfortable—impossible, but I'm a creature of habit, even if that habit is *fucking* pointless—but the Ticks, too, have realized how screwed we are. That, or they know at least one of them will get a shot at me when the sun sets.

A sob curdles in my throat, making a strangled sound I'm grateful everyone else in the room is too incoherent to judge me for. Tears rake rivers down my cheeks. Crying is a thousand blades to my chest, but I can't stop. I can't make this horrible, suffocating feeling go away.

Mara and I are going to die. Raisa and Noah are going to lose half their family. Me and Mara to the Pit, and Sam to her own cowardice.

After all of this, all of the fighting, I'm going to die. I hadn't realized how desperately I wanted a future until now, watching it slip through my fingers. Another sob pushes out of me. I slam my fist into the metal bars without thinking, hissing as my knuckles split open and pain ignites over my skin.

Beside me, the trembling form that half resembles Mara shifts. I know her gaze is on me before I meet it. For an agonizing, breathless second, there is nothing in her pewter eyes. Mara Knight is nowhere to be found, and this time, she might be too far to reach. Her eyes slide shut.

"*Mara*," I say.

I reach my bloody hand up and wrap it around one of the bars, tipping my forehead against it. If she wanted, Mara could snap the tops of my fingers clean off. She doesn't. Her pale hand rises, and her fingers curl around mine. Her forehead finds the bar, two inches away.

Her eyes meet mine, and *nothing* has traded itself in for an overpowering, excruciating *everything*.

33

MARA

Time and I slip back into place as I clutch Rory's warm fingers against the cold sting of metal. She could have been gone an hour or a year and I wouldn't know, but she's back now. Bruised and bleeding and wincing, but gripping my hand, too. Her lip is swollen, busted open, and I watch a drop of blood bloom and trickle onto her chin.

I pull my head from the bars but don't shift away, and neither does she.

"There's blood in your mouth," I mumble, and chide myself for it. As if she needs a reminder of what I've brought upon her.

The right side of her mouth lifts. "Yours, too."

"What happened?" I push farther up, putting us at eye level. "Mal . . . Did he—"

"That doesn't matter," she says, gentle. It's so unlike her yet so intoxicating, and if she is lulling me into a trap, I'm walking with eyes wide open. "Just leave it."

"Are you hurt?"

"I said leave it," she says, colder, more like the girl I know.

"Haven't we done this already?" I ask, more tired than instigative. "Find another punching bag, Rory. See how long they put up with it."

She pauses. It sounds curious when she says, "Why have you?"

Frustration surges like a wave, but I tug it back. If I'm dying tonight,

I won't spend the last hours of my life arguing with Rory Blake. Being with her is luck enough.

The words I have cradled close for so long find their way forward, as if they've been waiting, as if they knew we were headed here.

"Because I love you, you absolute fool," I say.

And for the first time in our lives, I manage to render Rory Blake speechless. If cameras were still around, I'd take a photo. All rapid blinks and parted lips and bulging eyes, like I've spoken another language.

"What?" she breathes.

All of a sudden, I can't remember the paralyzing fear that nailed my feet to the floor and kept my mouth shut. So many years I wasted, and now time is up, and the list of things I never said to Rory is miles long.

"I love you. I loved you when we were ten, and twelve, and fifteen, and I love you now. And if I die tonight, I need you to know that I don't regret any of this."

"Don't say that—" she stammers, and I'm not sure which part she's referring to, but I don't care. I don't care that she can't, could never, love me back. I just care that she knows I do, always did, before it's too late.

"It's the truth."

Flecks of gold in her eyes I've never noticed catch the dim lights, like a sunrise poking through the dark night. Anyone who says brown eyes aren't beautiful has clearly never seen Rory Blake's. I reach for her through the bars before my brain can warn me not to and brush her perfect mouth with my treacherous fingers.

These fingers have broken more than they could ever try and repair, but she's letting them stay. Sharp, quick, heated breaths pulse against my hand, and adrenaline smells sour in the air.

The urge to turn fingers to talons, to peel those lovely lips off her teeth, is a stinging splash to the face. I pull my fingers back, but

Rory's hand flies up, and her fingers close around my wrist, and I am stuck, drowning in a deep brown sea.

"Don't let it take me," I whisper.

She decides something then, and if I weren't fighting to stay balanced, I might know what it is.

"Never," she says.

A sigh tumbles out of me, and I sink into the bars, as close to her as I can reach.

"I wish it was . . ." I stop, lose the words, but Rory effortlessly picks them back up. *Better, different*, fill in the blanks; the sentiment is the same.

"I know," she says. "I do, too."

Her breathing is labored, her eyes glassy. I can smell her pain in the air, tangy and buzzing like electricity. A dam as close to breaking as I am. A tremor rolls through me, loosening my grip on sanity, but again, Rory's voice hoists my head above water.

"I lied," she says. "I don't wish you were dead. And that's not even the worst part." Her eyes fall shut. "I don't even wish you were still alive. When you walked in the door that day, I only cared that you were here. And I hated you for it as much as I hated myself."

"Somehow, I doubt that," I say.

Fierce brown eyes snap open. Her fingers take my chin, pull it toward the bar, trap me in her gaze.

"Look at me," she says. "Tell me if I'm lying." Her nostrils flare, a muscle twitching in her jaw. Warm breath grazes my cheeks. "I've tried so hard to hate you, but I don't. I *can't*. I love you, and I always have." Her grip softens, calloused fingertips caressing my scarred skin. "You're my fucking heart, Mara Knight."

Heart cracks in her mouth, and the rapid thudding of my physical heart flushes me with euphoria. I have never felt closer to life. I could swear the heat in my veins is blood, moving as it should. Or maybe it's her.

"You mean you don't hate me even a little bit?" I ask.

Her smile doesn't belong here in this rusted room, but it is dazzling still.

"Obviously a little bit," she says.

Her hand falls, but she doesn't pull it back through the bars. Fingers twine into mine, and she releases a heavy breath. The silence lasts a second before the numbness edges its way over my ears.

Rory tenses beside me like she's sensed the shift.

"It's almost over, isn't it?" she asks simply, like she's asking whether I want syrup on my pancakes.

"I think so."

"What does it . . ." She pauses. "Does it hurt?"

I give a hazy smile. "Do you remember that last Thanksgiving when Carter let us have a few of her wine coolers? She said as long as we didn't get her in trouble . . ."

"Not our finest moment."

"We broke into the pool down the street, fell asleep in the lawn chairs, got caught by some housewife the next morning. That next day, we laid in the backyard, miserable, drinking water straight from the hose."

"I thought my head was going to explode," Rory agrees. "You puked on my favorite sneakers."

"Those weren't your favorites." I shake my head. "You only said that *because* I puked on them."

"Oh? And what were my favorites?"

"Those checkerboard Vans," I say. I can see them still, the faded canvas patterned with pale green lines, the rubber soles flecked with dirt. My name was Sharpied across the back heel, as hers marked the toe of my Converse. "You wore 'em until the bottoms fell out, and then taped them back together."

It seems ridiculous now, that we didn't see it. More ridiculous that we're a hair away from too late, too close to do us any good. I must be smiling, not at all appropriate for the circumstance, because Rory stills, drags her tongue across her bloody lip.

"You really remember that," she says.

A shrug is all I give her, like answering that is somehow more exposing than anything else I've said. That I didn't just love her—I held on to her.

Hunger rumbles up my chest.

"Anyway, it feels like that, almost. And I don't even mind the pounding in my skull or the empty—" I stop. It feels like ages since my tongue went rogue on me, and I struggle to form the words. "I don't care that it hurts. It's the voices . . . this *thing*, sitting behind me, telling me what to do, and it doesn't want me to go for a midnight swim or cheat on a test. It wants me to—" I pause, swallowing the copper on my tongue. "It just wants me."

Rory's head jerks, and the ferocity that was born long before the Tick flares in her eyes.

"It can't have you," she says. Her ring finger catches the fraying strings of the bracelet on my wrist. "You're mine." A frown ghosts her lips. "You know, *until.*"

And with a blink, it is Rory's turn to crumble, mine to be strong, and we switch without thought. The pressure or the reality or both put her in a trance, and she drifts, expressionless. "We're going to die tonight."

"I don't believe that."

"Well, it's true. My ribs are broken, my leg is killing me, and I probably have a concussion. You're barely staying human." There is no venom to it, not like all the other times, but a sadness, a resignation. "You were right. We're out of moves."

"I said *no.*"

Her smile is mournful, and her eyes are sadder than I've seen them. "Come on, Mara. We finally stop fighting, and you want to start again?"

"I can't let you die."

"And you can't do anything to stop it," she says. I've never heard her talk this way. "I didn't get to say goodbye before. I'm not making that mistake again."

Dread unfurls spiky talons, shredding through my armor, and I know she's right about one thing. Someone is dying tonight, but not her. Anyone, everyone in that Pit, but not her.

"We're not dead yet," I say. She hums a disapproving tone but closes her eyes. "And who knows. Maybe we'll get lucky."

The retort I anticipate doesn't come. She's following her own rules.

"Maybe," she says.

And despite the underlying sarcasm, there is a trace of something more, of wanting and not being able to admit we do. Like acknowledging that we want things to get better will make it worse when they don't.

There is no hope left in this world, but we shuffle toward it anyway, believing someday maybe our fingers will close around it. Maybe they won't. Maybe hope is long gone, erased by the monsters we made and became. We're still searching for it, though. Human and monster alike.

●

My grip on everything but Rory's hand slips and slides as time creeps by, her voice my tether to this reality. Through the tinted windows, the sun has set, and the generator has kicked into gear, the lights brightening above us. I can barely keep my eyes open.

I'm getting worse. By the time the sun rises, I'll be three days without a dose. There may be nothing left for Rory to hold on to anymore.

If I had a choice, I'd choose to be right here, leaning against Rory through the bars, listening to her tell story after story. Each time the

Tick tries to push forward, I reopen the wound inside my mouth, letting the bitter, acidic taste of my own mutated blood numb the craving. With all her storytelling, Rory's split lip stays bloody, and I do my best not to stare.

"—Carter nearly took my head off when she saw the stain, but you told her—" Rory's dazed tale slams to a stop.

The door whines open, six pairs of boots smacking the ground as Mal enters with Lily and four other soldiers. Not a single set of eyes drifts to us, but Mal's presence answers the unspoken question: We are out of time.

"Showtime," Rory says, easing back into the arrogant rebel she's made them—made me—believe she is.

"Headliners," Mal says. "The great Rory Blake versus seven unmedicated Ticks. Shouldn't be an empty seat in the house."

Seven on one. I have no clue whether I can keep six starving Ticks off her, and less of a clue what to do when it's the two of us standing. My hope shrinks but doesn't evaporate. It won't, can't, until Rory stops breathing.

Soldiers come for my crate first, and a set of metal cuffs dangle from one's hand. In a way, putting all my focus into not lunging for throats as the cage door swings open makes not thinking easy. I understand Rory then, and her reluctance to give in to the future. It is easier like this. Not thinking beyond your next breath.

Rory's emergence from her crate, her struggle not to be cuffed, douses my reliance on instinct—trades it in for a different kind, maybe. Rory and I, held back by two soldiers apiece, lunge for each other and somehow manage to pull from our captors' bonds.

Every weapon in the room finds a hand, but neither Rory nor I stop, not until we're a foot apart.

"Hold it!" Mal barks, raising a hand to stall the others. As shocked as I am, I don't waste the sliver of time we've miraculously been given.

The soldiers in the room fade into nothing. It's only her, brown eyes flecked with black and gold, expression fierce, bravery unfaltering. My hands, bound at my front, catch Rory by the shirt and draw her to me.

There is no gentleness, no caution in this kiss—there is consumption, desperation, the knowledge of the sand spilling from the clock. My tongue sweeps her russet-stained lips, her blood sparking every nerve ending, and I wish I had free hands for a million different reasons, all of them bad, half of them monstrous. The delicious, heady thrum of copper in my mouth turns biting as the slow drawl of my blood mixes with it.

"Rory," I say, and the name melts like butter into my breath. A smile halts her mouth on mine for a heartbeat.

Kissing her is coming home and coming apart all at once, and the sting as she is wrenched back by a uniform is like a swarm of angry bees.

This time, only she pushes forward, reaches me once more, tips her forehead against my temple.

"You're Mara Knight," she says. "Don't you dare forget it."

Hands catch her by the elbows, dragging her to the door, into the hall, and I am pulled after her.

Like I wouldn't have followed Rory Blake into hell on my own.

34

RORY

Death is different when you know it's coming. It isn't death anymore, but a game, and you get so tired of playing you don't care who wins.

It's pretty damn clear how this game will end, if it wasn't already. I'm delusional with pain, Mara is craving a brain burrito, and neither of us is ready for what we're walking into.

The stabbing pain in my leg pulses to the rapid beat of my heart, and every breath pushes the knife deeper into my lungs, but somehow I'm better off than Mara. *Mara.* I'm on a death march, and all I can think about is her and the fierce, intentioned press of her mouth to mine. My lips still taste like—

I ram my heels into the concrete, stalling Lily and my other captor's progress long enough for Mara to catch up. She's tugged back and away fast, but I see what I need to.

Blood so dark it's almost black, swirled with scarlet, blurred across her mouth. And staining my own. The wound in my lip throbs, and realization hits me like a bird shot to the leg.

I lost everyone I ever knew to the Ticks.

Blood. Saliva.

Exactly what of Mara's I have in my mouth and in my wound. The ringing in my ears grows deafening. A strangled, mirthless laugh tears out of me, ripping through my tender ribs and putting tears in my eyes, but I don't care. I was already going to die tonight. It's fitting, and ridiculously ironic, that it may be Mara who pushes me into the grave. Or, I guess, to the edge of one.

Kissing Mara Knight may prove to be deadlier than I thought.

"Pull your shit together, Blake," Lily barks in my ear, lugging me forward. I crane my head, seeking out Mara, and catch her eyes.

It's her, and then she's gone. Gone like all the rest. Like Aria and Mara's parents and everyone else who will never come back.

"Your name is Mara. Mara Josephine Knight," I say, words booming down the hall. "You were born eight months before me. Your parents were Michael and Josephine. She was named after your great-grandmother—it's where you got your middle name."

I say everything but the words *Come back to me.*

"Is this for my biography?" a hoarse voice murmurs behind me.

A lump forms in my throat. "Depends. You still here?" It is a marvel my tone is steady.

"I'm here," Mara says, but the unstated hangs over us both. *For now.*

She is slipping more and more with each step, and the closer we get to the doors leading to the pool deck, the more I realize how different this fight will look depending on which part of her is driving the car.

35

MARA

Hunger is not a feeling. It is a creature, unfolding like liquid in a vase, filling me up and encompassing all my empty spaces. The overwhelming stench of life in this small hallway is like being sat at a buffet table and not allowed to lift a fork.

Seven hearts. Seven names. Seven lives, blooming and bustling around my head like static turned all the way up. The quiet is nowhere to be found.

At my sides, two men push me forth. One soldier to my back. Another at the head of the pack. Two on either side of the girl with the bloodstained blond hair—hers is the name I make an effort to find.

A nail scrapes along my arm, and I snap, narrowly avoiding the man's jugular as I'm wrenched back, slammed into the wall.

"I told you we needed more hands on the feral ones."

A rifle butt slams into my spine, but my arms are pinned, my motions restricted. I'm walking. Walking is what matters. Biding the seconds until my leash is loose enough to reach someone's throat is what matters—

"Don't hurt her," the girl with the fierce eyes snarls, sending me a glance over her shoulder.

No—she is what matters. *Her.*

"You're going to burn for this, you cowardly pieces of—" she says.

The man at the front of the group strides to the girl and knocks her jaw back with the force of his punch.

Her pain is sharp. It stabs at something far away, brings flickering images too blurry to make out.

You're mine, says the voice, but it is different. Softer. Hers. And outside my head, she is hurt.

I wrench out of one pair of hands, and three weapons rise before I've taken a step.

The girl spits a gob of blood onto the floor, shakes her head, says, "Don't," and when I try to move, my feet don't respond. Like they know the girl better than they know me.

"I'm about done with this guard-dog bullshit—" someone says. I growl.

"Mara, don't," the girl huffs, leaning heavily into her captors' arms. I can't look away from her. Can't see around her.

"It's dorky," she grumbles, a newly installed retainer giving her a slight lisp. "It means, like, dawn. What's so exciting about a new day?"

"Better than mine," I say. "Mara is a goddess of death."

"Are you kidding? It's cool as hell."

I shake my head. "Besides, that's not the only thing Aurora means."

"Oh? And what else does it mean?"

"It means resurrection."

"Mara," she says, and I am. The Tick's control falters, and I stamp it beneath my feet.

Rory's brow furrows as she registers the change that no one else notices. One of many worry lines fades, and she gives me a tiny nod.

"There you are," she says, softening for a breath. Her next words are for Mal, and hard as steel. "You should be careful, Mal. The dog bites." Her teeth are still stained scarlet from Tara's blood, along with her own. "So do I."

At my side, one of the men stiffens.

"Keep moving," Mal says, continuing down the hall. The rapidly approaching door turns my senses into overdrive. The intensity of it makes clinging to consciousness harder than it already is, but the Tick knows what's coming as well as I do.

In front of me, Rory puts up a solid front, but she's favoring her left leg more than usual and winces with each step on the right. Her breath is loud and strained, and bruising has already begun forming over her face.

We're screwed floats into my head, and for once, the voice is my own. It is in no way reassuring.

36

RORY

Before it became a place for despondent survivors to work out pent-up energy on Ticks or pay off crimes, the Pit was an Olympic-sized pool for young athletes and the occasional housewife who paid to swim laps. Over a hundred and fifty feet long, ten feet deep all across, it was a great place to hold practices. It's a better place to hold death matches.

Rickety fencing edges the pool, tall enough to lean into and flecked with grime no one bothered to wash away. Someone took all the bleachers from inside the gym, stacked them alongside those wrapping the pool, and doubled its capacity.

I've only ever seen fifty people in the metal stands. There are over a hundred tonight. All of them seeking revenge for the attack at the school. The attack Mal caused. If I didn't know I'd get shot again before I could finish a sentence, I'd scream the truth until my throat bled.

The chatter reaches a thunderous roar as we step into the night sky. I try to scan the faces, find one I recognize, but the bright stadium lights hanging over the pool shine mercilessly on us.

Mara and I both stumble, but we're dragged forward like potato sacks. Mal waits near the ledge. The yelling is so loud I can't hear the pounding of my heart, but it threatens to shove through my throbbing ribs. If I'd eaten recently, I would puke.

Lily and the soldier manage to maneuver me to the edge, where Mal has positioned the thick metal ladder in place. He's far too pleased to have me in his hands, gripping my shoulders so tight I have to bite my tongue to keep from snapping at him the way Mara did in the hall. And I don't even have a parasite in my head to excuse it.

"It isn't too late, Aurora," he says. "You know how to make this stop. Where is Samantha?"

I want to tell him that she's gone, screwed off to who knows where, but I refuse to give him that.

"You'll let me go?"

"You have my word."

An exaggerated sigh spills out of me. "Fine. I'll tell you."

His brows lift, eyes incredulous. It almost makes dying here worth it.

"Up my ass, around the corner, and to the—"

Mal wrenches me around, jams the key into my cuffs, releases them. He yanks me close and whispers in my ear, "This is for my daughter. For *Juliette*."

Then he shoves me forward. I barely keep from tumbling over the edge, landing hard on my hands and knees with my fingers curled around the ledge. I suck in a breath, refusing to give these people the satisfaction of seeing me break.

Climbing the metal rungs, painful on a good day, feels like knowingly walking into a room on fire. And I just ran out of one of those.

Sharp pangs run up my calves as I land on the pool floor, and while I may have been annoyed at being dropped in first, I'm grateful for the moment to catch my breath. In minutes, the Ticks who have spent the day fantasizing about a Rory risotto will be here, and one hundred fifty feet may as well be zero.

A thud sounds behind me. Mara joins my side. Her eyes, gray and haunting, are clear.

She's still here. But not for long.

She sweeps the pool with a look—like the booming crowd above us doesn't matter, like they aren't placing bets on how long it'll take me to die. The walls are baby-blue tiles, half of them cracking like vines that snake their way up to the surface. A long-ruined floor is stained with browns and reds and colors with origins I don't let myself think about. Not thinking is how I survived the first time.

At the opposite end of the Pit, a pile of rusted weapons waits for the gunfire that starts the round—that, or whenever a Tick is on the ground and realizes it has a free meal.

"Don't," I warn. "You go for a weapon before it starts and you're dead."

"Any more rules I should know?" she asks. Her pupils dilate and shrink, and the trembling of her limbs makes her clenched teeth chatter.

My hand curls into her tee, and she stills, her skin cool beneath my knuckles. Wholly Mara for a moment. The butterflies in my stomach give an untimely flutter, and I stamp them into submission.

"Gladiator rules," I say, swallowing the bile burning up my throat. "The weapons on the ground when the game starts are fair game. No help from the audience."

"And, you know, the whole fight-to-the-death thing," Mara says, eyes on the ladder.

God, I love her. It's like I opened floodgates when I spoke it aloud, and now the thought batters around my skull like a pinball machine.

"Gladiators didn't always fight to the death. Misconception."

She arches her brow. "Is now really the time to discuss the historical inaccuracies of gladiators?"

"You brought it up."

A smile ghosts her lips, but her gaze strays again, and she blinks, transforms. She's still Mara, but it's like the Tick is there, too. I guess even the virus knows we're at the end of the road.

When I hear the moans, I understand.

I don't think I'll ever forget that sound. A hollow, thin song that gets stuck in your head.

Instinct sends me back, Mara beside me, until we bump the wall on the opposite side. Seventy-five feet between us and the ladder, and it feels like an inch.

The first over the edge are a milky-skinned old man with vibrant purple veins and a pale yellow bucket hat sagging over one eye, and a middle-aged man missing one eye and most of his teeth.

Four more bodies tumble down as Bucket Hat and No Teeth begin struggling to their feet. Next to rise, Dolly and a gray girl who can't be much older than Carter with piercings through each brow. Not to be forgotten are Emir, who is certainly not Emir right now, and a woman Sam's age in a floral dress.

It takes all of three seconds for No Teeth to notice me. Another second for Mal to fire a shot.

Mara breezes past me in a blur, shoving Bucket Hat to the side as she goes. She beelines for the weapons across the Pit, and while I'm grateful Emir and Dolly are distracted enough by it to trail after her, it still leaves four starving, drooling Ticks.

Bucket Hat, to my relief, has a weak ankle, but I am not as fast as Mara. I won't make it to the weapons in time, and she won't make it back to me quick enough.

The Pit is empty on purpose—any advantage would be too much, I guess—but that doesn't mean I'm useless.

Think, Aurora, think.

Time staggers to a halt, my surroundings flying in all at once and organizing. The overwhelming calm I've missed settles like an old coat, and my fear goes silent beneath it.

The empty sheath for my sword was made crudely from collected parts—a welded metal cup, leather belts to strap around my leg, and thin steel pipes holding it together.

Clenching my teeth, I stretch down, grip two of the bars as tight as I can, and wrench them off. The shoddy sheath comes apart with the bars, belts falling to the ground.

The first Tick reaches me as I lift the bars, one gripped in each hand. I can't hear the pounding of my heart or the thundering roar of the crowd over the snarling and snapping as Piercings gnashes her chipped teeth inches from my face. One bar held up between us is the thing keeping me alive, but her strength is unmatched, and she quickly shoves me back, back, all the way into the wall.

My head smacks the tile, but I don't have the time to feel the pain, too busy keeping Piercings's teeth off my skin and trying to get the other bar up. A rough hand curls around my arm and yanks me sideways, the momentum pulling Piercings and me into a pile on the ground.

No Teeth swats for me from atop Piercings's back. Two pairs of empty gray eyes stare at me, snapping their jaws and screeching.

"Aurora!" Mara's voice, echoing through the din, slams my fear back into its cage.

A bar in both hands, and a Tick for each. I resist the urge to close my eyes. Take a breath. Bring both bars together like a mismatched clap and jam each into a skull.

Two bodies go limp atop me. The weight forces a strangled gasp out of my mouth, and I pull myself out from beneath them, retching bile onto the ground.

A moan brings me back a heartbeat from too late. Bucket Hat and Flowers, still progressing on me, the latter a few feet away. Across the pit, Mara jams weapons under her arms and lands a swift kick to Emir's chest before she darts my way.

At my feet, one of the flat bars from the sheath is in reach. Three leather belts rest curled in a heap a few feet away.

Nails graze my cheek as I lurch for the bar, the stinging pain throwing me off balance. Flowers, her dress splitting at the seams, grabs my wrist as my fingers close around the flat bar. I scramble back until I hit the wall.

Flowers stumbles after me, her hands outstretched like a zombie from an old Romero movie.

Using the wall behind me as support, I push to my feet, all my weight on my right leg, and wait for her to reach me, then swing the bar right into her temple. She drops like a sack, and I don't wait for confirmation that she's dead, bringing the bar down once, twice, until her skull cracks open like an egg.

If Bucket Hat didn't reach me at that moment, I'd keep hitting until I split the ground open beneath us.

Bucket Hat wrenches me to the side, hooking his claws into my shoulders. One of his wrinkled hands loops around my ponytail, and he tosses me into the wall. I throw my arms up uselessly over my head, and fire unfolds in my elbow as it collides with the tile. I slide down to the ground. Everything disappears but the ringing in my ears, the copper on my tongue, and the blaring lights above me.

I let the anguish stay for three seconds before I throttle it into submission. Pain is nothing but signals from the brain to the body and back. The Ticks are ignoring their signals, and I will ignore mine.

Back on the ground, I draw my right knee up and kick out when Bucket Hat reaches me. He stumbles back a yard and comes forward again. All I can do is hold him back, sweep the ground with my free hand, and wait for one side of the scale to tip.

A steel bat collides with the Tick's skull, sending a spray of black blood into my face. He staggers to the side, turns for Mara, and gets another crack to the head. This one puts him down and keeps him there.

Relief is a warm and heavy syrup in my veins as Mara ducks to hoist me up. Her gaze skates over my stinging cheek. I must be bleeding. She meets my eyes, gives me the tiniest, most untimely half smile, and hands me the gore-covered bat. Littering the ground at her feet are weapons: a pickaxe, a scythe, a hammer.

Her lips part to speak, but before she can, another gunshot splits through the air.

At the edge of the pit, where we were dropped in, Mal stands with a pistol pointed upward. The message is clear. Keep the show moving, or it ends now.

My own message is clear, too. A single finger to the sky.

Fingers tighten around my arm, dipping into broken skin, and I yelp, attention flying back to Mara. She stares blankly at her grip on my elbow. Her hand, painted in red, in shreds of my skin—like road rash, but instead of falling to the ground, I was chucked into it.

"Mara," I say, but it isn't Mara looking back at me. Her eyes are hollow pools of silver and black.

Her nostrils flare. Her head cocks as if she's listening. The girl who kissed me in the dark and kept an old bracelet is nowhere to be found, and I am alone, really alone.

Cold prickles up and down my spine, stretching out into my limbs. Something old and forgotten inside me screams *run*. I've heard that voice before.

"I'm sorry," I say, and step back, swinging the bat into Mara's knees. She hits the ground with an echoing thud, instantly rising again, snarling.

Don't let me go. She isn't all gone, not yet. She doesn't have to die, not yet.

A scarier thought flutters through my head, drenched in dread and panic. If she comes for me again, do I have the will to stop her?

The most dangerous thing in the Pit is not the remaining Ticks or Mara. The most dangerous thing is what I feel, and the fact that no one else in this drained pool feels at all.

A screech ripples through the air, and a light-haired figure flies past me—the one-armed girl, Dolly, Emir a few yards behind her.

The pickaxe is more practical, but if Mal wants a show, he'll get one. The scythe, rusted and probably dirtier than the inside of a Tick's mouth, is heavy and awkward in my hands.

When I swing it, I can't look at the teen girl it slices through. I don't need to know it's another red stain on a bulging ledger. Dolly crumples, a limp pile of limbs, and I jerk my head around, searching for Emir. Silence has fallen over the bleachers above, the onlookers holding their breath as the fight moves into its finale. If only I had that luxury.

Stars dance in my vision, and the glaring lights above and sweat dripping down my brow make it harder to see. My heart pumps steadily in my bleeding arm, like a song with a beat that gets faster as it goes on.

Sucking in gasp after gasp, willing my screaming body not to give in on me yet, I struggle to free the scythe from the girl's stomach. It refuses to give, but the other weapons are too far away, and Emir is—

Where the hell is Emir?

A heavy form barrels into me, sending me crashing into the ground. Emir scrabbles to pin me down, drool sliding down his cheeks. He grabs my cheeks as if he's going to kiss me and slams my head down.

Everything splinters, light splitting and twirling above me, snarling teeth moving in and out of focus. I am the feral creature now, writhing and fighting beneath him uselessly.

A set of pearly teeth catch the light and drop toward me. All the fight goes out of me, a cold numbness taking its place. And then, pressure below my collarbone, so much pressure I think my entire body will pop like a balloon, and my skin tears beneath Emir's teeth. It takes a long moment for me to realize the guttural, piercing sound is my own scream.

Years of running and fighting and bleeding and losing, and this is really, truly it. The end of the road.

Whether Emir kills me this second or not, I'm dead. If the bite were small, on my hands or feet, far from my heart, I'd have hours. With this one, I can't have more than twenty minutes. I may have already been on my way to turning since I kissed Mara.

All the pain I've been pushing aside slams back into me, and I can't think, can't hear, can't do anything. The weight, so heavy atop me, is turning me to ash and dust.

Goodbye, Mara.

37

MARA

The light, the noise, the heat of a hundred beating hearts and pumping veins. So much life you could drown in it.

I want the quiet, the numb, the constant, the cold. Not this overwhelming stench of life pulsating around me. There is nothing but noise and scent, all of it meaningless.

And then, an agonized scream. The girl, blond hair dyed with her blood, and one of the quiet ones like me, pressing her into the ground, rearing back with blood and skin in his mouth.

Her noise peters out for a blink, and it is not the relief it should be.

My feet carry me forward. Until the moment my hands land on the boy rather than the girl, it's her noise I plan on snuffing out.

You are mine, the darkness reassures.

A silken voice stirs the girl slumbering in my skin, embraces me in suffocating memories.

It can't have you, she says. The girl with the dark eyes and the fierce smile, the one I know even when I don't.

I rip the boy back. I think I know him, think I care about him, but he wants the girl. He lands beside the blond girl, and I launch onto him. He expects me and brings his hands up, dragging me sideways, sending us rolling across the floor. Sharp objects dig into my back, and *belt* flits into my head.

It means nothing until it does, and while I have a grasp on the word, I tug the leather strap from underneath me, loop it around the boy's neck, and *tug*. He keels over, deserting his attempts to claw my eyes out in favor of freeing himself, but the girl on the ground is dying, and this boy wants to kill her.

Death cannot have her. She is mine. And I am hers.

The boy and I go tumbling away, his nails digging into every inch of exposed skin he can find, but I don't release the belt. Tighter, tighter, tighter on the leather until something in his spine gives a great *snap*.

Even this doesn't stop him, not completely, the limbs he can still control thrashing. I catch him by the shoulders and smash my elbow into his nose. His balance falters, and his knees hit the floor.

His eyes are vacant when I slam my heel into his skull. It cracks wide open, the crunch of cranium like a pallet of wood splitting. Blood and bits of brain scatter across the stained floor, and the boy becomes nothing but another body on the ground.

Not the one that matters. Her ivory skin is splattered with red, her trembling hands slipping over the mess of her throat. She's covered in blood, in bruises. Tears trace tiny rivers down her face from eyes squeezed shut.

Pain, *hers*, stings my nostrils, and the sound of her life, skipping like a scratched record, is so loud, too loud.

It would be so easy to make it stop.

I kneel beside her, and big brown eyes peer into mine. She does not scream, or cry, or shake with fear. Her eyes are an endless ocean, and I am a boat caught in a hurricane, sinking into her.

Rory.

Words and letters flit around my head, none sticking but the ones that belongs to her.

I rip the sleeve off my shirt, balling it up and shoving Rory's bloody fingers out of the way, pressing the fabric into the wound. She stiffens, grits her teeth, catches my arm in a tight grip, but relents. Her hand falls atop mine, and I lift her other hand from the ground, positioning both on the fabric.

"Mara—" It tickles at something I don't want to remember—someone I can't be. One of her hands reaches for me, and I push it back down, along with the urge to bite her fingers off.

"Hold," I choke out, forcing her to keep pressure on the bite.

Part of me, the slowly growing part, reminds me of the pointlessness of such a move, but that same part is also desperate to keep her heart beating.

A gunshot ricochets six inches from my sneaker—from *Rory*—and I whirl, standing with a foot on either side of her, finding the man with the gun aimed our way.

"It's last man standing, Mara," Rory says. "One of us has to die."

Ice creeps into my chest, and an old sensation I don't have a name for tightens around my throat. Fingers curl around the hem of my tee, pulling me down, and I crouch over Rory, keeping one eye on the man above.

Delicious copper seeps into my nose, and a hand finds my cheek, drawing my gaze down.

"Do it," she says. "End it."

I look at you, and I see the end of the world.

That can't be the last thing she sees. It won't be.

My name is Mara Knight. And Rory Blake will not die by my hand or anyone else's.

"Nothing ever ends," I say, and straighten, lifting my eyes to Mal's at the ledge of the pit.

Me, Emir, the other Ticks at least have excuses for our hollow hearts.

Mal's hand shakes with anger as he aims the gun between my eyes. It's a long shot, but I have no doubt he'll make it.

"Mara, it's *over*. I'm bitten, it's over—" Her voice is raw and lilted.

"Quiet," I say, and to my shock, she listens.

A second later, I realize the true reason for Rory's silence. The reason Mal hasn't shot me yet.

Soldiers, their boots stomping along the deck, surround the pool and come to the far edge; across the Pit is Sam.

The cavalry has arrived. But it's too late.

38

RORY

She came back. Sam came back.

She stands across the Pit, flanked by Thalia O'Neill and at least one hundred soldiers scattered around them. They don't wait a beat before wrangling Mal's crew into cuffs, slamming them into the ground—half the people in the bleachers flee.

The other half, though, watch us.

"Aurora." Sam pushes through the gate and slips over the edge of the pool and into the body-littered arena. Her movement triggers the rest, and Thalia slides down after her, a dozen soldiers breaking from their positions. No one bothers with the ladder, too busy with the bomb under the spotlight.

Mara is a statue standing over me, half monster, half girl—her chest heaves, though I'm pretty sure she doesn't need to breathe. The addition of bodies to the Pit saps any trace of human from her, and every inch is a rigid, dangerous predator. The slender and beautiful fingers that traced across my skin have become talons.

Beautiful isn't the right word for the girl covered in blood. Mara isn't beautiful. She's devastating.

And I'm dying, to which I can put the blame for the sappy, ridiculous train of my thoughts.

I am not a scientist, or a high school graduate, but I know how it works once it's in you. The virus functions like any other disease, moving through the blood to the heart and up to the brain. Closer to the heart, faster to the brain.

Up on the deck, a soldier wearing the dark RPA fatigues is in a heated discussion with Mal. What I wouldn't give to hear her chew into him.

"Aurora!" Sam cries again, sprinting toward us, soldiers and Thalia on her heels. Mara's head snaps their way. They're still too far to hear the low, soft growl that rumbles from the back of her throat. It prickles fear deep in my gut, but there is another feeling, too, a safety.

I can't let you die, Mara said, and for a single second, I believe her.

Sam reaches us first, but before she comes within five feet, Mara lunges—a warning in the gnashing of teeth. Sam stops, and the soldiers gather behind her. At least a dozen tranquilizer guns train on Mara.

"Don't touch us," she growls. Sam's wide eyes flick to mine. I press the fabric harder against my neck, pushing up onto my elbows with a groan. I fumble a hand out to grab onto Mara's pants and tug. Her chin drops slowly, reluctantly.

Her gaze is focused as it skates across me, and when she looks at Sam, the threat in her stance has even me stamping down the urge to reach for a weapon. My heart hammers against broken ribs, like it's trying to bust through and scale the Pit walls. I'd go with it if I could.

Go back to the backyard between my and Mara's houses on the night before the end. I'd tell her all the things I waited too long to say. When Carter came outside to call her in, I would make her stay.

Meeting Sam's eyes, I give her a nod and a thin-lipped smile that is probably more grimace. She's not happy, but she nods back. She doesn't have to like it; she just can't stop it.

Fear is a pit of scorpions in my belly, snapping at my insides while the Tick pushes through my veins. I think I feel it spreading, a hot rush up to my head. Like a grenade without a pin attached to my sanity. Every hit I took during the fight lands all at once as the adrenaline sputters out.

"Mara," I say. She kneels begrudgingly beside me and uses one hand to push me to a seated position. My ribs scream in protest, and a groan catches behind my teeth.

Her hand stays on my back, and the other comes to replace my own on the soiled T-shirt. Dark brows furrow as she pulls it back, like she's making sure it's still there.

I almost have to look away when she meets my gaze, choking on the despair pooling in the gray. A sob lodges in my throat, and Mara's hand moves to my cheek. To her credit, she doesn't look at the blood once.

"It'll be alright," she says. "We'll get you Dyebucetin."

"Don't let me hurt anyone," I say, fingers climbing to the hem of her tank and twisting. I meant to say *Don't let me turn*, but it's like my tongue makes the choice for me. Or maybe the choice was already made, and I didn't know until now.

I don't want to die. I'm not done here.

"Look at me," she says, and I do. "I won't let you hurt anyone. And I won't let anyone hurt you." She glances back at the people all around us.

I thought the Ticks were the scariest thing left on this earth, but they aren't. We are. The Ticks didn't choose to forget their humanity, but we did.

I want to remember.

I swallow dryly, and my bruised throat throbs with my heartbeat.

"I should have been faster," she says softly. "I'm sorry."

"Don't be. I was probably done for the second you kissed me," I say, and I mean for it to be a joke, but Mara doesn't take it as one.

She stiffens and sits back, confused until a hand rises to her mouth. When her fingers come away stained in dark reddish-black blood, I think she might start crying.

"It's okay," I say. I lean toward her, trying to find the brilliant gray of her eyes in the blur.

Her brows pinch together, and I can tell she wants to argue with me. Instead, she slips her arms around me, and in a move so human I forget she isn't, she drops her head onto my shoulder.

"How long, do you think?" I ask. "You *are* the expert."

Her sad, low laugh is muffled against my shoulder. She lifts her head, sweeps a look around—no one's moved.

They're waiting for the inevitable. Whether I take the Dye or not, nothing changes until my heart stops beating.

"What do you feel?" She taps the skin a few inches above my busted arm gently.

"Like I got hit by a truck."

"You're really going to be difficult on your deathbed?"

"One hell of a deathbed," I say.

She purses her lips and sighs, raising a hand to my forehead. "The fever sets in a few minutes after the bite no matter where it—" Her jaw goes slack, and the blood drains from her already-pale face. "It—" She presses her hand to my head again and moves it to my cheek.

"There should be—" She tugs the tee from my neck, peers at the bloody flesh. Clearly not a fatal bite, or I'd have bled out, but that isn't what matters, is it? Those are the old rules.

"You don't have a fever." She looks back at Sam, like she has some answer, and at me, accusatory. "Emir bit you. You should be—should *feel*—" She gives her head a tiny shake. "Right now you should feel like someone stuffed you in a deep fryer and turned the heat up all the way."

"Like I said." I gesture at the mess of my body. "Just the truck thing." It's the concussion, or the pain, or the Tick itself numbing my edges. That, or the things Mara is saying don't make sense.

She shakes her head again. "That's not possible. You're infected."

"Maybe treated Ticks—*Altered*, whatever—can't infect people," I say, but I know it's not true. We were all given the welcome pamphlet for resettlement. The warning was in writing, clear as day.

While the Altered have complete control over their condition and the viral load they carry is minimal, they still pose a threat through traditional means of infection.

A bite. A deep enough scratch. Blood, or saliva maybe. For a long time, we didn't waste the time to see—you had to assume anything that could lead to infection would.

"Mara?" I ask, like she's some scientist or god that can tell me what's happening. Back when we *were* a we, Mara was the cool cucumber in the chaos, and I was the instigator of said chaos. I had to adapt and fill the gaps she left—gaps I never bothered to fill on my own.

I became someone without her, but it's nice to lean into someone else for a minute.

"I don't know. I—" She stops, clamps her eyes shut, and tears her hands from me.

The gravity shifts, and I draw her back, fingers curling around her wrists. "Stay with me."

Her lips part, and a shudder rolls through her. The noise, like a cry but not quite human, tugs at something deep inside me.

"Like I ever left you," she says, and opens her eyes, fully Mara for the moment. She pauses, turns to Sam. Her hands curl into fists, veins flexing against my palms, and uncurl.

"Sam," she says. She addresses the soldiers and Thalia on the ground. "Only Sam."

"Or what?" pipes some stupid, unfortunate soldier.

Mara trembles, and my grip on her wrists tightens.

"Or I let her kill you," I say. For some reason, it calms her. Mara fixes the soldier with an icy smile.

"Thalia," Sam says, and the woman nods, barking a command at her soldiers. Though they aren't technically her soldiers. They wear RPA badges but follow Thalia's command.

Sam drops at my side, tossing the tranquilizer gun aside. Mara perches next to me in a crouch that makes me think she's trying not to run. Her nostrils heave with each of our movements, and every shift in the breeze makes her cringe, but she doesn't move an inch from my side as Sam's attentive hands skate over my injuries.

"You came back," I whisper, low enough only Sam, and by default, Mara, can hear.

Sam's cheeks flush. She meets my eyes briefly and says, "I came back."

"Why?" I ask.

"Later," Mara says. Sam, for once, seems grateful Mara is there.

Sam isn't a doctor, but we all learned battlefield medicine because we had to—trial and error. She runs through the same fever checks, and more, asking questions that remind me of doctor's visits as a kid: sitting on exam tables disguised as plastic elephants and placing Hello Kitty Band-Aids on my skin after shots.

"This isn't possible," Sam says. "We're past fifteen minutes. With a bite that close to the heart, the virus should be in your brain by now."

"What are you saying?" I ask. "Other than the fact that I haven't turned yet."

Sam's mouth falls open and stays that way. She closes it, tries again.

"I'm saying . . ." Sam's eyes are wide. "I'm saying you're not *going* to turn, Rory. I don't know how or why, but you're not showing any signs of infection. It's like you . . ." She waves a hand. "Like you're immune."

"No one's immune," I say. "It's why they never found a—"

"A vaccine," Sam says. "I know. But Rory—"

Mara's eyes glaze over, and her hand rises to her mouth. Her fingers are stained red and black—my blood and hers on both our lips.

"What does that mean?" I ask.

"It means you're not dying," Sam says, a tear sliding down her cheek. "Not today."

39

RORY

You're not dying.

I repeat the words over and over in my head until they lose meaning.

For all these years, the rules have been fixed. I'd barely gotten used to them. And now I'm upside down again. I'd resigned myself to dying in that pit, to turning into a Tick, like Mara, and then becoming Altered, also like Mara.

The clock in my head ticks on and on, and I get no closer to monstrosity than I already am. Which, to be fair, is pretty close, but I'm not feeling any urges to bite the people around me, and I'll take that as a victory.

After thirty minutes of no change, it's Mara who makes the call. And she does it without request or any actual authority. She simply pushes to her feet, hoists me into her arms like I weigh nothing—if I wasn't currently fighting against the pain raging a battle through my body, I'd smack her—and starts to the wall. I can't blame the soldiers for raising their tranquilizers.

"Mara, you—" Sam begins. Mara stalls, addressing Sam with a stern look.

Please let Fatimah have brought the Dyebucetin.

"The ladder." Mara's voice doesn't waver, but she speaks through gritted teeth. Her hold on lucidity slips more with each minute. "Now."

She scans the soldiers at the edge of the pool deck. One, a boy not much older than us, with a nasty scar across his jaw, jerks forward and wrangles the metal ladder into place.

She lowers me gently when we reach the rungs, hands steadying me.

"Can you?" The words are soft, for me alone, and something in the act makes the butterflies in my stomach bust from their cages.

Everyone still on this pool deck watched me get the ever-loving crap beat out of me and watched me say what I thought were my last words. My injuries aren't in question. Resilience, though, is a never-ending battle.

I want to say no, but the eyes boring into my back make me swallow the bile and reach for the ladder. The first step makes my injuries scream.

A hand touches my back, giving a small but firm push, and my surprise has me up another rung without thinking. I don't look down, but somehow the knowledge of Mara below me gives me the strength to climb the final steps. At the top of the ladder, a soldier slips his arms beneath mine and lifts me up and onto my feet. Mara is there in a blink, shoving the soldier out of the way and sliding an arm around my waist. She shifts my weight into her unnoticeably and turns, waiting for Sam and Thalia behind us.

"Fatimah—" Sam says.

"I sent one of the guys for her before we got here. She's set up in one of the classrooms. Follow me," Thalia says, all business as she gestures for us to join her, heading for the exit to the pool deck. I met Thalia once, when she visited the Island over six months ago, but she seems older. Stiffer.

The walkway between the deck and the gyms, separated by a gate, has been slashed through, and we duck through the twisted metal to the concrete sidewalk. One right, a left, and we reach a courtyard backing up the high school.

Three stone tables scatter the ground: one is split in half, its pieces canted to the side; one is upturned; and another is stained with grime. Light beckons through the cracked door of an old classroom. Thalia crosses the courtyard confidently, Mara and me limping after, Sam on our heels. Soldiers surround us, but they stop halfway through the courtyard.

"Rory," Sam says from behind me. I pause, glancing ahead at Mara and Thalia as they pass through the doorway into the classroom, and let Sam catch up to me.

"You're here," I say. "I thought that you . . ." I clear my throat.

I thought you ditched us.

Sam swallows. "I know what you thought. And you weren't wrong for thinking it. When I left the house, I was . . ." She closes her eyes for a beat. Opens them. "I was going to leave for good. There's no other way to say it. I was running. I went to the station to steal a boat key."

I was right, then. She did try to ditch us. But she didn't go through with it.

"When I was in there, I saw the frequency jammer. I realized why transmissions off the Island were so bad, and I knew that there'd be no way of getting help for the Altered—for Mara—if someone didn't do something. I almost walked away. But do you know what I asked myself?" It's clearly rhetorical, but I don't think I'm capable of a response right now anyway. Sam lets out a sad laugh. "What would Aria think of me? What would she see when she looked at me? Would she look at me the way you do?"

I open my mouth—to protest or to agree, I'm not sure. I'm not sure how it is I look at her, either. Before I decide, she keeps talking.

"I had no idea what I was going to do when I got to the mainland. Didn't know until I was pulling up to the Bay. Daphne helped me reach Thalia, who got in touch with the RPA. I guess they don't get their hands dirty, but they weren't happy about Mal, so they gave Thalia temporary command of some of their soldiers."

I say nothing, taking a page out of Mara's book. It's quite effective.

"Look, Rory . . ." She tucks a fallen strand of hair behind her ears. She keeps meeting my eyes and looking away. "I know that there is nothing I can say to change these last few years. No apology I make can erase everything you've had to do. But I—" Her eyes glisten with unshed tears, but she keeps herself composed. "I know that I hurt you, and that you had to grow up much faster than you should have. I wasn't there when you needed me. And I'm so, so sorry."

"Thanks," I say lamely.

I don't know what else to say. Because she's right, and nothing can change what's happened or what we've become, and it's not okay. The only thing we can do is keep going. Relief and shame and guilt and all the twisted feelings I have toward her swirl around in me, and I can tell Sam is waiting for me to say something, but all I can force out is "Mara is waiting for me."

She almost looks like she wants to say more, or hug me again, but fortunately decides against it. Before she can change her mind, I make a beeline for the cracked classroom door Mara and Thalia walked through a minute ago.

The desks are gone, but old, faded math equations linger on the now-gray whiteboards, and old flyers are tacked to corkboards along the walls. College pendants hang dusty below the ceilings.

The lights above us flicker, clinging to life. With electricity, this place could be a million things. Apartments for survivors, a makeshift mall for us to trade or barter. Maybe a real school. One day, we could have enough students to fill a building. The images come out of nowhere and from a place I didn't realize still existed.

In lieu of an exam table, an old wooden table sits in the center of the room, and Fatimah stands above it, unpacking a medical bag. Her full lips are pursed, and deep bags sit beneath her sunken eyes.

She glances my way. "Give me two minutes, Rory," she says, pulling a stack of gauze from her duffel. "Can you stay alive that long?"

I snort, wave a hand, and almost fall over. Mara catches me and pulls me back into her side. Her gaze lingers a little too long on my bloody arm.

"Two minutes?" Mara asks, eyeing the small office door a few feet away.

Fatimah's brow furrows. "Not literally—"

"Two minutes," Mara says, and tugs me gently through the doorway to the office, slamming the door behind us. The window facing outward is covered in blackout curtains, and for the first time in a day, we're alone.

Mara turns to me, catching my face in her hands. For a full twenty seconds, she is silent, scanning the injuries she couldn't on the Pit floor, and by the time her eyes find mine again, I want to scream. Her fingers, like ghosts on my skin, are too quick to catch.

"Please stop trying so hard to die," she says, thumb tracing a line over my cheek.

"Isaac says I'm a death magnet," I say, unsure why I do—it makes her smile.

She lets out a breath, tips her forehead into mine.

I close my eyes for a beat, reveling in the pressure of her fingertips on my cheeks, but when she stiffens, nearly imperceptibly, I lean back to meet her gaze.

"Fatimah. She should have Dye—"

"I'm fine," Mara says through gritted teeth.

"I'm not bleeding out. I'd be dead by now."

"You should be dead."

"Not, though," I say. She scoffs. "How are you?"

"I'm—"

"And if you say you're fine, I will stab you."

She shuts her mouth. Considers for a moment. "I'm me right now."

She stops, gaze darting down to my mouth and back up, and I think she's going to kiss me. She doesn't.

Fine. She doesn't have to. Maybe it's the concussion, or the almost dying, but I don't hesitate to lean in, letting my fingers settle against her collarbone. She lets out a staggering breath and stays statue-like, even when my lips graze hers gently.

I inch back, nose bumping hers. My pulse races for a different reason, and the stone in my gut turns to shame.

"Rory," she says softly, in that tone I have feared hearing for a decade, with that expression on her face I've imagined so many times I could read this script myself.

I thought we'd passed the point of needing it, but maybe I was wrong from the start. One of us was always supposed to die, and the promises you make on a deathbed don't always hold up if you leave it.

I step away, immediately woozy, but when she reaches for me, I squirm out of her arms. The pity in her eyes is more than enough to keep me steady until I wrench the door open and step back into the classroom.

●

"You're saying I'm cured."

Fatimah looks up from the biology-lab microscope she's been peering at a drop of my blood through and crinkles her nose.

"Not really," she says, stepping around the edge of the table to where I'm propped up. She balls up the bloody gauze left from cleaning my wounds and tosses it into a cracked plastic bin. "There was nothing to cure. The virus is in your blood, but the levels aren't what we'd expect from an infection."

"I was bitten," I say.

"And the sky is blue," Mara adds. I'm not sure if she's being sarcastic, helpful, or simply delusional. I've badgered her twice about getting a dose, but she's refused until she's sure I'm not going to turn. I can't tell if her concerns are valid, or if she's stalling.

Either way, the compromise was no dose until Fatimah took a look at my blood, a rickety chair propped next to me, and a rope around Mara's torso. I thought it was excessive but was outvoted.

"I think we have established at least six times now that Rory was bitten," Sam says. "And should be dead but isn't."

She leans against the wall with her arms folded. She gives me room, as everyone but Fatimah does—Mara maintains a pocket of space around us and the doctor—and her disapproval is evident. I'm not opposed to it, though. I'd gotten comfortable on Sam's and my footing over the last few years, and now she's shifted the continents.

"It isn't death," Mara says. "It's a coma." She squeezes my hand, tight. From where she sits, and with the binds, she has to reach up to keep a grip on my hand, but it and the rope seem to be her only tethers.

The humans in the room share perplexed looks.

"The Tick kills its victim," Sam says.

Mara is a hair too defensive when she says, "Not victims. Hosts."

"What's the difference?" I ask.

"The Tick is looking for a home, not a hotel. Kill the host, you have to find another one."

"When did you become an epidemiologist?" I ask.

Mara's jaw sets. It takes considerable effort for her to force out, "The Tick brings us to the point of dying, but then it keeps us in some kind of stasis."

"Whether it's death or almost death . . ." Sam pinches the bridge of her nose and readjusts her eye patch; the skin beneath is irritated. "It's been a very long night for all of us. And all of us want answers." She licks her lips, nods at Fatimah.

Fatimah's mouth is a thin line. "Somehow, in some way, it's as if Rory was inoculated. Not immune—asymptomatic."

"And you claim you aren't a real doctor," I say.

"You can thank a certain showrunner and a medical textbook for the big words," she says. "But as for the rest, all I can do is guess. If you could get to someone with real experience, real equipment—" She shakes her head. "This is out of my area of expertise. Which, if you will recall, was running a small boutique."

"Fatimah's Fashions was a goddamn treasure," I say.

"Give us your guess, then," Thalia says. No one is more interested in my sudden humanity than the representative. I'm betting she has the whole RPA to answer to, and their soldiers watching her every move.

"My best guess"—Fatimah's face twists as she thinks—"and it *is* a guess," she says, "is that you were exposed to a small enough— we'll call it an *attenuated*—dosage of the virus. And if that happened, the exposure acted as a vaccination. Introducing the disease to your body in a quantity small enough to fight."

"The body remembers," I say. Fatimah's words back in the infirmary after the gunshot, each time she caught me waking from nightmares of horrors I thought I'd forgotten.

Mara squeezes my hand.

Fatimah nods. "Exactly. The same way you get a measles shot. Your cells learn what to look for and how to keep it out." She inclines her head, eyes glassy with thought. "Or perhaps it worked as camouflage. The pathogen recognized some remnant of itself in your blood and didn't try to split into another host."

"Where would she have been exposed? A scratch, or a . . ." Sam waves a hand, gesturing at nothing. "How?"

"Keeping in mind my total lack of schooling on this . . ."

"We've established that, too, Fatimah," I say.

She gives me a condescending look and presses forward. "A scratch too deep would turn you, and plenty of those who were eventually bitten and turned were scratched light enough before." She taps her chin, untangling the thread. "It would have to be a small amount of saliva or blood, I think."

Mara turns my way as I turn hers—only I'm capable of blushing, but I'm sure she would be, too, if she could.

"What about both?" I ask.

"Both?" Fatimah inclines her head.

"Saliva and blood," I say, looking at Mara. "A few times."

"Saliva and . . ." Sam pauses. Sucks in a breath and lets it out. "Oh, you have got to be *kidding* me." She looks between us like we've been caught in some foggy car.

Fatimah's shoulder rises and falls once in a half shrug. "In theory, it's possible."

"Could someone elaborate, please?" Thalia asks. I'd forgotten she was here.

"She's saying making out with Mara saved my life. Literally," I say.

"Simply speaking, yes," Fatimah says. "If you were exposed to the virus multiple times through"—she clears her throat—"intimate contact—"

"A kiss—" Mara says.

"More than one," I say.

"Girls," Sam says. I throw her an irritated look, and she swallows, shoulders slumping a bit.

"I do believe it's possible Mara's saliva, and any of her blood from open injuries, that ended up, for lack of a better word, in your mouth, is the reason you're still here, Rory," Fatimah says.

"Does that—" Sam stops. She isn't one for hope, either, but she's brimming with it. "If Rory is vaccinated, does that mean this same concept could apply to someone else?"

"Is Altered blood the vaccine?" I ask.

We are all on the edge of our metaphorical seats, Thalia especially.

I kind of wish Fatimah wouldn't speak. The definition of insanity is doing something over and over and expecting the same result, and hope is that thing. It will drive you mad if you let it.

Fatimah pulls in a breath. She looks at us, one by one, and by the time she speaks again, I am seconds from smacking the words out of her mouth.

"Yes," she says. "I believe it is."

40

MARA

With Rory off the table, it is my turn on it. Thalia, unconcerned with the medicating of a Tick, dips into the hallway to assist with the frequency-jammer issue so she can get in contact with whoever sent the soldiers. It doesn't shock me that the RPA sent Thalia on their behalf. At first, I thought whoever was in charge, whether it was a few old government interns who got a big head or an actual surviving senator, stayed away from the facilities because they thought they were above it. Now, though, I wonder if they're hiding. Letting us do the dirty work, clearing the path to a safer world for them to step into.

Sam takes off in search of Isaac and the kids; Mal's assertions they weren't harmed were *not* assuring.

Rory unties me from the chair, looking a bit sheepish as she does it. She grabs my hand and squeezes once.

You're Mara Knight.

I release her hand and ease up onto the tabletop, the soles of my shoes brushing the carpet, and eye the small box of syringes Fatimah pulls from her bag. To say it's the Tick alone who wants to run far from those drugs would be a lie.

The Tick is seething, banging its fists against my skull like a monkey against the glass wall of the zoo, and I, too, am suddenly unsure. The numbness is more appealing than I'd care to admit. There is no light at the end of that tunnel, but I still want to crawl down it, fade into nothingness.

I killed my friend today. I killed Emir. Dolly, too, is dead, and neither deserved it.

The door handle facing the hallway jiggles, and I'm grateful for the interruption of Thalia, but it is not Thalia who opens the door. It is Carter.

Before I have a chance, Rory, in her limping, shaking glory, lunges toward her but is quickly wrangled back and into her chair by Fatimah.

"If you think you get to show your face here—" she snarls.

Carter, leaning heavily into crutches, sporting as many bruises as Rory, maneuvers away from where Rory is being pinned to her chair. Her eyes seek me out, nervous like I haven't seen in a long time. One hand strays to the thick wrapped bandage around her arm tucked in its sling.

A memory of the *crack* of her bone sings a melody in my ear.

"What do you want?" I ask dryly.

Carter swallows and darts a look at Fatimah and Rory. "Could we . . . Do you have a minute?"

"No, she does not—" Rory starts, but Fatimah cuts her off with a push to her rolling chair.

"Mara," Fatimah says, "it's your call." There is a warning in her words, as if I'm unaware how close I am to slipping away.

But I kind of doubt Carter would agree to a rain check, and I want to know what she has to say.

I nod.

"You have two minutes," Fatimah says. It's stern, but there is an assurance in it, too, unnecessary but kind, that she's not leaving me alone.

"Fatimah, don't you dare shut that—" The door swings shut on Rory's protest, and even if they are a few feet away, Carter and I are the only people on the planet.

"Mara," Carter says after a full thirty seconds of my silence—always effective. "Look, I . . . I don't know how to say this, but—"

"Sure you do."

To my surprise, and irritation, she laughs. Tilts her head back ever so slightly, like our mom did. Like I do.

"God, you really are her, aren't you?" she asks. "My annoying little sister."

Isaac's words, days old, echo in my ears. *You're not a monster. You're Mara Knight.*

He was partially right. Maybe I am a monster. I am also Mara.

"I always was."

"You didn't exactly—" She stops, culls the anger from her tone. "No. I'm not here to argue with you."

I don't respond.

"I have something I need to say to you. Just one thing, and I'll leave you alone. You okay with that?" she asks, jutting out her chin. She looks nine years old again, folding bony arms over her chest and telling me she was going first on the Slip 'N Slide.

I wave a hand at her as if to say *go ahead*. Pink creeps up her cheeks.

"Do you remember that night?" she asks.

I answer truthfully. "Mostly."

Her gaze clouds. "I dream about it all the time. I can still hear the banging on the bathroom door and see the look Mom gave Dad in that hallway when they realized what it meant, like they were so *tired*. We barely made it to the weapons by the time you broke through—"

"I remember," I interject, holding back the blood-soaked images. They, along with the scent of Carter's life enfolding me, make my mind drift places I can't let it go.

Mara Knight. You are Mara Knight.

"Not this part," she says, and her voice is cutting. "After—" She stops. Clears her throat and blinks away moisture. "Before I could get out, I managed to trap you in the guest bedroom long enough to grab that damn bag Dad was always on us to have packed. And long enough to go back to their bodies and—" This time, when she stops, she doesn't start again. She doesn't need to.

I wondered why they never turned. I thought I simply destroyed too much of them for the Tick.

"And then I left, and I locked you inside. I shoved whatever I could to hold the front door from the outside, and when I was done, I looked up, and you were staring at me through the front window. For this horrible second, I could see you, and you looked . . . I don't know, *relieved*—" She shudders. "Then you were gone, and I ran. I kept running until Lily found me, half-dead, on one of the early supply runs.

"We're not kids anymore, but we are still blood. And we were family once." She sucks in her cheeks, blinks rapidly. "I need you to know that I'm sorry." She takes a long breath. "I thought you were gone, even though you were right in front of me, but when I saw you in the Pit, the way you saved Rory, and when we thought—" She stops. "I don't want to spend the rest of my life hating you. So I forgive you."

She swipes a tear from her eye as it falls, and jams her free hand into her pocket. "For what it's worth, I really am glad you're still here," she says, and leaves before I get the chance to reply. I'm not sure I would have.

"Time's up," Rory says, having freed herself of Fatimah and rolling the chair into the room. The doctor enters behind Rory with a pointed look.

"Is everything alright?" Fatimah asks.

My eyes are on Rory, and though she doesn't speak, it's clear she wants an answer to the question.

I nod.

A frown plays on Rory's lips; she doesn't buy it.

Fortunately, Fatimah is determined, and she takes my arm, swiping at the skin with a gauze pad. Disinfection seems pointless, but I don't protest. If I speak, move, breathe, I'm scared I'll run or do something worse.

While Fatimah uncaps the needle, I hold Rory's eyes. She's beautiful, even covered in blood and dirt and grime. The most beautiful thing I have been lucky enough to see.

I'm luckier to love her, I think. To know that she loves me, too.

The liquid slithers into my veins, but where there is usually a sharp pressure, a burst of sensation in every nerve ending—pain and pleasure and warmth—there is instead a sharp heat.

Not the warm flicker of a lighter, but a raging wildfire. And within seconds, it drags me into the flames and out of consciousness.

The last thing I hear before I slip away is my name off Rory's lips. That sound, like a melody, is as beautiful as she is.

41

MARA

Bright lights turn the darkness a vibrant red, and I keep my eyes closed against it. My thoughts slog like molasses, and a soft fuzzy feeling pushes through my body. It takes a long few seconds to piece it all back together.

A piercing pain in my belly that pulled me awake in a knot of blankets on Rory's bedroom floor. A sleepover that ended in the emergency room and then an OR. Two families, Knights and Blakes, jammed into a waiting room.

"How long until she wakes up?" Carter asks, somewhere to my left. I'm still too tired to bother opening my eyes, but on the inside, her impatience makes me smile.

"Could be up to an hour," my mother says. I can hear the smile in her voice. "Why don't we run and grab something from the cafeteria? I could go for some powdered eggs. Mike, do you want anything?"

"I'm good. I can stay with her and grab something in a bit."

"You go. I'll stay with her," another voice says. Aurora.

The steady beep of my heart on the monitor lurches and settles again. Carter doesn't try to hide her snort.

"I can't argue with that," my dad says, which is worse than Carter's laugh. Even weighed down by anesthesia, the buzzing electricity that runs through my veins when Aurora is near heightens. Right now everyone can hear it. She can hear it.

I'm not sure I want to open my eyes.

"Want anything, Aurora?" Mom asks. "Crappy coffee, on me?"

"Yes, please. And no—"

"No sugars, no creams, the way no one intended. Coming right up."

"We'll be back in five minutes," my dad assures. The room quickly grows silent with their exit. I hold my breath for ten seconds and open my eyes.

In the chair beside the bed, Aurora has her legs pulled up and crossed beneath her and deftly weaves the beginnings of a bracelet. It's a familiar sight, one that sends a heavy ache rolling down my back. Only a few rows are completed, unflawed like always, but I get caught on the colors. Red, blue, and pink.

She stiffens, and her head snaps up. Her fingers tremble around the bracelet as she sets it in her lap.

"Hey," she says, like I'm not in a hospital bed with three sets of tiny stitches and one less organ.

"Hey," I say.

A tiny smile spreads across her lips. It's rare; I've seen this smile a handful of times, and only ever directed at me. The heart monitor screeches again, and I take three deep breaths.

"How do you feel?"

My tongue is thick and dry in my mouth. I struggle to swallow. "A couple of ounces lighter."

She scoffs, rolls her eyes. The smile slips from her face.

"What is it?" I ask.

Her eyes fall to the long bracelet strings she's fiddling between her fingers. When she looks at me again, it's through feathered lashes.

"You scared the hell out of me," she says. "The way you screamed when you fell out of bed—I thought—" She stops. Her expression turns fierce, and she looks away. "Don't you dare do that again."

"Scream?"

"Almost die." She pauses. "Leave me."

A sudden rush of bravery makes me take her hand and squeeze it. Her eyes snap to mine.

"I'm not going anywhere," I say.

Her fingers tighten around mine, and the next smile she gives feels dangerous.

"Promise?"

"I promise."

42

RORY

After three days holed up on a cot beside Mara's comatose form, I am threatened with a head-shaving if I don't *get the hell out of my infirmary and take a damn shower*. Three days of pestering, of failed attempts to coax Mara out of whatever state she's in, and Fatimah is a live wire.

I've stopped asking, mostly because Fatimah has stopped engaging, but I got all the answers I needed two nights ago. I kept on with the questions because I thought the response might change if I did. Still, Mara hasn't moved a muscle in nine days.

"How do you know you didn't kill her?" I asked, standing over a motionless Mara on the cot.

Fatimah, pulling a blanket up over Mara's legs, averted her gaze. "Because she would be *rotting* by now."

Rotting. My stomach rolled. Fatimah materialized a bucket to puke into. From the concussion, the stress, the trauma, or all of the above, she said.

"If not for what she herself said regarding the Tick's behavior," Fatimah said, "I would think she was dead. It's as if she's preserved in amber."

"In stasis," I said. She nodded. "Is that what's wrong with her?"

Fatimah chewed on her lip. "I'm not so sure anything *is* wrong with her. Not that I can see, at least. But the Dyebucetin is supposed to be taken on a consistent schedule. We have no way of knowing what missing so many doses and taking it again did."

"Clearly something is wrong. She's . . . well, *look* at her. She *looks* dead."

Gently, she said, "She always did, didn't she?"

Yes. No. Both.

"Is she going to wake up?"

Fatimah took a deep breath, and said, "They're sending one of the doctors from the facility Mara was treated in. I'm hoping she'll have the answer to that question."

Her proposal of a shower and a nap isn't exactly a bad one. Fatimah hosed the blood and gore from the Pit off me, but it hardly did me justice. It's not like Mara is complaining, and other than Fatimah's mother-hen hovering, no one apart from my parents and I have been in the infirmary in days.

"Let me tell her I'm leaving. Just in case."

She doesn't point out that Mara likely can't hear me, or that if she was going to flat-out die—finish dying, I guess—it would have happened already. "Fine." She waves a hand dismissively. "But I want you out in five minutes, or I will kick you out."

"Doubt you could," I say, easing my weight onto my left leg. The RPA gifted me the brace as a *thank you for not dying*, I guess. Technically, Thalia gave it to me on their behalf. So far, I've yet to meet the faces behind the RPA, but it sounds like I'm not the only one.

I'm sturdier than I have been in ages. I lean and tap my fingers against where the metal is locked around my thigh. "I'm rocking updated gear now."

"You're not invincible because you're still alive, Rory Blake," Fatimah warns, and slips into the hallway, pulling the door behind her.

I ease onto the cot, nudging Mara back slightly and leaning into her hip. Solid and supportive, even with her eyes shut.

"I don't know if you can hear me, wherever you are," I say, brushing the black hairs from her forehead, letting my pointer finger trace down the bridge of her nose. The skin is bumpy where the slashes intersect, but it isn't as monstrous anymore. *She* isn't as monstrous anymore. Still a little bit, of course, but I am, too.

"I need you to know you were right," I say, speaking through the stone lodging in my throat. "You were right, and I couldn't see it. I'm sorry I figured everything out too late." Tears rake down my cheeks, and I let them, not bothering to swipe them away. Tiny drops slide off my chin to land on Mara's shirt.

If we were in a fairy tale, a teardrop would be enough to wake her. But we aren't in a fairy tale, and a tear is saline, and Mara isn't Sleeping Beauty—which was a problematic story to begin with. There is no quick solution to make her wake up.

"You didn't ruin my life. You saved it. And it's not fair that—" I stop to wrangle the dread before it drags me away. "You should be here. You should be here to see it." A sob claws its way up my esophagus, and I drop my forehead onto Mara's torso. Her body, still but warm—not human warm, but warm enough—is firm beneath me, and I inhale, uncaring that the scent is all sweat and blood and grime. It is Mara, too, beneath the surface.

"You promised. So I need you to come back to me, okay?"

Pulling away from her and pushing to my feet is like ripping off a patch of skin, but I do it anyway. Standing at her side, I bend down once more, pressing a kiss to her forehead—sappy as shit, but fortunately, no one is here to witness it.

"I've got to go, Mara. Whenever you're ready, come find me again," I say. Each step weighs a thousand pounds, but I push away from the cot and into the hall.

I have one more stop to make before I can actually leave. My focus is on the Cells, past the infirmary and record room, and left down the far hallway. Standing guard are Lily and Tara; Tara's head is wrapped half like a mummy, and she doesn't look thrilled to see me.

"The hell do you want, Blake?" Tara says. On the other side of the door, Lily shifts, a hand moving to her knife and falling away.

"None of your business," I say. "How's the ear? Or . . . sorry, lack of one?" My brows waggle, and Tara's nostrils flare. If Lily weren't here, I'm pretty sure she'd go for my throat. I kind of wish she would. Ever since Mara closed her eyes, I have been buzzing with anger. Punching one of Mal's clones sounds like the perfect antidote.

Except they aren't Mal's clones anymore. They were given a choice: join Mal in a cell or submit to the RPA soldiers for judgment. Not a single one chose Mal. It turns out more people are on hope's side than we thought.

"It's like you're actively trying to get yourself killed," Lily says, shaking her head. "What are you doing here, Rory?"

"Just give me five minutes—"

"Not a chance," Tara says.

"Wasn't talking to you, Dumbo—"

"We'll see if that nickname stands when I slice your tongue right out—"

"Tara, walk away," Lily says. Tara jerks toward her, shocked, but Lily's expression is unwavering. "Now."

To my surprise, Tara listens, trudging past me. She knocks her shoulder into mine for effect, knocking me off balance. Just as she steps away, I whirl, bring a hand up, and smack it into her bandaged head.

She lets out a howl, stumbling and catching herself on the wall. She whips to face me, all rage—and I'm eager to meet it, to release the anger stirring in me like a monsoon—but another sharp glare from Lily has her retreating down the hallway.

"Your girl's gonna be pissed if she wakes up to find out that you egged half this island into killing you," Lily says, though it's more amused than anything.

If she wakes up.

I really, really want to hit something.

"I'm not here to make small talk," I say.

"Clearly," Lily says. She cocks a brow. "What do you want with Mal?"

"I'm not here to kill him, if that's what you're thinking."

"Can you blame me?" Lily leans back against the wall, folding her arms over her chest. Waiting.

"I just . . . I need to look him in the eye. To . . ." I trail off, the words piling up behind my teeth in all the wrong order. I don't know what I want from Mal, if anything, but he's the reason Mara isn't beside me, the reason all of this happened, and if I can't talk to her, I sure can lay into him.

Lily's brow furrows, and she clears her throat, stepping back from the door. Her fingers curl around the hilt of a blade tucked into her belt; carved into the wood, in tiny letters: L+C.

Carter.

I guess Mara and her sister are more alike than I thought. Similar tastes, at least. If Mara were here, she'd smile.

I lift my chin and catch Lily's pink cheeks. She clears her throat again and jams a key into the lock, tugs the door open, and gestures for me to go inside.

"Five minutes. And I swear on my life, Rory, if you so much as touch your weapon—"

"Yeah, yeah, *no killing.*"

"Five minutes," she says sternly.

A gross, soggy feeling blooms in my chest. I have to chew on a *thank you* so it doesn't breach my lips, and step over the threshold. I stop the moment I cross, looking back at Lily.

"Thank you," I say, and I'm not sure which of us is more surprised to hear it.

She drops her head, nods dismissively, and tugs the door shut behind me. For a second, I think she's going to lock it. She doesn't.

The Cells, previously temporary holding for jaywalkers or teens caught smoking on the beach, are the same as they used to be. Six individual holding cells with rusted bars, flimsy cots, and horrendous metal toilets.

And one Mallory Gordon, looking pathetic as ever in civilian clothes, his jaw lined with days of scruff, propped on the cot in the first cell. Once Thalia returns to the Island—my blood, apparently, took precedence over Mal—he'll be dragged onto a boat and carted away to the RPA headquarters, which is apparently only a two-hour drive away. To stand trial. Not that we have courts yet, but I'm not all that opposed to Mal rotting for however long it takes.

As I walk to the cell, a grimace finds a home on his chapped lips. He looks like a child, curled cross-legged on the cot, head tilted to one side.

"Rory Blake," he drawls. "What brings you to my part of town?"

I step up to the bars and fold my arms over my chest. Hunkered in the dark and bruised from a beating I'd bet was given by some RPA soldier, Mal doesn't seem the persuasive giant he has been for so long. Even locked in a cage, he still infects this island with his hate.

"I hear you've been on lockdown. Didn't get the daily paper, I'm guessing," I say. "Pretty good stuff."

"Ah, come to rub your victory in my face." He sneers. "You truly are a child."

"You've really got to find some new material. If you've got enough time left." Deep breaths, Rory. "But no. I'm not here for that. I wanted to let you know that you lost, not because it's satisfying as hell to see the look on your face as you realize your kingdom fell—which it is—but because I thought you should know what Fatimah figured out. Turns out, when you don't have a megalomaniac breathing down your throat and jamming your radio frequencies, there's a lot about the Altered we didn't know."

I lift a hand to the bars, tracing a finger down a curling piece of rusty paint. "Fatimah's been talking on the radio with the other communities, even a doctor from one of the RPA facilities. Want to know something interesting?"

Mal seethes, his shoulders rising and falling quickly. Maybe this *was* mostly for my own satisfaction. It's pretty damn satisfying, too.

"All of them say the same thing. That the Altered are coming back to life." I leave out the fact that they never really died, either—that Fatimah swears Mara has somehow aged at least a few months past when she was bitten. It's still too weird to wrap my head around. She and the others aren't cured, and will probably need the meds as long as they un-live, but they're less dead than they were. "The Dyebucetin, it's working. Slowly, really slowly, but it's working."

"Are we nearing a point anytime soon?" Mal asks. His jaw is wrenched tighter than a corkscrew.

"You missed it, actually," I say. "That's the point. All this time, you've been looking over your shoulder. And *you* missed what was right in front of us.

"And for a long time, I thought you were right, Mal. The world was done for, and we were, too, and I was no better than you. Just another cockroach hiding under a rock. But I won't be like you. I'm not like you."

"You think you understand this world, but you—"

"*Enough*," I snap, smacking a hand into the bars. Mal stiffens, jaw tight—he's afraid of me. Satisfaction rots in my belly. "Don't you get that? It's over." It would be so easy to ram the blade home, but he's already in a cell, damned. Alone. "It's been over for a long time."

I am not like him. I won't be.

"I'm sorry about your family. I'm sorry about Juliette. I'm sorry that you lost everyone," I say. "But we're still here. And I'm sorry you can't see that. I couldn't. But I do now."

The mention of his family is the spark to a match, and he rises to his feet, anger swelling his chest, but I realize I have nothing more to say to Mal, if I had anything at all.

"See you in hell," I say with a wave of the hand, turning for the door. Whatever. Growth isn't always linear.

I push through the door and into the hall, letting Mal's protests fall on indifferent ears.

"Blake," Lily calls, making me pause. I turn to face her, and indecision twists at her expression. "We got word from Thalia and the RPA. About Mal. What they're doing with him."

"I thought they were taking him up to their headquarters to toss him in a cell and let him rot. Stick some stupid sentence on him."

Lily's cheeks flush a sickly pink in the flickering fluorescent lights.

"I guess they don't want to bother," she says. She drops her chin. "He's being . . ." She doesn't finish the sentence, but her gaze trained on the blade at my hip is answer enough.

Executed. The word she can't say.

"What happened to a trial?" I ask, not sure why I'm inching anywhere near defending him.

Lily shrugs, frowns. Ashamed, maybe, though it wasn't her who made the call.

"Guess the apocalypse is harder to shake than we realized," she says.

Dread pools like acid in my belly, and I press down the hallway before I puke on Lily's shoes.

Days ago, I wanted nothing more than to watch the life leave Mallory Gordon's eyes. I wanted to do it myself. For all he's done, there had to be a price, but now that it's come time to pay, it's too high. Because this isn't about justice. This is about the RPA punishing Mal for stepping out of line and letting his demise serve as a warning to the rest of us. The rest of the Alliance.

In some ways, we're better than we were before we stopped running for our lives. In others, we're still worse than the monsters we spent so long fighting.

The street is busier than I have ever seen it when I push out into the sun. Families, straggling survivors, hardened warriors, all lugging bags and boxes and weaponry toward the residential streets.

New residents. A whole two hundred of them. Mal hasn't allowed anyone new since my family, and even that was tenuous. But the gates are open now. The newbies have been sorted into houses along the residential streets that are as run-down as ours was when we moved into it. With a little work, they'll be homes again. New residents brought new Altered, too. Ten of them, plus the nine others who Mal tried to throw into the Pit. They all missed days of Dyebucetin; Mara is the only one who fell into a coma.

I was warned of the inevitable return of Thalia, who is officially the go-between for the Alliance and the RPA, and a gaggle of RPA scientists for more samples; I am the only vaccinated human anyone has heard of, apparently, and it makes me fairly popular. Hence the back path I take through the Island, away from the newcomers' eyes. Even without the assistance of photos and video, my name has made its rounds faster than expected, and half the state knows about the blond girl with the sword who should be dead but isn't. I plan on avoidance for as long as possible, and with an island still so empty, it's easily done.

Even the abandoned streets, the ones we haven't yet started to rebuild, shine a little brighter in the afternoon sun.

It feels so suspiciously like . . . not normal, because normal flew the fuck away before the bombs fell. Like hope, maybe.

●

The bridge is still one of few places I'm likely to find any peace. Anything to escape Sam's tension and Isaac's sympathy and Noah's endless questions.

Where is Mara? When is Mara coming back? Can we go see Mara?

I lasted a full hour, including a shower, before heading through the front door with the half-hearted promise of returning before dark. It's been weeks since I ventured onto the bridge, since the day I learned Mara was coming home, but the city looks different than it did last time I was here.

For over three years, I have seen the city as a wasteland, nothing but ash and dust and bone. I don't know if I've never looked long enough or simply couldn't see, but it isn't the same place beyond the bridge—behind it.

Greens are woven into the grays and browns of decaying skyscrapers and streets: trees growing beyond their limits, vines busting through windows, wildlife retaking its kingdom.

I have spent so much time waiting for the world to end, I missed every clue that it was putting itself back together. That we are, too.

Slipping a hand into my pocket, I tug out the worn thread bracelet I pulled from Mara's wrist before I left. Her wrist is smaller than mine, and forcing the threads over my thumb almost breaks it, but the bracelet, worn and faded and stained, rests easily around my wrist.

I lost Mara Knight when the world lost itself. This time, I plan on holding on.

I was wrong about the world being long over, about catching up to the end of the road. It was Mara who got it right. And if—when—she wakes up, I might admit that to her.

Nothing ever ends.

EPILOGUE

MARA

The first things I notice are the straps digging into my ankles and wrists. It isn't pain, necessarily, but discomfort.

The second thing I notice is that I'm noticing anything at all. Like I've ripped back some curtain and let sunlight flood into a big dark room, all of it filled with mold and cobwebs.

"Can you tell me your name?" a woman asks. I didn't notice her until now, and I wonder how long she's been there, standing in the corner of the small room. I wonder how long I've been here. And who I am.

Name. That word means something, but the next word that flies to my tongue, Aurora, doesn't fit well enough to be the answer. I think it's some answer, though.

My lips part. It takes a long second to realize the croaking sound is me.

The woman, still hesitant, shifts toward me. Her furrowed brow smooths.

"My name is Dr. Benitez. My friends call me Isadora." She points to herself, and then to me. "What is your name?"

I recall a woman not much older than this one, with raven-black hair and kind green eyes, and her hushed whispers: It's going to be okay, Mara.

"M . . ." The letters coil and snap on my tongue. Frustration surges through me, red and sharp, and it makes the woman, Dr. Benitez, stiffen and lean back.

I huff in a breath of stale air. "M . . . M-Mara."

She relaxes. Nods. "Mara," *she says.* "It's lovely to have you back, Mara."

Back. Back, as in, I was gone.

More images—not images, but memories—claw to the surface, and my cool body hardens to ice.

"Wh-when?" *I ask.*

"I'm sorry?" *Dr. Benitez frowns, but recognition dawns in her eyes, and she steps closer to me.* "Oh. We can't know for sure, as everyone stopped keeping track at one point or another, but the general consensus is the world ended around two and a half years ago."

That can't be right. I was counting the days. I don't remember what I got to, but the number wasn't that high.

I've lost more than a year.

The binds. The doctor's hesitance. The fuzzy red-soaked memories sliding into place alongside clear ones.

I press my head back into the gurney, clenching my eyes shut. An odd tingling starts up in the corners of my eyes, but no tears come. This makes me want to cry more.

"N-no," *I say.* "No. N-no, n-o—"

Warm fingers graze my own, and my eyelids snap open. Dr. Benitez jumps back, but she doesn't remove her hand.

"I have one more question for you. I understand it may be a difficult one." *She purses her lips.* "What do you remember, Mara?"

The first face I see when I open my eyes is Dr. Benitez's, and for a brief, horrible second, I think I'm back in the facility, tied to a gurney. I think these last weeks have all been a hallucination or a dream.

Then Fatimah and Isaac step up beside her.

"I don't understand how I'm awake," I say after thirty minutes of being poked and prodded by Dr. Benitez, who made the trek when she heard I slipped into a coma—or whatever it was—and has taken up residence in the infirmary. From the looks of things, her tools and equipment scattered everywhere, she has no intention of leaving anytime soon.

"A few years ago, I might have been able to give you a clear answer," Dr. Benitez says. She and Fatimah sit on one of the cots opposite me, while Isaac stands at the foot of my bed. It reminds me so much of Rory that it's hard to think straight.

"But . . ." Isaac says.

"*But* a good half of our resources were lost after the Fall. Medical equipment, machines, knowledge itself. Most of it is gone," she says. "All I can give you is a hypothesis."

"A guess," Isaac says, less combative, more curious.

"Science has always been a guess. Some of it is more well informed than the rest, but still, at its core, a guess," Dr. Benitez says.

"What's your best guess, then?" Isaac asks.

Dr. Benitez purses her lips. "The Dyebucetin acts as a bulldozer, forcing the virus back, eventually shrinking it. When Mara stopped taking the medication, the virus rebuilt, regained control. How she didn't completely regress, I haven't the slightest clue," Dr. Benitez says to Isaac.

"But I did," I say. "In the Pit, I was . . ." I can't feel much, but shame still burns. "I would call that *regressing*."

"Rory told me what happened in the Pit. What you did," Isaac says. "You may not have been entirely yourself, but you weren't a Tick, either. You saved her life."

Dr. Benitez says, "It's as if, for a little while, the parasitic relation-ship became"—she crinkles her nose—"*mutualistic*. It adapted long enough to survive, and it didn't, for lack of a better term, kill you to do it. And do not ask me how or why, because I can't begin to guess."

"What about the coma?" I ask. Dr. Benitez inhales, probably to cor-rect me, and I quickly add, "Or whatever it was?"

Dr. Benitez closes her mouth. It's Fatimah who answers the question.

"When I gave you the injection, it—" Fatimah pauses. "Shocked your system. The virus panicked. It shut you down."

Dr. Benitez nods.

"I'm assuming that's not the official diagnosis," Isaac says.

It makes me think of being a child in a doctor's office, looking to my parents to give the answers.

"It's not the most official of answers, but it is as good as we're going to get right now," Dr. Benitez says. She gives me a gentle smile. "There's nothing like the end of the world to trade a decade's worth of education for assumption."

"What's stopping it from happening again?" Isaac asks.

"She is," Dr. Benitez says, catching my eye. "Mara kept herself human in the Pit as the Dyebucetin left her system."

"I got lucky," I say, and in an instant, I'm back in that chair in the facility sitting across the desk from Dr. Benitez, terrified of losing my grip on the world I've so recently grabbed hold of again. "And I wouldn't have lasted another day without it."

"Maybe. Maybe not. But it wasn't luck," Dr. Benitez says. "It was you."

●

It takes another hour until Dr. Benitez and Fatimah are convinced I'm not going to lose consciousness on the spot and give me permission to leave. Before I ask the question, Isaac tells me Rory is at the high school with the kids.

"I'll see you at home," Isaac says for the third time, pulling me into a hug. I hug him back, letting out a deep breath.

"I'm so glad you're okay, kiddo," he says, voice muffled by my hair. He pulls back, hands giving my shoulders a squeeze before he steps back and heads down the stairs.

I linger at the bottom of the concrete steps, watching as he heads toward the main blocks.

Across the road, the park I followed Rory to that first night is bathed in golden afternoon light. A mother watches her children climb atop the old playground. The playground is missing pieces, and its slides are half-rusted away, but the children don't mind. Their laughter carries all the way over to me.

Home.

Footsteps echo inside the station, tearing my attention from the park. The doors whine open behind me. I don't have to look back to know who it is.

"Mara," Dr. Benitez calls. She jogs up to me, and her smile is kind. "Would you mind if I walk with you for a minute?"

I shake my head, letting her fall into step beside me. The school is two blocks away, and though I'm anxious to see Rory, it's clear the doctor has something on her mind, so I slow our pace.

"There's one more thing I wanted to talk to you about," Dr. Benitez says after a moment. When I say nothing, Dr. Benitez laughs softly and presses on. "During one of our very first sessions back at the campus, you asked me a question that I didn't have the answer to. It was the first time you spoke more than four words to me." She flashes me a soft smile. "Do you remember what you asked me?"

The first few weeks at the facility were a haze. Turning the lights back on was one thing. Remembering who I was before they went out, and while they were out, was another.

42,381.

42,381 bumps above me on what I now remember is called a popcorn ceiling, and I've counted them all.

I sleep. I wake up. I count bumps on the ceiling. The doctor talks. She asks questions. I don't answer them.

"I know you're in there," Dr. Benitez says from her spot in the chair a

few feet away from my cot. She comes closer than any of the others who venture into this tiny room. "Your little fugue act works on Dr. Caldwell and the others, but I don't believe it. You're wide awake."

I risk a glance at her. Her scrubs are pink today. They're always some pastel color. I haven't seen colors like that in a long time.

"And I know you don't want to spend the rest of your life strapped to this bed," she says.

My head snaps her way. She doesn't flinch.

Life? I can't tell if she's joking. She doesn't seem to be.

"You have to work with me here," she says. "Talk to me, and I can see about getting those cuffs off your wrists at the very least."

I haven't been able to do much more than shift side to side in the ankle and wrist cuffs. The stiffness doesn't hurt, but it is somewhat uncomfortable.

I inhale, though I haven't yet decided if I need to breathe anymore.

"Am-m I . . ." My tongue trips over itself. I fight it back into place. "Still d-dead?"

Dr. Benitez pales. Sits back in her chair. She swallows visibly. Not the kind of talk she was hoping for, I guess.

"Would you like me to be honest with you?"

I lift my brows, and I swear Dr. Benitez wants to smile.

Then she says, "I have no idea."

I nod.

We're coming up on the block the school sits on. I stop at the corner and turn to face Dr. Benitez.

"I couldn't give you an answer then, but I can now," she says.

I frown.

"I conducted physical exams from the day you were brought in to the day you left," she continues. "And three days ago, when I arrived, I conducted another."

Her tone tilts with something I haven't heard in years. Hope, maybe.

"Every inch was documented," she says. "Height, weight, hair length, estimated bone density. The Dyebucetin had proven to prevent more deterioration, but the goal was always more than that. In theory, the drug could stimulate regrowth of all those dying cells."

A warm, uncomfortable feeling spreads through my belly.

"And?" I ask.

"And we're seeing evidence that supports that theory. Moreso in the younger medicated survivors, those who hadn't completed puberty and had more substantial growth ahead, but we're seeing it."

It takes me a moment to realize that when she says *survivors*, she means me. Me and the other Altered.

"You've aged, Mara. Not at anywhere near the normal rate, but you have aged at least a few months since you were bitten."

I shake my head. I feel like I did in the beginning, when words refused to order themselves on my tongue.

"Every day, you're getting a little bit better," Dr. Benitez continues. "Just a little, but eventually, it won't be so little."

"Does that mean—I don't . . ." I stop.

Do you remember what you asked me?

"Am I still dead?" I ask.

Dr. Benitez smiles.

"No," she says. "I don't believe you are."

It hasn't been more than a few weeks since I last set foot on the school grounds, but the entire back section is closed off. What's left of the Pit hides behind tarps and mismatched pieces of chain-link fence. I avoid it still, taking the front entrance.

The debris on the rest of the grounds is substantially less. An electric humming rises in my ears as I pass through the courtyard and a tunnel with a large glass mosaic mural above it. The colors are long faded, and most of the glass is gone, but I imagine it was a lovely piece once upon a time.

The generator's buzz steadies as I near the thick metal door that leads into the classrooms Rory is redoing.

Isaac said it's been her personal passion project since I went unconscious. When she wasn't at my bedside, she was here.

I stop when I reach the door, the voices inside momentarily nailing my feet to the concrete.

"I'm much good at this," announces Noah.

"Very good at this," Rory says. My heart pushes out a thump. "And, yeah, you're a prodigy."

"Prodigy," Noah says, and I can tell he's pleased with the label.

"And you are, too, Rai," Rory continues. "Both of you, whiteboard-cleaning enthusiasts."

"We're enthusiasts, Raisa!" Noah elongates the *th*. His next words are heavier, more hesitant. "I wish . . ." He sniffles. "You-know-who was here."

A brief silence follows before Rory says, "You can say her name. It's okay. No one will explode."

Another silence, and the soft uncapping and recapping of a marker. Raisa must have written something on one of the whiteboards.

"I wish she were here, too, little monster," Rory says.

"Are you sure she's not gone? Dead gone?"

"I'm sure," Rory says with a fierceness that makes something in my ruined insides twist. She sounds so sure, surer than I feel now, and I've been awake for two hours. "She's taking a really, really long nap. We don't know when she's gonna wake up. Sam's with her now. I'm going to stay with her tonight."

"She's not alone," Noah says. "Good."

I reach for the door handle, fingers stalling on the metal.

I shouldn't be avoiding her. I'm not entirely sure why I am. Maybe part of me is afraid that I woke up to a different world once again.

It can't have you, Rory said in the locker room. *You're mine.*

Taking a breath I'm not sure I need, I open the door and step into the classroom.

The first thing I see is Rory's hand fly to her sword, and all of my fears slip away like grains of sand through my fingers.

The three of them are surrounded by desks and chairs and cleaning rags. They look as they did when I left them. Alive and well. An unrealized weight falls off my chest.

"Mara!" Noah exclaims, crossing the room with impressive speed. He throws his bony arms around me, squeezing tight, and I pull him close, ducking my chin to press my lips against his curls.

Raisa is quick to join us, pressing her face against my ribs and curling her fingers into my shirt. I hug her tight, and don't mind all the elbows and chins jabbing into me.

Noah leans back. "We thought you weren't gonna wake up!" He grips my shirt in his little fists. "But you did! You woke up!"

I smile, smoothing a curl off his forehead. "I'm sorry it took me so long." I risk a glance at Rory and quickly drop it back to the kids. I brush the hairs behind Raisa's ears and cup her face in my hands. I want to tell her that I'm sorry for leaving them, that I won't leave them again. Raisa nods, like she understands. She always was smarter than she had any right to be.

"Are you staying?" Noah asks.

I nod.

"For good?"

I thought running away, hiding at the Bay, was the only option I had left. But that day, when Vivian asked me to come with her, I was wrong about Aurora being the path I had to follow. Rory is part of it, a large part, but not the whole of it. Isaac and Noah and Raisa, and even Sam, are just as much what I've been scrambling to find.

I look at Rory and say, "For good."

Apparently satisfied, Raisa pulls Noah away, leading him to the door to the connecting classroom. She swipes the pile of rags from one of the desks and sends Rory a meaningful look, glancing between us once before she and Noah are gone.

"She'd have made an incredible wingwoman," I say, because the air is so thick with tension Rory could slice into it with her sword. "Maybe there'll be bars again by the time she's old enough."

Rory says nothing. She stares at me, and I know she's thinking about the last time we were in this room—when she tried to kiss me and I pulled away.

"You're awake." She cinches her expression tight, and it's so forced I have to resist the urge to smile.

"And you're still human," I say. It was my first question when I woke up in the infirmary. Whether or not I had killed her.

Rory fights her smile, but it slips through long enough for me to see it.

"No thanks to you," she says.

"I would say it's entirely thanks to me."

Rory folds her arms over her chest. She clears her throat and asks, "Are you . . . How are you feeling?"

"Like death," I say.

"Well, yeah, that's a given." Rory's lips pull thin, but a smile breaks though, and I smile back through this odd wall that slid up between us. Once again, we are fifteen and nervous around each other.

Rory twists the bracelet around her wrist. I glance down at my own wrist and find it bare. She must have taken it when I was in the infirmary.

"Back in the classroom—" I start.

"Don't," Rory says. She grinds her jaw. "It's fine. We don't need to talk about it."

"Rory—"

"I said don't. I'm glad you're awake, and we can leave it at that. Okay? You don't want to kiss me, that's fine. We don't—"

"Is that what you think that was?" I ask, and swallow a laugh. I've wanted to kiss her since I was ten years old.

Rory snorts. "What would you call it?"

I shake my head, crossing the short distance between us until we're a foot apart.

"It wasn't about not wanting you, Rory," I say, and my voice is gravellier than normal from disuse. I shake my head again, giving her a sad smile. "That has never been the problem, trust me."

Rory's mouth opens and abruptly shuts again.

"Then . . ." She waves her hand, gesturing at nothing.

"I didn't kiss you because I didn't want to hurt you. Because I'd watched you almost die, and if something happened to you . . . if I did something to you, I'd never—" I stop, pinching the bridge of my nose above the intersection of the slash marks. I force my gaze back to Rory's. "Because I thought you deserved better than me."

"You don't get to decide that." Rory's nostrils flare, and she jabs a finger at me. "And you sure as shit don't get to decide what I deserve."

Even after everything, the fire I saw in her eyes the first day we met still burns bright and strong.

"But you were right every time you called me a monster." I press my lips together for a beat. "I was, because I believed I was."

"I was wrong." Rory halves the space between us. Her eyes are frantic. "I was wrong, okay? You showed me I was wrong. And I can't take back the way I was when you first got here or get rid of all the shit I've done, but I can try to be better." Her lips turn up in a sad, hopeful smile. "That's all we can do, right? Try to be better every day."

Every day, you're getting a little bit better. Just a little, but eventually, it won't be so little, Dr. Benitez said.

"Dr. Benitez told me what they've discovered about the Dyebucetin. That it's working. That I'm . . ."

"Coming back to life," Rory says.

My mouth attempts a smile. "Trying to, at least."

Rory's gaze flicks around my face before returning to my eyes.

"Mara," she says, and something about hearing it makes all of this a little more real. My eyes fall shut, and I'm not sure how much time passes before I open them again.

And Rory is still there, inches away.

"Do you still see the end of the world when you look at me?" I ask.

Rory's breath hitches. She bites down on her lip, takes the final step toward me, and takes my face in her hands.

"No," she says firmly.

I reach for her before I've made any conscious decision to, pulling her into my arms and burying my face in her tangled hair. Rory stills, then sinks into me, gripping me so tightly that it would hurt if I were entirely human.

"No," Rory says again, her voice muffled by fabric.

My heart gives a hard thump, and Rory jerks back, pressing her palm to my chest. As if cued, my heart sputters out another beat.

Rory's eyes find mine, and in an instant, I see a million different versions of the girl in front of me. The Aurora I met and lost and loved, and the Rory I found on the other side.

"What do you see, then?" I ask.

"I just see you," Rory says, and brings her lips to mine.

ACKNOWLEDGMENTS

The physical act of writing may be solitary, but writing a book is not. To start, I have to give endless thanks to the people who helped take this book to a level I could never have imagined. My agent, Penelope Burns, whose passion, support, and knowledge are immeasurable, but so appreciated. And my editor, Rūta Rimas, and the entire PRH team, for the enthusiasm since day one. It means more than even I could put into words.

To my parents, who fostered my love of books from my literal day one. Thank you for pretending not to realize I was faking it all those days I stayed home "sick" from school inhaling books, and for not panicking (at least, not outwardly) when I told you I wanted to study writing. You may not have understood, but you stood by me, and that was enough.

To Jeannine, the strongest woman I've ever met, who I'm lucky enough to call an aunt and who has read everything I've written. The resilience I've written into this novel, and which has carried me through my own tough times, is largely inspired by you.

To the Writer Youngin's group. I can say firmly and without a doubt none of this would be possible without all of your support, brainstorms, workshops, and plain old excellence. I can't wait to see the incredible dreams you all achieve. Thank you for helping me achieve my own.

To the readers of my early writing, who supported me as I learned to write, and helped me gain the confidence to step out of other worlds and create my own.

To Jenny Howard, who showed me that writing could be more than simply a hobby and gave me my first insight into the industry.

To Liz Harmer, who helped me see fiction in an entirely new way and made me feel like I had a shot.

To Jodi, who taught me to stand up for myself and helped me find a voice off the page.

To Autumn, who taught me everything I know about friendship.

To Katie, who taught me vulnerability.

To Linh. Without you, I'd have set my metaphorical pen down a decade ago.

To you, the readers. You have a place in this world. Fight for it. Fight for yourself.

And lastly, to little me, who never believed she could be anything, drowning under her own insecurities and fears. We made it, B.